THE SCENT
OF
VIOLETS

A NOVEL

JOE REGENBOGEN

MILFORD HOUSE

an imprint of Sunbury Press, Inc.
Mechanicsburg, PA USA

MILFORD
HOUSE

an imprint of Sunbury Press, Inc.
Mechanicsburg, PA USA

Copyright © 2025 by Joe Regenbogen.
Cover Copyright © 2025 by Sunbury Press, Inc.

For information about special discounts for bulk purchases, please contact Sunbury Press Orders Dept. at (855) 338-8359 or orders@sunburypress.com.

To request one of our authors for speaking engagements or book signings, please contact Sunbury Press Publicity Dept. at publicity@sunburypress.com.

FIRST MILFORD HOUSE PRESS EDITION: July 2025

Set in Adobe Garamond Pro | Interior design by Crystal Devine | Cover by Rebekkah DeKok | Edited by Anaiah Davis.

Publisher's Cataloging-in-Publication Data
Names: Regenbogen, Joe, author.
Title: The scent of violets / Joe Regenbogen.
Description: First trade paperback edition. | Mechanicsburg, PA : Milford House Press, 2025.
Summary: One summer evening, a bomb rips apart the home of an older couple in Bloomington, Illinois, targeting two Holocaust survivors who first fell in love in the Sobibor extermination camp during World War Two. Motivated by antisemitism at a time when the American Nazi Party Supreme Court's challenge made daily headlines, the bomber ultimately undergoes a transformation raising questions about redemption and forgiveness.
Identifiers: ISBN : 979-8-88819-309-9 (paperback).
Subjects: FICTION / Historical / 20th Century / World War II & Holocaust | FICTION / Jewish | FICTION / Crime.

Designed in the USA
0 1 1 2 3 5 8 13 21 34 55

For the Love of Books!

To Dana,
the source of everything good in my life.

"Forgiveness is the fragrance
that the violet sheds on the heels
that crushed it."

—MARK TWAIN

CHAPTER 1

GRANT

June 1977

A massive explosion rocked the quiet, oak-lined streets of Bloomington-Normal early on Monday, June 6. Those living closest to the site were jolted from their sleep. Some grabbed their robes and slippers, racing outside to uncoil garden hoses and extinguish the embers that had floated onto their roofs. The impact echoed further away as window panes shattered and car alarms blared. Emergency services arrived at the scene within minutes, their sirens wailing from all directions.

A mile south, Grant Parker's eyes sprang open. His initial thought was that a lightning bolt must have struck outside his bedroom window, followed by a clap of thunder. After all, thunderstorms frequently bowled through Central Illinois' flush cornfields this time of year. Grant glanced at the illuminated digits on his nightstand, which showed it was only 1:30. He rolled over and instantly fell back asleep.

Ten minutes later, the sudden cry of the phone ringing next to his bed roused him again. This was a more familiar sound, and at this time of night, he was conditioned to hearing Jim Davenport's scratchy voice on the end of the receiver. Jim worked the night desk at *The Pantagraph*, the daily newspaper where Grant was a veteran reporter, and a call from him at this hour always meant breaking news he would have to cover. Grant flipped on a lamp, snatched up the phone, and launched their conversation without waiting for Jim to utter a word.

"Hey, Jim?" Grant moaned, rubbing sleep from his eyes. "What's up?"

Grant could picture Jim at his desk with an ashtray full of residue from a night of chain-smoking. Jim was divorced, childless, and for many years had been married to the job. In his youth, he had been a hard-nosed reporter in St. Louis, as old-school as they came. Now, in the twilight of his career, Jim preferred the quiet evenings of a midsized college town.

"Did you hear the explosion?" Jim asked, and then added without waiting for a response, "Both the police and the fire department have been dispatched to a residential house in Normal. Let's see. The address is 210 Highland Avenue. I believe that's close to you, isn't it? I know it's early, but can you check it out?"

Grant stiffened as he recognized the address. He had visited it multiple times over the past few months. The parents of his girlfriend, Rachel, had recently moved into the cozy cottage at that address. A year earlier, they had relocated to Normal from Skokie, a predominantly Jewish suburb just north of Chicago, to be closer to their daughter. Her father, Benjamin Abramowicz, had opened a shoe store in Bloomington's Eastland Mall while his wife, Miriam, worked from home as a seamstress.

Although their home was modest, it had a charming appearance that would fit into any Norman Rockwell landscape. The house had just been painted an ivory-white and was accented by imposing deep blue shutters flanking each window. The porch was guarded by a picket fence that ran the entire width of the front facade. Inside, a high ceiling towered above solid hardwood floors. The interior walls were buried beneath Judaica paintings and family photos, mostly depicting Rachel from diapers up through her doctoral graduation. Notably, Grant had never observed any pictures of extended family.

"All right," Grant replied. "I'll head over now. It's less than a mile away, so it shouldn't take long. If it turns out to be a major story, I'll aim for tomorrow's front page since it's already too late for today."

"Sounds good," Jim responded. "I'll pass this on to Dutch when he arrives."

"Thanks, Jim. Talk to you later."

Grant absentmindedly leaned on his elbow while staring at the phone he had just hung up.

He collapsed onto his back and lay in bed for a few more seconds to plot his next steps. First, and most importantly, he would inquire about Rachel's parents' condition. Second, Grant would talk to the police at the explosion site to gather facts and quotes for his story. Finally, he would stop by Rachel's apartment to provide her with the latest information before she heard it from a stranger, such as a policeman or an ER doctor. Or even worse, someone at the morgue.

Satisfied with this plan, Grant climbed out of bed, threw on a button-down shirt and a pair of slacks, and headed into the bathroom to brush his teeth. While rinsing, he was startled by the screaming of nearby sirens. Creeping past Michael's closed door, he wondered how his son could sleep through the piercing uproar. But then again, Grant knew a meteor strike would not awaken his seventeen-year-old son at this hour.

Grant briefly considered brewing a cup of coffee but concluded he did not have enough time. He would just have to rely on adrenaline. On his front porch, he paused long enough to study the horizon. The Abramowicz home lay directly to the west. The sky in that direction glowed like a brilliant sunset capped by dark, puffy clouds resembling burnt marshmallows. At least the wailing of the sirens had finally subsided.

As Grant squeezed his lanky frame into a beat-up Honda Civic, he wondered what had caused the blast. His first thought was that it may have been an accident, perhaps a gas explosion from an aging stove or water heater. One nagging thought, however, made Grant suspect it was a deliberate act. Benjamin and Miriam Abramowicz were not just Jewish; they were also Holocaust survivors. The community had recently learned their gripping story, thanks to Grant. After hearing Benjamin address a public symposium, he interviewed the couple and wrote a lengthy front-page feature about them for the paper's Sunday edition. Was it a coincidence that their home was bombed just two weeks after the story was published?

Grant knew anti-Semitism could appear anywhere without warning. This ancient prejudice had resurfaced recently in the national headlines, generated by a First Amendment lawsuit filed by the ACLU on behalf of the American Nazi Party. Still, its epicenter had been the South Side of Chicago, not the more enlightened hamlet of Bloomington-Normal. After all, this twin city in the heartland of Central Illinois was primarily home to middle-class, well-educated, and open-minded people.

If anyone understood this, it was Grant Parker. He was born in Bloomington, graduated from Bloomington High School, and lived his entire life in the area except for the four years he spent at Northwestern

University. And Grant had developed an even deeper understanding of his hometown since securing his position as a reporter. Located halfway between Chicago and St. Louis, Bloomington-Normal was Grant's utopia. In this town, he could enjoy Shakespearean theater, classical music, delicious dining, plentiful shopping, and the latest Hollywood releases without enduring a big city's noise, crime, and pollution.

In addition, Bloomington-Normal was home to two universities. Illinois Wesleyan was a liberal arts college, and its picturesque campus was only a few blocks from Grant's two-bedroom bungalow. And just to the north, beyond Division Street, was the town of Normal, home to the Illinois State Redbirds. With an enrollment of just over 20,000 students, ISU was initially named Illinois State Normal University, the state's premier teachers' college. When Illinois State became a comprehensive university, it dropped "Normal" from its name, but the surrounding town picked it up.

Grant knew there were other reasons why Bloomington-Normal was not the breeding ground of fascism. Since it was the corporate home of State Farm, the nation's largest insurance provider, another 10,000 well-educated people made Bloomington their home. In addition, some unique historical features have influenced the local culture. Abraham Lincoln once argued cases in downtown Bloomington. Adlai Stevenson, the senator who lost two presidential elections to Dwight Eisenhower, was raised in the area and buried here. Even the character Henry Blake from the hit series *M*A*S*H* was originally from Bloomington.

This might be the heart of flyover country to many people living on the East and West Coasts, Grant thought, but he believed it was the last place that would produce neo-Nazis. If someone had deliberately blown up the Abramowicz home, they may have been anti-Semitic terrorists, but if so, they hailed from somewhere else; they were *not* homegrown. This, more than anything else, was why Grant was happy to have Michael once again living under his roof. Regretfully, his son had been residing with Gretchen, his ex-wife, on the South Side of Chicago for the last ten years. This poisonous environment had taken a toll.

As Grant drove north on Linden Street, he reminisced about the day Michael was born. He vividly recalled the bottle feedings, the diaper changes, and the nightly bedtime stories. Grant had given Michael his first bath and was the one who sat up all night with him when he had the croup. Later, Grant taught his son how to throw a baseball at Miller Park and how to swim at Evergreen Lake. Shortly before the unexpected divorce announcement, Grant had taken off the training wheels from his son's bicycle and witnessed the wide grin on his face as Michael whizzed by on the sidewalk in front of their tiny apartment.

One of Grant's fondest memories was taking Michael on a backpacking trip to Rocky Mountain National Park when the boy was six. For almost a week, his son quietly endured the afternoon showers and the frigid nights. Michael diligently lugged his small pack full of energy bars, drinking water, and a beaten-up teddy bear up and down the roller-coaster trails for thirty miles, including twice over the Continental Divide. On the final day, Michael almost burst out of his skin when he saw a bull moose grazing in a shallow pond. Grant smiled, remembering the sparkle of wonderment in his son's eyes.

Michael was now a teenager, and since moving back in with his father, living with his erratic mood swings was like riding a rodeo bull. Grant never knew what to expect at the breakfast table or when he came home each evening. One moment, Michael could be chatty and effervescent. The next, he might be angry or sullen. Grant mostly chalked this up to hormones and adolescence, but it still added significant stress to his life.

Grant also noticed how Michael avoided political conversations, which were frequent occurrences in the home of a news reporter. Once, though, after Grant told his son about *Bakke v. California*, a Supreme Court case he was writing about, he was stunned by his son's reaction. When Michael learned the petitioners in the case were white medical school applicants who maintained that they were victims of "reverse discrimination," Michael shocked his father with a sudden outburst railing against affirmative action. Although Grant disagreed with his son's arguments, he was still impressed by his passion and the clarity of Michael's reasoning.

Despite his obvious intelligence, Michael had never excelled as a student. Grant recognized that this was mainly due to a lack of discipline and effective study habits. Despite his best attempts, Grant had been unable to instill in his son the motivation to work harder for better grades on his report card. However, there were numerous instances where he witnessed Michael demonstrating a remarkable level of critical thinking.

Mulling over his relationship with Michael during these predawn hours, Grant acknowledged that, in many respects, there was a side of his son he still did not know. After all, he was currently living with a combustible seventeen-year-old infused with testosterone. But was Michael just a typical adolescent? Because of his unique history, that question was more challenging to answer.

Grant first met Gretchen during his final year at Northwestern while she was working as a waitress at his favorite diner in Evanston. Ready to launch her adult life, she had traded her parent's flat near Comiskey Park on the city's southern end for an apartment crowded with roommates near Wrigley on the north side. As a result, she was like a recently uncaged bird. Grant found her seductive and spirited. Gretchen was a magnetic change of pace from the pretentious coeds he usually encountered on campus. She was aggressively flirtatious, even asking him out on their first date.

Defying his parents' expectations, Grant was attracted to Gretchen's rebellious streak and eagerness to challenge authority, not to mention her long blond hair and curvaceous figure. This was 1959, and the nation was about to explode into a countercultural revolution. Grant thought Gretchen was electrical excitement, someone openly flouting the traditional 1950s expectations for single women. He had never known anyone quite like her. She took him to an Elvis Presley concert for their first date and then back to her bedroom to cap off the evening. A month later, Grant packed his bags, deserted the single bedroom in his fraternity house, and moved into a small efficiency with Gretchen.

Unfortunately, she dropped a nuclear bomb on Grant the month before his graduation: she was pregnant. Gretchen may have had a rebellious streak, but some rules were too sacred and deeply ingrained to violate. Her Irish Catholic background, coupled with Grant's desire to "do the right thing," dictated that marriage was the only option for the young couple. Grant wed Gretchen in a small ceremony that summer, and Michael was born the following January.

At the time, this appeared to be a happy outcome. Gretchen agreed to move to Bloomington with her husband when he got a job with the local newspaper, believing his modest salary would still be enough for her to stay home in their cozy apartment and raise their son. While this was not the original blueprint Grant had sketched for himself, in the end, he still landed in his hometown with the job he had always dreamed about. Grant had always planned to be a husband and father, just not so soon.

Shortly after Michael's seventh birthday, Gretchen shocked her husband by telling him she was tired of living in "Dullsville." She wanted to return to Chicago. Grant offered to take her home for more weekend visits, but that was not enough. Gretchen thirsted for the excitement of daily life in a big city. After a gut-wrenching fight one night, Gretchen unflinchingly packed her bags and caught the next Greyhound to the Windy City. A week later, she reappeared with her brothers in a Chevy Bel Air to retrieve Michael. With the extra muscle, Grant had no choice but to go along with it.

A few months later, a divorce settlement made it official. Grant agreed to an uncontested breakup, reticently complying with Gretchen's terms regarding custody and visitation rights. He would get to spend one weekend a month with his son. Immensely frustrated, there was little Grant could do since if he contested these terms, besides wasting a lot of money, he knew he would ultimately lose.

On the first Saturday morning of each month, Grant drove to Chicago, checked into the same modest motel, and then took his son to museums, playgrounds, or movie theaters showing Disney films. Time spent with Michael in Bloomington was more pleasant, but that required two trips to Chicago within three days, one to pick up his son, the other to bring him back. Unfortunately, that meant over 500 miles of driving since Gretchen and her family were unwilling to help.

This routine might have lasted forever, but by the time Michael began high school, he started to get into trouble. One afternoon, when Gretchen was unavailable, an assistant principal called Grant about a spray-painting incident on the school grounds. This led to a meeting with his counselor, where Grant learned about Michael's marijuana use and his recent habit of cutting classes.

Gretchen maintained their son was just being "a typical teenager" who lacked close friends because he was "too independent" to fit into any tenth-grade cliques. She also expressed little concern when Michael shifted from having long, stringy hair and donning bell-bottom jeans and tie-dye shirts to sporting a crewcut and wearing only jeans, white tee shirts, and a grubby leather jacket. Grant believed his ex-wife took pride in Michael's "James Dean" manner, focusing more on being his friend than a parent.

In addition, Grant heard rumors that Gretchen was drinking heavily and had become seriously involved with a man who, according to Michael, had a swastika tattooed on his bicep and kept a sawed-off shotgun in the trunk of his car. Grant had finally had enough. He dipped into his savings for a private investigator and a family law attorney and took his wife to court. This time, a judge agreed that, in "the best interest of the minor," a change was in order.

The final result was a reversal in their child custody arrangement. The new plan called for Michael to move in with his father, attend Bloomington High School, and spend breaks and one weekend a month with his mother in Chicago. Initially, Michael challenged the change, but his son hesitantly agreed when Grant offered to buy him a used car for his sixteenth birthday. Of course, a few months later, the price of the used AMC Gremlin, along with its high maintenance and insurance costs, siphoned off even more of what remained of Grant's savings.

Grant wasted no time loading his Honda Civic with Michael's belongings. He bolted from his ex-wife's apartment like a high school student darting out of school on the final day of classes. At first, Michael was soberly quiet, responding to his father's questions with only yes or no answers. Driving south on I-55, he stared vacantly out the car window. Grant refused to give up, however, and by the time they passed Joliet, his elation about reuniting with his son had become infectious. Their conversation grew livelier as they approached Pontiac, and they were soon making plans to eat pizza that night, followed by watching *Jaws* at the Normal Theater.

For the first month or so, Michael appeared to thrive. He spoke favorably about his teachers, especially in math and chemistry, and he tried out for the cross-country team. Michael also mentioned the names of friends at school, although Grant had never met them. At the open house in September, Grant learned from his son's homeroom teacher that Michael started each day by devouring books he had checked out of the school's library. He seemed to possess an unquenchable curiosity. It appeared Michael was flourishing in his new home and that the money and effort Grant had expended to retrieve his son was a good investment. After a few months, though, the situation began to sour.

No matter what Grant did in Bloomington, Michael could never escape the negative influence of Chicago's South Side. For example, when he talked about going to college and pursuing a career in medicine or science, Michael quickly lost interest after spending a weekend in the Windy City. After he seemed to develop a mutual crush on a quiet Latina girl—an A-plus student—he returned from winter break unwilling to even call her. Any progress he made in Bloomington was quickly undone after just a few days with his mother.

So now, as Grant approached the fiery remains of the house on Highland Avenue, he wondered how Michael would respond when he heard the news about this morning's explosion. On the one hand, his son had met the Abramowiczs and appeared to sympathize with their story. On the other, there was no telling what adverse influence the lurking specter of Chicago might hold. Grant hated to think his son might know any of the criminals behind the devastation that now lay before him.

As Grant scrambled out of his Civic, he ended his thoughts about Michael, at least for now, by concluding that his son was a typically confused teenager. Michael occasionally liked to shock people with bold talk, and maybe he sometimes wrestled with the conflicting values inherited from two highly different parents. But Grant was convinced that, in the end, his son was just trying to make sense of the world. With one more year of high school left, Grant still had another twelve months to polish Michael's rough edges. Then, he would hopefully launch his son off to college.

Parked down the street from the crime scene, he saw two fire trucks, several police vehicles, and an ambulance occupying most of the block, which made it impossible to navigate any closer. The Abramowicz home had been reduced to charred studs, debris, and a few remaining flames tossing embers into the night sky. One fireman still had a hose trained on the smoldering ruins while police officers worked to secure the area with a perimeter of yellow police tape.

Grant was ready with his press ID, but since the first cop was a familiar face, it was unnecessary. High-intensity lights from the fire trucks transformed the expanse from night into day, reminding Grant of the searchlights used at Hollywood film premieres. In addition, the cherry lights swirling above each emergency vehicle added a bizarrely festive atmosphere.

Grant quickly assessed the situation and noticed that while most of the fire had been extinguished, the explosion and resulting flames had destroyed the entire front section of the house. Only burnt beams were left to support the remnants of the second floor. Grant had seen photographs of Dresden taken near the end of World War II after the Allies had destroyed most of the German city with high-explosive bombs, including incendiary devices. At least 25,000 people died in a single night, and fifty percent of the city's residential buildings had been obliterated. The Abramowicz home looked like it belonged in one of those pictures.

Grant approached the supervising police lieutenant at the scene. Charles Maddox, known as Chuck to his friends, was slightly older than Grant and had worked with him numerous times. Over the years, they had built a mutual respect and camaraderie typical of professionals who frequently collaborated at the same tragic sites. Although they had often discussed going out for a beer after a long night, they had never actually done so. When Chuck spotted Grant, he left a group of officers and walked over, extending his hand to his friend from the local newspaper.

Chuck pointed to an area just to the right where he asserted the bomb had exploded. The working theory was that someone had deposited a short-fuse explosive on the porch. Shortly after the bombers ignited the fuse, they raced down the steps, and a few seconds later, the device exploded. An oak tree in the front yard was painted with black scorch marks, and the bomb blasted a gaping hole through the front wall where Miriam and Benjamin had been fast asleep.

The bomb, which firefighters believe was planted next to a small container filled with a combustible fluid, probably gasoline, ignited a vicious fire that swiftly engulfed the front of the house. It worked like a Molotov cocktail but on a larger scale. As they talked, Grant cautiously approached the area, inspecting the damage. In his years with *The Pantagraph*, he had seen the jaws of life used to extract survivors from the twisted ruins of a head-on car collision. He once examined the remnants of a farmhouse plowed under by a tornado. And he had seen more than his fair share of house fires. But this was potentially Grant's first terrorist bombing. With palms perched on his hips, he stood before the debris and slowly shook his head.

Grant looked at Chuck, hesitating to ask the one question he had been avoiding until now. Before he could speak, he was startled by an engine roaring and the wail of a siren. After the emergency vehicle turned the corner, Grant quickly turned back to the police lieutenant and took a deep breath.

"So . . . who's in that ambulance?"

"His name is Benjamin . . ." Chuck paused to gaze down at his clipboard. "Benjamin Abramowicz. Age sixty-two. He lives here with his wife, Miriam. Benjamin should be okay. From what we could tell, he was further away from the window, and his wife may have shielded him partially from the blast."

Grant remained quiet, waiting to see if there was more. From his experience, he knew most people were uncomfortable with silence and would inevitably fill the vacuum. His patience soon paid off.

"I'm no doctor, Grant, but from what I saw, Benjamin's injuries were mostly superficial. There was some blood, but he was fully conscious and coherent. Once the first ambulance left with his wife and the EMTs calmed him down, we convinced Benjamin that the fastest way to join his wife would be to ride in that second ambulance to the same hospital. Miriam had already departed before you arrived."

Once again, Grant paused, afraid to ask about Rachel's mother. He feared the worst. However, Chuck had run out of steam, so Grant had no choice but to broach the subject.

"What about his wife? What's her condition?"

"Hard to say," Chuck replied, as though he was suddenly the focus of a press conference. "There was still a weak pulse, but she never regained consciousness. One EMT thought the blast may have hurled her across the room because it appeared she had suffered a major head injury. We sent her right away to St. Joseph."

Grant turned to face Chuck squarely. "Have you contacted the family yet?"

"No, but Mr. Abramowicz gave us his daughter's phone number." Once again, he checked his notes. "Rachel's her name. Rachel Abramowicz. She lives here in Normal."

"Yes, I know her," Grant replied, noticing the policeman's eyes widen in surprise. "We've been dating for about nine months. I also know her parents. In fact, I've been here on several occasions."

"Oh wow, Grant, I'm sorry," Chuck responded, shaking his head in disbelief. Then, after a brief pause, he added, "Where're you headed next? The hospital?"

"Yeah," Grant answered while glancing downward.

"And I assume you'll be checking on their condition?" After Grant nodded, the cop added, "Officially, Grant, we're supposed to contact the immediate family. But under the circumstances, it might be best coming from you. It'd be better than hearing it from a stranger."

"Yes, *absolutely*," Grant agreed. "After I check in at the ER, I'll drive straight over to Rachel's apartment to give her the news in person."

"Sounds like a plan," Chuck responded.

"Before I get going," Grant uttered, "I should snap a few photos."

He set down the leather satchel strung over his shoulder, squatted, and pulled out a camera. Of course, a big city newspaper would have sent a photographer to a major crime scene. However, journalists in smaller markets like Bloomington-Normal often had to shoot their own pictures. So, after checking to be sure there was film in the camera, Grant stood and started snapping photos from various angles.

Finally, when he was done and the camera was secure, Grant strode back toward Chuck to say goodbye. That's when it hit him. Due to his initial alarm about Rachel's parents, Grant had overlooked the first question any journalist would have asked.

"Hey, Chuck, any idea who did this?"

"I wondered when you'd get around to that," the cop answered wryly.

He paused as though trying to add to the suspense. When he finally continued, Chuck summarized what they had learned so far.

"Since the crime occurred at such an ungodly hour, we don't have any eyewitnesses. As for physical evidence, so far, there's not much. And let's face it, anything with prints on it was blown to smithereens or destroyed by the fire. Forensics might be able to tell us something about the explosive, but otherwise, short of a lucky break, this one would be a dead end." After a brief pause, Chuck added, "However, there's one reason why this crime might be solvable."

Like a cat that had just trapped a mouse, Grant observed a sparkle in Chuck's eyes. He waited expectantly for the cop to continue.

"The bomber or bombers were neo-Nazis."

Grant's eyes widened, and his jaw dropped. "You're *shitting* me. How do you know that?"

"Because, when we first arrived," Chuck answered, "The fire had not yet spread to the other side of the house. For just a moment, we could see that the bomber had spray-painted a huge swastika, stretching from the floor to the ceiling. I'll tell you, Grant, it was the most surreal image I've ever seen. Right here, in the heart of America, flames were engulfing a giant swastika. It was like a scene from, what was that Nazi propaganda film, *Triumph of the Will*?"

"No kidding," Grant reacted.

"What's more, the swastika was well-drawn. The lines were thick, proportional, and perfectly straight. Can you *imagine*? Someone actually stood on that porch in the middle of the night, carefully painting their calling card."

"*Wow* . . ." Grant responded. Then, almost as an afterthought, he added glumly, "You know they're Jewish, right? Benjamin and Miriam? They were both Holocaust survivors."

Chuck snapped his fingers. "Oh, that's right, they're the ones you wrote about a couple of weeks ago. I don't know why I didn't make the connection." Then, he grinned, "Don't be so surprised, Grant. Some of us actually read *The Pantagraph*."

"You guys can read?" Grant teased.

Chuck smirked but remained silent. Meanwhile, Grant turned back to face the horrific scene. He needed a few seconds to process the news about the swastika. Suddenly, Grant froze. Then, through tightened lips, he sighed, releasing air like a deflating balloon.

Chuck noticed something was amiss from the corner of his eye. When he turned to face the reporter, he gently reached for his shoulder and twisted him so the two men faced each other. Since they were roughly the same height, about six foot two, Chuck could see a hint of moisture gathering beneath Grant's arctic blue eyes.

"Hey, what's wrong?" Chuck inquired.

His tone had softened. In all the years they had known each other, this was the first time their friendship crossed from professional to personal. Grant did not answer at first. He was touched by the policeman's concern.

"I think this was *my* fault," Grant finally whispered. "I introduced these people to the world. I'll bet anything the monster who did this learned about the Abramowiczs from *my* story."

Chuck examined a smoldering beam on the second floor like a man studying the dancing flames of a fireplace. He appeared to be hypnotized. Grant realized, however, that as a cop who often had to console victims, he was probably preparing the appropriate response. Finally, Chuck turned toward his reporter friend, inhaled deeply, and gazed at him.

"Grant, you're not responsible for what happened. Yeah, there's a good chance this house was targeted because of the people who live here, and yes, there's a chance the animals who did this learned about them from your article. But that doesn't mean you did anything wrong. You were just doing your job. I read your article, and as much as I hate inflating your ego, it was outstanding. The Abramowiczs had an inspiring story that needed to be told, and that's all you did. Most people who learn about them will be less likely to hate, not more."

Grant nodded appreciatively but said nothing. Then, he was struck by an inspiration.

"What about Frank Collin and his Nazi stormtroopers up in Chicago? They've certainly been in the news enough lately. You think they could be behind this?"

"Very possible," Chuck answered. Then, he added, "Grant, according to your article. Benjamin Abramowicz was originally from Skokie and had long been an outspoken critic of those hoodlums from the South Side. Right? He wrote letters to the editor, badgered local politicians, and circulated petitions. He did whatever he could to keep those assholes out of his hometown. It wouldn't have been hard for them to find his new address. And, what's more, they probably figured it would be safer to do this downstate than in a Jewish suburb currently in the national spotlight."

Grant recognized his cop buddy was thinking aloud. From the focused look on Chuck's face, he hoped their conversation was contributing to his investigation.

"So, you'll check it out?" Grant inquired.

"Absolutely. It'll be the first item on the agenda when I speak to the FBI."

Grant nodded approvingly. "Alright," he asserted. "I better get going. After I write the story, I'll give you a call to confirm the details. And Chuck . . . Thanks for your kind words. They're greatly appreciated. When this is over, let's be sure to finally grab that beer."

"Sure, happy to help," Chuck responded. "And the beer sounds good, especially if you're buying."

After a warm handshake, Grant grabbed the camera, threw the strap over his shoulder, and spun around to leave. However, after taking only a few steps, he froze.

Across the street, a sizable assembly had gathered. Despite the early hour, this was unsurprising, given how the explosion had jolted the neighbors out of their beds. Since then, the blinding lights and deafening sounds had ended all hope of going back to sleep. But standing in the rear of the pack was a tall, slender boy wearing a midnight-black tee shirt.

Like the others in the crowd, the boy was gazing at the steam rising from the wreckage. The detailed features of his face were not easy to make out in the early dawn's opaqueness, but his lips were drawn wide open in astonishment. For some bizarre reason, the boy was also wearing dark sunglasses that reflected the orange glow of the smoldering house.

To Grant's dismay, the boy looked like Michael. Could that be his son, who he assumed was asleep back at their house? If so, why had he joined these inquisitive neighbors gathered like the chorus of a Greek tragedy? Was he just curious? Maybe the sirens had woken him after all. Grant stepped into the street for a better view.

Unfortunately, he marched directly into a tangle of fire hoses and stumbled before regaining his balance. Halfway across the street, Grant looked up, trying to find his son. However, like a ghost, the face he had seen at the back of the crowd had disappeared.

CHAPTER 2

MICHAEL

September 1976

Michael wondered if his personality had split in half, like Sybil Dorsett, the girl he had recently read about with dissociative identity disorder. Of course, Sybil had been diagnosed with sixteen distinct personalities. So far, Michael only had two he knew about, and they were not full-blown identities. Rather than becoming a textbook example of a psychotic disorder, Michael had divided into two identical entities, like a cell experiencing mitosis.

Part of this, of course, was simply due to the schizophrenia of adolescence. In Michael's case, though, he suspected that his parents' divorce had profoundly exacerbated it. His mother and father were *so* different, each inhabiting utterly dissimilar worlds. Traveling back and forth between them was like Neil Armstrong returning to Earth after walking on the moon. One day, Michael was lugging a backpack around the college town of Bloomington-Normal, where an ocean of cornfields surrounded an island of strip malls, Methodist churches, and sprinkler-watered lawns. The next day, his head was spinning in the urban landscape of Marquette Park, where he dodged traffic while crossing busy streets, rode the L train, and was occasionally awakened by the sound of gunshots.

Shortly after the court had ordered Michael to live with his father, he invented what seemed to be a harmless fantasy after climbing out of his twin bed one morning. Since a recent growth spurt had propelled him above six feet, almost as tall as his father, Michael had a full view of his face and torso whenever he stood in front of the bathroom mirror. One day, he simply began conversing with his reflection. Why not? Since he frequently felt like two distinct people, why couldn't one provide companionship for the other?

At first, Michael felt self-conscious about his morning ritual. Was he going insane? Was he suffering from some mental issue? He reassured himself that both identities within him were fully aware of each other and that, unlike Dr. Jekyll or the Wolfman, he would never find himself wondering what his twin had done the night before. He believed most people talked to themselves when they were alone and that this could even be a healthy practice. If nothing else, it made him feel a little less lonely.

After the first few times, Michael decided to let geography dictate their roles. The Michael in the mirror always represented the city he had just left, while the one standing in front of the sink embodied where he currently resided. Soon, Bloomington Michael was engaging in stimulating conversations with Chicago Michael daily. Sometimes, they even argued, although he kept his voice down to avoid raising suspicions from his father downstairs.

The routine usually began with an assessment of his physical appearance. Sometimes, he wrestled with whether to shave since, with jet-black hair, Michael's one effort to grow a beard made him look like Charles Manson's much taller brother. On other days, though, he simply popped a pimple or two. The one given was that Michael would always experiment with his hair. Shortly before moving to Bloomington, he had shaved it off, but now that it had grown back, long enough to lay flat at least, he was continually brushing it in different styles.

On a Thursday morning in late September, Michael stumbled sleepily into the hall bathroom, wearing nothing but a checkered pair of underpants. This was the only bathroom in the house, located upstairs between the two bedrooms. He shared it with his father, but Michael had the facility to himself since his dad was an early riser and had already gone downstairs to prepare breakfast. As usual, the room reeked of his father's aftershave and cologne. Michael was also annoyed at the wave of dampness that always engulfed him after his dad's showers. At least the mirror's fog had dissipated enough to allow the Chicago Michael to greet his Bloomington counterpart.

Michael decided to focus this morning's conversation on the conference scheduled after school today between his dad and U.S. History teacher, Mrs. Reynolds. After a heated discussion a few days ago, Michael was aware of the reasons for her concerns. On the surface, Mrs. Reynolds was unhappy with the oral presentation he had given in class; she interrupted him halfway through and refused to grade it. However, Michael believed the real issue lay in the underlying tension between him and his teacher. She may have sensed that he could not respect anyone with dark skin.

"Good morning, handsome," exclaimed the reflection in the mirror. Chicago Michael smiled sarcastically and slowly shook his head. "Looks like you could use a few more hours of beauty sleep."

"Let's just say it's been a long week," Bloomington Michael countered. "But tomorrow, for the first time, I'll get to drive to Chicago. Then, at least for the weekend, you and I will trade places." After briefly pausing to glance around, he added, "And I can't wait to get out of this shithole."

Michael leaned closer to the mirror, tilting his head and using his fingers to probe where he had recently popped a pimple. Of course, Chicago Michael mimicked the same moves. Then, they simultaneously stood erect and exchanged smiles.

"Looking *good,*" Chicago Michael pronounced. "That should be completely gone by the weekend."

To finish their bathroom rituals, the two Michaels brushed their teeth, gargled with mouthwash, and spent an inordinate amount of time combining water with a brush to force down the stubborn tufts of hair that came alive during the night. Finally, it was time to address this morning's topic of conversation.

"Before I can think about this weekend," Bloomington Michael intoned, "I have to deal with that American History bitch."

"You mean Mrs. Reynolds?" inquired Chicago Mike knowingly. Before his counterpart could answer, he added, "Who is *she* to judge *you?*"

The two Michaels nodded in agreement. The face in the mirror continued.

"You know, your idea to do an oral report on William Simmons was brilliant, right? You used *her* stupid-assed assignment to spread *your* message. It was beautiful. By explaining how a preacher single-handedly restarted the Klan forty years after it was suppressed, you gave yourself a platform to safely talk about the sanctity of the white race. When you're in Chicago, you should tell Frank about your report. He'll be impressed."

Bloomington Michael grinned smugly as he listened to his Chicago colleague. While the contrasting environments had sculpted two different Michaels, they shared the same core values beneath the surface.

"And I *did* spread the message," Bloomington Michael agreed. "After class that day, Jerome, this quiet kid the size of a truck who blocks on the offensive line, approached me and said how much he liked my presentation. He was also pissed that Mrs. Reynolds would not let me finish it."

"Nice!" Chicago Mike exclaimed. "You should buddy up to Jerome. Who knows? Maybe you can sign him up as the first member of the Bloomington Bund. That's how it's done, you know, one person at a time."

"Yeah," Bloomington Michael agreed, "But first, I need to get past today's conference. Mrs. Reynolds will probably tell Dad that my report was *really* a personal attack on her. It was, of course, but Dad can't know that. If she succeeds in upsetting him, he'll probably pull the plug on my driving to Chicago tomorrow. That'll mean riding that damned bus. Again. *Man*, I'm so sick of Greyhound."

Michael and his reflection nodded in unison. Just then, a voice wafted up the stairs. Michael's father was calling him down to breakfast.

"I have to go," Bloomington Michael told his colleague in the mirror. "Don't worry; I'll figure something out."

The two Michaels grinned at each other. The same inspiration had placed an identical gleam in their eyes. That was the beauty of this fantasy ritual. Sometimes, Michael and his twin were like a close-knit married couple, capable of telepathically sharing ideas.

Three minutes later, Michael was dressed and downstairs in the kitchen, diving into a plate of pancakes that he liked to drown in maple syrup. Across the wooden table sat his father, finishing a bowl of Frosted Flakes that he liked to drown in skim milk. When Michael glanced up, he was shaken by the furrowed brow on his dad's face. A ray of sunlight from the window above the kitchen sink accentuated his father's sober expression.

"What?" Michael asked, his voice muffled by a mouthful of fluffy pancakes.

"I asked you last night why your history teacher wanted to meet with me today, but you were as evasive as a politician."

Grant placed the spoon in his bowl, stood up, and started to clear the table. Meanwhile, he never took his eyes off Michael, stubbornly waiting for a response. Finally, after he had swallowed, Michael peered up with a defiant expression.

"Mrs. Reynolds wants this meeting because she hates me, and nothing would bring her more joy than getting me in trouble with you."

"*Really?*" Grant countered. He paused briefly to calm his tone, hoping to avoid a confrontation. "Why do you suppose she hates you?"

"Because I refuse to kiss her ass."

Grant stared at his son blankly, waiting for more explanation. Meanwhile, Michael sliced into his last pancake, which looked like a saturated sponge, stabbed a large piece with his fork, and shoveled it into his mouth. He sat back in his chair, brazenly glaring at his father.

"Come on, Michael, give me *something*. I don't want to walk into the meeting this afternoon without knowing what it's about. I doubt Mrs. Reynolds will say she hates you because you won't kiss her ass. Give me a clue what she *is* going to say."

Michael nodded, acknowledging that he understood his father's request. After chewing and swallowing, he leaned forward, clasped his hands on the table, and looked up at his dad as though he were about to address a confused man in a nursing home.

"Dad," Michael stated evenly, "Mrs. Reynolds gave us an assignment at the start of the year. She asked us to choose someone we considered a hero in American History, do some research, and then put together an oral presentation on that person. She planned that we would each have a day to give our report in the final ten minutes of class. I gave *mine* on Monday."

"How'd it go?" Grant inquired in a deliberately conversational tenor.

"It went well until she interrupted me," Michael immediately answered.

Grant remained silent, but the quizzical arch in his eyebrows begged for more explanation.

"Dad, she gave us complete freedom to choose our hero for the presentation. Mrs. Reynolds never required us to clear the choice with her in advance. About half the class had already presented, and I didn't learn anything new. Who wants to hear the same boring facts about Ben Franklin, Abraham Lincoln, or Helen Keller? Everyone already knows about those people. I wanted to pick someone that no one had heard of."

Suddenly, a familiar sound echoed throughout the kitchen. It was the school bus honking for Michael to come out and board. Grant frowned at his son, who looked like he was seeking permission to be excused. After his father nodded reluctantly, Michael jumped up, grabbed his book bag, and turned to leave. Then, as an afterthought, he spun around to make a final pronouncement.

"You know, Dad, I wouldn't have to rush off if you'd let me drive to school."

"Yeah, yeah, yeah . . . ." Grant uttered, shaking his head. "I don't want to pay the parking fee when the school bus is free."

Then, before Michael could vanish, his father called after him with a surprising last-minute request.

"Michael, why don't you join us for the conference?"

"*What?*" Michael uttered as though his father had just asked him to go outside and play in traffic. "She didn't invite me, Dad; she just wants to talk to you."

"I get that," Grant countered. "She wants me to hear her side of the story. But I'd also like to see how she responds to *your* side of the story."

Grant had recently taught his son to play chess, and Michael quickly picked up the game. Whenever he meditated over a move, Michael intensely glared at a piece like he was trying to move it telepathically. Now, the same penetrating expression was plastered across his face.

"*Sure,*" Michael finally answered. "Why not? This could be fun. I'll meet you in her classroom. It's room 210, on the second floor."

Before Grant could respond, Michael whirled around and disappeared from the kitchen. Shortly afterward, the front door slammed, followed by a diesel engine revving as the school bus pulled away, carrying its human cargo for another day of learning at Bloomington High School.

Michael quickly climbed the steps and scurried to his usual seat on the last bench of the bus without acknowledging the driver, who had been waiting patiently. The other students knew Michael's preferred seating and avoided the last three rows. As the yellow school bus rumbled toward North Linden Street, Michael turned toward the window and caught his reflection in the glass. He smiled to himself and nodded. Both Michaels silently agreed that this afternoon would be a cakewalk. Why had he not thought of this strategy earlier?

Michael grew progressively excited about the upcoming conference as the school day dragged on. At the end of his history class, he approached Mrs. Reynolds and gleefully told her about his father's request that he participate in the conference. Michael observed how her eyes enlarged as if staring at an oncoming train. Before she could respond, though, he gave her a snide salute, spun around toward the door, and walked out as fast as he could.

Michael realized he was happier at Bloomington High School. Unlike the urban fortress back in Chicago, there were fewer minorities and minimal racial tension. Everyone seemed to get along. It was like he had left the Sweat Hogs of *Welcome Back, Kotter* behind and enrolled in the Jefferson High School of *Happy Days*. Except in this analogy, the Sweat Hogs at his old school could be vicious, especially the gang members united by race. Despite his views, Michael did not miss the daily stress over when the next race riot might occur.

And here? The people in this school were so *nice* and so naïve that he often felt like they were puppets and he was their puppet master. He didn't mind taking shortcuts and occasionally cheating to earn his diploma. And while Michael loved to read, it would only be magazines and books of his choosing. Michael viewed this high school like a giant smorgasbord, where he could pick and choose what to learn, whom to hang with, and how to get by from one day to the next. As for dealing with Mrs. Reynolds, he could not wait for the end of school.

When his dad finally arrived, Michael was pacing in the hallway outside room 210. Unsurprisingly, he avoided waiting inside the classroom with his history teacher. Michael instantly flashed his father a welcoming smile and motioned him toward the entrance. Once inside, they spotted Mrs. Reynolds, a small Black woman sitting behind a big desk, grading papers. When Grant cleared his throat, she glanced up, displaying a no-nonsense expression like a drill sergeant awaiting a new squad of marines. Before anyone could speak, Michael kicked off the meeting.

"Mrs. Reynolds? This is my father, Grant Parker. He writes for *The Pantagraph*. Maybe you've read some of his articles? Anyhow, he's here for the conference *you* requested."

Mrs. Reynolds slid off her reading glasses, stood up, and offered her hand to Grant. Afterward, she circled the desk and invited her two guests to join her at a circular table in the back of the room. Along the way, they passed a series of historical maps placed chronologically along the wall. Above were pictures of the presidents, also laid out from first to last, beginning with George Washington and ending with Jimmy Carter. All the windows on the opposite side of the room were open, so the three-some could hear the whistles and shouts of an intense football practice, accompanied by the sounds of cheerleaders rehearsing their drills. Best of all, they could feel a cool autumn breeze refreshing the room.

Once seated, Mrs. Reynolds wasted no time wrestling control of the conference back from Michael.

"Thank you so much for giving up your afternoon to meet with me, Mr. Parker. And *yes*, I frequently enjoy reading your articles in the newspaper."

Even seated, Grant and Michael towered over the diminutive educator. Nevertheless, her tough-as-nails manner and the precise articulation of her words communicated instant control of the meeting. Despite her size, Mrs. Reynolds had few classroom management problems. Michael knew this and thought it best, for now, to let his father see him cower in her presence. Be patient and let her take the driver's seat. His turn would soon come.

"It's no problem," Grant declared. "On a beautiful day like this, it was nice to have an excuse to get out of the office. Besides, it's been a slow news day."

"Well," replied the history teacher, "I'm still sorry to get you out of your office under these circumstances. Let's get to the reason for this conference."

Grant nodded. Looking at Michael, he noticed his son's chest heave before he slumped back into the hard wooden chair with his arms crossed tightly. A scowl swept Michael's face as he stared angrily down at the wooden table. He would maintain a quiet but intransigent demeanor for now. Michael had recently read about using gambits to open games in a chess book he had recently checked out of the library. Sacrifice a pawn initially and then get a checkmate thirty moves later.

"Did Michael tell you anything about his class presentation on Monday?"

"Yes, he did," Grant answered, shifting awkwardly in the straight-back chair, trying to get more comfortable. He finally settled on lifting one leg to rest just above the knee of the other.

"And did he tell you," Mrs. Reynolds continued, "What person he chose to be the American hero for his presentation?"

Grant glanced at Michael, who faintly shrugged his shoulders. He was still leaning back as though relaxing on an open recliner.

"We were discussing that this morning," Grant answered, "But Michael had to leave for school before telling me the name. I know, however, that he was determined to pick someone unique, someone the other students would not know."

"I see," replied Mrs. Reynolds in a teacher's voice, which she had perfected over many years in the classroom. "Well then, I guess he should be commended," she added, this time with a touch of sarcasm, "Because I had never heard of William Joseph Simmons. Have you?"

Grant shook his head while sporting a self-conscious grin. He looked over at his son, who once again shrugged his shoulders with an "I told you so" expression.

"It was only from the content of his presentation," Mrs. Reynolds continued, "That I finally understood who William Simmons was. Mr. Parker, are you familiar with the movie *The Birth of a Nation*?"

Grant smiled and nodded, apparently pleased to know the answer to one of the history teacher's questions.

"Yes, it broke new ground as arguably Hollywood's first feature-length film. It came out early, though, so it was a silent movie. But I also know that it was DW Griffith who directed it, not someone named William Simmons."

"That's all correct," Mrs. Reynolds responded, continuing to speak in her teacher's voice. "William Simmons was just one of the fifty million people who viewed the film; he had nothing to do with producing it. However, unfortunately, the movie did such a terrific job of glorifying the Ku Klux Klan that after viewing it, Mr. Simmons was so inspired that he restarted the KKK after it had been inactive for forty years. He then declared himself the Imperial Wizard of the rejuvenated Invisible Empire. Within a few years, his Klan had a membership of four million. One out of every twenty-five Americans had a white robe hanging in their closet. Fifty thousand racists openly marched in the streets of our nation's capital. They also continued to burn crosses, terrify minorities, and lynch Blacks and Jews."

Realizing her lesson about Michael's choice was becoming a lecture, Mrs. Reynolds paused to let Mr. Parker digest her words. Then, before Grant or Michael could respond, she resumed her invective.

"This was your son's hero, Mr. Parker, one of America's all-time bigots. And he chose to deliver this presentation in front of a class that included three Blacks, two Jewish students, and one recently arrived immigrant from Honduras. Not to mention one teacher who was deeply offended by his choice and what he attempted to teach the class. I hope you understand why I had to interrupt and could not allow Michael to complete his report."

Mrs. Reynolds had made a compelling case against Michael. Grant then swiveled in his chair toward his son like the turret of a tank training its gun on a target. His face had reddened with anger and embarrassment. He leaned forward, placed his hands on the table, and clenched them so tightly they soon turned as crimson as his cheeks.

"Why?" he demanded, "Why would you deliberately choose a topic that would be *so* hurtful to others?"

Michael sat upright in his chair and placed his hands on the table two feet from his father's. Ever since this morning's conversation with Chicago Mike, he had expected this accusation from his father and was ready.

"For starters," Michael began, "William Simmons was simply a product of his time. That's one of the problems with how history is so often taught; we always judge people from the past by the standards of the present. That's hardly fair."

He glared over at Mrs. Reynolds but continued before either of the adults sitting at the table could respond.

"Half the country saw *The Birth of a Nation*, and most thought it was a fantastic film. Simmons wasn't the only one. President Woodrow

Wilson screened it in the White House and afterward said, and I quote, 'It's like writing history with lightning. My only regret is that it is all so terribly true.' President Wilson then went on to fully segregate the federal government. Of course, when a girl in our class gave her report on Woodrow Wilson, Mrs. Reynolds never said a word."

Michael observed his father exchanging glances with his history teacher. In the patronizing approach employed by so many grownups, they probably were thinking the same thing. Why couldn't Michael apply this thinking acuity to develop arguments *against* racism? Of course, they were both brainwashed by the same Civil Rights bullshit that had been gaining momentum ever since Rosa Parks had refused to obey the law in Montgomery, Alabama.

Maintaining her composure, Mrs. Reynolds turned back toward Michael. After all, she probably viewed him as another challenge. How many years had she been handling clever but misguided students?

"Michael, when Jenny gave her report on President Wilson, she focused on his Fourteen Points, his plan to create a League of Nations, and his vision of a world without war. She never said anything about his racism."

"True," Michael conceded, "But if she can focus only on the good and ignore the bad, why can't I?"

Mrs. Reynolds expelled an exasperated sigh. "Michael, what in the world was *good* about William Simmons?" She must have known this was a perilous question since it opened the door for Michael to say anything in his response.

"In the 1920s, the Klan that Simmons restarted became a powerful political force. And not just in Southern states. At its height, the KKK controlled the Indiana, Colorado, and Oregon state governments. Simmons' Klan also played a profound role in passing federal legislation that addressed one of our nation's greatest problems."

Out of the corner of his eye, Michael observed a subtle grin cross his father's face. He appeared to be enjoying this debate about how to interpret the past. Grant's head swayed back and forth like he had a center-court seat at Wimbledon. If Grant was taking pride in how his son was holding his own against a seasoned educator, however, Michael knew that, ultimately, his dad could never accept the defense of a racist position. His father would not allow Michael to win. Therefore, it was no surprise to Michael that Grant finally entered the fray.

"What was the nation's problem? And how did the Klan help resolve it?"

"The *problem*," Michael answered, as though speaking to a second-grader, "Was the same as it is now. *Immigration*. Except that back then, the nation's door was wide open. Not counting the one law restricting the Chinese, anyone else who could reach the United States could remain in the United States. Millions were pouring in—Poles, Greeks, Italians, and more than two million Russian Jews. They took away jobs and were used as strikebreakers to keep wages low for hardworking Americans. Thanks to the Klan's help, Congress passed the nation's first major immigration restrictions."

"Yes, and thanks to your Klan's help," Mrs. Reynolds interrupted in a tone shaded by more sarcasm, "Millions of Jews who were later murdered in Nazi death camps were denied entry into the United States. Michael, you've heard of Anne Frank? Had Congress not passed those immigration quotas in the 1920s, she and her family would have been allowed to immigrate to the United States. Who knows? Her grandchild could then have been one of your classmates."

Michael turned back to face his history teacher squarely. It was evident he was not about to back down. His response was immediate and delivered in the same sarcastic pitch.

"I'm *sorry* about Anne Frank, Mrs. Reynolds, I truly am. But she was a German-born Jew, not an American Christian. No one gets to choose their place of birth, and we all have to play the cards we're dealt. And by the way, it was the German Nazis who were responsible for Anne Frank's death, *not* William Simmons."

Finally, Grant, who had realized this debate could go on all day without either side convincing the other, raised his hands in exasperation to pause the argument.

"All right, Michael, that's enough. You're still the student in Mrs. Reynolds' classroom. And if your words are racist or hurtful to others, Mrs. Reynolds is fully within her right to pull the plug."

Michael physically shifted his entire body toward his dad. Even his hands, with their fingers still interlaced together, swung over to aim in his father's direction.

"But Dad, I've got the First Amendment on my side. And the ACLU, which you love to tell people you're a member of, says that the Constitution supports Frank Collin and his right to lead marches in Chicago. And now they're going to court to defend his rights."

Mrs. Reynolds' mouth fell into an O-shape, and her eyes widened. Her aghast expression temporarily froze the muscles of her face. Finally, she managed to respond.

"But those are *Nazis*," she proclaimed. "And they want to march in full uniform with swastikas on their arms. Michael, the free speech rights of every American citizen *are* protected by the First Amendment, but there are limits. Every one of our constitutional rights comes with restrictions and responsibilities. As I'm sure you know, Supreme Court Justice Oliver Wendall Holmes said, and I quote, 'Free speech would not protect a man falsely shouting fire in a theatre.'"

"That's what the Supreme Court said over fifty years ago," Michael coolly responded. "We'll see what the courts say about those limits today."

"Even if the courts come to the Nazis' rescue," Grant piped in, speaking with the authority of a journalist who had made his career under the protection of the First Amendment, "That doesn't mean you have those same rights as a high school student."

"Actually, Dad, I *do*," Michael countered arrogantly. "You ever hear of *Tinker v. Des Moines*?"

Grant peered over at Mrs. Reynolds as though seeking help, but she was too busy shaking her head and scowling at Michael to notice.

"It was a Supreme Court case seven years ago," Michael continued in the same teacher's tone Mrs. Reynolds had employed earlier. "When some high school students wore black armbands to school protesting America's involvement in the Vietnam War, the principal suspended them out of fear it would be disruptive. The kids took their case to court on the grounds that the principal had violated their First Amendment rights. Dad, they *won*. The Supreme Court stated that the students do not 'shed their constitutional rights to freedom of speech or expression at the schoolhouse gate.'"

Michael held up his fingers to indicate air quotes when speaking the final words. Then he sat back in his chair, locked his hands behind his head, and proudly smiled like a lawyer who had just rested his case. Grant glanced over at Mrs. Reynolds once again, and this time, she was looking back. They both wore the same perplexed expressions while simultaneously shaking their heads. Finally, Grant interrupted the silence hovering over the circular table.

"Nevertheless, Michael, I don't want you to do or say anything hurtful to others."

A cloud of silence floated above the round table for a few seconds. Then, seeing that Michael was about to launch another passionate diatribe in support of his position, Grant quickly interrupted.

"Look, Michael, I don't know if I should even say this, but I have strongly mixed feelings about this whole situation. On the one hand, I'm proud of your intellect and tenacity. On the other, though, I'm dumbfounded at your choice of a Grand Wizard for a history presentation and your defense of neo-Nazis."

Then, before Michael or Mrs. Reynolds could reply, Grant pivoted toward Michael's history teacher with a proposal he thought might appease both parties. Michael had always known that his father considered himself a master of mediation and compromise.

"Mrs. Reynolds, would you agree to let Michael have another chance to do his presentation if he chose a different person? And this time, subject to *your* approval in advance?"

"*Dad*," Michael interjected, "What about *my* approval?"

Grant calmly turned toward his son and replied, "You'll still get to make the initial proposal." Then, momentarily glancing toward Mrs. Reynolds, he added, "And after you and I brainstorm some ideas together, we're going to have an at-length discussion about why William Simmons was *not* an appropriate choice."

The history educator began nodding, and Michael thought he saw a faint smile appear on her face.

"That's acceptable, Mr. Parker." Then, as she began to stand, Mrs. Reynolds added, "This is a reasonable plan under the circumstances. However, I'd like us to communicate again in a few weeks. We should touch base at that time about Michael's progress."

Grant stood up, followed by his son. Both shook hands with Mrs. Reynolds over the round table, although there was a slight hesitation on Michael's part. Once in the hallway, Grant and Michael did not speak until they were well out of hearing range from Mrs. Reynolds' classroom. Then, just as Michael was about to raise a question, they heard a jocular voice from behind.

"Hey, Michael, you're here late today. And is that your father with you?"

Michael recognized the voice. Mr. Kaczynski was his chemistry teacher, and because of his deep interest in the subject, Mr. K was probably his favorite teacher. However, Michael also knew from previous conversations with his father that he had gone to school with Lyle Kaczynski. According to Grant, Mr. Kaczynski had always been a bit of a bully. At one point, though, they had been on the brink of becoming friends. That abruptly ended at the start of their senior year when both were interested in Marcia, a junior cheerleader. Mr. Kaczynski won the contest, but according to his father, Lyle eventually impregnated, married, and finally divorced the former cheerleader.

Over the years, Michael's dad occasionally ran into his former classmate, but neither had ever moved past their high school friction. Unfortunately, now they would meet in a location where their one common interest was Michael. The next few minutes had the potential to be highly awkward for all three participants.

"Mr. *Grant* Parker," Lyle added, "It's been a long time."

As the two men guardedly shook hands, Michael observed how his father stared a little too long at the beer belly that had settled over his former schoolmate's midsection. Then, Grant looked up at Lyle's thin hair, where gray strands had blended with the auburn. A large swath was plastered over the beginning of a bald spot. Michael also noticed how his father wrinkled his nose, probably at the funky chemical smell wafting from Mr. Kaczynski's apron.

"What brings you to our neck of the woods?" Mr. Kaczynski inquired, wearing a smug expression, as though Grant were trespassing on his territory.

"A conference with my son's history teacher," Grant answered. Michael knew that wild horses could not drag out any further explanation.

"Well, I hope everything is all right with Mrs. Reynolds," Lyle said. "Between you and me, she can be a tough broad." Mr. Kaczynski followed his comment with a childish grin and a knowing pat on the arm.

"We worked things out," Grant finally pronounced after a moment of awkward silence.

Before Grant and Michael could turn to leave, Lyle added, "Well, you know, in Chemistry, your son's one of my star pupils."

Lyle hesitated, waiting for a positive response. When none was forthcoming, he continued.

"In fact, Michael is one of the best students I've taught in years. He learns everything so quickly that I sometimes use him to help teach the slower students. Michael also asks insightful questions and appears to have an insatiable thirst for knowledge." After briefly pausing, Mr. K added, "At least in chemistry; I can't speak for history."

"*Oh*," Grant chuckled, "He's managed to learn quite a bit of history lately."

As Grant gazed at his son with a mixture of pride and vexation, Michael smiled despite his best effort to maintain a serious facade. Both father and son silently agreed to use the chemistry teacher's praise as an antidote for the toxic tension that had followed them out of Mrs. Reynolds' classroom. Then, swiveling back toward Lyle, Grant offered his hand and shook more vigorously this time.

"It was good to see you again, Lyle. And thanks for your kind words about my son."

At that, Grant tapped Michael's shoulder, indicating it was time to leave. They walked into the blinding sunlight, raising saluting hands to shade their eyes. As they strode in lockstep across the empty parking lot, Michael noticed a line of weary, grass-stained football players slowly walking in the opposite direction. Most were too fatigued from their practice to even look up. One, though, who must have weighed over 300 pounds, glanced up at Michael, grinned, and gave him a friendly wave.

As they approached the tiny Civic, Grant pulled out his keys, unlocked the car, and paused to glance at his son. At that moment, he could not help but smile.

"I know it's early, but maybe we should begin discussing possible topics for your presentation. Since I fear this may involve more negotiation than brainstorming, the sooner we start, the better, right?"

"No worries, Dad, I already have two names in mind. I'll share them with Mrs. Reynolds tomorrow and let her choose."

Grant was just about to squeeze into his small clown car, like he did every day, when he froze in place and stared intently at his son, who was preparing to get into the passenger side. They locked eyes and smiled at each other simultaneously.

"Wait, wait, don't tell me. Let me guess. Benedict Arnold and Aaron Burr? Or how about Jefferson Davis and Robert E. Lee? Maybe John Wilkes Booth and Lee Harvey Oswald?"

Grant sighed deeply, although he managed to preserve an increasingly forced smile. Meanwhile, Michael shook his head while maintaining a more genuine grin.

"No, Dad," Michael finally pronounced. "Why would I pick a traitor or an assassin as my hero?"

"All right, smartass, who do you plan to propose?"

"Charles Lindbergh and Henry Ford," Michael answered without delay.

Grant smiled and nodded in satisfaction. However, as he jammed his body into the car, he failed to notice the devious grin on his son's face.

CHAPTER 3

RACHEL

October 1976

Rachel's alarm went off at 6:30, even though it was a Saturday morning. She leaped out of bed, excited like a child on Christmas morning. The night before, she had brought home a 10-speed Trek bicycle. The bike was new, and so was the Wisconsin company that had built it. Painted ruby red, it was sleek, lightweight, and capable of climbing walls with its advanced gear shift, or so the salesman had told her. Of course, Rachel would seldom need this feature on the smooth plains of Central Illinois.

Rachel knew that there were only a few autumn days left when she could ride the bicycle, and today was forecast to be one of the best. While she had been advised to gradually build up her endurance for longer rides, Rachel had been an avid runner for many years and was in exceptional shape for someone who had just turned thirty. Before going to sleep the night before, she had consulted an Illinois road atlas, mapping a thirty-mile circular route that would take her out onto country roads before finishing up in Bloomington's Miller Park. Her plan included a relaxing break along the grassy slopes encircling the park's lagoon, after which she would pedal the short distance back to her apartment.

After dressing in record time, Rachel paused momentarily in front of a full-length mirror to study her image. Her new uniform was tailored for cycling. She wore sleek black shoes designed to slide into the bicycle's toe clips. Above were dark, padded pants, covered by a bright yellow jersey that made her look like the current leader in the Tour de France. Finally, a polished navy blue helmet crowned her head. Her wavy chestnut hair was tied back into a ponytail that tumbled out of the helmet from behind. Rachel's olive complexion made her look like she had just returned from a Mediterranean cruise. And the final piece de resistance was the streamlined new sunglasses she delicately placed over her aquamarine eyes.

As Rachel rolled her bicycle out of the apartment's mudroom and into the parking lot, she listened to the ratatat of the bicycle's sparkling new wheels. Once past her pine green Chevy Vega, Rachel stepped back to behold her new prized possession at arm's length. It was a beautiful piece of workmanship. For Rachel, an only child who had always lived modestly, this was the first time she had treated herself to a relatively expensive material possession. But why not? She was now an associate professor in the history department at Illinois State University, and while she would never be a millionaire, Rachel could afford a new bicycle.

She massaged the tires one last time. They still felt rock solid, just like the night before. Rachel then double-checked that the miniature bike pump was stowed correctly and that the tire repair kit was secure in a small bag beneath the bike's saddle. One of the greatest worries of distance cyclists was getting a flat tire miles away from home. Rachel had always been a cautious person and a meticulous planner. Today was no different.

Once she had raced beneath the I-55 overpass, Rachel pedaled out onto a county road aimed directly at the tiny hamlet of Danvers. With a population of less than a thousand, this little farming community was barely a dot on the map. The sun rose behind Rachel, casting her shadow onto the path. Her legs pumped like pistons. Surrounding her were eight-foot stalks of corn that guarded both sides of the empty roadway, waiting to be harvested. They reminded Rachel of German soldiers marching with rifles and fixed bayonets.

The air was crisp, and Rachel's cheeks turned red from the frosty breeze massaging her face. When she glanced down at the bike's digital speedometer, it read eighteen miles per hour. The speed was exhilarating, fueled chiefly by adrenaline. However, Rachel realized she could not maintain this pace with twenty-seven miles left. She reduced her speed but unknowingly resumed the same blazing pace shortly afterward.

As expected, the combination of speed, the bicycle's swaying motion, and the serene setting lulled Rachel into a semi-hypnotic trance. She decided to reflect on her current state of affairs to keep her mind active.

At moments like this, Rachel liked to review a mental checklist, essentially taking a personal inventory of her life.

She began by reviewing the positive side of the ledger. First and foremost, Rachel adored her parents. She was familiar with their background story, how they had somehow met and developed a romance in a Nazi concentration camp and then miraculously went on to survive the Holocaust. After the war, Benjamin and Miriam Abramowicz trekked from Poland to Sweden to New York and finally to Skokie, a predominantly Jewish suburb north of Chicago, where they had distant relatives.

Unfortunately, complications during birth kept Miriam from conceiving any more children, so Rachel was raised as an only child. At first, she wondered if this belonged on the negative side of the inventory. After all, there were many times when Rachel wished she had had a baby brother or sister—especially a sister.

On the bright side, Rachel knew that being their only child meant she had a monopoly on her parents' affection. Since Benjamin and Miriam were the most adoring and attentive parents she had ever known, Rachel considered this an asset. Many parents of only children often smother them with excessive attention, but Benjamin and Miriam always seemed to strike the perfect balance. Additionally, her early exposure to Yiddish, which was commonly spoken at home, likely helped Rachel develop advanced language skills that gave her an advantage over her peers in school during her formative years.

Rachel, conceived in Sweden but born a U.S. citizen, was also grateful for her Jewish heritage. However, as she came of age, she gradually drifted from a rigid belief in God. Rachel also rejected some of Judaism's more archaic traditions, such as separating men from women in Orthodox shuls. Still, there were elements of the Jewish faith that held a magnetic attraction for Rachel. She was particularly drawn to the moralistic components, such as the value placed on family, the evenhanded application of the law, and the sanctity placed on every human life.

Two other defining characteristics of Judaism also shaped Rachel's mindset. The first was tzedakah, which means "righteousness" in Hebrew but is often understood as "charity." However, Rachel understood tzedakah to mean more than a spontaneous act of goodwill. To her, it was an ethical obligation, a moral compass to guide her life. This value was so deeply ingrained in her sense of identity that Rachel was sometimes criticized for not being able to recognize the moral ambiguities in certain situations.

To Rachel, for example, John Brown, the antebellum abolitionist, was guilty of murder, plain and simple. She would readily concede that slavery was America's original sin. However, she believed that its abolition still did not justify the bloody massacre of five pro-slavery men in their cabins along Pottawatomie Creek in Kansas. Tzedakah had instilled a strong didactic tendency in Rachel, often leading her to see situations as strictly black and white, without recognizing the subtle shades of gray. However, she was fully aware of this aspect of her personality and would never apologize for it.

The other feature of Judaism that Rachel strenuously valued was its emphasis on history. Dating back over 3,500 years, she took great pride in belonging to the world's oldest monotheistic faith. Even though Rachel considered herself an agnostic regarding her belief in God, she knew the Torah had bound Jews together for several millennia. It enabled them to hold onto their traditions regardless of where they lived. The Torah, that is, the first five books of the Bible, had always been the key to the survival of the Jews.

Rachel knew there had been a Torah in every shul scattered across Poland, a nation inhabited by three million Jews before the Nazi invasion. She also knew they were in the arks of her synagogues in Skokie and, now, in Bloomington. Regardless of where a Jew fell on the continuum, from the most secular to the most orthodox, this provided a commonality amongst all Jews, an inseparable bond.

Rachel also appreciated the vital role that the modern state of Israel had played in securing this bond since its birth shortly after the end of World War II. She was an ardent Zionist and had always wished her parents had settled in Tel Aviv rather than Skokie. "Next year in Jerusalem" was the phrase she loved repeating during every Passover seder. However, her parents were deeply rooted American patriots. They might leave Skokie to follow their daughter to the plains of Central Illinois, but they would never give up their American citizenship. It was second only to their daughter as their greatest source of pride.

Benjamin and Miriam followed Rachel to Bloomington-Normal, and for this, she was deeply grateful. Since her father had once repaired footwear, it was only natural that he would establish a shoe store in Skokie. When Rachel landed the position at ISU, he happily traded one shoe business for another, this time opening a new store in Bloomington's Eastland Mall. Miriam, who worked at home as a seamstress, taking in clothing and sewing hems, could do that anywhere. Rachel was appreciative of her parents' willingness to move. It would allow them to maintain their symbiotic relationship for many years to come.

Finally, under the positive side of the ledger, Rachel was pleased with the person she saw in the mirror each morning. Never lacking in confidence, Rachel knew she was intelligent, attractive, and a fundamentally decent person. She never had many friends, but that was mostly by choice. Rachel hated the silly gamesmanship young girls played to fit into a desired clique. Instead, she had gradually assembled a few close friends over the years whom she knew could always be counted on.

In high school, Rachel steered clear of the tables filled with jocks, cheerleaders, and even the bright, nerdy students. Instead, she chose to sit with the girls whom others considered social misfits. When she attended Northwestern for college, she completely refused to consider joining a sorority. During the years Rachel took to earn her doctoral degree from the University of Chicago, she only formed two close friendships.

Rachel also applied this highly selective approach to the boys in her life. She had one serious relationship in high school, but that ended when Mark chose to attend UCLA, knowing she planned to remain in Chicago to be closer to her parents. There was also just one in college, but Rachel ended it when John took a position with Mayor Daley's office after graduation. To her, the Daley Machine was unconscionably corrupt. In graduate school, Rachel was almost engaged to a young physician, but Philip's late discovery of his sexual attraction to men abruptly ended that relationship.

As Rachel neared her thirtieth birthday, she would hesitantly list the absence of a meaningful love interest as the one negative item on her checklist. At least in Rachel's view, though, her new position at ISU outweighed the lack of a serious boyfriend. She loved lecturing to her survey classes in European history, had already begun to develop a strong reputation for her electives on twentieth century Europe and Nazi Germany, and especially enjoyed researching the sociological factors behind Hitler's rise to power in the 1920s and 1930s.

As Rachel steered her bicycle south and then east, back toward Bloomington, she finally slowed her pace. The sun had risen higher in the sky, and she was beginning to compete with more traffic on the roadway. It was time to bring her private reckoning to an end and pay more attention to her surroundings. As a final moment of closure, Rachel acknowledged that the only significant piece missing from her puzzle was a love interest, especially because she wanted her parents to become a Bubbie and a Zadie one day.

Twenty minutes later, Rachel was seated cross-legged on a lawn sloping toward the lagoon in Miller Park. She had briefly entertained the thought of touring the Bloomington Zoo since she had heard that what it lacked in size, it made up in "adorable critters," like red pandas, river otters, and a giant tortoise. But since she had neglected to buy a bike lock, this option would have to wait for another day. Instead, while Rachel gazed down at a young mother and toddler feeding bread crumbs to a flock of ducks, she decided to return to the subject of that one missing piece.

Rachel had always been picky about admitting new people into her life, or as she preferred to say, she was "selective." Should she now loosen her standards? Rachel had recently made the momentous decision to remove Judaism from the checklist for a future spouse, although her parents could barely mask their disappointment when she mentioned this. Rachel had convinced herself that what mattered most were the values held by her husband, not whether he was circumcised.

Maybe she should expand her options to nearby cities, like Peoria, Springfield, or Champaign-Urbana. They were all within an hour's drive. And what about age or education? Mary, a graduate student working as her teaching assistant, had invited her to a party tonight. Of course, most attendees would be a bit younger, and Rachel had always hated social situations defined by heavy drinking, loud music, and people striving too hard to impress each other.

Down the road, the only other option Rachel could think of would be to leave Bloomington-Normal and look for a position in a larger city like Chicago, St. Louis, or Cincinnati. Given that her parents had already uprooted themselves to follow her to Central Illinois, though, she could hardly expect them to do so again. Rachel expelled a large sigh, telling herself that while she would keep trying, her options were growing increasingly limited. Perhaps a husband and children would have to be shelved, at least for a while, in return for maintaining an intellectually stimulating career and an already tight-knit family.

Rachel stood up, strapped on her helmet, and reached for the bicycle lying in the grass. As she wheeled it toward a nearby asphalt path, she observed that the rear wheel made a thwacking sound as it turned. Reaching down, Rachel squeezed the tire, felt the rubber give, and shook her head in exasperation. Her worst cycling fear had been realized. The tire was flat. Rachel had never repaired a bike tire before, and while she knew the basic steps, the back tire presented some particular challenges. Taking off this tire meant dealing with the chain and a pyramid of sprockets.

Rachel stripped off her helmet, gently laid the bike on its side in the grass, and sat down to begin the delicate operation. Removing the tire took a few minutes, and pulling out the rubber tube proved easier than expected. After pumping air into the tire to locate the leak, Rachel pulled out the tire repair kit, spread some glue around the hole, and carefully secured the patch onto the black rubber. So far, so good.

The next step also went smoothly. Rachel squeezed the uninflated tube into the tire and slid its axle back into its permanent home. Now came the hard part. How do you get the chain secured onto the tire's sprockets? Rachel maneuvered the wheel at several angles, but the chain refused to catch. She shook her head in exasperation. Then, a shadow fell over her.

"It might help to have a second pair of hands," a deep voice suggested. "May I help?"

Rachel glanced up and raised a hand to shield her eyes. Towering above her was a man, but it wasn't easy to make out his features with the sun glowing behind his head like a halo. After Rachel nodded her assent, the man knelt on one knee and, using the tire lever from her repair kit, guided the chain onto one of the tire sprockets with one hand while slowly rotating the pedals with the other. It worked! Once secure, Rachel stood up to pump air into the repaired tire. While sliding the pump's handle up and down, she snuck a peek at the man holding the bike up for her.

He was tall, with a wiry frame and forearms that were muscular but not too brawny. The man had the body of a distance runner, and this was further confirmed when Rachel observed his nylon shorts and Saucony running shoes. His dirty blond hair was in disarray, with some of the tufts plastered down by sweat. Clearly, he had interrupted his long run to help her with the tire. When Rachel finally looked up, he smiled radiantly, and when he stripped off his sunglasses, probably to get a better view of her, the man unmasked a pair of soft blue eyes that resembled those of her father.

"Thank you *so* much," Rachel gushed while securing the bike pump back into its bracket. "Now I'll know how to do this in the future."

"No problem," the man responded. "I was ready for a little break, so this was good timing."

Realizing the man would soon resume his run if she did not say anything, Rachel blurted out the first question that came to mind.

"Are you training for something?"

"Yes," the man answered. "The New York Marathon. It's in three weeks."

"On my gosh," uttered Rachel, "Did you just interrupt your long run to help me?"

The man momentarily looked down and wiped away the sweat streaming down his face. Then he glanced at his digital wristwatch, touching a button that issued a low beep. Finally, he looked back up at Rachel, and the sunny smile returned to his face.

"Actually, that's next week, and it'll be twenty miles. Today was only supposed to be eighteen."

"Did you finish the eighteen?" Rachel inquired tentatively.

"No," the man answered, as though he could not tell a white lie, "It was about seventeen. But I don't think the training gods will care if I skip the last mile."

"Well, thanks again," Rachel uttered as she leisurely climbed onto her bike's saddle.

"What's your name?" the man suddenly asked. He was clearly looking her over, although trying not to appear too obvious.

"Rachel. Rachel Abramowicz. You?"

"Grant. Grant Parker. It's nice to meet you, Rachel Abramowicz." Then, after a brief pause, he extended his hand to shake. Rachel found that she was attracted to Grant's old-fashioned style. He was indeed a gentleman. On closer examination, Grant appeared to be a few years older, but Rachel did not see a ring on his finger. She briefly recalled her recent self-inventory. Maybe it was time to take a chance.

"Hey, Grant," Rachel asserted, "I'm basically done with my workout, and you sound like you're finished with yours. Would you let me buy you lunch? You know, to thank you for helping me with my tire?"

Rachel observed how Grant cocked his head as though he was earnestly considering her invitation. Then she glanced down self-consciously, realizing that her outfit made her look like one of the boys. Rachel also suspected that Grant might be concerned about their age difference. However, if it didn't matter to her, it hopefully would not be an issue for him. Of course, they knew nothing about each other, but an hour or two over a decent meal would quickly change that. If nothing else, it was just lunch, not a marriage proposal.

"Sure," responded Grant. "Where would you like to take me?"

"How about Avanti's? In Normal? Do you know it?"

"Of course," Grant answered. "You'd have to live under a rock not to know Avanti's in this town. Whatever you order, it's absolutely delicious if served on their bread."

The corners of Rachel's mouth turned upwards, and her dimples deepened, acknowledging Grant's assessment of her restaurant choice. She glanced down at her watch. "How about we meet there in an hour? That should give us enough time to go home, clean up, and then drive to the restaurant."

"Sounds like a plan. I'll see you in an hour, Miss Rachel Abramowicz."

And with that, Grant turned away and started jogging down the asphalt path. Rachel watched as he accelerated to an impressive speed. She smiled impishly, wondering if he would maintain that pace all the way home or was just showing off. Either way, Rachel was pleased with herself. To her memory, she had never asked a man out on a date. But this was the 1970s, and the Equal Rights Amendment only needed a few more states to be ratified. The times were indeed changing.

Ninety minutes later, Rachel and Grant were chowing down on Avanti's famous Gondolas, cold sandwiches with ham, salami, cheese, and lettuce. The key, however, was the homemade bread. With a slightly sweet taste, the crusty buns concealed a soft, doughy interior that would melt in your mouth. Rachel and Grant were familiar with the iconic restaurant and ordered the same item off the menu without hesitation.

In addition, they both cleaned up well. Rachel took a few extra minutes to blow dry her hair and threw on a yellow sundress that was a bit low cut and short enough to show off her shapely legs. This was an outfit Rachel saved for occasions such as this, not when she was going to synagogue with her parents. Grant chose a pair of jeans instead of his usual cargo shorts, topped by a plaid button-down shirt tight enough to accentuate the musculature of his shoulders and chest. Rachel and Grant had dressed to play up their best assets.

The conversation over lunch mainly focused on their biographical backgrounds. Grant loved that Rachel was a history professor since he had minored in that subject in college. He was also intrigued by her Jewish background. Despite Rachel's self-description as a "secularized Jew," Grant was still a little concerned about the barrier their religious differences might pose in the distant future. Rachel subscribed to *The Pantagraph* and was already familiar with Grant's work. And, while she respected his fervent commitment to Michael, his teenage son, she still had questions about the story behind his divorce.

Due to the restaurant's popularity, Rachel and Grant noticed the stares from some people in the crowd waiting in the foyer for a table. Shortly after their plates had been cleared, Grant offered to buy dessert down the street at the Baskin-Robbins. They strolled up Main Street, spooning their ice cream from cups as they walked. Rachel and Grant then made their way to the ISU quad, where they sat on an empty bench under the shade of a white oak tree to savor their melting treats and extend their date.

By late afternoon, Grant mentioned he had had such a lovely time that he wanted to continue their date over dinner at Biaggi's. He suggested they walk back to their cars, drive home, and change into clothes more suitable for a swankier restaurant. This time, however, he asserted that he would like to pick Rachel up at her place and that dinner would be on him. Rachel readily accepted, just as eager to keep the magic going for as long as possible.

During their hike back to the car, Grant mentioned something that placed a blip on Rachel's radar. It seemed inconsequential at the time, but afterward, she made a mental note to look into it further.

"You know," Grant commented when talking about his son, "Michael moved in with me a few months ago, but there are times when I still feel like I'm living with a stranger."

"Yes," Rachel agreed, as though she had extensive experience as a parent. "Teenagers can be like that."

Grant nodded in agreement as they made their way up South University Street. But then he added, "In this case, I think it's more than just hormones."

"Well," Rachel conceded, "I've never met your son, but from what you've told me, I'd guess his parents' divorce at an early age, combined with being bounced back and forth between here and Chicago, might weaken the normal father-son relationship. Right?"

"That's true," Grant replied despondently. "But I think there's something else going on, and I can't quite put my finger on it."

He glanced over at Rachel, who was gazing straight ahead. Then, he casually reached over to touch her arm, indicating he wanted to stop walking for the moment to face her. As Rachel came to a stop, she was shocked by how quiet and deserted the street was. There were times when automobile and pedestrian traffic jams choked University Street. But this was a Saturday afternoon. Since there were no classes, it probably helped that at least the offshoot footpaths to the classroom buildings were deserted.

"I don't know why I'm sharing this with you, Rachel. And I hope it won't scare you off because I definitely want to see more of you going forward."

Grant paused momentarily and looked away. When he returned his gaze toward Rachel, an unexpected grimace appeared on his face. He glanced downward and clenched his hands together.

"I know we only met a few hours ago," he continued, "but I need to get something off my chest. I enjoyed talking to you today, Rachel, and I want to see a lot more of you in the future. However, I'm worried about how Michael will fit into all this."

Vertical lines creased Rachel's forehead as her lips tightened. "Why?"

"I'm worried," Grant paused and then bit his lower lip, searching for the right words.

"I'm worried because of the years Michael spent in a hornet's nest in Chicago. It's not just his mother. Her entire family is in Marquette Park, and they're nothing but a bunch of racist bigots."

"I see," Rachel responded pensively. "And has Michael done anything to make you believe he's come under their spell?"

"Maybe," answered Grant hesitantly. "I recently met with his history teacher at school. She was upset that he not only chose a KKK leader to do an oral report on but that he also tried to convince the class that this guy was some kind of hero."

Rachel nodded knowingly and sighed, wrestling with a mix of emotions. On one hand, the past few hours had been magical—perhaps the best time she had spent with a man in years. On the other hand, as she learned more about Grant's family situation, she began to see red flags warning her to stay away. A woman who prided herself on being objective, Rachel found herself utterly confused. For once, she decided it might be best to follow her instincts rather than her intellect.

"Well," Rachel finally commented, searching for something to say, "Some sixteen-year-olds will do almost anything to garner attention."

At that moment, Grant shocked her. He reached out and took her hand. Then, after interlacing his fingers within hers, he gently prodded her forward, and they began to walk back toward Avanti's. Silence ensued as the pair pondered the day's developments. By the time they returned to their cars, Rachel had convinced herself that the perfect man simply did not exist at this stage in her life. Any relationship would come with baggage. She would have to go slow with Grant and take things one step at a time.

Rachel had settled on the next step by the time they reached the restaurant's parking lot. If Grant was concerned about his son developing racist or possibly anti-Semitic feelings, how would he feel about her parents and *their* story? Would he turn and run in the other direction after hearing about her mother and father's experiences at Sobibor? Rachel would find out tonight when she shared their story with him over dinner.

As Grant walked Rachel to her car, she decided to share her plan for that evening, partly to give him an advanced warning but also to build up a little anticipation for what was coming. He nodded politely and stated that he looked forward to hearing all about Benjamin and Miriam. This was followed by a quiet moment as Rachel and Grant stood facing each other beside her Chevy Vega.

They were still holding hands, reluctant to let go. Then it was Rachel's turn to surprise Grant by taking another audacious risk. With her free hand, she reached up, placed it behind Grant's neck, and pulled him in for a passionately bold kiss.

CHAPTER 4

MIRIAM AND BENJAMIN

September 1942

The door suddenly slammed open, allowing brilliant sunlight to spill into the crowded boxcar. Although the journey had taken only a few hours, the people crammed inside needed a moment for their eyes to adjust. Benjamin Abramowicz roused his wife and three-year-old daughter from their empty numbness and gently prodded them toward the exit. On the horizon, Benjamin spotted an alluring line of pine trees bathed in the sun's mid-afternoon glow.

In the foreground, though, a daytime nightmare transpired as an SS officer with a megaphone and a leashed dog shrieked at the Polish refugees to disembark from the railcars. There was mayhem on each exit ramp as a combination of soldiers and camp workers attempted to organize the newly arrived Jews into orderly groups. While Benjamin and his tiny family awaited their turn to venture out, he glanced to his left. A column of dark smoke punctuated the turquoise sky. Benjamin wondered what was burning in this work camp that was supposed to be his family's new home.

With a hand on their shoulders, Benjamin tenderly guided his wife and daughter down the ramp. More than anything, he was determined to keep his family together. Benjamin could feel his heart pounding beneath his shirt like a jackhammer. He was only 27 years old, but something told him the remainder of his life would be decided by what happened in the next few minutes.

Once on the ground, Benjamin stood at the back of a rectangular cluster of people. An SS officer sporting a lightning bolt insignia stood menacingly facing the group. Behind him, someone who appeared to be the commanding officer waited impatiently on a wooden platform for the crowd to settle down. A megaphone dangled in one hand while the other held a leash attached to a massive St. Bernard. Benjamin knew this breed was famously trained for mountain rescue operations during avalanches. The savage animal lingering above, however, looked more like Cerberus, the monstrous watchdog of the mythological underworld.

Most people were on the verge of mass hysteria. Grandparents mixed with a wide assortment of younger men and women. There were also infants, toddlers, and children of all ages. Although their civilian clothing ranged from rags to expensive suits, everyone was required to display a yellow six-pointed star on their shoulder. Using his taller height to sweep across the panoramic scene, Benjamin, who had worked as an accountant because of his talent with numbers, estimated the crowd to be more than a thousand.

Several camp workers, wearing uniforms made of coarse grey-blue striped material, cautiously circled around and behind each group, attempting to quiet the restless audience. Benjamin knew they were Jewish because they also sported the familiar yellow stars. One of them, an older man with dark wavy hair and powerful shoulders, slowed behind Benjamin and leaned in to whisper a message. There was no way to know it then, but this man was about to save Benjamin's life.

"When they ask if you have a skill, step forward and say you're a shoemaker."

Before the man could drift away, Benjamin leaned back while still facing forward, responding under his breath.

"I'm an accountant. I don't know anything about making shoes."

The man paused and casually moved back toward Benjamin. He glanced around to be sure he had not attracted any attention.

"It doesn't matter. Just *do* it."

Benjamin observed that the crowd had grown quiet as the man moved away. Then, finally, the commandant lifted the megaphone to his mouth and spoke. As he did, Benjamin observed something for the first time. It was glaringly obvious; why had he not noticed it before? Behind the camp commander was a broad sign with seven letters painted across its width: SOBIBOR.

The commandant explained that everyone must shower for sanitary reasons before settling into their family barracks. He then ordered males to separate themselves from females. This command created further chaos as Benjamin and several other men objected to separating themselves from their families. The camp commander lifted the megaphone, spoke with surprising reassurance, and calmed the crowd by stating they would all be reunited soon. Besides, he proclaimed, it was only proper that the crowd segregate by sex for the showers.

It took a few minutes to reorganize the mass of people, but when finally accomplished, there were now two large assemblies directly facing each other. Benjamin eyed his wife and daughter in the opposite crowd. He nodded and forced a weak smile to comfort them. Benjamin observed that the wind had shifted because some charcoal-colored smoke from the distant fire drifted over their heads. A new smell had also replaced the sweet aroma of the pines, something mildly repellent.

Before deploying his vast audience toward the showers, the commandant had one final request. He asked tailors, seamstresses, metal workers, carpenters, electricians, plumbers, and anyone else with unique skills to step forward. Benjamin, who had been brought up to believe honesty was a virtue, hesitated. Then, he spotted the Jewish camp worker who had advised him to lie about being a shoemaker. The man was glaring at Benjamin. With his eyes, he pointed toward where those with special skills were gathering.

Benjamin glanced back at his wife, who had picked up their daughter and was straining to keep her still. Ada was not tall, but she was uncommonly strong. Her auburn hair framed a young woman's face, highlighted by gentle almond-shaped eyes. Even from a distance, Benjamin could observe the discrepancy between Ada's strained smile and the tears streaming down her cheeks. Benjamin and Ada had heard rumors about what happened in these camps, so they appreciated the moment's significance. Finally, Ada nodded. Only then did Benjamin step forward to join this small gathering of men and women.

Benjamin married Ada five years ago, and their union was based on love, breaking away from the traditional practice of using a matchmaker. Two years later, they welcomed their daughter, Sonia, adding even more joy to their lives. However, their situation took a turn for the worse in the fall of 1939 when the Soviet Red Army occupied their village. Over time, many residents began to feel thankful that they did not live in the western half of Poland, which had been invaded by the Nazis.

In July 1941, when Hitler turned against Stalin and launched the largest invasion force in history into the Soviet Union, Benjamin considered evacuating his family to the East, past the Ural Mountains, to escape the SS and their plans for Poland's three million Jews. However, Ada opposed this idea, as many of her extended family members were reluctant to leave.

Now, the moment of reckoning had arrived. Benjamin told himself that if the showers were a ruse for something more insidious, he could do nothing to help his wife and daughter. Joining the massive crowd of men as they marched to their fate would not save Ada and Sonia. Nevertheless, as he restlessly swayed within the smaller crowd of young men and women, Benjamin was on the verge of retching.

Shortly afterward, the enormous mass of men and women marched off to the showers, leaving only a few dozen claiming to possess skills valued by the SS. Then, with its freight cars emptied, the train steamed away on the tracks behind them, leaving a sea of suitcases and other personal belongings. Benjamin still naively hoped that when the Jewish camp workers began to collect this baggage, they would take it to the barracks of the massive crowd heading for the showers.

Shortly afterward, two SS officers led Benjamin and the others to a sprawling dilapidated barrack crowded with young men and women. They were curtly ordered to eat, sleep, and be ready for a full day of work beginning at sunrise. After a meal of stale bread and watery soup, Benjamin strode outside to inquire about his wife and daughter. Certainly, they should have returned by now. Standing before the barrack, Benjamin observed that it was a picturesque, tranquil evening. Nevertheless, he noted an eerie light glowing in the east while the sun's radiance barely lingered in the west. Was something still burning?

The evening's stillness was suddenly disturbed by a man approaching from behind. His familiar voice prickled the hairs on the back of Benjamin's neck. "You're wondering about that light, aren't you?"

It was the camp worker who had told Benjamin to lie about being a shoemaker.

"Yes," Benjamin answered. After pausing, he added, "And I'm worried about my wife and daughter. They never returned from the showers." Then, after another brief interlude, he asked, "Do you know where they are?"

The camp worker met Benjamin's question with silence. The longer it lasted, the queasier Benjamin felt. For a moment, the two men trained their parallel gazes on the sinister glow above the shadowy profile of the pines. Finally, the camp worker turned to his new acquaintance. He reached out and gently pivoted Benjamin so the two men squarely faced each other.

"My name is Leon," the man pronounced. "Yours?"

"Benjamin. Benjamin Abramowicz."

Leon nodded, indicating he wanted to know more than just a name. Taking his cue, Benjamin continued.

"My family and I are from a village in eastern Poland near the Russian border. The Red Army originally occupied our region. That was bad enough, but when the Nazis invaded the Soviet Union last year, the situation grew even worse."

"Yes, I know," Leon interjected. "The Russians have always hated the Jews, but compared to them, the Germans are the epitome of evil. They plan to kill us all."

Benjamin was just over six feet tall and looked down slightly at his new friend. He brushed aside a strand of blond hair while considering what Leon had just said. Then, suddenly, terror inflated Benjamin's eyes as he realized Leon was not exaggerating. When he'd said, "Kill us all," he meant it literally.

"Listen, Benjamin, there's no easy way to say this. Unfortunately, your wife and daughter will not be coming back."

A tear leaped from one of Benjamin's eyes and streamed down his stubbled cheek. He remained quiet, patiently waiting for Leon to continue.

"They did not get a shower. No one did. That's just a lie the Nazis say to keep everyone calm. Instead, once they were locked inside the shower chamber, they were all gassed."

Benjamin placed a hand over his mouth. "*Gassed*? What do you mean?"

"Everyone strips naked, believing they're about to get showers. Once locked inside, though, the Nazis pipe in the exhaust from old Sovieengines."

Leon paused so Benjamin could process his words. He had engaged in this conversation many times since arriving at Sobibor. No matter how often Leon shared this horrific information, it never got easier. Meanwhile, Benjamin gazed downward, cupped both hands above his eyes, and sobbed. He abruptly collapsed onto his knees, and his entire body began to quake. When Leon reached down to touch his shoulders, Benjamin stood and embraced his new friend. Leon had grown up the son of a rabbi, so he did not shy away from assuming this role as a consoler.

When Benjamin finally pulled away, he glanced at the glimmering light above Leon's shoulder. A look of understanding flashed across his eyes.

"The smoke I saw earlier today?" Benjamin inquired, "And the light I'm looking at right now?"

"They have ovens to cremate the bodies," Leon stated matter-of-factly.

Once again, Leon paused to allow Benjamin time to absorb the indescribable horror of his new home. He knew that for people unfamiliar with the mechanics of Hitler's Final Solution, the concept of efficiently running killing factories was beyond their comprehension. While Benjamin gazed toward the crematoriums, Leon broke the silence.

"When you're ready, my friend, we should talk. The Nazis did not build this place to leave anyone left alive. Ultimately, they intend for all of us to end up as ashes floating up those chimneys." Again, he intentionally hesitated so Benjamin had time to grasp the surrealism of the moment. "That is, unless we do something first."

Benjamin stepped back, attempting to understand the meaning of Leon's words. At this moment, any talk about resistance or escape was meaningless to Benjamin. He was still visualizing what had just happened to Ada and Sonia, wishing he had joined them.

"*Look*, my friend," Leon pronounced, "You should not spend too much time grieving over what's already happened. Trust me; there was absolutely nothing you could have done to prevent it. So, cry if you must, but when you're done, please understand that your survival is the *only* way to ensure that anyone will ever remember your wife and daughter."

Benjamin calmed his breathing and nodded. Then, for the first time, he gazed up and locked eyes with Leon.

"At first glance," Leon continued, "Breaking out of this place would appear impossible. There are only about fifteen SS officers, but over a hundred Ukrainian guards back them up. The Ukrainians don't particularly like us, but they're not cold-blooded murderers like the SS. Most are just a bunch of mercenary lackeys who can't lace their boots without Nazi instructions."

Benjamin kept nodding, though it was difficult to gauge his understanding. At least Leon had diverted his attention from thoughts of Ada and Sonia for the time being.

"And then there's the double set of electrified barbed wire fencing. And beyond the fences are the minefields."

Benjamin suddenly awoke from a daze. Signs of life returned to his eyes, and his dry lips parted into a sardonic smile.

"That's all there is?" he chuckled. "I'm surprised you didn't break out a long time ago."

"Believe me," Leon responded, "Many have tried. But we'll only have a chance if we're patient, organize ourselves properly, and wait for the right moment. Besides, we have nothing to lose, right?"

Benjamin inhaled deeply and nodded. He forced an appreciative smile, patted Leon on the arm, and circled past him to file into the barrack. Once inside, Benjamin crawled into an unoccupied wooden lower bunk in a corner and curled into a fetal position. A few minutes later, a short, stocky man tapped his shoulder, introduced himself as Max, and said Leon had sent him. Max indicated that he ran the camp's shoe repair shop and told Benjamin where to report the following morning, assuring him he would teach him everything he needed to know.

Benjamin hardly noticed when the barrack went dark. He was wide awake, though, and could not stop thinking about the mournful expression on Ada's face the last time he saw her. Even though he tried not to, Benjamin kept resurrecting the vision of his wife carrying his daughter into the shower chamber, wishing against all hope that water would soon flow from the nozzles overhead instead of exhaust fumes. But then, the vision faded so that all Benjamin could see was the crowd of women shrieking and climbing over each other, frantically trying to breathe. For hours, this nightmarish scenario continued to replay in Benjamin's mind.

Shortly before dawn, Benjamin recalled Leon's description of the electrified fencing surrounding the camp. He came to a decision. With his mind made up, Benjamin fell at last into a dreamless sleep. An hour later, however, he suddenly awakened and absentmindedly trudged outside, following the line of zombies to the open compound for the morning roll call. Afterward, while everyone else dispersed in a dozen directions, Benjamin paused to fix his bearings. He studied a line of barbed wire fencing that stretched between two guard towers. Next, he spied the machine gun barrels jutting from each tower's nest.

Suddenly, by some quirk of fate, Benjamin spotted an older man cautiously approaching the fence. There was a blank expression on his face as though he was under hypnosis. Threats hailed down from one of the guard towers. A machine gun peppered the soil before him as a warning. When he still didn't retreat, bullets from above ripped into the man's throat, spurting blood from his carotid artery like a fountain. Still, the man's body convulsed, unwilling to let go of life.

Benjamin was in a complete state of shock. Nevertheless, he was grateful for the lesson he had just learned. The best one could hope for was a quick and painless end. Benjamin made an instantaneous decision. He would *run* toward the fence. That way, the electricity would quickly end his life. It would all be over in a matter of seconds.

For a moment, Benjamin examined the macabre scene in front of him. The man's body ceased trembling while a pool of blood gathered around his head, turning the dry dirt into a reddish circle of mud. Benjamin spotted puffs of smoke dissipating from the machine gun nest at the top of the tower, but otherwise, the camp grew eerily silent. He assumed the man's body might remain there all day to serve as a warning.

Benjamin looked up at the electrified fence like it was the portal he would have to cross through to rejoin his family. He visualized Ada and Sonia's smiling faces. Just yesterday morning, they trusted him when he led them to the railway station on the edge of the ghetto as it was being liquidated. Later, bathed in angst, he recalled their expressions as they joined the crowd of women, unknowingly preparing to march to their deaths. Benjamin had already missed them *so* much that he couldn't breathe. What's more, his sorrow blended with guilt. How could he live another moment without them?

Benjamin scouted around in every direction. Except for the guards posted in the distant towers, he was alone. Thanks to the freakishly odd coincidence that another person would intentionally approach the electrified fencing just before he could take his turn, no one noticed Benjamin at this particular moment. He fixed his gaze on a nearby section of fencing equidistant from two towers. This would be his target.

Before he could take the first step, Benjamin felt a hand on his shoulder. He froze, fearing it was an SS guard. Benjamin slowly glanced over his shoulder and was stunned to see the face of an attractive young woman. Where had she come from? Barely over five feet tall, she was almost a foot shorter than Benjamin. To get a better look, he spun around to face her directly. As if reading his mind, the woman squinted her eyes, tightened her lips, and slowly shook her head.

"Don't *do* it. You'll just make their job easier. If you want to avenge the murder of your wife and daughter, then *stay alive*. Survival is your best revenge."

Benjamin studied her face. She had dark hair that fell just to her shoulders, round chocolate-colored eyes, and a deep olive complexion. Even while enduring his worst nightmare, Benjamin couldn't help but recognize her captivating beauty. Additionally, her straightforward manner had captured his full attention.

"How did you know about my family?" Benjamin inquired.

"Leon told me. He asked me to keep an eye on you." Then, pausing to nod toward the nearby corpse, she added, "I saw what happened to him. I don't want you to make the same mistake."

"I see," Benjamin replied, unknowingly nodding in agreement. For a moment, he was at a loss for words. Then, finally, he thought to ask a simple question.

"What's your name?"

"Miriam. Miriam Rosenfeld. And I already know yours." She glanced around as though someone might be listening. Then, Miriam looked up directly at him and asked, "Can I trust you will not do anything foolish? At least for now?"

Benjamin peered over her shoulder toward the fence. He had been only seconds away from throwing himself on the barbed wire with its invisible, lethal current. For now, he remained silent.

"Look, Benjamin," she stated as though issuing an order, "I want you to wait a day. That fence will still be here tomorrow. In the meantime, you need to get to your shoe repair shop, the position Leon secured for you. And I also need to get to my job. We can talk more later tonight."

Benjamin remained quiet, but this time, he nodded in agreement.

"Good," she replied, and then Miriam broke into an understated smile. "Now, Benjamin, get to your shop and learn everything you need to know to *survive*."

Benjamin unknowingly smiled for the first time since his arrival in Sobibor as he stepped toward the shop on the other side of camp. However, an unsettling numbness soon churned within his gut. His encounter with Miriam had lasted only a few seconds, but Benjamin felt oddly disloyal. One moment, he was on the verge of running toward the electrified fencing to join his wife and daughter. The next, at the behest of an unknown woman, he was marching toward the shoe repair shop, bent, at least for the time being, on survival. Try as he might, for the rest of his long life, Benjamin could never fully process what took place the first time he met Miriam.

For the next twelve hours, Benjamin worked diligently in the shop with Max, a good-natured Lithuanian, who guided him in the repair of boots and shoes. In particular, Max stressed the need to work extra hard on the SS footwear. One unintended blemish on their shiny jackboots could easily provoke a mortal thrashing. The work was relatively easy compared to most other jobs within the camp, but it still required his complete attention since it was all new to him.

Benjamin mulled over his last 36 hours while shuffling back to the barracks at the end of the day. Before arriving at the camp, people had always ribbed him for his sunny disposition and eternal optimism. Therefore, nobody would have predicted what he almost did that morning. Now, he was in a complete state of flux. Part of him still wanted to sprint to the electrified barbed wire at top speed. Another part, though, kept replaying Miriam's words: *Survival is your best revenge.*

Benjamin also appreciated the relativity of the situation. He now understood that most people arriving in Sobibor would be murdered and cremated within a few hours after disembarking from their railcars. Benjamin, on the other hand, was still alive. Moreover, despite the dystopian environment surrounding him, kind people were looking out for his welfare. Leon had saved his life yesterday, and Miriam did the same this morning. So, without realizing it, Benjamin accelerated his stride.

Later that evening, after gagging down the same tasteless meal of soup and bread, Benjamin crept back into his dark bunk to curl up into a cocoon. He was physically and emotionally exhausted and prayed that sleep would soon come. Then, shortly after closing his eyes, Benjamin felt a gentle touch on his back. He remained motionless, hoping the interloper would think he was asleep. The hand didn't move, however. Finally, Benjamin rolled over and lifted his head slightly to see who stood beside his bunk. It was Miriam.

"Care to take a walk?" she asked. "You know, to burn off that big meal." Miriam smiled at her own sarcasm.

Benjamin propped himself up on one elbow to study her face. Miriam's gaunt cheekbones were the same as those of all the other famished workers in the camp, but there was a gleam in her eyes. Her body may have been slowly wasting away, but Benjamin could see that her spirit was still fiercely alive.

"Come on, Benjamin," she nagged. "It's too early to sleep." After a brief pause, Miriam added, "Besides, the best thing you can do right now is talk, not brood."

Benjamin nodded tentatively and slowly climbed down from his bunk. Once on the ground, he again towered over the young woman. Benjamin then lazily lifted a finger and pointed toward the exit.

"Lead the way," he mumbled.

Once outside, a stillness filled the space between them. They breathed in the sweet scent of the surrounding pine forests that dominated this sparsely populated section of the Lublin district. The night sky was a sea of stars engulfing a brilliant full moon. The only aberration was the glow to the east. In another time and place, this might have felt romantic. But the pungent aroma of burning flesh was also in the air, the shadowy silhouette of towers brisling with machine guns intruded into the horizon, and the memory of recently departed loved ones haunted everyone's consciousness. Survival. It was the *best* revenge. Survival itself had become the only point to their lives.

"So," Benjamin uttered, dragging out the word. "You seem to know a lot about me. What about you? How did you come to live in this paradise?"

Benjamin glanced at his companion, but she was hidden in the shadows. A distant light occasionally illuminated where they were strolling, but he could barely make out Miriam's face due to their height difference. For a moment, the only sound came from a soft breeze whistling through the nearby barbed wire. Miriam eventually stopped and turned to face her companion. Benjamin could see a tiny pearl rolling down her cheek in the faint light.

"I arrived here in June with my parents and six younger brothers and sisters. At nineteen, I was the oldest. Like you, my family was led away to the showers shortly afterward, and I never saw them again."

Miriam paused to wipe away the moisture from her cheeks with a weathered sleeve. She inhaled deeply and continued.

"I was part of a huge shipment. Judging from the length of our train, there must have been at least 8,000 in my transport, and to the best of my knowledge, I was the only survivor."

Once again, Miriam hesitated. She looked away as though searching for her next words.

"You see, shortly after we disembarked from the railcars, some Ukrainian guards spotted me. I was petrified because I didn't know why they'd singled me out. But then one of them shouted, 'Hey, you over there.' He pointed to me and said, 'You can do our washing.' Then he pulled two other young girls and me out of the line. After the huge crowd, including my family, left for the showers, the guards took us to a small barrack. My first night in Sobibor—*what* a nightmare. The Ukrainians each had their way with us. They dragged us out the following morning and said it was our turn for the showers. At the time, I still didn't know what that meant."

Benjamin noticed Miriam staring blankly at his chest. She paused once more, and he observed her shoulders rise as she took another deep breath. Then, Miriam looked up at Benjamin, and their eyes met.

"At the last moment, this man, one of the camp's Jewish workers, rushed up and announced to the guards that we should not be sent to the showers because we were all seamstresses. It was a crazy thing to do, and he's lucky they didn't shoot him on the spot. The other two girls couldn't have been older than twelve or thirteen, too young to have perfected their sewing skills, so the guards laughed and prepared to drag them away. However, when they looked at me, I started spouting off about cuffing pants, taking in dresses, and attaching buttons. It worked. Instead of the showers, one of them escorted me to the tailor shop. I later learned the man who saved my life was Leon."

"Hmmm," Benjamin uttered. He looked down at Miriam admirably and said, "You must've been very convincing."

"It wasn't hard," Miriam explained. "You see, Benjamin, I *am* a seamstress. Or at least, that's what I was training to be before the Nazis shipped us to the ghetto."

Benjamin nodded knowingly. He was beginning to understand how much luck played a vital role in deciding who lived and who died.

"Come on," Miriam finally whispered, "We should probably get back. It's got to be almost curfew time."

Over the next few weeks, Benjamin settled into an endurable routine. While he spent most of his time in the shoe repair shop, the SS frequently drafted him and other camp workers to help with the chaos when the trains arrived. There, Benjamin would whisper to a young man or woman to "volunteer" whenever the Nazis requested that people with valued skills step forward. Otherwise, each day was filled with long hours of tedium peppered with unexpected moments of fear and horror.

Eventually, the weeks grew into months; before anyone knew it, 1942 turned into 1943. Each evening, Benjamin spent an hour or two socializing with Leon, Max, Miriam, and others, who all shared the same raging determination to survive. And more and more, to ensure their survival, the talk turned toward the prospect of escape. There had been several attempts, but always by individuals and never successful. After all, the Nazis did not build this camp to house long-term residents, and its guards thought nothing of taking the life of any worker who attempted to flee.

During the nighttime conversations, Benjamin learned that Sobibor had opened in May 1942 as one of five death camps, along with Belzec, Treblinka, Chelmno, and the most notorious, Auschwitz-Birkenau. These extermination camps were part of the Nazi conspiracy to murder Europe's Jews systematically, otherwise known as Hitler's Final Solution to the "Jewish Question." Sobibor was not a work camp. Its only purpose was to kill as many Jews as efficiently as possible. By its closure in October

1943, the camp's gas chambers had murdered 250,000 Jews, mainly from Poland and the German-occupied areas of the Soviet Union.

The camp relied on the slave labor of approximately 600 Jews to keep its killing machine operational twenty-four hours a day. Most workers lived strictly in the present, doing whatever was necessary to survive from one day to the next. For the few who dreamed of a future, it was like staring at a mirage in a desert. There could be no future if the Nazis successfully carried out their plan to murder every last Jew in the camp.

In hopeless desperation, some individuals stopped eating or approached the electrified fencing like the man on Benjamin's second day. Even if an escapee somehow managed to cut through the barbed wire, they would be mowed down by the guard tower's machine guns or blown up in one of the surrounding minefields. To do nothing, however, was also not an option. It was only a matter of time before each of the 600 fatigued workers would be selected for extermination after being replaced by fresh arrivals.

Leon and the others who dared to think about a future knew their only hope was a well-orchestrated effort that would free as many prisoners as possible. But, for the time being, their plans remained vague and theoretical. None of the Jews were trained as soldiers, and most were not mentally prepared to kill anyone, not even SS guards. That all changed, however, in late September 1943.

The catalyst for planning a big breakout appeared with the sudden arrival of a transport from Minsk that included eighty Jewish Red Army POWs. Their leader, Lieutenant Alexander Pechersky, also known as Sasha, was tall, striking, and charismatic. His chiseled features and battle-hardened confidence inspired the Jewish workers of Sobibor. Under his leadership, there were now experienced soldiers who could train, organize, and motivate the civilian workers to do everything necessary to gain their freedom.

Shortly after their arrival, Sasha and his officers began huddling with Leon's cohorts to formulate a viable plan. Recognizing that the SS formed the brains of the camp, they determined that if they could assassinate all or most of the Nazi officers at roughly the same time, the Ukrainian guards, the camp's muscle, would be mostly incapacitated. Cut off the head, and the body will die, or so they believed. The conspirators gradually began to visualize the details of a feasible escape plot.

Then, circumstances changed, forcing them to accelerate their time-line. The coming of October meant the Polish winter was approaching, and soon, the surrounding forest would be carpeted with snow. Additionally, the camp leadership noted that the transports had dropped sharply, indicating the Germans were running out of victims and, consequently, would soon liquidate the camp's workforce. As a result, the inmates had to act fast. They chose to carry out their escape on October 14 after learning that several high-ranking Nazis would be gone from the camp that morning.

By this time, Benjamin and Miriam had progressed beyond a platonic friendship. Initially, their mutual attraction stemmed from the belief that two people had a better chance of surviving together than an individual alone. As time went on, their grieving for the past evolved into planning for the future. Benjamin and Miriam encouraged each other to let go of mourning and to focus on reasons for hope. At the center of these reasons were the romantic feelings they were developing for one another. They spent every free moment together, and as they learned more about an upcoming breakout, their belief in the possibility of a hopeful future grew stronger.

Miriam and Benjamin soon became the subject of teasing among the others in the barack, who lightheartedly joked about what looked like an adolescent infatuation. Their roommates frequently noticed them holding hands and compared them to lovesick schoolchildren. Despite the teasing, everyone else looked away at night whenever Miriam climbed into Benjamin's corner bunk. The fact that love could flourish in such a barren desert renewed their hope that anything was still possible.

Miriam and Benjamin would play a critical role in the escape plan since the assassination of the SS was to occur inside the workshops. The action was scheduled to begin precisely at four in the afternoon, relying upon the Germans' renowned punctuality. At that exact moment, the SS officers were to be lured into the shops by recently acquired coats, jewelry, boots, and other lucrative goods intended to be used as bait. Once inside, the shop workers were to dispatch the soldiers with axes, knives, and other tools. They would then take the guards' rifles and distribute them to Sasha's men, who would use them during the second part of the breakout.

When Hans, a burly SS officer known for his unstable and sadistic behavior, entered the shoe shop to pick up some refurbished boots, Max motioned him toward a bench to try them on. But, since Max was older and smaller in stature, Benjamin was chosen to approach the guard from behind with one of the hammers commonly used to repair shoes. Benjamin was young, relatively stout, and had the element of surprise. The question, however, was whether he had the stomach for such a ruthless undertaking.

At first, Benjamin hesitated. Although Sasha had assiduously provided instructions and pep talks on multiple occasions, the thought of plunging the head of a hammer into a man's skull was entirely foreign to Benjamin's psyche. To get moving, he finally forced himself to think of Ada carrying their daughter into the gas chamber. That's all it took. Afterward, Max and Benjamin dragged the large corpse behind the work table, secured the guard's rifle, and quickly sopped up most of the blood. Until then, Benjamin had never killed anything larger than a fly.

Unfortunately, some SS guards had ignored their invitations and were still on the prowl somewhere in the camp. However, this fact was unknown to Leon and Sasha, who proceeded with the plan's next stage. First, they commenced distributing the captured rifles. Second, they cut the telephone and electricity lines. Finally, as the evening roll call approached, they positioned their sharpshooters to aim for the armed guard towers.

At this juncture, the plan called for the remaining 600 inmates, who typically gathered at this time for the day's final count, to rush the front entrance en masse, overwhelm the Ukrainians guarding the gate, and flood the roadway leading into the woods. This was the safest route to avoid the camp's lethal minefields. Precise timing was critical.

Unfortunately, two SS officers appeared near the front area at the worst possible moment, discovered what was happening, and assumed command. A vicious battle erupted. The two officers, some Ukrainian guards on the ground, and a few still alive in the towers fired on Sasha's armed soldiers. Bullets flew in every direction, and the thunderous noise was deafening. Meanwhile, pandemonium broke out in the common yard, where most of the 600 camp workers had assembled. While the crowd began to move with trepidation toward the front gate, Benjamin attempted to find Miriam. For a moment, he froze, paralyzed by the fear that he was about to lose the second love of his life.

Then he spotted her. Miriam dashed from the direction of the tailor shop with a raging resolve in her eyes. Benjamin screamed at the top of his lungs, but she could not hear him over the sounds of battle. He ran toward her, weaving through the panic-stricken throngs. When Miriam spotted Benjamin, she fought her way in his direction. Once they reunited, the couple held each other tightly amid the bedlam.

Suddenly, they heard a man's voice. It was Leon, who had somehow managed to get his hands on a megaphone. Seeing that the front gate had not been cleared, he resorted to his only other option. Leon bellowed, "Charge the fences. The electricity's been cut. Now, it's everyone for themselves." As he shouted these words repeatedly, Sasha and his cohorts stepped into the crowd, shepherding people toward the fencing. Some led the way with wire cutters, while others shoved the masses from behind. They were purposefully trying to start a stampede.

Still embracing Miriam, Benjamin stepped back far enough to gaze into her eyes. Then, without saying a word, they nodded, agreeing to take the plunge. With bullets still buzzing around them, they spotted perhaps 200 rushing toward the nearest fence. Benjamin and Miriam followed in their wake.

First, there was a brief pile-up while the men with the wire cutters sliced through the first fence. Then, while the larger mass pushed through the openings, the men leading the way cut through the second line of fencing. Suddenly, the crowd froze like it was teetering at the edge of a cliff. Then, without uttering a word, they simultaneously rushed into the minefield.

Within seconds, deafening explosions began hurling bodies into the air. Sprinting towards the distant forest had become the ultimate crapshoot. Benjamin intentionally paused after crossing the threshold of downed wires, gripping Miriam's arm hard. He held up a finger, signaling the need for patience. Finally, he leaned toward Miriam and shouted into her ear.

"Follow precisely in my footsteps."

Benjamin waited until a small group passed him, racing toward the woods. For the remainder of his life, he would grimace whenever thinking about that moment when he used others to clear a path through the minefield. Still, he reminded himself that they would have raced across that field regardless of whether he and Miriam followed from behind. There was nothing that would have prevented their actions. And his plan worked. Benjamin and Miriam safely crossed the minefield into the forest. Then night began. For the next several hours, the blue light of a full harvest moon lit their way.

Benjamin and Miriam would later learn that the uprising at Sobibor, along with similar events in Treblinka and the Warsaw Ghetto, is considered one of the most courageous moments in recent Jewish history. In each instance, the Jews resisted, refusing to accept death on the Nazis' terms. On that day in mid-October, half of the 600 Jewish workers in the camp managed to escape alive.

Unfortunately, the Nazi manhunt began at dawn the following day. Mounted police, Wehrmacht soldiers, SS forces, and Ukrainians patrolled the woods around the camp while surveillance planes circled overhead. Of the 300 prisoners who escaped, only 53 survived until the end of the war.

Miriam and Benjamin entered Sobibor as the sole representatives of their families, each being the only survivor of their respective clans. Their survival can be attributed to a combination of remarkable luck, a strong determination to live, and the help of one man, Leon Felhendler. Although Leon was killed in Lublin just as the war was nearing its end, he played a crucial role in ensuring that several others lived. Among those survivors were Miriam and Benjamin Abromowicz.

CHAPTER 5

FRANK

February 1976

Frank lowered his head onto the armrest of the Naugahyde couch in his tiny efficiency apartment, sighed loudly, and shut his eyes. He was so exhausted that, for a moment, he forgot he had a guest sitting just two feet away. Though Frank was thirty-one and Harold, his latest protege, was only twenty-two, the two men recently realized they shared a mutual attraction.

Since early morning, Frank and Harold had been working the polls on Chicago's southwest side. With the votes finally tabulated, they knew that Frank Collin had lost his bid to win a seat on the city's Board of Aldermen. This was no surprise since, as the founder and leader of the National Socialist Party of America, the N.S.P.A., better known as the American Nazi Party, Frank was not expected to win. Nevertheless, earning only 16 percent of the votes was a depressing outcome. No one liked to lose.

Harold, seated stiffly on the straight-back chair he had brought over from the kitchen, mindlessly stroked his jet-black goatee and studied his mentor. Had Frank fallen asleep? Should he wake him or slink out of the apartment and let him get some shuteye? Harold delayed the decision by yanking off his glasses, holding them up toward the one bare bulb glowing in the center of the room, and wincing at how smudged they were after such a long day. Shortly after arriving in the dingy apartment, both men had loosened their ties, untucked their shirts, and removed their swastika armbands, now lying haphazardly on the kitchen table. Harold used the tail of his button-down brown shirt to polish his glasses.

Frank mumbled in disbelief, his eyes still shut, "I can't believe how badly I lost."

Harold, who had just slid his glasses back onto his broad face, looked up in astonishment. Since Frank had just been snoring like a growling bear, Harold assumed he had fallen asleep. Frank's eyes remained closed, but Harold decided to respond when he saw Frank wipe his mouth with the back of his hand.

"Well," Harold countered, "I actually think you did quite well. After all, it was only forty years ago that your country defeated the Nazis in the worst war in history. When you think about it, it's amazing how many people voted for you."

Frank's eyes sprung open, and his lips parted into a devious smile. He sat up, swung his legs over the edge of the couch, and leaned forward with his hands clenched between his knees. Frank stared at his new friend with piercingly dark eyes. The intensity of his gaze reminded Harold of the original Fuhrer. Frank Collin could almost pass as Hitler's twin if he lightened his dark hair and grew a truncated mustache beneath his nose.

"That's a good point," Frank replied. "You know, the best the Nazis ever did in German elections before Hitler was appointed chancellor was 37 percent, and that was during the height of the Great Depression. When you think about it, Harold, it's not the quantity of your support that matters; it's the *quality*."

"Well, as I see it," Harold responded, inching his chair a little closer, "Many of the white people in this city have grown tired of racial integration. They're sick of the government trying to make everything so equal. These people don't give a rat's ass if you're a Democrat, Republican, Communist, or Nazi; they just don't want to live next door to Blacks; they don't want their kids going to school with their little monkey children; and they definitely don't want their daughters marrying one of them."

"That's true," Frank affirmed, "But that's just the starting point. Ultimately, we've got to sell them on our total vision."

"And what's that?" Harold asked naively.

Frank looked up, his brow furrowed in confusion. Then, he smiled as a thought occurred to him.

"You've got quite an accent, Harold. Where did you say you were from?"

"Rhodesia," answered Harold, with a slight hint of pride.

"Rhodesia?" Frank inquired, his curiosity rising. "Isn't that the African country where the whites are trying to hold onto their power?"

"Yeah, that's the place," Harold promptly responded. "My family's been there since Cecil Rhodes first established the colony named after him in the late 1800s."

"So, why'd you leave?"

"Because the place has become a sinking ship," Harold exclaimed. "Blacks make up over 90 percent of the country, and they're becoming increasingly aggressive. There's no way the whites can stand up against those odds. If my family didn't get out, it could turn into a bloodbath when the munts take over. They're already talking about changing everything, including the country's name. Once Rhodesia becomes Zimbabwe, my family will count their blessings for having left."

"I see," Frank commented, beginning to tire of the conversation. "It sounds like you were smart to get out when you did. But, I take it you're not that familiar with the situation here in Chicago, are you?"

Harold shrugged, smiled awkwardly, and shook his head. Then he added, "What I do know is that your country also has a growing problem with its munts, and when I read about George Lincoln Rockwell, I wanted to learn more. After hearing that you're connected to him, I decided to join your Bund." Then, as an afterthought, he added, "Did you personally know Rockwell?"

"Did I *know* Rockwell?" Frank echoed. "By the time of his murder, we were like brothers."

"Was he truly as great as everyone claims?"

To add a little drama to his response, Frank stood up and raised his hand, appearing to give a Nazi salute. Holding his hand in place, he continued, "There's the Fuhrer." He lowered his hand about six inches and stated, "Then, there's Rockwell." Next, he dropped his hand to chest level and uttered, "Then, there's me." Finally, after lowering his hand to his belt, he proclaimed, "Here's everyone else. Including you, at least for now."

Harold's eyes widened. "How did you and Rockwell meet?"

Frank sat back down. "Okay," he proclaimed, "Time for a little history lesson. All right?"

Harold nodded, his expression a mix of humiliation and gratitude. He felt embarrassed for not understanding what everyone else seemed to know, yet thankful that someone finally offered to provide some background information.

"It was almost ten years ago, 1966 to be exact when Martin Luther Coon first came up to Chicago."

He paused. "You've heard of him, right?"

Harold nodded awkwardly, and Frank continued. "The king of the Sambos decided to bring his movement from the Deep South up to the Windy City. He wanted to lead a march right through the heart of Marquette Park. In those days, even more than today, Marquette Park was mostly Lithuanian, Polish, German, and Irish. In other words, *all* white. And those children of immigrants didn't want to make room for any more outsiders, especially the Spooks, most of whom were smart enough to stay away from Marquette Park."

Frank glanced away for a moment. When he looked back, a smile had creased his lips, revealing a begrudging look of admiration.

"You got to give King some credit, though; that coon had the courage to lead parades in the places that hated him the most. But I think even he was surprised by the reception we gave him in Marquette Park. Hundreds turned out to greet him with bricks and bottles. One rock struck King himself on the head. He later said that even after everything he'd seen in Alabama and Mississippi, his welcoming party in Marquette Park was the most violent and hostile he had ever experienced."

"You were there?" Harold asked, like a child listening to his grandfather tell a war story.

"Oh *yeah*," Frank exclaimed with a proud grin. "I was only about your age at the time, but I was the one who organized the counter-protest. I'd just been appointed Midwest coordinator of our original organization. Back then, it was officially called the National Socialist White People's Party, although most people just called it the American Nazi Party. Let me tell you," Frank added with a nostalgic look of satisfaction, "That was one *glorious* day."

"I bet it was," Harold affirmed. "So, then what happened?"

"All the hoopla in Chicago caught the attention of Mr. George Lincoln Rockwell. He was the man who'd created the American Nazi Party and was its national leader. Rockwell lived in D.C., where he maintained some impressive barracks staffed with dozens of uniformed stormtroopers. However, he decided to come here after he heard about our little riot. Soon, he was handing out pamphlets and White Power T-shirts with swastikas on them. In a later rally, Rockwell confronted King face to face. Shortly afterward, he led his own White People's March. During that time, he and I became close friends. Harold, let me tell you, Rockwell was the greatest man I ever knew."

"What was he like?" Harold inquired, as though asking Peter to describe Jesus.

"In person, Rockwell was incredibly charismatic. He was tall, striking, and very passionate. At the same time, though, he could be like a fatherly figure. The man was always smoking a pipe, for God's sake. But it wasn't only the man. It was also his ideas."

"Yeah?" Harold asked, waiting patiently to hear more.

"He didn't just organize a little political party, Harold; it was an entire movement built around protecting the white race from the Sambos and the Christ-killers. Rockwell was the first to point out that desegregation was really a Jewish plot designed to weaken the white race through genetic mixing. He called Hitler the 'white savior of the twentieth century' and wasn't afraid to tell the truth about the Holocaust. Rockwell pointed out that the Hymies invented the whole thing just to get the UN to create Israel. He also pointed out that Martin Luther Coon was a tool of the Jewish Communists."

Frank paused to catch his breath. He loved discussing Nazi ideology and would continue all day if he could. After expelling a deep breath, he resumed.

"Rockwell viewed the Sambos as a lazy, primitive race that only cared about simple pleasures. He created a whole plan to resettle them in a new African state funded by the American government. Some of his ideas were not all that different from those of militant spooks like Malcolm X. They all agreed it would be best to separate the races. To his credit, though, even though Rockwell worshipped Hitler, he didn't push for an American Final Solution to exterminate all the vermin. He simply wanted to deport the darkies back to Africa. As for the Hymies, he'd get rid of them through a forced sterilization program."

"Sounds like an excellent plan," Harold remarked. "How did he carry it out?"

"Well," Frank responded, "Here's an example. Rockwell knew those Jew bastards in the Jewish Defense League had made a deal with the media not to cover Nazi Party rallies. They didn't want to give us a platform. But Rockwell was smart enough to get around their quarantine by using other tactics to get attention. He'd march his uniformed stormtroopers out onto the National Mall for thousands to see. Then, he'd drive them around the country on a bus draped with swastikas and racist slogans. He made it impossible for us to be ignored."

Harold sat back in his chair, locked his fingers behind his head, and glanced up at the paint chips dangling from the ceiling. He needed a moment to digest everything packed into Frank's lecture. Finally, he looked back at his mentor.

"So, what happened to Rockwell?"

"The following year," Frank answered ruefully, "He was shot in Virginia by a former party member. Rockwell had kicked the guy out because of his Bolshevik leanings, so the asshole took revenge."

"Ah, man," Harold complained as if the assassination had just occurred, "That's too bad. So, who took over in his place?"

"We had an election. Considering my recent success in Chicago, I thought it should've been me, but they chose Matt Koehl. At first, I was okay with that choice since I was much younger than Matt. But then, because he still saw me as a threat, Matt dug up some crap about my father and tried to use it against me."

Frank hesitated and looked away momentarily as if wrestling with something from his past. Then, he sighed loudly and turned back to face Harold squarely.

"Matt said he had something published by my father claiming he was a Jewish Holocaust survivor who later changed his last name from Cohen to Collin. I knew it wasn't true. Furthermore, I believe Matt made it up since he conveniently discovered it just when he was looking to drive me out of the party."

Harold's lips tightened, and his forehead furrowed into parallel lines of concern. Frank observed that his mentee could wear many masks, all displaying larger-than-life expressions.

"So, what'd you do?"

Frank hesitated to answer at first. After all, how well did he know Harold Covington? His pupil might not be happy with the answer to that question. Finally, Frank formulated a response that placed himself in the best possible light.

"Here in Chicago, I convinced everyone we needed to break from Matt's party. The old National Socialist White People's Party wasn't the same now that Rockwell was gone; besides, it was located on the East Coast. We needed a more central location. So, our new party was called the National Socialist Party of America, and it was based right here in Chicago. No one really paid much attention to the name change. Most people still thought of us as the American Nazi Party. And we've been doing just fine ever since."

"Hmmm," Harold purred, this time bearing a mask with exaggerated empathy. "I fully understand what you did." Then, after a brief pause, he added, "So, what are your plans for the future?"

"My immediate goal is to find us a place for our headquarters. I'm tired of working out of my apartment, and holding meetings in an open tavern's a pain in the ass."

A screaming siren punctuated Frank's final statement. Both men ignored it since they were accustomed to hearing these sounds around the clock in this neighborhood. As the piercing noise subsided, Harold grinned broadly.

"I've got an idea," he exclaimed.

"Yeah?" Frank asked. "I'm all ears."

"My uncle just bought an old house on 71st Street that he plans to rent. It's a two-story redbrick building we could have for a dime. The place needs a little work, but there's enough space for several of us to live upstairs. You could charge a little rent, which should be more than enough to pay the bills."

Frank nodded and began to smile. He could visualize a structure with a red flag fluttering above, sporting a giant swastika. On the exterior walls, they could post racist banners. Then, Harold added the piece de resistance.

"And, Frank, you know what we should name our headquarters?" Before his mentor could respond, Harold blurted out the answer. "Rockwell Hall!"

Frank was thrilled and agreed to tour the property the following day. He enthusiastically shook Harold's hand and offered to buy him a celebratory drink. Twelve hours later, Frank signed a lease, put down a token deposit, and started the long process of packing.

A few weeks later, Frank entered their new headquarters, which buzzed with activity. About a dozen young men had moved in along with Frank and Harold, and sleeping bags and worn-out couches were scattered throughout the upstairs rooms. It resembled a boys' club but was far less orderly. Empty potato chip bags and candy wrappers littered the floors, indicating that the residents primarily relied on junk food from vending machines.

In addition to the permanent occupants, other people regularly hung around Rockwell Hall, including some of the girlfriends of the Neo-Nazis. Several pre-adolescent boys came and went, especially after Frank and Harold organized their "Hitler Youth Group." As Frank walked through the front foyer, he passed the donation jar and the table exhibiting the White Power T-shirts and other merchandise for sale. Over the years, Frank had learned much from his original mentor.

Additionally, Frank and Harold introduced several new features, including a printing press to churn out flyers and newspapers promoting white power and an answering machine that played a recorded "white power broadcast" with news and announcements. Frank had purposefully avoided items intended to provide leisure comfort, like a television set. Instead, the residents listened to Frank's speeches, which were recorded on audio tapes.

Frank also spent a lot of time conducting meetings. The more participants, the better. There was always another march or rally on the horizon, and Frank constantly sought new ways to improve their operations. Demonstrations in their neighborhood or on the streets of Marquette Park usually went well, but they attracted little attention. Frank realized the most successful activities were those that incited opposition, thereby leading to more widespread media coverage.

Recently, their rallies in communities like Cicero and Berwyn had encountered a new problem: too much opposition. These predominantly white areas had attracted few counter-protesters in the past, but now, Buzz Albert, the new chair of the Chicago Chapter of the Jewish Defense League, had recently recruited a rough band of young Jewish men who would physically attack the Neo-Nazis during their marches and rallies through these neighborhoods.

The other day, Buzz and his Jewish warriors attempted to prevent Frank, Harold, and their stormtroopers from entering Berwyn. Buzz single-handedly reached out, grabbed both fascists by the throat, and lunged at them. A fight broke out, and despite being outnumbered two to one, the JDL managed to turn the Nazis back. Frank was shocked and humiliated to be defeated by the Jews. His only consolation was that he appeared in the newspaper with blood dripping from his face.

Later that night, the main room on the ground floor was already packed when Frank marched in. The recent shellacking in Berwyn had aroused the fury of anyone connected to the Bund. Everyone was dressed in their version of a Nazi uniform: brown shirts, black ties, and swastika armbands. Many were carrying guns and military-style side arms. The agenda consisted of just one item, but it was a dilemma that was not easily resolved. The spectacle of street fights may have helped the Neo-Nazis gain attention, but there was a limit to how much Frank and the others wanted to be bloodied. And while firearms made an impressive show on their home turf, they could not pack heat when the Chicago police were around.

The meeting commenced as always, with a mass salute to Hitler's photograph on the wall, followed by a recitation of the Pledge of Allegiance as everyone faced the American flag draped next to the Fuhrer. Then, as though he was addressing a class of third-graders, Frank explained the issue. The ensuing discussion quickly turned raucous. Some in the audience talked about employing firearms against the JDL. Others corrected them, pointing out that guns would churn out the wrong kind of publicity. It appeared the meeting might soon get out of hand.

One of Frank's henchmen, Gary Lauck, further confused the issue by complaining that the city of Chicago had just passed a new ordinance requiring demonstrators to post large insurance bonds, knowing this was beyond the financial reach of the American Nazi Party. A verbal explosion then denounced the unfairness of this new law. After the crowd had settled down, a teenager standing along the back wall signaled that he had something to say.

For a moment, Frank gazed at the new kid. He was tall and relatively thin, and despite looking like a hippie with long dark hair, bell-bottom jeans, and a tie-died shirt, a fire was burning in his eyes. It was only a first impression, but Frank immediately liked what he saw. He had always been drawn to the younger boys who had just achieved puberty, and this kid was overflowing with magnetism.

"Yeah?" Frank asked, pointing at the kid. "What've you got to say?"

The kid glanced around, suddenly realizing the spotlight had fallen on him. He wiped his mouth with his hand and unknowingly took a step backward. The boy looked like he might bolt out the front door and never return. Then, he rallied, and the room grew silent.

"Mr. Collin," the kid uttered in a barely audible voice, "The Chicago ordinance is clearly unconstitutional."

"Yeah?" Frank smiled. "You an attorney?"

After the snickering subsided, the kid continued, this time in a louder, more confident voice.

"The city does not have the power to restrict our rights. As long as we avoid violence, we have the right to free speech and peaceful assembly. It says so right there in the First Amendment of the Constitution. What's more, it's not our responsibility to pay for insurance against the possibility of violence. Instead, the city must provide enough police protection so that no one gets hurt. We'd win if we challenged this ordinance in a federal court."

A hush fell over the audience. Frank smiled while simultaneously shaking his head. Before he could respond, though, Harold interceded.

"And how do you suggest we pay the lawyers to take our case to court? Most are Jew shysters who would charge thousands of dollars we don't have. And I seriously doubt any of them would want to defend *our* rights."

The kid calmly pivoted toward Harold. "The lawyers might be Jewish, but they won't charge a dime, and believe it or not, some probably *would* take our case."

Looking to reclaim the spotlight, Frank asked, "Kid, what are you talking about?"

"Have you ever heard of the ACLU?" the kid asked, glancing around the room. "The American Civil Liberties Union? They're a nonprofit organization dedicated to protecting our Constitutional rights. *Everyone's* rights. Many of their lawyers are indeed Jewish, but they supposedly don't care who their clients are. They'll go to court to protect *anyone's* free speech, not just those they agree with. And, if they accept our case, they won't charge anything. They get their money from membership fees and donations."

An eerie quiet filled the crowded room. For a moment, most faces oscillated back and forth between the kid and Frank Collin, nervously waiting to see how their leader would respond. Finally, a smile exploded across Frank's face.

"Holy shit! If this kid's right, can you imagine the optics of Jew lawyers representing *Nazis*? That could put us on the front page of every newspaper in the country."

"Yes," the kid confirmed while, for the first time, a smile creased his face. "But I've got an even bigger idea."

Frank glanced around the room. As suspected, most of the brown-shirted stormtroopers were murmuring among themselves, exhibiting excited smiles and widened eyes. Who *was* this kid?

"Go on," Frank assured, "You've got our undivided attention."

"Well," the kid responded, now basking in the limelight, "Why Chicago? Nazis marching in the Windy City don't even break the front page anymore. Why not copy what Martin Luther King did and take our message to where they hate us the most?"

"Where is that?" Harold asked, his skepticism fading.

"Skokie," the kid immediately responded. "It's just to the north of the city, has a population that's more than half Jewish, and for some reason, is home to 7,000 Holocaust survivors. That's more than anywhere in the world outside of Israel."

Frank and Harold instantly rotated to face each other, mirroring the same expression of astonishment. Who *was* this kid? Meanwhile, the kid ventured on without waiting for anyone to respond.

"If we threatened to march peacefully in Skokie, I guarantee they'll pass something to keep us out. When they do, we'll take our case to the ACLU, sit back, and wait. Pretty soon, we'll be drowning in free publicity. Since the courts are so slow, it'll drag on for months, maybe years. The story that will be repeated endlessly is that of American Nazis attempting to exercise their constitutional rights and the Jews of Skokie striving to limit their freedom. Without spending a dime, we'll get publicity worth millions of dollars. And it will be *good* publicity."

"Holy *shit*," Frank Collin pronounced again. "This kid's a *freaking* genius. What'd you say your name was again?"

"Michael. Michael Parker."

"Well, Mr. Michael Parker, welcome to the American Nazi Party. Now, I've just got one command for you."

Michael nodded. While he smiled bashfully, his eyes conveyed mounting confidence.

"Yeah?" he finally inquired, unable to remove his slaphappy grin.

"Cut your hair. *Short*. Get rid of those hippy clothes. And help yourself to one of our armbands. The next time I see you, Michael Parker, I want you to look like us."

CHAPTER 6

GRANT

January 1977

The winter in Central Illinois had been brutal, one of the worst in recent memory. Temperatures had remained below zero for several days, and the blistery wind had piled snow into every corner and crevice. Grant had memories of making giant snowmen as a kid, but back then, the deep white carpet had always lain flat over the endless prairie. Now, the winterscape looked more like Central Siberia than Central Illinois. When Grant left for work this morning, his small cottage looked like the frozen house in the movie *Dr. Zhivago*.

Toward the end of the day, Grant peered out the window of his office cubicle to see that at least four more inches of fresh snow had covered his Civic. He knew the temperature was predicted to climb above zero for the first time in a week, but only by a couple of degrees. Grant inhaled deeply and then expelled the air from his lungs. In the background, he could hear the tiny black-and-white television set broadcasting from across the expansive room. The small crowd that had initially gathered to watch Jimmy Carter be sworn in as the 39th president had lost interest and returned to their desks, but no one bothered to turn off the inaugural parade. Grant tightened his lips and slowly shook his head. He had voted for Gerald Ford.

Suddenly, he was startled by the phone ringing from behind. Grant reached for the receiver on his desk and was thrilled to hear the musical tenor of Rachel's voice.

"Hey, babe, are we still on for tonight? Or should we cancel?"

Grant glanced out the window again, even though he already knew what he would see. He had enjoyed snow days as much as anyone as a kid, but since then, Grant took an obstinate pride in not letting the weather interfere with his plans. Besides, he had been looking forward all day to seeing Rachel.

"Yeah," he finally responded. "Why don't I pick up a pizza at Garcia's and bring it to your place?"

"You sure?" Rachel inquired. "It's pretty sketchy out there."

Grant reminded himself that his next car would be a four-wheel drive vehicle. For now, though, his little Honda Civic, with its front-wheel drive, was better than Rachel's crappy Chevy Vega. He would call in a phone order and pick up a pepperoni pizza on the way to Rachel's apartment. Altogether, he would only have to drive a few miles, so if he took it slow, it was doable.

"Yeah, I've got this. I'll get the usual and see you in about an hour." Then, even though he had only started saying this recently, Grant added, "I love you."

Rachel promptly replied, "I love you too."

Exactly one hour later, Grant used his key to enter Rachel's apartment, carrying their pizza in a cardboard box. He immediately noticed that rather than setting the dining room table as she usually did, Rachel had placed paper plates, napkins, and empty wine glasses on the coffee table in front of her leather sofa. The television was already on, and the local news from Peoria was showing.

Grant looked down at the arrangement and grinned. He did not see Rachel but could hear her in the kitchen. When she strode into the living room, Rachel was carrying a bottle of wine she had just uncorked.

"This looks *nice*," Grant commented. "There's nothing like a warm, cozy dinner on a snowy day." He glanced over and nodded approvingly at the fire burning in her gas fireplace. Then, observing the bottle of red wine in her hand, Grant asked, "Did you go out to buy that?"

"It's the least I could do," Rachel answered. "Since you had to drive in this mess to pick up dinner, I could walk a few blocks to get some wine." Then, nodding toward the TV, she added, "I thought we'd watch a movie with dinner. WGN's showing *Mr. Smith Goes to Washington* at six. I guess it's their way of honoring today's inauguration. Have you seen it? Even if you have, it's such a great classic; I figured you wouldn't mind watching it again."

"You know," Grant began, "I have seen it, but it was a long time ago, and I'd love to watch it again." Then, flashing a smile, he added, "Of course, you Jimmy Carter liberals love movies like this, don't you?"

Rachel feigned a pouty frown while hanging Grant's coat. "Jimmy Carter? I told you I didn't vote for *him*."

"Oh, that's right," Grant countered, "Carter's too conservative. You threw away your vote on Eugene McCarthy, didn't you? You know, although Gene challenged LBJ in '68 over our involvement in Vietnam, he didn't have a prayer last fall. If anything, you probably helped Ford stay in office."

"Maybe," Rachel replied as she opened the pizza box and sat behind one of the place settings. "But, as I saw it, there was no difference between tweedled-dee and tweedled-dum. So, every vote for McCarthy made a statement that this country badly needed someone to restore dignity to the White House after the Watergate Scandal. We also need someone who can address problems like poverty and racism."

Grant loved that he and Rachel could openly debate politics without making it personal. In his view, this kind of discourse was healthy in any viable democracy. Although Grant considered himself a moderate who preferred to vote for the candidate rather than the party, he was far to the right of his new girlfriend on the political spectrum.

"Fair enough," Grant contended, "But that's exactly what Ford would've done had he won the election. Nixon chose him to be vice president because of his spotlessly clean background. He definitely would've restored integrity to the presidency."

Rachel almost gagged on her bite of pizza. After managing to swallow, she cackled momentarily before rebutting Grant's point.

"You're joking, right? 'Spotlessly clean?' That's what you call the man who pardoned the most criminal president in American history?"

Since Grant had just taken a large bite of pizza, Rachel took advantage of the lapse in conversation to grab the television remote and change the channel. Her timing was impeccable. Before Grant could explain that Ford had only issued his pardon for the good of the country even though he knew it might cost him the election, the image of a woman holding a blazing torch, the Columbia Pictures logo, appeared, indicating the movie was starting. This side-tracked Grant from their political discussion, and within minutes, he was more focused on Jefferson Smith's tribulations than those of Gerald Ford.

Three hours later, Grant awoke from a brief nap. He was lying naked in Rachel's bed with the soft comforter cozily nuzzled beneath his chin. When Grant extended his arm to draw Rachel in for a cuddle and possibly a second round of love-making, he was startled to find her side of the bed empty. His eyes sprung open, and Grant raised his head to gaze around the room. He spied Rachel standing by the window. With her back turned to him, Grant could make out her shapely silhouette framed by the soft snowflakes dancing outside in the frozen breeze. Despite the winter scene, Rachel had not bothered to dress. She stood beside the window, studying the falling snow in her natural glory.

"Now, *that's* a vision," Grant exclaimed. "Although I'm not sure it should be shared with the whole world."

When Rachel glanced over her shoulder and smiled, Grant thought he had never seen anyone so beautiful. The diffused light from the snowy-white world brightened her alluring smile while her dark, wavy hair hung past her bare shoulders. To Grant, Rachel's statuesque curves reminded him of Camille Claudel's erotic sculptures, which he had obsessed over during his semester abroad in Paris. He patted Rachel's side of the bed, inviting her to rejoin him. Her bottom lip emerged into a childish pout as she glided away from the window.

"Grant, are you sure you can't stay the night? The snow has lightened, but it's accumulated again where they'd cleared the streets."

"No, I'm sorry," he answered remorsefully. "We talked about this. I need to get back to Michael. As long as I'm home by midnight, I can look in on him before he goes to sleep." Then, after briefly pausing, Grant added, "I haven't seen the kid all day."

"Well, then, why don't I follow you home?" Rachel asked cheerfully. "We can spend the night at *your* place."

"Because," Grant answered edgily, "The first time I introduce Michael to my girlfriend shouldn't be right before she and I climb into bed."

"Fair enough," Rachel conceded, expecting this response, "But maybe it's time for me to meet Michael under more proper circumstances. Have you even told him about me?"

Grant propped a pillow beneath his head, disappointed that a sober conversation was about to occur instead of a second romp beneath the sheets. Meanwhile, Rachel skirted beneath the covers and lay on her side facing Grant.

"I've told him I'm seeing someone," Grant answered. "Other than teasing me once for 'finally getting some,' Michael's shown little interest."

"So," Rachel complained, "You obviously haven't told him about my religious background, have you? Don't you think, in light of what you shared on the first day we met, that Michael should know his dad's dating someone Jewish?"

"You're right," Grant admitted. "I guess I've been avoiding the subject."

Rolling onto his side to confront Rachel face to face, Grant continued. "Rachel, I'll admit, the kid scares me sometimes. No matter what I say or do, I can't penetrate the barrier between us. I know Michael's a smart kid, brilliant even. But we haven't had much of a connection lately. And, to be perfectly honest, I'm afraid if I scratch the surface, I won't like what I find underneath."

"Grant," Rachel uttered in a more lecturing tone, "Don't you think if your son's a racist, you need to address the situation?"

"You make it sound so simple," Grant answered like a child being scolded, "But in reality, it's not that easy."

Rachel stayed silent. Grant could see her lips pressed together in exasperation even in the dim light. The only sound came from her breathing through her nose. Finally, Grant decided to break the silence.

"I tell you what," Grant whispered. "I'm taking Michael out for dinner for his seventeenth birthday tomorrow night. I'll tell him all about you then. I promise."

Seeing a smile break out across her face, Grant reached out to pull Rachel in for a long, intense kiss. Moments later, they began round two of the love-making he had anticipated. After they finished, Grant took a quick shower, threw on his clothes, and drove home through the deserted, snow-laden streets. There were only a few flurries, at least for now, and he enjoyed the crunching noise his tires made as they compressed the soft snow into packed ice.

Along the way, Grant could not help but smile. He had finally met the woman of his dreams. Rachel was acutely intelligent, stunningly attractive, and morally grounded. He knew that, in all likelihood, he could live out the remainder of his life and never meet a more perfect mate. It seemed like there was only one potential obstacle in his path.

Grant left work early the next day to get home before his son returned from school. He was seated at the kitchen table behind a large flat package when Michael walked through the door. The gift's wrapping was uneven, a result of a rushed effort, but Grant had attempted to compensate by placing a large red bow at its center. Hopefully, Michael would appreciate the effort. Grant had also attached a birthday card containing only a few scribbled sentences, but their sentiments were genuine.

When Michael entered the kitchen and glanced down at the table, a tight-lipped smile crossed his face, and he nodded in satisfaction. Grant suspected that his son knew what was in the package. After all, Michael had been hinting about a black leather jacket for months. Grant knew his son could use a new coat, especially in the harsh winter weather they had recently experienced. He would have preferred buying him something cheaper and more practical, like a heavy parka with faux fur or even a dressier overcoat. However, he knew this coat was more of a fashion statement for Michael. He thought it was part of his son's new style that Grant didn't understand, which included a shaved head, khaki button-down shirts, narrow black ties, and steel-toe work boots. Teenagers. Grant told himself this was no different from his desire to dress like James Dean when he was seventeen.

Michael sat down to open and read his birthday card. This and the enclosed twenty-five dollars immediately made him stand for an affectionate father-son hug. Then, Michael ripped off the wrapping paper, opened the cardboard box, and feigned over-the-moon surprise when he held up the leather coat. When he tried it on, Michael pranced about like a model in a fashion show. He briefly disappeared to examine his appearance in the full-length mirror upstairs. Once he returned, Michael was in an unusually joyful mood.

"So," Grant asked, "Where would you like to go for your birthday dinner?"

"Tobin's," Michael answered without hesitation.

"Pizza? *Really*?" Grant countered. "We eat there all the time. Wouldn't you like somewhere nicer?"

Michael shook his head. There was a boyish grin on his face. "I *love* Tobin's. I always have. They've got the best pizza in the world. What's more, I've got some good memories from that place."

Grant could not argue. He had always thought the pizza was exceptionally greasy, but the stringy cheese almost made up for it. Besides, he had learned to sop up most of the grease by dabbing each slice with a napkin like a sponge. And while Grant could not recall many good family memories from his marriage with Gretchen, he had to acknowledge there had been at least a few at Tobin's.

"All right," Grant proclaimed. "Tobin's it is. Are you hungry now, or would you rather wait a while?"

"Let's go now," Michael answered. "I've got plans later tonight with a friend."

Grant raised an eyebrow at the mention of a friend. Nevertheless, knowing the boundaries, he didn't ask. Then, to his surprise, Michael made an unusual request.

"Dad, let's take separate cars. That way, I can leave directly from Tobin's afterward."

The restaurant was only about six blocks away, and if the weather had been better, Grant would have suggested they walk. Since the drive was at most five minutes, Grant was unclear why they could not travel together in one car. Nevertheless, this was probably just a matter of Michael asserting his independence, so Grant did not argue. His seventeen-year-old son was probably preparing mentally to leave the nest. The next year or two would require even more patience and understanding.

"Okay," Grant sighed. "I'll meet you there in about five minutes."

Fifteen minutes later, Grant was seated alone at a table, nursing a beer. Tobin's had not changed one iota over the years. The tables were still covered with worn blue and white checkered tablecloths overlaid with clear plastic, and the same ancient pinball machines guarded the restrooms in the back. Festive lights, the kind used to adorn Christmas trees, were glowing on one of the walls. Grant could see a layer of dust on some of the bulbs. The lights had always been strung haphazardly, creating a mood more fitting for an abstract art museum than a cozy Italian bistro.

The decorations were a valiant effort, but overall, Tobin's was still depressing. It did not help that Grant was currently the only patron. The snow may have lifted, leaving clear, aquamarine skies behind, but the extreme cold still kept most people at home. Grant glanced at his watch.

Where was Michael? He had made a promise to Rachel the night before and was anxious to keep it.

When his son finally strode into the restaurant, he appeared oblivious to the time. Michael also seemed distracted.

"Where've you been?" Grant inquired in a weak effort to sound casual. "I thought your time was limited."

Michael peeled off his new leather coat, draped it over the back of his chair, and fell into his seat. His lips were clenched in irritation as he shook his head.

"Well, *not* anymore," Michael barked. "The plans fell through. That's why I'm a little late. I was tied up on the phone."

"I see," Grant said with a touch of sympathy. He looked up beyond his son at the waitress emerging from the kitchen and nodded for her to come by their table.

"The usual?" Grant asked his son. Then he recalled that this meant another pepperoni pizza for the second day in a row. Oh well, chalk it up to the sacrifices of parenthood. Fortunately, Grant liked pepperoni pizza.

"Sure," answered Michael, still appearing distracted.

After giving their order, Michael excused himself to the men's room. He was gone for almost ten minutes. When his son returned, it was as though he had traded his temperament with someone else. How was that possible? Michael had been moody and distressed when he left the table but returned relaxed and ebullient. Whatever. At least now, Michael might be more receptive to his news about Rachel. First, though, Grant thought it might be better to start by focusing on a seventeen-year-old boy's favorite subject.

"So," Grant began, "Let's talk about *you.*"

"Yeah? What'd you have in mind?"

"As I see it," Grant continued, "You're already halfway through your junior year of high school. It's not too early to think about what you'd like to do after graduation. Have you given it any thought?"

At that moment, the waitress, old enough to be Michael's grandmother, interrupted their conversation by setting down a plastic glass filled with Pepsi and a frosty beer mug. She smiled warmly but quickly vanished after glancing at the teenager she had just served. Meanwhile, Michael looked down at his soda and then eyed his dad's beer. When he then peered back up questioningly, Grant nodded and slid over the sweating stein of Michelob.

"Just one sip."

Michael eagerly picked up the mug and began gulping beer like he was competing in a chugging championship. Before Grant could say anything, the tankard was half empty.

"*Whoa*," Grant hollered. "You call that one sip?"

When Michael finally came up for air, he set the mug down on the table, wiped the foam from his mouth with the back of his hand, and belched loudly. Grant snatched back what was left of his beer.

"Good one," Michael proclaimed proudly. Then, seeing his dad's annoyed expression, he pronounced, "That *was* one sip. But then again," he added with a devious smile, "I guess it depends on how you define a sip."

Grant sighed loudly. "All right, we were just talking about your future," he declared, attempting to overlook his half-empty beer stein. "So, what do you think you might want to do after graduation?"

Michael nodded thoughtfully, acceding to his father's attempt to restore a more sober tone to their conversation.

"I'm thinking college. Maybe study chemistry or business. Who knows, maybe I'll even major in both."

Grant grinned. His son's response had caught him off guard. He knew Michael's grades were mediocre, but maybe he could do well enough on the ACT exam to offset his low GPA.

"Where would you want to go?" Grant inquired, sounding like any proud father discussing college plans with his almost-grown child. "ISU?"

"No," Michael snapped, "I've had my fill of Bloomington-Normal. I'd prefer a bigger city." After briefly pausing, he added, "I was thinking about Chicago State."

Grant nearly spat out the beer in his mouth. Chicago State University? He knew it was only a few miles from Marquette Park. His son would end up in the same den of wolves he had worked so hard to drag him out of. Michael would be in Gretchen's clutches and those of her bigoted family. And once he was eighteen, Grant would lose all custody rights and probably see little of his son. This was unacceptable, but what could he say?

"Well," Grant muttered, "There's still time to think about this. Maybe we could look at colleges in other big cities besides Chicago."

"Maybe *you* can," Michael retorted. "I want to return to Chicago. Hey, *you* asked." Then, after seeing his dad's furrowed brow, he added, barely repressing a smile, "Anyhow, enough with me. Let's talk about *you*, Dad. Why were you out so late last night? This has become a regular occurrence."

Grant was still reeling from the news about Michael's plans to return to Chicago. He admitted to himself there was nothing else he could say for now. After all, his son had just surprised him with plans to attend college, and there was nothing wrong with Chicago State. At least not for anyone else. Grant would have to give this some thought. Rachel might also have some insight. Speaking of Rachel, since his son had just decided to interrogate him about where he had been the previous night, perhaps now was a good time to finally address that subject.

"I told you," Grant answered, "I've recently been seeing someone."

Enjoying the sudden reversal of roles, Michael continued with his examination. "And who are you seeing?"

"Her name is Rachel," Grant replied, happy to play along. "She's a history professor at ISU, and we've *really* hit it off."

Michael paused. Grant could see the mixed emotions in his son's eyes. He knew that Michael had initially asked about last night to change the subject, to get the spotlight off himself. But his son had never been comfortable talking about his father's interest in any other woman besides his mother. What had begun as light-hearted banter had the potential to become a more profound conversation.

"Do you have a picture?" Michael inquired, still attempting to keep the mood light.

Grant reached for the wallet in his rear pocket. "Actually, she just gave me one."

He removed it from its plastic casing and presented it to his son as if he were handing over his driver's license to a traffic cop. Michael studied it for a moment while Grant held his breath. Why did this make him so nervous? Finally, his son looked up and smiled.

"Dad," he whispered, "She's *beautiful*."

Before Grant could agree, Michael held up the picture again for a closer examination. He positioned it near his face to inspect every detail.

That's when Grant remembered the photo was a couple of years old and had been taken during a trip to Israel. A friend had snapped it on a beach in Tel Aviv. What Grant loved about the picture was Rachel's vivacious smile. What Michael had noted, however, was the Israeli flag fluttering in the background—the flag with its blue Star of David.

Michael looked up. His smile slowly evaporated, and his eyes narrowed. Grant had seen this look before. He could tell that his son was struggling to find the right words to say next. "Think before you speak" was a maxim Grant had repeated from when his son first learned to talk. Michael glanced around the restaurant. The entire room was empty. Even the waitress must have disappeared into the kitchen.

"Dad," Michael finally asked in an eerily calm tone, "Is Rachel Jewish?"

Grant briefly felt like a child caught red-handed with forbidden candy. This was absurd. He was the adult in this relationship and had done nothing wrong. The wording of Michael's question was harmless and innocent, but his tone was undoubtedly anti-Semitic. He was the one who should be reprimanded, not Grant.

"Yes, she's Jewish," Grant answered with increasing conviction. "Is that a problem?"

Grant could feel his anger rising slowly like the mercury of a fever thermometer. In September, he had hoped Michael's history presentation was just a colossal misunderstanding. Despite the evil influences swirling around him in Chicago, Michael was not really a racist, was he? If so, Grant must acknowledge that his son had done a marvelous job masking his bigotry. In subsequent communications with Mrs. Reynolds, they both agreed that Michael had become a model student. So, now, where was this question about Rachel coming from?

"Dad," Michael began, assuming a lecturing tone that always sounded condescending, "It's best to keep Jewish people at a distance. They're out there, of course, and as a newspaper reporter, you probably have to deal with them all the time. But you don't have to be friends with them, and you definitely shouldn't date one of them."

Grant unknowingly tilted his head back and squinted his eyes. He did not know how to respond. One moment, he was discussing college plans with his son, who had just turned seventeen. The next, he was sitting across from a Nazi storm trooper. Finally, he reacted with the only question he could think to ask.

"What in the *hell* are you talking about?"

Michael squirmed in his seat. The die had been cast, so there was no turning back now. Realizing he needed to take a different tack, Michael doubled down by throwing a hypothetical at his father.

"Look, Dad, say you and Rachel get married sometime in the future. I can see from her picture that she's probably younger than you, and I assume she'll want children. Since I'm your only offspring, you'll go along with this plan, right? Then, suddenly, I've got a mixed-breed half-brother or sister." Michael paused to inhale a deep breath. "That's entirely unacceptable."

"Mixed-breed?" Grant echoed. "Where's this coming from? Judaism's a religion, Michael, not a different breed of humanity. Rachel and I both believe in one God. The only difference between us is that she doesn't refer to God as Jesus."

Michael grinned and shook his head in disbelief. "Dad, her people don't want her to marry you any more than I'd like you to marry her. Don't you know that? They're very clannish. That's how they've survived for thousands of years. By only marrying other Jews, they've never assimilated into the larger population. As a result, they've developed their own unique gene pool. Dad, most Jews *want* to remain apart. And they're right to do so. It's only natural."

"That may be true for some Jewish people," Grant conceded, "But it's only because they're trying to hold on to their unique culture. It has nothing to do with race." After a brief pause, he added, "And on an individual level, each person should decide for themselves if they want to marry outside their faith."

Before Michael could respond, Grant decided to go on the offensive. "And where is this ugly anti-Semitism coming from? You weren't raised with these beliefs."

Michael leaned forward and clasped his hands together on top of the table. He glared at his father and slowly shook his head in frustration. Before he could respond, the waitress emerged from the kitchen, tentatively approached their table, and placed the pizza pan between them.

"Can I get you two anything else?" she inquired sheepishly.

Still gazing intently at his son, Grant finally looked up and said, "I could use another beer."

The waitress nodded and quickly vanished, leaving an awkward silence. After looking around to confirm they were still alone, Michael spoke.

"Where is this coming from?" Michael parroted. "Dad, it's been around for thousands of years, and it's *not* ugly. It's just a reality. Look, over four billion people share the planet today, and it's incredibly naïve to think we're all the same. There are many different races, just like there are various animals who share the forest. And, yes, some of the animals *are* superior to others. Should a wolf stop hunting a deer out of the mistaken belief that all animals are the same?"

Grant opened his mouth to respond, but before he could, Michael interceded. "And frankly, Dad, I take offense at your assumption that someone has influenced my beliefs. I'm not the victim of some indoctrination program. Don't you think I'm capable of thinking for myself? That's what *you* taught me to do. I've read quite a bit on this subject, talked to many people, and worked these ideas out on my own. Now, maybe for once, you can listen to *me*. I've had to listen to your sermons my entire life."

Grant looked down at the pizza. Neither had placed a slice on their plate, and amid this surreal argument, pausing to take a bite of pizza now, knowing that the stringy melted cheese would probably dangle from his mouth, was the last thing Grant wanted to do. The pizza would have to wait. He could always ask for a box and take it home. Grant was determined not to let his son win this debate.

"All right," Grant allowed. "Let's go with your nature metaphor. In the woods, there are carnivores, and yes, they feed on the herbivores. But after millions of years of evolution, humans have risen to the top of the food chain. And that's true for *all* humans. Whether they live in Europe, Africa, or North America, every human walks on two feet, uses opposable thumbs, and has an enlarged brain capable of limitless innovation. To distinguish between people because of superficial differences like skin color, hair texture, or religious faith only contributes to hatred and intolerance. It's been the source of many wars throughout history."

While his father was speaking, Michael grabbed the spatula to slide a slice of pizza onto his plate. He picked it up, blew on it, and took his first bite. He then glanced at the front door past his father, as if someone had just entered the restaurant. Whether intentional or not, the implication was that the food mattered more than his dad's dull lecture. When Grant finally noticed his son's dismissive attitude, he stopped talking mid-sentence. Realizing this, Michael looked up from the triangle of pizza hanging from his mouth.

"What?" Michael asked, his voice muffled by the food he was chewing. "I'm listening. It's just not anything I haven't heard before."

Grant gazed at his son in disbelief. He was speechless. On the one hand, Grant knew he could never give up on Michael. He was his son, his flesh and blood. Michael could burn crosses in Klan rallies or march in Nazi parades with a swastika wrapped around his bicep, and Grant would still have to love him. On the other hand, Grant was tempted to stand up, reach across the table, and slap the face of this insolent racist. How far should a son or daughter be allowed to go to test the limits of a parent's unconditional love?

"I'm done," Grant pronounced dolefully. "I'm just going to say one more thing for now." He paused to clear his throat. "This night was supposed to be a celebration of your birthday, and I'm sorry about how it turned out. However, I will *not* apologize for anything I've just said. If you were anyone other than my son, I'd walk out and never speak to you again. To me, there's nothing more repugnant than bigotry and racism. That's what I meant, Michael, when I said you weren't raised with these beliefs. I can only hope you'll soon come to your senses."

For a moment, father and son silently glared at each other. Then, without uttering a word, Michael stood up, tossed the remnants of his pizza slice onto the table, and grabbed his leather jacket. He held it up as if examining it for stains and then, with a fixed stare, tossed it back onto his chair.

"First of all," Michael growled, "I'd rather endure the cold than wear this piece of crap. Second, *Father*, I hope you enjoy my birthday meal. If there's anything left over, take it home and stick it in the fridge. I'd rather eat it cold by myself than stay here and listen to any more of your self-righteous bullshit. And finally, if you want to take up with your little Yid girlfriend, don't let me stop you. You're a grown man. You don't need my approval."

Michael turned to leave. Before he could take a step toward the front door, Grant stood and called after him.

"Michael," Grant pleaded. "Don't leave yet. Let's talk about this some more. We can work something out."

There was desperation in Grant's voice, and he knew it. Instinctively, he understood that if Michael walked out the door, he would lose all hope for a meaningful relationship with his son. Michael turned back, and the two men scrutinized each other. His son's glare gradually melted into pity when he saw the look of despair in his father's eyes. Then, without uttering another word, Michael turned and marched out of the restaurant.

Grant sat down, despondent. His first thought was silly, almost whimsical. Now, he understood why Michael had insisted on driving his own car to Tobin's. He evidently wanted to keep his options open. Next, after the waitress emerged from the kitchen like a mouse ensuring the cat had gone, Grant requested the check and a take-home box. After leaving behind cash that included an overly generous tip, he stood and put his coat on like a man moving in slow motion. With a black leather coat draped over one hand and a pizza box balanced on the other, Grant walked out into the frozen darkness.

Once seated behind the wheel of his Civic, Grant stared ahead at the clouds of mist forming with each breath. He glanced up at the rearview mirror and didn't recognize the eyes staring back. Grant didn't know how to begin processing everything that had just happened; he needed to talk to someone. He started the engine, exited the parking lot, and turned north on Main Street toward Rachel's apartment.

CHAPTER 7

MICHAEL

March 1977

Michael squirmed his way to the back of the Greyhound bus and placed his knapsack filled with all the essentials for the upcoming week onto the overhead shelf. With an angry scowl, he settled into an empty window seat. It was a Saturday morning in mid-March, the start of Michael's spring break. He had wanted to drive his ratty AMC Gremlin to Chicago, but his dad had said no, stooping so low as to take away the keys. According to his father, the Gremlin might not survive the trip. Michael was convinced, however, that his dad simply wanted to curtail his freedom in the big city.

Within minutes, the big bus lumbered up I-55, heading northeast for the three-and-a-half-hour trek to the Windy City. The trip was just over 130 miles, but the stops in between added to the length of the journey. Michael had made this same trip aboard this same bus countless times, and he knew it was like watching paint dry. Now, as he gazed out the window at the endless flat fields waiting to be plowed with corn and soybean for the spring season, he seethed with anger and resentment.

Unbeknownst to his father, Michael had been getting high with Jerome until three in the morning. With the bus departing at 7:45 a.m., he was exhausted. Unfortunately, Michael could never sleep on a moving bus. Instead, he leaned against the window and gazed at his reflection in the glass. The eyes staring back at him were filled with regret.

"Why do you hang out with Jerome?" Chicago Mike whispered. "He's such a loser. You could engage in a more stimulating dialog with a dishrag."

"He's not so bad," Bloomington Michael rebutted. "He looks up to me, and it doesn't hurt to be friends with the biggest kid in school.

Yeah, sometimes our conversations sound like Lenny and George from *Of Mice and Men*, but so what? And Jerome is fiercely loyal. He'd do anything for me."

"Maybe so," Chicago Mike conceded, "But did you have to stay out so late with him? You knew the bus schedule."

Michael straightened up and nodded. "True enough," he agreed, "But I didn't feel like going home." Then, after a brief pause, he added, "I can't wait 'til next year. Once I have my diploma, I'm gone. Bloomington's where fun goes to die. And Normal? There's never been a more apt name for a place."

Michael noticed a restrained smile spread across the face reflected in the windowpane. He closed his eyes, hoping to give both Michaels a brief rest. When he opened them a few minutes later, he saw the jagged blades of razor wire encircling a mammoth correctional facility. Shortly afterward, the Greyhound pulled into the bus terminal in Pontiac, and five new passengers filtered on, scrambling to find vacant seats.

Michael heard the grunt of someone dropping into the seat next to him. He glanced over and saw the face of a young man with wavy blond hair and a bristly beard. Michael's new travel companion was short-statured, but after he pulled off a faux leather jacket, his sky-blue tank top revealed impressively sculpted biceps. He nodded toward Michael with a witless grin as though he was already inebriated.

As the bus began to crawl in reverse, Michael sighed noisily. He was disappointed to lose the extra space beside him and squirmed in his seat to find a more comfortable position. Just as Michael was about to turn away from his seat buddy, he noticed a blood-red swastika tattooed just above the man's wrist. Michael froze. He then glanced up and locked eyes with the young man, who knew his tattoo had been spotted and was searching Michael's eyes for a reaction. Finally, the young man broke the silence.

"Is there a problem?" He asked, the innocuous smile gone from his face.

"No," Michael quickly responded. He took a conciliatory tone, wanting to disarm the moment. "No problem at all. I was just admiring your tattoo."

"*Really?*" the man asked. "That's not what I expected from the first person I met on the outside."

"The outside?" Michael echoed.

"Yeah, man. If someone boards a bus in this town, you gotta figure there's a good chance he just got out of prison." Then, after a brief pause, he added with a grin, "Don't worry, dude, I was just paroled. You're not sitting next to an escapee."

"I'm not worried," Michael proclaimed. "But, can I ask you a question?" Without waiting for a response, "Why were you locked up?"

"Before I answer," the man responded, "Tell me your name."

"Michael. Michael Parker." He then flashed a friendly smile and extended his right hand.

"Dale O'Connor." And as they shook hands, Dale added, "Armed robbery. I was locked up for armed robbery. I was just the driver, though, and since it was my first felony conviction, I only had to serve three years. Now, I'm headed home."

"Chicago?" Michael inquired, settling into a conversational rhythm.

"Yeah. Well, actually, Cicero. You?"

"I've got another year to go with my dad in Bloomington, but after that, I plan to move back to Marquette Park."

"You make it sound like a prison sentence," Dale replied with a grin.

"Yeah, that's how it feels." Then, after a pause long enough to indicate a change of subject, Michael asked, "So, if you don't mind, can I ask about your tattoo? Is that something you got in prison?"

"Yeah," Dale replied, "It told everyone I was an Aryan. That meant I had a brotherhood watching my back. Since there are several gangs in prison, if you're smart, you'll join one of them. I chose the Aryans."

Michael sank back into his seat and glanced at an 18-wheeler passing on the left. For a moment, he tried to visualize what life would be like in an Illinois state prison. He took comfort in knowing there was an Aryan Brotherhood he could join and that it was there to provide a new family, like a fraternity offering refuge for a homesick college student. Michael glanced back down at Dale's tattoo.

"So," Michael began, "I get why that was important in prison. But, will it mean anything on the outside?"

"Hmmm," Dale mused, "That's a good question. On the one hand, I need to find a job, you know? Which is never easy for an ex-con. Let's just say I'll be wearing long sleeves to the job interviews."

"On the other hand?" Michael inquired.

"On the other hand," Dale repeated, slowly drawing out each word, "I don't know. It'd be nice to find some kind of brotherhood on the outside."

Michael twisted in his seat to face his new friend directly. He scrutinized Dale while trying to determine what to say next.

"I'm going to be blunt," Michael stated hesitantly. "How do you feel about Blacks, Jews, and other minorities?"

"Well," Dale answered as though thinking aloud, "For the most part, I don't like 'em. But as long as they stay in their place, I don't have any problem. Before I entered the pen, though, the Blacks were getting pushier and pushier about wanting a larger share of the pie, even though mine always seemed to be getting smaller. And in Pontiac, the Panthers were our arch-enemies. We only got along because we stayed on opposite sides of the yard."

Michael looked at Dale as if trying to decide whether to hire him to fill a job. Then, with a slight nod, he plunged ahead.

"Dale, you said you were looking for a group like the Aryans on the outside? And possibly a job connection as well? I might be able to help you with both."

Dale lifted his eyebrows and smiled. "Oh yeah?

"There's a place up in Marquette Park called Rockwell Hall. It's the headquarters of the American Nazi Party, and they have a meeting and rally planned for tomorrow night. I know their leader. His name is Frank Collin, and he's a good guy. I think you'd like him. I could introduce you, and I bet Frank could hook you up with a job. He might even have a space for you in Rockwell Hall until you find something more permanent. Also, you'll meet a lot of people like the Aryans you knew in Pontiac. What do you say? Do you want to join me?"

Michael and Dale talked nonstop for the next two hours. In almost every respect, they complemented each other. Dale was older, but Michael's height and physical stature compensated for the difference. Michael was the smarter of the two, but Dale's maturity and street smarts put them on an even keel. And their plans for the following night posed a win-win for both of them. While Dale stood to gain the most by attending the rally, Michael wanted to earn even more approval from Frank Collin by showing up with a new recruit.

When they reached the Chicago bus station, Dale and Michael traded contact information. Then, as they stepped off the bus, they exchanged sheepish grins as their mothers greeted them. Before parting ways, the two new friends agreed to meet in front of Rockwell Hall the following evening, about a half hour before the start of the meeting.

Twenty minutes later, Gretchen and Michael climbed from her ancient Ford Mustang and scurried down the steps to her basement efficiency apartment. Gretchen still worked as a waitress, and since losing the monthly child support payments from Grant, money had been tighter than ever. Space was also at a premium whenever Michael came to town, and he always slept on a couch that was so torn up it was permanently covered with an old quilt Gretchen had picked up at a garage sale.

When Michael walked through the front door, he was immediately greeted by the powerful aroma of cigarettes. This was no surprise since his mother had always been a chain smoker, but it still never failed to stop him in his tracks. So far, at least, Michael had not picked up this vice, and it always took him a day or two to adjust to the smell that would soon be embedded in his clothes, hair, and skin.

When Michael closed the door, Gretchen turned around to face him directly. She was at least a foot shorter, so his mother had to reach up high to wrap her arms around his neck for a tight hug.

"I've missed you, baby," she whispered.

Michael embraced his mother for a moment before gently pulling away. He glanced around the claustrophobic apartment and sighed. The place was dingy and dark, with the only natural light stealing in from the two upper windows that flanked the front door. Gretchen had used her furniture to divide the one room into a small kitchen, dining area, and den, but the effort had not worked. Michael knew that when he tried to sleep that night on the couch, he would hear his mom coughing and snoring from across the room.

"I've missed you too, Mom," Michael uttered, inspecting her for the first time since his arrival. Gretchen was painfully thin. Her stringy blond hair draped around hollow cheeks, and her eyes were tired, as though she could barely keep her lids open. Michael could also detect a deeper hoarseness in her voice, probably resulting from years of heavy smoking. His mother looked years older than his father, something that Michael could not help but resent. Even though he knew that Gretchen was the one who had bailed out of the marriage, Michael still blamed his dad for her poverty.

"We're having pizza tonight," Gretchen announced. "Your grandfather and uncles will join us. They said they'd supply the beer if I ordered the pizza." Then, she added with a wry grin, "Sounds like a good deal since I plan to drink a lot more than they'll eat."

Michael forced a smile while he studied his mother. She conveyed a pathetic aura, one that broke his heart. The best years of her life were clearly behind her, and the more he thought about it, the more he blamed his father. Michael instantly decided something he had been mulling over for a long time.

"Mom, in a year or so, I'll graduate, and I'll be eighteen. At that point, I'd like to come here for good."

Hearing his words aloud confirmed the decision, and he instantly felt good about it.

"And when I do," he added, "I'll find a job so we can move someplace nicer."

A huge grin spread across her face, creating deep lines around her lips. Michael observed a dark space toward the rear of her mouth. He immediately thought that if his new Chicago job paid enough, he would look into getting some dental work done for his mother.

"Wait," Gretchen proclaimed, her smile quickly evaporating. "What about school? I thought you were planning on going to college?"

"We'll see," Michael answered. "Depending on the job and its pay, maybe I can take some classes part-time at Chicago State."

The hint of a smile returned as Gretchen nodded thoughtfully. Michael could make out a sparkle in her eyes.

"Hey, Mom, whatever happened to that guy you were seeing a few years ago? What was his name, Tim? Jim?"

While Michael tumbled onto the couch that would later be his bed, Gretchen strolled over to the kitchen wall phone and peered at a number posted on a small bulletin board next to the antiquated Frigidaire. Michael assumed it was the number of her favorite pizza delivery service. He could feel his stomach growl at the thought of a thick, Chicago-style slice of sausage and pepperoni. Without looking up, Gretchen answered his question as though describing tomorrow's weather forecast.

"Oh, he's in Joliet. Aggravated assault with a deadly weapon. Jim pistol-whipped some Black son-of-a-bitch and almost killed him. He could never control his temper, especially when he was drunk."

Gretchen glanced up, and the grin on her face confirmed that this news did not upset her. Not in the least. As she began to punch the numbers on the phone, she added, "I don't miss him, Michael. Sure, he was a lot of fun sometimes, but I was getting sick of being his punching bag."

Michael nodded in approval. Realizing it would be a while before the pizza showed up, he reached into the knapsack he had brought from Bloomington and pulled out a half-eaten bag of pretzels. This would have to be tonight's appetizer.

Several hours later, Michael fell back onto his couch, thoroughly inebriated. His uncles had not brought over a couple of six-packs as expected; instead, they had carted over an entire keg. After the pizzas were devoured, the party expanded onto the street. Gretchen's apartment may have been sparsely furnished, but years ago, she had sprung for a stereo with gargantuan speakers. These were now positioned near the front windows, and a stack of LPs was placed on the turntable broadcasting tunes by Led Zeppelin, Pink Floyd, and Black Sabbath. Throughout the evening, no one had noticed or cared that Michael had regularly visited the keg, pumping suds into his plastic cup until the barrel was finally empty.

By one a.m., Michael fell into a comatose sleep that lasted over nine hours. When he finally awoke, his mother was grilling pancakes. At first, Michael felt too hungover to eat anything, but his appetite returned with a vengeance after a half pot of coffee. A long, steamy shower inside his mother's cramped bathroom also helped to restore his circulation. By seven that evening, Michael had dressed in his newest black slacks, a khaki button-down shirt, and a dark tie.

Before sliding on the black leather jacket he had finally agreed to accept from his dad, Michael reached for the armband he had stowed in his knapsack. Gretchen happened to walk in at that moment, having returned from an afternoon shift at her restaurant. She saw the crooked black cross of the swastika on a circular field of white, enshrouded in blood red. Pretending not to notice as she passed through the living area toward the bathroom, a slight smile parted her thin lips. She knew where Michael was going. In fact, for months now, Gretchen had been hearing good things about her son filtering out of Rockwell Hall.

Dale was already waiting outside when Michael arrived, and the expression on his face reflected a blend of apprehension and joy. Michael glanced at his watch and was relieved to see there were still thirty minutes before the rally started. This would give him time to show Dale around. Ten minutes later, the downstairs assembly room was still mostly empty as the two new friends settled into their seats.

"So," Dale began, "I've got a question."

Michael glanced over, expecting to be interviewed more about their upcoming meeting. Instead, after nodding his head, Dale surprised him.

"Remember how we talked about race problems in this country yesterday?"

Dale hesitated as though embarrassed to continue. He glanced around the room. Michael got the impression that he was about to ask a question and was ashamed not to know the answer.

"What's the big problem with the Jews?" he asked finally.

Michael could not help but smile. Dale's inquisitive expression did not change, however. He was serious. Michael's grin evaporated, replaced by a more sober countenance. Before answering, though, he thought to himself how much he liked Dale. His new friend was direct and honest, like a curious child.

"For starters," Michael asserted, "The Jews are Christ-killers. I've no idea if they *really* murdered Jesus, especially since he was one of their own, and frankly, I don't care. But that's why people first started hating them 2,000 years ago. That, and their stubborn refusal to accept Jesus as their lord and savior."

"But," Dale wondered, "Nazis aren't especially religious, are they? That's not the reason why Hitler killed so many of them."

"No," Michael answered, "Hitler saw the Jews more as a race. And he may not have been wrong, considering how long they'd been keeping to themselves. To Hitler and his Nazis, the Jews were pure evil. They needed to be exterminated the way you'd get rid of rats or other vermin."

Dale momentarily studied his new friend. Finally, he asked, "Do *you* believe this?"

Michael scanned around the room. He knew that Frank Collin and his henchmen had a pat answer to this inquiry. But Dale's question was so earnest that Michael felt it deserved a more honest response.

"I'm not sure," he said. "But I know this much. Jews seem to dominate certain fields, giving them much greater power than they deserve. You can't turn over a rock in law, medicine, finance, or even entertainment without finding a Jew. What's more, they're incredibly clannish. They go through life with an unmitigated arrogance, always acting superior to everyone else."

"I've never known a Jew," Dale confessed. "Have you?"

Michael grimaced as though conjuring a regretful memory. He twisted in his chair to face Dale directly.

"Yes. About five years ago, I spent the summer with my father down in Bloomington. I was twelve at the time. He had enrolled me in this academic summer program on the Illinois State campus. We did a lot of writing, but most of the time, it was pretty dull. However, there was one reason I enjoyed attending the class. Her name was Deborah Cohen."

Dale's lips instantly parted into a broad "you dog" smile, showing teeth already yellowed by excessive smoking.

"I *loved* Deborah Cohen. She had already developed nice round breasts and purposefully unbuttoned the top of her blouse after her parents dropped her off each morning to show them off. She also had long dark hair and the widest brown eyes. But it wasn't just her body. Deborah was brilliant. She always gave us the best feedback when we'd read our poems and stories aloud, even better than the teacher."

"But," Dale interrupted, "She was Jewish?"

"Yes," Michael answered, "But it didn't seem like such a big deal. It came up once or twice in her writing, but otherwise, Deborah was like everyone else in the class. And, what did I know? Sure, my family in Chicago always complained about the Jews, but since there were none in my school back in Marquette Park, I never actually knew any. So, Deborah was the first I'd ever met, and from what I could tell, she didn't have any horns on her head."

"So," Dale asked, clearly engaged, "What happened?"

"We were good friends for most of the summer. But eventually, I wanted more. I finally got my chance in mid-July when Deborah invited me to her birthday party. This was an especially big deal because it was her thirteenth birthday, so her party followed a service called a Bat Mitzvah. For Jews, it marked their entry into the adult world. Seeing my chance, I put on a coat and tie, had my dad drive me to the synagogue, and brought what I thought was a special gift."

"Special?" Dale echoed. "What made it special?"

"I know this sounds hokey," Michael uttered sheepishly, "But it was an ID bracelet. You know, the kind you used to give a girl when you wanted to go steady? When I gave it to her that night, Deborah threw her arms around my neck and gave me my first real kiss. I'll never forget the feel of her wet tongue in my mouth. I still get a boner thinking about it."

"*Nice*," Dale exclaimed. "So, I guess Jews weren't so bad after all."

Michael began to shake his head with a scowl. "Maybe the younger ones aren't, but Deborah's parents went ballistic when they saw my brace-let on her wrist. One moment, I thought I was in love; the next, I was forbidden from ever seeing Deborah again."

"Did it *really* matter, though?" Dale queried. "You were about to return to Chicago, right?"

"True, but I'd still be back to see my dad during school breaks, and in the meantime, Deborah and I could've written letters or talked on the phone. But that's not the point. These assholes decided I wasn't good enough for their little princess. They didn't know me. All they knew was that I wasn't Jewish. So they ended our relationship, and I never saw Deborah again."

"Well," Dale stated, almost as if apologizing for Deborah's parents, "Maybe they were just looking out for their daughter. Granted, it wasn't fair to you, but that doesn't mean all Jews are evil, does it?"

"Yes," Michael instantly responded, "It does. You see, after that sum-mer, I started researching the Jews. It turns out that Deborah's parents fit squarely into the larger pattern."

Michael paused and glanced around the room, half full by now. He nodded to familiar faces before turning to look at his new friend directly.

"Dale, have you ever heard of *The Protocols of the Elders of Zion*? This theory has been around since the turn of the century. According to The Protocols, the Elders of Zion, that is, the Jewish leaders, have been secretly plotting to rule the world. This may sound unbelievable, but it's true if you think about it. By manipulating the economy, controlling the media, and encouraging conflict, Jews are slowly and quietly taking over everything. Henry Ford understood this. Besides building cars, Ford published a series of articles in his newspaper based on *The Protocols*. They were later combined into his book called *The International Jew*. Hitler read it and thought it was spot on."

"*Damn,* son," Dale reacted, "You've done your homework. I should start reading more."

"They have literature about all this right here," Michael asserted, pointing toward the table in the front foyer.

Before Dale could respond, Frank Collin approached the front podium, switched on a microphone, and called the meeting to order. At once, everyone stood in unison, raised their right hands in a Nazi salute, and barked, "Sieg heil" three times. Michael glanced at his new friend and observed the gleam in his eye. He was clearly impressed by the spectacle of fifty people, all adorned in khaki uniforms, black ties, and swastika armbands, acting with such precision.

This was followed by reciting the Pledge of Allegiance to the American flag draped behind the podium. After the minutes from the last meeting were read and approved, Frank Collin addressed the two most essential items on the agenda. The first was an update on the Supreme Court's decision to hear their case involving Skokie. Frank said this was fantastic news because it meant several more months of basking in the media spotlight. The second item was a planned demonstration downtown outside the Chicago Federal Building the following week.

While both of these topics garnered several questions and comments, the highlight of the evening was Frank's speech toward the end of the rally. He knew how to whip up a crowd like a preacher leading a Back-to-Jesus revival. Tonight's subject was Holocaust survivors, particularly those who lived just north of Chicago. According to Frank, bringing the swastika to Skokie sent a symbolic message to the world that he and his fellow Nazis intended to finish the job Hitler had started. By the end, the crowd was again on its feet, bellowing "Sieg heil" repeatedly, each chant growing increasingly thunderous. Michael glanced over at Dale, gazing straight ahead with his arm raised, screaming as loud as everyone else in the room.

After the meeting, Michael waited for the crowd around Frank to disperse. He had two items on his agenda. First, he wanted to introduce Dale to Frank and facilitate his new friend's absorption into the party. Second, Michael had something else he wanted to discuss. Despite his youth, he understood his value to the party. Most people attending tonight's rally would never become rocket scientists or brain surgeons. Therefore, it was not hard for Michael to stand out intellectually. He wanted to be sure Frank knew this.

The first part of Michael's plan worked even better than anticipated. Frank offered Dale a bed in the upstairs "dormitory" for as long as he wanted and stated that he knew of a restaurant looking for a short-order cook. Since the two men were closer in age, they seemed to hit it off immediately, leaving Michael feeling like a student eavesdropping on a conversation in the teachers' lounge. Michael bit his tongue, patiently listening to the same backstory Dale had shared on the bus the day before. Finally, Frank, who appeared highly pleased with the party's latest recruit, turned toward Michael to thank him for bringing Dale to the meeting.

"Once again, Mr. Parker," Frank pronounced, "You've outdone yourself." Glancing over at Dale, he added, "Recruiting someone for the party during a short bus trip from Bloomington shows outstanding hustle on your part. You've made yourself indispensable to our organization in such a short time."

Michael couldn't help but grin at the praise he received. Even though he still had a year left of high school in Bloomington, he was already looking forward to his new life in Marquette Park. Additionally, while he often despised his biological dad, Michael was increasingly starting to view Frank Collin as his true father.

"Well," Michael replied with growing conviction, "There's something else I'd like to run by you."

He scanned the room. Most people had left the Hall, probably heading to the nearest tavern. Dale was still within hearing distance, but Michael had no problem entrusting his proposal to his new friend. After Frank nodded, he continued speaking.

"I've become the top student in my chemistry class," Michael proudly declared. "And my teacher loves me. Therefore, I now have access to a number of chemicals that can be used to make explosives."

Leaning in conspiratorially, Michael inquired, "I've also been doing a lot of research about how to build bombs that are easy and safe for us to detonate but highly destructive for our purposes, if you know what I mean. Would any of this interest you?"

Frank Collin's eyebrows shot up as he exchanged a devious smile with Dale. Like the villain in a silent movie, he stroked his chin, deep in thought. Finally, he turned back toward Michael, crossed his arms across his chest, and patted the swastika armband encircling his bicep.

"Build and test, Trooper Parker, build and test. But do so with the utmost care and caution. The last thing we need is to lose one of our most promising members to an accident or to law enforcement. At some point in the future, we may find the right opportunity to use your skills."

After a brief pause, Frank added, "However, for now, you need to stay extremely vigilant and cautious. We definitely don't want any of this traced back to our organization here in Chicago. Therefore," he emphasized, "please do not take any action without checking with me first. Do you understand?"

CHAPTER 8

RACHEL

April 1977

The morning light filtered through the vertical blinds in Rachel's bedroom, casting dark stripes across Grant's dead-to-the-world, unshaven face. His bottom lip trembled slightly, making Rachel wonder what he was dreaming about. Fortunately, if demons were haunting Grant, they hadn't invaded his subconscious the day before. Like a couple of teenagers, Rachel and Grant celebrated their first date's six-month anniversary with a day trip to Chicago, culminating in a steak dinner at a downtown restaurant.

Rachel scooted up in bed and propped her head on a pillow to better examine every feature of Grant's face. A couple of horizontal lines wrinkled his forehead, the only visible evidence of their age difference. Otherwise, he was indeed a beautiful man. Rachel loved Grant's high cheekbones, the cleft in his chin, and how his hair haphazardly fell back over his pillow. As she often did at moments like this, Rachel decided to take a quick inventory of their relationship.

Even more than his strikingly handsome features, Rachel adored Grant's personality. He was clever, even-tempered, and possessed a witty sense of humor. Rachel never grew tired of his company, no matter how much time they spent together. When they were apart, even for just a few hours, she missed him. Rachel made it a practice to memorize the highlights of her day so she could share them with Grant later in the evening. She was grateful to have finally found the one man with whom she could share the rest of her life. Rachel could happily grow old with this man.

In addition, Rachel admired Grant. She respected that he was a dedicated journalist, committed to investigating any problem or issue and bringing it to the community's attention. Grant represented the embodiment of the printed press, the fourth branch of the government, a necessary component in any functional democracy. Rachel knew Grant chose his profession because he genuinely wanted to make a difference. He was not concerned about making money or acquiring material possessions. Grant was indeed an honorable person.

Sudden movement within the room disturbed Rachel's concentration. The recent spring weather had been so mild they had been sleeping with open windows. An unexpected gust of wind had rattled the blinds, causing parallel shadows to dance around the room. When Rachel finally refocused on Grant, she noticed the start of an oval age spot on his left cheek, directly beneath his eye. Rachel would generally care little about such a minor blemish, but in this case, it once again reminded her of their age difference.

Ten years. Was this a deal-breaker? When Rachel turned forty, Grant would already be fifty. She acknowledged that it would be worse biologically if she were the older one in the relationship. After all, a man could generally become a parent later in life than a woman. Still, this age difference put Grant into a different orbit. While she was looking forward to having a baby in the near future, Grant was already the father of a teenager. This reminded Rachel of possibly the most significant obstacle in their path: Michael.

No matter how much she tried, Rachel could never connect with Michael. Their brief conversations were mainly superficial and completely one-sided, with her asking the questions and Michael responding with one-word answers. Even though she had never said or done anything remotely offensive, Rachel sensed nothing but hostility from Michael. This alone might have doomed their relationship. However, she and Grant shared an understanding that Michael would probably flee the nest in the next year or two. Rachel kept reminding herself that enduring this bad seed for just one more year was worth it for a lifetime with Grant.

For now, at least, the positives of this romance far outweighed the negatives. Rachel deeply loved Grant, and from his words and actions, she was convinced he felt the same. She could visualize a timeline extending over the next few years that included first living together, followed by a brief engagement, then a simple wedding ceremony, and finally, her pregnancy leading to the start of their own family.

Another burst of wind created more movement within the room, like someone shaking a snow globe. When Rachel returned her attention to Grant, she was shocked to see him staring back at her with a lustful grin. She did not hesitate, reaching out to wrap her arms around his neck and draw him in for a fiery kiss. Almost like a wrestling maneuver, he flipped from his side to his back, dragging Rachel on top. Twenty minutes passed before they exchanged words beyond their amorous moans and groans.

"So," Grant enquired while rolling onto his side and using his hand to wipe away the moisture on his forehead, "Now that we've satisfied one craving, should we address another?"

"Are you offering breakfast in bed?" Rachel teased, "Or are you inviting me somewhere for brunch?"

Rachel already knew the answer. Since neither liked to cook, the only question was what restaurant they would choose.

"How about Shannon's out on Veterans Parkway?"

Rachel could see moisture gathering on Grant's lower lip. Was he already drooling at the thought of a Belgian waffle? She smiled, thinking about how quickly they had settled into a comfortable rhythm of daily habits and routines.

Rachel suddenly leaped from the bed and grabbed her clothes from the day before, which were piled in the corner. Then, turning back toward Grant with an exuberant smile, she issued a challenge.

"Let's bet on who can get ready the fastest. Loser buys."

Since Grant and Rachel both had a competitive streak, neither bothered to shower. Rachel started in the lead, but Grant passed her when an awkward bra held her back. By the time Rachel climbed into the passenger seat of his Civic, Grant was already sporting a spirited grin from behind the steering wheel.

Ten minutes later, they started their brief wait for a table. Fortunately, Shannon's was a large restaurant with a quick turnover, so it wasn't long before the waitress set down two heavy plates on their table: one topped with an oversized waffle dusted in powdered sugar and the other featuring a steaming omelet. Then, as he smothered his breakfast in syrup, Grant raised a potentially explosive question.

"So," Grant asked after swallowing his first bite, "Have you been following the latest news about Skokie?"

Rachel had just cut into her cheese omelet and glanced up warily, sensing they were about to enter a minefield.

"Yes, of course," she answered, "As you know, that's where I grew up. However, I'm not sure I understand the most recent legal maneuvers."

"It's complicated," Grant agreed, "But at the risk of oversimplifying, I think the state courts, including the Illinois Supreme Court, have supported Skokie's effort to keep the Nazis out. Now, the case is headed to the US Supreme Court."

Rachel sipped her coffee while glancing at Grant from across the table. She strongly suspected they were on opposite sides of this volcanic issue. Would it be better to steer away from this subject? On the other hand, this might be a good time to test their relationship. After all, if she was going to spend the rest of her life with this man, Rachel wanted to be able to discuss hot issues without a debate turning into mortal combat. So, after swallowing another bite of her omelet, she pressed ahead.

"I've read that some of the ACLU lawyers representing the Nazis are *actually* Jewish." After a brief pause where she shook her head, Rachel added, "I just don't understand that."

"Really?" Grant asked, his tone doubtful. "Why do you suppose more Jews live in the United States than any other country? Don't you think many immigrated here because they knew the First Amendment would guarantee their freedom of religion?"

"So?" Rachel inquired, echoing Grant's argumentative tone while forking another bite of omelet into her mouth. "I agree that many craved freedom. They came here to escape pogroms, the Holocaust, and other forms of anti-Semitism in Europe. But why would they then turn around and defend the very people from whom they had just escaped?"

"Because many Jews have come to understand that the best way to guard their freedom is to protect *everyone's* freedom, even the most despicable in our society. Even the Nazis. To do otherwise creates a dangerous slippery slope."

Rachel began to roll her eyes before catching herself. She understood that insulting mannerisms might appeal to an audience, but they were a disgraceful way to engage in an intelligent debate. Still, there was no harm in throwing in a bit of sarcasm, was there?

"Okay, Clarence Darrow, just to clarify, you support the ACLU's decision to represent the Nazis? Because I've read that this has already cost them a significant percentage of their membership."

"*Support* them?" Grant echoed. "I've been a member of the ACLU for over a decade. And," he added with conviction, "I've got no intention of withdrawing my membership."

"So, you believe the Constitution gives those Nazi thugs from Marquette Park the right to terrify the Jewish residents of Skokie? Thousands of them survived the Holocaust. Do you realize the nightmares they'll experience when they see swastikas paraded on the streets of their own community?"

"Terrify?" Grant asked, unable to hide his skepticism. "They may call themselves Nazis, but most are just pathetic clowns. They're hardly the German stormtroopers who brought Hitler to power. And," he added after a brief pause to catch his breath, "if the counter-demonstrators, who will outnumber Frank Collins' supporters at least ten to one, react violently, then that's on them. To be safe, though, Governor Thompson might want to call in the National Guard. However, if he does, they need to remember their purpose is to maintain peace, not to prevent the Nazis from marching. Telling the Nazis they can't march is a form of prior restraint, plain and simple. It would violate not only their First Amendment rights but everyone else's as well."

"You should've been a lawyer, Grant. Then you could've delivered that speech before the Supreme Court."

The hint of a smile on Rachel's face evaporated when she did not see it reflected across the table. After pausing briefly to steady her tone, she responded.

"You're right, Grant; most Jews in this country do value their Constitutional rights. That's why so many joined Martin Luther King in the civil rights struggle. However, this situation is different. Telling the village of Skokie that they must allow a group of individuals wearing Nazi uniforms and displaying the swastika is a blatant form of terrorism. While it may not involve physical violence, this so-called 'peaceful protest,' as you call it, is just as harmful, if not worse."

By now, Rachel and Grant understood they were engaged in a full-scale debate. So far, it had been civil, but Rachel knew that she and her boyfriend could sometimes be fiercely competitive. The next few minutes would determine if they would pass her test.

"I'll admit," Grant conceded, "That a Nazi demonstration in Skokie would upset many people. And that's perfectly understandable. But it's the price we pay to live in a free society. There's a reason why the Lady Justice statue is holding a scale. It's all about maintaining the ideal balance. When it comes to protecting our civil liberties, though, it's always best to tip the scale in favor of protecting rights even if it might result in a few nightmares."

"That's easy for you to say," Rachel countered. "You're not the one suffering from the nightmares. Grant, there have to be some limits. The Constitution is *not* a suicide pact."

"That sounds familiar," Grant commented. "Where's it from?"

"Most people believe Lincoln used this phrase to justify his restrictions on habeas corpus rights during the Civil War," Rachel explained, adopting her professorial stance. "However, the phrase was actually mentioned in several recent Supreme Court cases. It fits, though, doesn't it?"

"Maybe," Grant allowed. "And I'll admit there must be guardrails on our Constitutional rights. But in this case, keeping the Nazis out of Skokie simply because their message is offensive to the community doesn't justify the exercise of prior restraint. According to that reasoning, the state of Alabama could've legitimately kept Dr. King from leading his march from Selma to Montgomery."

"*No*," Rachel rebutted, her anger growing. "It's not the same."

She paused momentarily to calm herself. Grant had hit a nerve, but if they were to pass her test, Rachel would have to avoid getting emotional. She inhaled deeply before proceeding.

"It's not the same," Rachel repeated in a more composed tenor. "You cannot equate the Nazis to our civil rights leaders. To do so means there are no absolute moral standards. All human behavior would then become relative. Martin Luther King represented the highest level of moral decency; Frank Collin and his disciples stand for nothing but evil. One is virtuous; the other is wicked. You cannot say they both deserve the same rights."

"There is no question," Grant agreed, "That the Nazis are on the opposite end of the moral spectrum from Martin Luther King. But in the end, the righteous side usually prevails. Why? Because in a democratic society, public opinion will resolve these moral conundrums. The public acts like a jury. In a trial, neither the prosecution nor the defense cares about the truth; they just want to win. But it's the jury's job to decide the truth. It'll be the same in Skokie. Let the American people hear both sides and then trust them to decide who's right."

"You can't be serious. Trust the public to determine what's morally right? Grant, you're being remarkably generous." Rachel scoffed, disregarding her decorum. "And maybe a bit naïve. How well did that work for Germany's democracy after World War I?"

"A democratic government was imposed on Germany by the nations that had just defeated it, and it was only barely established by the time Hitler came to power." However, we live in a Constitutional Republic that's just celebrated its 200th birthday. The roots of our democracy reach much deeper than theirs ever did." Grant added, "And besides if the residents of Skokie *really* want to deal the Nazis a blow, they should simply ignore them."

Rachel's eyes widened in disbelief. Momentarily, she shook her head, mouth agape and speechless. Finally, she responded in a slightly higher pitch.

"Grant, the Second World War just ended a little over thirty years ago. Do you honestly expect Jewish people to ignore Nazis?"

"So instead," Grant countered, "By passing this ordinance to keep the Nazis and their swastikas out, Skokie's handed them what they crave the most, free publicity. This legal battle is playing out on the national news practically every night. And while I trust most Americans to see the Nazis for who they are, there are still thousands of racists and mentally disturbed people out there who will be drawn to them. No," Grant pronounced in conclusion, "I say let them march and don't turn this into an issue. That way, the First Amendment will be upheld for *everyone*, and the Nazis won't be given a platform to spread their propaganda."

To Rachel, it sounded like Grant had concluded his part of the debate and was now allowing her the opportunity to have the final word. If she could finish it off civilly, it meant they would have passed her test. But what approach should she take? It was tempting for Rachel to personalize their debate by reminding Grant of her parents' experiences at Sobibor and how disturbed they would be to see the swastika paraded in the community where they had lived for the past thirty years. However, she decided to appeal more to his logical mind than his emotional heart.

"You made a valid point," she began, "By talking about all the free publicity the Nazis have garnered from this issue. However, why blame Skokie? It takes *two* sides to create an issue. If the ACLU had never brought this case to court, the Nazis wouldn't be able to march, no one would be paying attention, and they would not be getting all this free publicity."

Rachel paused and took a deep breath. Her expression indicated that she was not quite finished.

"One more thing. I believe we've overlooked the most pertinent point in this case. Our Constitutional rights can and should be restricted if the speech threatens society's safety. I'm sure you're familiar with the famous Oliver Wendell Holmes claim that free speech does not give you the right to shout fire in a crowded theater, right? To do so could start a riot where people might be hurt or killed. The same can also be said about allowing the swastika to be paraded through Skokie. If allowed, there's a good chance somebody will be hurt or killed. It's in society's best interest to keep the Nazis out."

"Well," Grant replied, grinning and shaking his head, "As they say, I guess we'll have to agree to disagree."

Then, as though someone had thrown a switch, Grant's smile faded. Even though half his Belgian waffle was still uneaten, he pushed his plate away. Grant ceased making eye contact with Rachel and shifted his focus toward his intertwined fingers resting on the table.

"Is something wrong?" Rachel inquired with raised eyebrows. "I enjoyed our discussion this morning. I wish most of my students could debate as well as you just did. It was quite stimulating."

Grant peered up with a conciliatory smile. "Yeah, I enjoyed it, too. It was enlightening to hear a different viewpoint expressed so well. It reminded me of the debates we used to have in my history classes."

"So then, what's the matter? It seems like something's bothering you."

Rachel had recently started noticing this expression on Grant's face. Whenever this occurred, his eyes turned downward, and the corners of his mouth fell into a heart-wrenching frown. She began to fear their discussion had triggered the one anxiety Grant consistently harbored: Michael.

It did not take a genius to figure out that all their talk this morning about Frank Collin and his Chicago-based Nazis likely reminded Grant that his son could be caught up in this neo-fascist farce. At the very least, Grant could be worried about whether the situation in Skokie would reinforce the racist baggage Michael had inherited from his past.

"It's nothing, *really*," Grant finally answered. "It's just that I feel a bit hypocritical when I think about what I've just said to you."

"Why?" Rachel asked, genuinely confused. "In what way were you hypocritical?"

Grant glanced at Rachel, clenching his lips and combing his fingers through his hair. "Well," he began slowly, "Here I am smugly defending the Nazis' right to march through Skokie while, at the same time, I'd like to strangle every last one of them."

When Grant stalled again, Rachel decided to help him out. "This is *really* about Michael, isn't it?"

Grant nodded but remained silent. Rachel took this as a green light to continue.

"So, in theory, you support the collective right of the Nazis to march, but you're concerned that one of those parading through Skokie could be your son. Is that what you're thinking?"

"You know," Grant answered, "I wouldn't have had this concern a few days ago. In fact, I would've been bragging about Michael."

Rachel tilted her head back in surprise. "*Really?* Why?"

"Several reasons," Grant said, even now unable to conceal a bit of paternal pride. "First, I started hearing some good things from his teachers, including that history teacher he'd butted heads with. Then, I just got his latest report card. Rachel, it's all A's and B's."

"No kidding," Rachel uttered encouragingly. "That's *terrific*."

"And that's not all," Grant added. "Recently, Michael's actually been a nice kid to live with. I don't know what got into him. The other day, he sat down next to me on the couch, and we actually watched a movie together. *Butch Cassidy and the Sundance Kid*. Afterwards, we went out for a pizza. It's the most fun we've had together in a long time."

"*Really?*" Rachel queried, unable to mask her disbelief. "Why didn't you tell me about this?"

"I wasn't sure it was real," Grant replied with a faint smile.

Of course, if everything was going so well, Rachel thought, what had happened to darken the situation?

"So why are you upset?"

Grant's smile gradually faded as he searched for the right words.

"The other day," Grant responded, "When I was doing Michael's laundry, I went into his room to put away his clothes. What I came across was quite upsetting."

Rachel glanced across the table quizzically. She wondered why this was just coming out now. Why did Grant hesitate to share the details about Michael's life?

"You know how we've been watching those Nazi marches on the news? Have you ever noticed how Frank Collin and his disciples always wear the same khaki shirts with those thin black ties? And they're always sporting dark slacks with black boots. While putting away Michael's clean clothes, I suddenly realized the same items were right there in his closet. Rachel, they've been under my nose all this time. I never paid much attention to the kid's weird fashion statements. I just figured he was being a typical teenager. However, until *that* moment, I'd never thought about the significance of his latest clothing styles."

"*Really?*" Rachel asked, feigning disbelief.

"This was just yesterday, Rachel," Grant continued. "I've been wrestling with whether to tell you. And to be honest, it's incredibly embarrassing."

"And you're sure about this?" Rachel inquired tentatively. "You're sure it's a Nazi uniform and not just the clothes of a rebellious teenager?"

"Yes," Grant answered without delay. "I thoroughly searched his room since Michael was out with a friend. The clincher was finding the armband hidden beneath his underwear. It was emblazoned with a *swastika*. Rachel, there's no mistaking that symbol. It was right there in my son's chest of drawers."

Grant's face transformed into a mask of Greek tragedy. His lips parted, and the corners of his mouth turned downward. His eyes looked as if they were on the verge of releasing a stream of tears. For now, though, they merely widened, pushing his eyebrows up and distorting the rest of his face in an unnatural way. Rachel had never seen this before. The confident man she loved now appeared helplessly broken, and it made her heart ache.

Seeing Grant in such pain stirred every bit of compassion within Rachel. She believed there was goodness in his heart and recognized that holding the son's sins against the father would be unfair. She reached out to take his hands, now clasped in front of him on the table. But then the waitress appeared with a burst of energy, utterly oblivious to what had been taking place. Observing the half-eaten waffle on Grant's plate, she glanced uneasily in his direction.

"Was the food all *right*?" she asked in a Southern accent.

"Yes, it was fine," Rachel quickly answered. "Do you think we could have a to-go box? As well as the check?"

"Sure, sweetheart," the waitress answered. She forced a smile and disappeared.

Rachel again reached across the table, taking Grant's hands within her own and squeezing hard. This raised the corners of his mouth into a somber smile.

"So, Grant," Rachel inquired, "What are you going to do?"

"I don't know," he mumbled like a lost child. "What can I do?" Then, as if a light bulb went off in his mind, Grant continued. "Tonight, I'll confront Michael. I'll make him get rid of the Nazi clothes, and then I'll take away his car keys. Finally, I'll make him sit down for a heart-to-heart to help him understand why this is all so wrong."

The waitress suddenly reappeared. Astutely sensing the tension at the table, she quickly put down a Styrofoam container and the check. Grant started to reach for his wallet, but Rachel already had a credit card in her palm. She handed it to the waitress in a flash, who once again vanished without a word.

"I've got this," Rachel pronounced. "You were the first to get ready this morning, remember?" After briefly pausing, she added cheerily, "I always pay off my bets."

Grant pocketed his wallet, nodded slowly, and attempted to return her grin. He scooted his chair closer to the table, indicating he was not quite ready to leave.

"Thank you for breakfast," he began. While Rachel graciously nodded, a more restrained veneer returned to Grant's face as though he had again replaced his mask.

"As for Michael, I'm not going to kid myself. No matter what I do, Gretchen still has partial custody, so there's no way I can keep him from going up to Chicago. And the more time he spends in Marquette Park, the more those bastards will get their hooks into him."

Rachel nodded compassionately. She remained silent, waiting to see if there was more. After a brief pause, Grant continued.

"But what else can I do? Hopefully, with a little luck and a lot of patience, he'll grow out of this phase."

"And if it doesn't?" Rachel asked, sounding somewhat hesitant.

"That's a good question," Grant replied, slowly shaking his head. "But no matter what, Michael's my son. I can't just give up on him. Ultimately, I've got to separate the boy from his dreadfully racist ideas. If he joined a cult or became a heroin addict, I'd still have to be there in his corner, right? As I see it, this is no different."

Grant abruptly pushed back his chair, signaling he was ready to leave. Rachel assumed this also meant their discussion was over. This time, Grant had had the final word. She accepted this reality, understanding there was nothing more to say. The issue was not subject to further debate. However, as Rachel pushed back her chair and stood up to leave, a troubling premonition settled in her gut. For the first time, she realized that even if Michael moved out in a year or so, he might always be a wedge between her and the man she hoped to marry.

CHAPTER 9

BENJAMIN

May 1977

A blistering sun baked the half-empty parking lot of Eastland Mall as Benjamin shuffled toward his Oldsmobile station wagon. Abandoning his store in the middle of the day left him with a queasy feeling. Benjamin was unusually dedicated to his business, and leaving it in the hands of one of his salespeople, even if just for a few hours, made him uneasy. As he often said to Miriam, "Anything can happen while I'm gone." Nevertheless, Benjamin could hardly say no when his daughter invited him to speak at her World War II symposium, which could only occur on a weekday.

As Rachel explained, the event consisted of a panel of speakers considered "primary historical sources." She said the department wanted to enrich the traditional curriculum based chiefly on textbooks, lectures, and other secondary readings. Many professors tried to spice up their courses by including primary source documents, but, according to Rachel, there was nothing more intellectually stimulating than hearing someone talk about a historical event they had lived through.

Each year, the department selected a different period or event from the recent past. Last year's symposium focused on the Great Depression. As Rachel mentioned, finding grandparents with stories about unemployment, bank crashes, and the Dust Bowl was relatively easy. The challenge, however, was locating individuals from overseas who could discuss the impact of the Depression on other nations.

This year's subject was World War II. The speakers included veterans, women who worked on the home front, and even an English immigrant who had survived the London Blitz. Rachel told her father he was the keynote presenter and was scheduled to speak last. She explained that the department wanted to end with someone who had survived the Holocaust because they considered this the most consequential event of the war. Benjamin was a bit skeptical at first, but Rachel reminded him that with the threat of a Nazi march in Skokie dominating the news, the department felt the Holocaust had become even more historically significant.

Unlike many Holocaust survivors, Benjamin had always found satisfaction in sharing his story. Like others, he had endured an indescribable experience, including the heartbreaking loss of his first family. What made Benjamin somewhat unique, though, was his courageous resistance. Not only did he personally kill an SS monster with his own hands, but he also played an active role in orchestrating their escape.

Although he had never said this to anyone, not even himself, Benjamin knew there was another reason why he reveled in sharing his story. He had lost his wife and daughter in Sobibor, but that had occurred immediately upon their arrival. Benjamin always began his story as a poignant tragedy but slowly turned it into a heartfelt romance by the end. Many in the crowd grew teary-eyed when he concluded his narrative. Although Miriam was bashful and refused to join him onstage, when he pointed her out in the audience and asked her to stand, the crowd always offered them a warm ovation. Benjamin never grew tired of hearing the applause.

Benjamin also appreciated the historical value of his story. He had always subscribed to the George Santayana quote, "Those who do not learn history are doomed to repeat it." And since the Holocaust ranks as one of the worst acts of cold-blooded cruelty in history, Benjamin felt it must be thoroughly studied so it would never happen again. Upon his arrival in the United States, his desire to speak to audiences was a pivotal motivator for mastering the English language.

After a quick stop to pick up Miriam, who had never missed one of his presentations, Benjamin drove to one of the visitor lots, parked his aging but well-maintained station wagon, and entered Capen Auditorium in Edwards Hall. He had been here twice before but only as a member of the audience. The first time was during the previous year's symposium when he had occupied one of its more than 700 seats to hear a retired banker talk about bank runs during the early 1930s. The other time was when Rachel escorted her parents to a special viewing of *The Godfather*. Today, he would be up on the stage, the center of attention.

As Benjamin and Miriam entered the back of the auditorium, which was in the same building as the history department, they quickly spotted Rachel. Their daughter hurried over to guide them to their seats. Once Miriam was settled on the front row, Rachel ushered her dad up a few steps to the stage, where a couple of chairs and a podium with a microphone awaited. Between the chairs, a small table supported a glass of ice water. As usual, his daughter had thought of everything.

Since Benjamin had arrived early, Rachel left her father to attend to a few last-minute details. The stage lights were luminous, and due to their glowing heat, Benjamin stood up, took off his sports coat, draped it over the back of his chair, and loosened his tie. Once he sat back down, he looked around at the half-empty auditorium, beginning to feel like the only tropical fish in a brightly lit aquarium.

With his hands clasped between his knees, Benjamin watched as the crowd gradually began to grow. Rachel had told him to expect a large audience because not only had every member of the history department invited their students, but the symposium had been advertised locally and was open to the public. Furthermore, because Rachel had created and distributed a flyer briefly summarizing Benjamin's story, she anticipated a large crowd from the off-campus community.

Soon, Benjamin could not find an empty seat, and he began observing people standing in the back and along the side walls. Squinting for a better view, which only accentuated the crow's feet flanking his eyes, he noticed that the audience was a diverse mix of traditional college students and older members of the community. Since many of the boys had long hair, Benjamin could barely tell the males from the females. He smiled faintly at the thought of what had recently happened with the youth in this country.

Benjamin had spoken to many groups over the years, usually in smaller, more intimate settings. Here, there was even a balcony that also seemed to be full. He began to feel butterflies in his stomach, something that had not happened in years. Benjamin nervously stroked the loose strands of gray hair on his increasingly balding scalp, an old habit that had always helped to reduce his anxiety. He inhaled deeply and glanced down at the front row, where he could barely make out his wife's face. Seeing her give a little wave was momentarily reassuring.

Then Benjamin noticed Grant, who was seated next to Miriam. He had met the reporter from *The Pantagraph* a few times, and his daughter's new boyfriend seemed pleasant enough. Most importantly, Grant appeared to make Rachel happy. He was not Jewish, however. Benjamin smiled at the thought that the traditional matchmaking custom, as his parents experienced in the old country, might have been a better way to find a spouse.

Benjamin saw Grant lean over to speak to someone opposite his wife. Who was this? Again, Benjamin squeezed his lids tighter to gain a better view. It was a teenage boy with dark hair. He was slouching in his front-row seat with his legs crossed and extended. Even from up here, where he was bathed in bright lights, Benjamin could make out the scowl on the boy's face. His arms were also crossed. The posture of the boy's lanky frame communicated that he wanted to be anywhere but here.

From nowhere, Rachel reappeared carrying a projector. She glanced around, located an outlet, and then ran an extension cord to plug it in. At the same time, a college kid, probably one of Rachel's students, lugged up a large screen, set it up on a tripod beside the podium, and opened it like an umbrella. Benjamin flashed his daughter a curious look. He had never used visuals in any of his talks. What was Rachel doing? Seeing her father's furrowed brow, Rachel approached him and whispered in his ear.

"I have some slides to use during your talk, Dad. I'll be in charge of them; you don't need to worry."

"What kind of slides?" Benjamin inquired.

"Dad," Rachel answered, "I've heard you talk so many times that I know what you'll say before you say it. Therefore, to visually reinforce the information, I created a set of slides. They're primarily maps, timelines, and photographs. I even have some pictures of you and Mom when you were young."

Benjamin appeared skeptical. "I don't know, Rachel. How will I know when to go from one slide to the next?"

Rachel held up a small gadget. "You won't have to do anything. As I said, I know what you'll be saying, so when it's the right time, I'll use this remote to advance the slides on the carousel projector."

"*Huh*," Benjamin exclaimed. "Modern technology. What'll they think of next?"

Rachel smiled. Then she glanced at her watch and stood. "It's time to begin, Dad. Are you ready?"

Benjamin inhaled a deep breath and nodded. No matter how often he did this, he could not get past the jitters he always felt right before his talk began. Rachel stepped over to the podium, tapped the microphone to be sure it was on, and then started. After briefly introducing herself and thanking the audience for coming, she went into a more extended, detailed introduction of her father. Then, as the audience applauded, Benjamin shyly stood and exchanged places with her.

Benjamin began, as usual, at a low volume and a slow pace. It always took a few minutes to warm up to the crowd, and today, he was also a bit distracted by the visual images shifting behind him. Each time Rachel advanced to a new slide, Benjamin glanced over his shoulder and paused to examine the new image. With each one, he nodded approvingly. At the outset, maps and timelines accompanied the historical overview he always provided. During the middle of the presentation, Rachel displayed pictures of Sobibor, including a map of the camp's grounds. And finally, towards the end, Benjamin grinned when he saw the blown-up image of Miriam and himself as they looked thirty years ago.

Since Rachel had already explained during her introduction that her father had never seen the slides, the audience understood why he paused to look them over. There was even some chuckling at his surprised reaction to the visuals, especially when he gasped at the picture of himself and Miriam taken at their wedding. Benjamin's Polish accent, seasoned at times with a few Yiddish words, enabled him to charm the audience as well as to inform them.

As Benjamin approached the conclusion of his speech, he did what he always did: he asked Miriam to stand. The audience began to applaud. Then, starting at the front and moving toward the back like a rising tide, they stood from their seats, producing a thunderous ovation. Benjamin was taken aback. He smiled at the crowd, modestly waving his hands for everyone to retake their seats. Feeling embarrassed, he quickly reached up to wipe away a tear that had started to run down his cheek.

Glancing downward at the audience still on its feet, Benjamin noticed one individual who stood out like a clown at a funeral. The young man beside Grant was still seated, his legs extended and his arms crossed. He was glaring directly up at the stage. Benjamin had seen this look before. On a trip to Warsaw as a child, he saw it on the face of a man who had spit on his father. He had also seen it on the faces of the SS and some of the Ukrainian guards in Sobibor. And recently, Benjamin had seen it on the faces of neo-Nazis marching in Chicago.

As the audience finally settled back into their seats, Rachel approached the podium to ask if anyone had a question. At first, no one raised a hand. Then, after one finally went up, it was like a dam had burst. The first few inquired about the breakout from Sobibor. This was followed by two women who wanted to know more about how Benjamin and Miriam had managed to fall in love in such a dreadful place. Then, a young man up on the balcony asked a question that required a longer answer.

"Mr. Abramowicz," he politely inquired, "How did you and your wife manage to leave Poland? And how did you come to the United States?"

Benjamin repressed a smile. He always enjoyed answering this question, though it was seldom asked. Most people were content to know that he and Miriam had successfully escaped from hell and went on to live happily ever after. He understood, though, that dodging the land mines and fleeing into the woods was *not* the end of their story. Benjamin cleared his throat and gripped the microphone.

"For the first few days, Miriam and I fled eastward. We'd find an area where the trees were the thickest to sleep by day and then cover as much distance as we could at night. Miriam and I figured the Nazis were looking for us because our escape had to be a great embarrassment to them. It was only later we learned we were correct. Of the 300 that escaped from Sobibor that day, only about fifty were never captured or killed."

Benjamin reached behind him, grabbed the half-empty glass of water, and downed a few swallows. After wiping his mouth with the back of his hand, he continued.

"Fortunately, we encountered a group of Polish partisans on the fourth day. We were starving, and they gave us food. They had been living for months in the forest using guerilla tactics against the Germans. These people hated the Nazis and would do anything to drive them out of Poland. Judging from their combat skills and how they managed to survive in the wilderness, we could see these people were tough. They must've been a major thorn in the side of the Nazis. Miriam and I ached to join them."

Benjamin paused to catch his breath. As he scanned the crowd, he observed several people leaning forward with their arms resting on their thighs. He stifled another smile, thinking this was what it meant to keep listeners on the edge of their seats.

"As it turned out," he finally continued, "None of these people were Jewish, and when they learned who we were, some wanted to send us on our way. But when Miriam told them about how we'd killed several Nazis escaping from Sobibor, they finally voted to let us join them. Of course, she may have exaggerated a bit, but it worked."

Benjamin looked down at his wife. Those seated near the stage could see him nod toward her, smiling slightly, and then give her a little wink.

"For the next year or so, we fought side by side with these people. They trained us to use their weapons, employ hit-and-run tactics, and live under primitive conditions. I wouldn't want to live that way today, of course, but we were young at the time, and besides, life in the woods with the partisans was like heaven compared to Sobibor. Most importantly, we were *fighting*. These people gave us the chance to kill Nazis, and for that, I'll never forget them."

Benjamin paused again and glanced at his wife. She knew what was coming next. Even though Miriam had already given her permission, Benjamin always felt the need to gain her approval at this juncture before proceeding. As always, Miriam faintly nodded.

"Toward the end of 1944, the Red Army invaded Poland from the east on their way into Germany. We were initially thrilled to encounter one of their units on a wintry day in late November. Some of us even approached the Russian soldiers and kissed them on each cheek. I never thought I'd see the day when Poles would be happy to greet Russians. At first, the Soviet soldiers appeared pleased to join us. But then, a high-ranking officer arrived. When he learned who we were, this man, who was surprisingly obese for someone who had been fighting under such brutal conditions, callously ordered his troops to conscript us into his unit.

"We looked around and saw dread on everyone's faces. Join the Soviets? These were the same people who, five years earlier, had signed a treaty with Hitler and then joined him in invading Poland. Soviet POWs had indeed helped to plan our escape from Sobibor, but those people, like

Sasha, had been Jewish. These soldiers were different. They'd want to treat Poland like a doormat, just like they had done for centuries. You see, that happens when your smaller country is stuck between two giants like Germany and Russia, with no natural borders to keep them out."

Benjamin paused once again to reach for the water behind him. Then, as though it were a shot glass, he tilted it back and drained its contents in one swallow.

"Once the Russian officer had vanished, the remaining Soviet troops began barking orders at us about setting up their camp for the night. From their brusque manner, it was clear they were planning to treat us like slave labor. Some of the partisans looked around with panic on their faces. For a moment, everyone froze with indecision. Then, without saying a word, we split into two factions. The larger group started to comply with their orders and do as commanded. The smaller band mumbled words I cannot repeat here and began to run into the woods."

Benjamin glanced up at the young man on the balcony who had asked about what happened after escaping Sobibor. He grinned before aiming a question back at him.

"Can you guess which group we joined?"

"That's a no-brainer," the man hollered, returning Benjamin's smile. "You guys became track stars."

"You got it, young man. We may have even led the way."

Benjamin's smile evaporated before he added, "Unfortunately, we heard shots behind us. Those Russian bastards were shooting at us. We should've all been on the same side, fighting the Nazis. But the Soviets didn't see it that way. Unless we did their bidding, they considered us deserters. Anyhow, once again, Miriam and I were lucky. We got away, and we continued running deep into the woods. By now, we were getting good at this."

Benjamin paused again, this time deliberately. Over the years, he had learned that well-timed periods of silence heightened the suspense.

"Miriam and I set up our camp deep in the woods that night. It was bitterly cold, so we set out to gather firewood. That's when I encountered two Soviet soldiers. They'd apparently been sent out as one of several small patrols searching for the Polish deserters. I guess they wanted to make an example out of us. It was almost dark when they caught me, so they didn't see Miriam hiding behind a tree. For a moment, I didn't know what to do. Both soldiers had their rifles trained on me so that any resistance would've been futile. I considered my options. Let them take me back as a captured deserter, probably to be executed, or run and let them end it right there. Considering how far I'd come since arriving in Sobibor, either choice was unacceptable."

Benjamin fell silent, fully aware that this was the most suspenseful part of the story. He had no intention of rushing through it and wanted to maintain the tension. The auditorium was filled with over 700 people, and the only sound that could be heard was their collective breathing.

"*Suddenly*, I saw two flashes and heard two loud popping noises. First, one Russian, then the other, fell forward as though each had been clubbed from behind. They were dead. Shortly afterward, Miriam stepped out into the small clearing with smoke rising from the barrel of her rifle. I could barely make out the terror on her face in the dim light. She had just shot the two Russians at close range in the back of their heads. Miriam had saved my life."

Benjamin stopped momentarily to glance at his wife, who was sheepishly staring at the floor. A hush permeated the auditorium. Then, a young woman in the back ended the silence.

"Way to go, *Miriam*," she shouted.

This set off another round of applause. Benjamin beamed at his wife, still staring down at her lap. He finally continued when the applause died down.

"Well, I'm afraid the rest of our story's a bit anticlimactic. The following day, we began our journey to the north. Once again, by finding ways to live off the land and traveling only at night, we finally made our way to Danzig. Today, this Polish city on the Baltic is called Gdansk. We hid there for a few months, living like ordinary Poles. Then, the following spring, we took the money we'd saved working odd jobs and bribed our way onto a fishing boat that took us up to Sweden."

Benjamin paused, thinking he had answered the young man's question. He had forgotten, however, that there had been a second part. How did they manage to immigrate to the United States? Another individual in the audience remembered.

"So, how did you and your wife slip into *our* country?"

The brazen rudeness of the question created a buzz in the crowd. After everything Benjamin had experienced, who would dare ask such an offensive question? Benjamin was a hero, not an illegal alien. Before

Rachel, Benjamin, or anyone else could respond, the questioner, seated in the front row beside Grant, pressed on.

"There were immigration restrictions in place since the 1920s, established by the quota laws, which limited the number of immigrants allowed into the United States from each country. After the war, millions of refugees were suffering and sought to come here. However, you two were doing just fine in Sweden. How'd you manage to sneak into our country?"

Every eye in the auditorium was fixated on the young man in the front row who had asked the impertinent question. Benjamin could see Grant leaning over, attempting to silence him. He could also sense his daughter approaching from behind, probably wanting to take back the microphone so she could address the disrespectful question. Benjamin shifted a bit to place his body between Rachel and the podium. He wanted to answer the question.

"The young man makes a valid point. Since becoming an American, I have learned a great deal about this nation's immigration laws, and I know that the quotas set by Congress in the 1920s allowed in only a small percentage of those who had entered before 1890. This law was deliberately aimed at the huge number of immigrants coming in from Eastern and Southern Europe."

Benjamin hesitated as he glanced around the room. He knew that immigration was a thorny issue, and he wanted to choose his next words carefully.

"The result was that ten years later, millions of Jews who had wanted to escape Hitler were turned away and later died in the gas chambers. But, to answer this young man's question, President Franklin Roosevelt, listening to Henry Morgenthau, his Treasury Secretary, and a Jew, I might add, created something called the War Refugee Board. Miriam and I applied to this board, which secured our necessary sponsorship. We then *legally* entered the United States shortly after the war ended. By this point, we were married, and since Miriam had some distant family living in the Chicago area, that's where we settled."

Benjamin quickly added another point before anyone could respond, including the young man in the front row.

"I want to say that this is a wonderful country and that my wife and I are extremely grateful for the opportunity to live here. Unlike many nations around the world, this country gives us all the freedom to speak our minds. And that includes my friend sitting here on the front row."

Every person in the auditorium turned to gaze at Michael, who was staring intently at Benjamin. The crowd waited to see if there would be a response from the speaker's "friend." There was not. Instead, Michael refolded his arms, tightened his lips, and nodded. Benjamin had silenced the heckler in the front row. The young man apparently realized he could not gain any traction against the speaker, at least not in front of this audience.

The buzzing in the auditorium faded, leaving an awkward silence. Soon after, a few audience members began to applaud, unsure if it was the right moment. This gradually turned into another hearty ovation. Meanwhile, Michael quietly stood up and glided stealthily toward a side exit. Once the applause subsided, several people in the auditorium, including Benjamin, Rachel, and Grant, turned their attention to Michael, anxious to see what he would do next. They were taken aback to find that he was no longer in his seat.

Rachel concluded the event by taking the microphone to thank her father and request a final round of applause. Afterward, she stepped away to gather her slides and dismantle the screen. As the audience moved toward the exits, Benjamin looked around the spacious venue before leaving the stage to join his wife. Just as he was about to reach her, he encountered a familiar face marked by downcast eyes and an awkwardly forced smile.

"I'm *so* sorry," Grant pronounced. "I never should have brought Michael to your presentation."

"Oh," Benjamin replied, "So that was Michael? We've been hearing quite a bit about your son recently."

Grant tilted his head and raised his eyebrows, looking both confused and embarrassed. Then, without thinking, he glanced up at the stage in an attempt to spot Rachel.

"What did you hear?" he asked sheepishly.

"I hope you don't mind Mr. Parker since this is none of our business, but Rachel has mentioned that Michael has an extreme case of teenageritis."

Benjamin offered a smile, hoping his weak attempt at humor would ease any tension in their conversation.

"Please, call me by my first name," Grant replied, "Mr. Parker's my father. And, no, I don't mind at all. If Rachel's already told you about Michael's recent obsession, that only makes it easier for me to explain why I'm apologizing."

"Well," Benjamin graciously offered, "no apology's necessary. I'm sure you're not the only person currently dealing with a rebellious teenager, especially during *these* times."

Before Grant could respond, Rachel came down the steps from the stage. She had overheard some of their conversation and jumped in without missing a beat.

"Dad, I'd also like to apologize. You see, it was my idea for Grant to invite his son to your presentation. We both thought your story might help Michael develop more empathy for Jews and other minorities. But at the very least, I should have warned you he was coming."

"Yeah," Grant added, "I assumed he'd listen with an open mind and keep his mouth shut. I was mortified by the question he raised toward the end."

By this time, the auditorium was empty. Rachel had packed away the screen, projector, and slides. Before Benjamin could reply, he was interrupted by the soft, familiar voice that, even after all these years, never failed to bring a smile to his face.

"Well," Miriam asserted, "I think inviting Michael was a wonderful idea. And who's to say it didn't work? You just need to give the boy some time. After he's had a chance to think about what he heard today, he may change his attitude."

Benjamin turned toward his wife. He then casually rested an arm on Miriam's shoulder, a move that came naturally because of her short stature and the fact that he had been doing this for over thirty years.

"Have I mentioned to you, Mr. Parker—excuse me, Grant—that this woman is the center of my life?" Benjamin smiled while gently pulling his wife in for a loving embrace.

"I have to say," Grant remarked, "I'm truly impressed by both of you. Your survival story is incredible. I've never encountered a narrative filled with so much courage, hope, and even romance. Believe me, I've covered quite a few stories throughout my career. I'm also moved by everything you've achieved since escaping from Sobibor. And how did you both learn to speak English so fluently?"

Before either of the Abramowiczs could respond, Grant, suddenly struck by inspiration, broke into a wide grin, glanced at Rachel, and then turned to face his girlfriend's father directly.

"Benjamin, would you and Miriam agree to sit for an in-depth interview for a story in *The Pantagraph*? I think we could make the front page in the Sunday edition, especially if we included a mixture of photographs from the war as well as the present."

Rachel instantly echoed her boyfriend's excitement. "Dad, you're always saying everyone should learn critical lessons from the Holocaust. This would allow you and Mom to get your story out to thousands of people."

"Maybe even more," Grant added. "There's a chance a story like this could be picked up by other big-city papers, especially because of all the recent news coming out of Skokie. If nothing else, it'll probably make the *Chicago Tribune*."

Benjamin peered down at his wife. This had become his automatic response for the past thirty years whenever a consequential decision had to be made. With only the most subtle nod, Miriam communicated her assent. Benjamin then offered his hand to seal their agreement. After shaking, Grant issued his standard cautionary warning.

"Now, with this kind of story, I must remind you that you'll be putting yourself out there. You understand? Yes, I believe you and Miriam will win a lot of empathy and support by sharing your experience. But, as you see on the national news, there are some dangerous people out there, and a newspaper story like this might carry a certain amount of risk."

Benjamin looked down at Miriam, and for a brief moment, they exchanged a smile that only a couple married for many years could share. Then, Miriam wrapped her arm around her husband's waist so they stood side by side. They had just held an entire conversation without saying a word. Finally, Benjamin turned his gaze to Grant and Rachel, resembling a battle-hardened veteran observing fresh recruits.

"You don't need to worry, Grant. This interview's nothing compared to all the risks we faced in Europe."

CHAPTER 10

MICHAEL

May 1977

After slipping out of Capen Auditorium in a cloud of anger, Michael decided to walk home instead of waiting for his father, who had given him a ride to the session. However, the weather was perfect, and the cool breeze helped calm him down as he doggedly began the mile-and-a-half walk home. Nonetheless, Michael still felt a pit in his stomach, a mixture of frustration, embarrassment, and anger. He had told his father that he had no interest in hearing Benjamin Abramowicz tout his survival story about how he had "bravely" fought the Nazis. Given a choice, Michael would have preferred to remain in school.

Who did that Jew think he was? True, the Abramowiczs' tale of loss, romance, and escape had been devoured by the crowd, who vigorously applauded their "courage." To the audience, Benjamin and Miriam Abramowicz were heroes. Of course, that is not how Michael viewed them. From his perspective, it was not courage but simple luck. Most Jews sent to the concentration camps entered the gas chambers as though placed on a moving assembly line. The few who survived caught lucky breaks, such as when Leon randomly chose Benjamin and suggested he lie about possessing a valued skill.

What bothered Michael most was how Benjamin and Miriam Abramowicz had deceived the audience. They had pulled off the timeless Jewish magic trick of presenting themselves as ordinary people rather than who they really were. That is what made Jews so insidious. If a rat crawled into your house, it still looked like a rat. That wasn't true with the Jews. They could look like anyone else on the outside while secretly conspiring to take over the planet, just like rats infesting a junkyard.

Hitler's plans to exterminate the Jews had started to make perfect sense to Michael. Regrettably, he didn't finish the job.

It also infuriated Michael that the Abramowiczs had disregarded the law and deceitfully claimed refugee status to enter the United States. They were *not* refugees. They might've been in Poland, but once they arrived in Sweden, a neutral nation, they should have remained there. The United States already had enough Jews. Why did we have to accept two more from Sweden? The Abramowiczs could have built a happy life for themselves in that Scandinavian country. Why did they have to become our burden?

On a personal level, Michael seethed when he thought about Benjamin Abramowicz. While marching south on University Street, he felt increasingly bitter as he replayed the scene when Benjamin answered his question about skirting America's immigration laws. He sounded arrogant and pretentious, coming across with a snotty air of superiority. That goddam Jew had thoroughly hoodwinked the audience. Of course, that's what they do. They're masters of deception.

The more Michael reflected on the situation, the more he felt that the Abramowicz family represented every negative trait he had recently learned about Jews. They had even gained his father's approval, as he was now dating their daughter. Michael was aware that the Abramowiczs had moved to Bloomington from Skokie. Additionally, he suspected that even from downstate, Benjamin Abramowicz might soon become actively involved in opposing the Nazi efforts to march in his former hometown.

Michael grew increasingly distressed after seeing how easily Benjamin Abramowicz had swayed the crowd. If he could accomplish this once, there was no telling how often he could do it again. To Michael, this was war. The Jewish conspirators had been holding their own for thousands of years, and despite a significant reduction in their numbers during World War II, the conflict was far from over. Since then, the frontline had shifted from Europe to the United States. More Jews now lived here than in any other country, including Israel, the Jewish state established by the Zionist manipulation of the United Nations. And Benjamin Abramowicz was one of their leaders, at least locally. He needed to be silenced.

Michael suddenly stopped, struck by an inspiration. He could almost visualize a light bulb illuminating above his head. A smile gradually spread across his face as he quickly pieced together a plan that would meet multiple objectives. The more he thought about it, the more he was convinced it was not only foolproof but possibly even brilliant. Michael knew that before he could put the plan into action, though, there was one person he needed to speak to.

It would mean placing a long-distance call, however, and if he did this from home, his father would see a record of the conversation on his next phone bill. Michael reached down for his wallet and saw that he had a few singles. He veered toward the Shell on Main Street, where he could exchange the bills for change and then use the coins to place a call on the gas station's pay phone.

"Hello," Michael began uncertainly, "Can I speak to Frank Collin?"

"Who's calling?" a gruff voice responded.

"Just tell him it's Michael Parker. I'm calling long distance from Bloomington." After a pause, he added, "Tell him I've got another idea he'll *definitely* want to hear."

The voice at the other end was not familiar. However, he seemed to know Michael.

"Yeah, okay," the voice replied enthusiastically, "I'll go get 'em."

Michael glanced at his watch, reminding himself that the call would end when his coins ran out. A moment later, the gruff voice returned, except now, it sounded more casual.

"Hey, do you still have that other phone number we gave you?"

"Yeah," Michael replied, frantically searching for his wallet and letting out a sigh of relief when he found the scrap of paper he had tucked away inside.

"Give Frank five minutes," the voice continued, "And then call *that* number."

After hanging up, Michael continued flipping through his battered wallet and smiled when he discovered another dollar bill hidden deep inside. While waiting, Michael exchanged the paper money for four additional quarters. He would probably need those for his next call. On the one hand, Michael resented the paranoia that required this extra step. On the other, if there was even a slight chance that someone was tapping

Frank's phone, this security measure was fully warranted. When Michael finally dialed the number of a payphone down the street from Rockwell Hall, within seconds, he heard Frank's animated voice on the other end.

"Mr. Michael Parker, what can I do for you? And when are we going to see you up here in Chicago?"

"Um . . ." Michael stumbled, eager to speak as quickly as possible. "I'm doing fine. And I'll be coming up as soon as school gets out for the summer."

"Well, the sooner, the better," Frank replied. "The situation in the courts is becoming really complicated, and I'm actually considering organizing a march just to support our right to march." After pausing to chuckle at his little joke, Frank added, "So, I hear you have another genius idea for me. I can't wait to hear it."

Michael glanced at his watch again and figured he needed to cut to the chase quickly. Any minute now, the operator might interrupt, demanding more money.

"Okay, Frank, have you ever heard of a Jew named Benjamin Abramowicz?"

"Sounds familiar," Frank answered. "I think he was one of the older JDL guys who used to confront us at some of our demonstrations— tough bastard. However, I haven't seen him around in a while. "

"That's because he's moved down here to Bloomington," Michael immediately responded. "He lives here now."

"*Really*?" Frank answered. "Most Yids avoid the smaller towns. What brought him down your way?"

"His daughter," Michael quickly replied, nervously glancing at his watch. "She's a professor at Illinois State, and I suppose her parents followed her down here. Anyway, believe it or not, my dad's dating his daughter. This afternoon, my father dragged me to a packed auditorium to hear Abramowicz give a talk, where he easily won over hundreds of people."

"Hmmm," Frank groaned. "I got to tell you, Michael, I'm not too crazy about your hometown. Not long ago, a professor there who taught a course on political extremism invited me down to speak. A large crowd of protestors showed up, and even though I had a half dozen uniformed troopers with me, the mob chased us out into the rainy night."

"Yeah, I remember that," Michael reminisced. "It made the front page of our local paper. My dad wrote the story."

"Well," Frank inquired, "Your idea doesn't involve bringing me back to Bloomington, does it?"

Before Michael could respond, the operator interrupted him, requiring more coins to be fed into the phone before the conversation could continue. Michael quickly dropped in the last of his quarters and then hurriedly answered the question.

"No, Frank. But I think we need to stop Benjamin Abramowicz. He just won over a crowded auditorium, and to me, that makes him a threat. He'll keep doing it if we let him."

Michael paused despite the pressure to complete his call. He was ready to propose his idea and wanted to explain it as clearly as possible.

"Frank, I think I could build a powerful explosive. I have access to what we'd need in my chemistry class, and I've been researching how to do it. If we detonate a bomb on that Yid's front porch, it'll send a message all the way up to Skokie."

Michael only heard white noise on the other end. He smiled with relief at finally getting his proposal out. After what felt like an eternity of silence, Frank finally responded.

"That's an intriguing idea," he remarked. "How sure are you that you can pull this off?"

"I just have to get my hands on the materials," Michael answered. "Some are in my high school chemistry class. Believe it or not, the others, like a particular fertilizer, are easy to get because of all the farms in this area."

"Michael," Frank breathed, "This *absolutely* cannot be linked to any of us in Chicago. You understand our party cannot operate effectively from a jail cell, right?"

"Understood," Michael replied, nervously praying the operator wouldn't interrupt their conversation.

"And one more thing," Frank added, "You'll be strictly on your own. I can't spare anyone to help you."

"That's alright," Michael countered. "I won't need any help." After a pause, he added, "So, does this mean I've got your blessing?"

"Man," Frank jested, "It sounds like you're asking if it's okay to marry my daughter." Then, after chuckling again at his own joke, he added,

"Yeah, Michael, you've got my blessing. The way we'll spin it up here is that this is what happens when a Jew town like Skokie tries to keep us out. We'll deny having anything to do with it, of course, but we'll point out that the Skokie ordinance has generated a lot of anger." After another brief pause, he added, "Just be careful, you hear?"

"Yeah," Michael answered, "I will. And Frank, thank you. You won't regret it."

Before Frank could answer, the operator once again cut into their conversation. Michael smiled, realizing he had made it just under the wire. When the voice requested another $1.50 to continue, Michael addressed her for the first time.

"Hey, operator, why don't you stick $1.50 up *your ass.*" Before she could reply, Michael slammed the receiver into its cradle and strolled away from the payphone, sporting a glowing grin.

As Michael hiked the last few blocks home, he mentally reviewed everything he would need to execute his plan. First, he intended to sneak out some essential items from the chemistry lab at school tomorrow. By now, Mr. Kaczynski was so enamored with Michael's talent that he hardly paid attention to anything Michael did before, during, or after class.

Next, Michael would need some diesel fuel. That was more challenging. He knew he could use an empty five-gallon canister in the back of the shed that his dad probably did not know about. However, since he had been grounded, Michael did not have the transportation to fill it. His father had taken away the keys to his car, and despite his best efforts, he had been unable to locate them.

Fortunately, some friends at Rockwell Hall had recently taught him how to hotwire a car, which they called a valuable skill. He would have to use this "valuable skill" to drive his Gremlin to fetch the diesel fuel. Then, once the bomb was built, Michael would place the canister still half full with diesel fuel next to the explosive device. That should create a fire that would consume whatever the bomb left standing.

Finally, Michael would need ammonium nitrate. It was a common fertilizer but would become a lethal explosive when combined with diesel fuel and some other chemicals. The local hardware store would likely stock it, but if not, Michael was confident one of the farm boys at school could steer him in the right direction. Once again, though, he might have to steal his car to make the purchase.

Michael figured it should take only a few days to assemble the bomb. However, he wanted a little more time to confirm some essential information. Although he was 90 percent certain he knew how to build the explosive, he wanted to be 100 percent. That would mean spending more time in the ISU library. In addition, Michael wanted to scope out his target. He would need to get the Abramowiczs' address, locate their house, and then check out the ideal spot to place the bomb.

Finally, what should be his target date? Michael knew he was scheduled to spend a week with his mother in Chicago beginning Wednesday, June 8. Since it made sense to get out of town shortly after the explosion, he mentally circled the night of Monday, June 6, to do the deed. That way, Michael could still hang around for a day to monitor his accomplishment before boarding the bus for Chicago. Yes, this all sounded perfect. June 6 would literally be his D-Day.

When Michael walked through the front door, his father awaited him. He was sitting on the couch like a statue, sporting a stern expression and tightly clasped hands resting in his lap. Michael turned around to close the door. While facing away from his dad, he paused, inhaled deeply, and tried to think. For a moment, Michael visualized a chessboard. He thought of his favorite move, the sacrifice. Even a queen, your most potent offensive piece, could be sacrificed if it led to checkmate. Michael turned back to face his father with a conciliatory smile.

"Before you say anything, Dad, please let me tell you I'm *so* sorry."

Grant squinted, bewildered, but remained quiet for the moment. Michael took his silence as a sign to continue.

"I took the long way home to think about everything that happened today. For starters, I never wanted to attend the presentation, and I resented you for making me go. My mind was already made up before we entered the auditorium. No matter what Mr. Abramowicz said, I was never going to like him. However, I must admit, he turned out to be a terrific speaker. He really won over that crowd. In the short term, though, that only made me angrier. I was even more pissed when Mr. Abramowicz kept getting so much applause."

"Oh, *really*?" Grant asked. "So what happened? Did you suddenly get struck by a lightning bolt on the way home?"

Michael chose to ignore his dad's sarcasm and carry on.

THE SCENT OF VIOLETS 135

"I just know," Michael stated, "that while I was walking home, I replayed Mr. Abramowicz's entire presentation in my mind, and when I finished, I reached some conclusions that even surprised me."

Michael hesitated, but this time, his father just nodded for him to continue.

"First, it should be obvious to anyone that he had no reason to lie or make up his story. No one was paying him to speak or write a book, right? Second, I realized Mr. Abramowicz and his wife survived incredible risks and dangers. I should be inspired by their courage, not envious of it. Third, while his response to my question may have slightly bruised my ego, he convinced me they did not violate any laws when they moved here. Dad, Benjamin Abramowicz is an amazing man, and he contradicted every stereotype I believed about the Jews."

Michael could see his father's face begin to soften. He had delivered his pitch like a salesman trying to sell the Brooklyn Bridge, but it seemed to be working. Why? Because Michael knew that when push came to shove, his father truly wanted to believe him. His dad never really accepted that his son had become a neo-Nazi. Therefore, he desperately clung to any hope that his child might find redemption. Why not take full advantage? Michael felt further encouraged when his father patted the empty spot next to him on the couch.

"So," his father asked, "you really did have an epiphany?" When Michael feigned a confused expression, Grant continued, "You truly changed your thinking? This is for *real?*"

"*Yes,*" Michael answered, as though he was ready to come to Jesus, "I guess I did have an epiphany. Mr. Abramowicz proved to me that I was wrong about the Jews. He and his wife deserved all that applause. And I was such an asshole for giving him crap about how they'd come to the United States."

"What do you mean when you say 'wrong about the Jews?'" his father asked skeptically, still not quite ready to take the bait.

Michael paused to consider his next move. He was likely halfway there, but judging by the tone of his dad's last question, there was still a bit more convincing to do. Perhaps actions would speak louder than words.

"Dad, I've been saying that Jews are unlike everyone else," Michael remarked. "And in some ways, they are. After all, they've been forced to live separately for so long that they've developed many unique qualities. But what Mr. Abramowicz showed me is that even if they're different, it doesn't mean they're inferior. He and his wife are clearly intelligent and courageous. They're survivors. There's no reason to look down on them. Or any Jews, for that matter."

Grant was nodding without realizing it. Michael could tell that his words were resonating, but he knew he needed to provide more than just words to seal the deal.

"Dad, I think I should apologize to Benjamin Abramowicz in person."

A broad grin spread across his father's face. Michael could see that this performance was beginning to work.

"I think that would be great," Grant exclaimed. "In fact, how about tonight? I'm going over to their house after dinner to interview them for an in-depth article for the newspaper. They've agreed, and I've already got the go-ahead from *The Pantagraph*. It'll be on the front page a week from Sunday. Why don't you join me? That way, you can not only apologize, you can also hear more of their story."

Michael mirrored his father's beaming smile. It was natural, too, not forced. He had just knocked it out of the park.

"I *love* that idea," Michael declared. "That way, I'll not only apologize, but I'll also get a chance to see you in action. Would it be okay if I asked a few questions, too? I promise none of them will be offensive."

Grant tightened his lips as he silently nodded. Michael could see that his father was not only on board with the plan but also taking at least partial ownership of the idea. The more Michael thought about it, the more he was pleased with their agreement. On top of everything else, this would even allow him to scout out the target thoroughly.

"Sure, you can ask questions," Grant declared. "In fact, after I finish writing the rough draft, I'd like you to look it over to see if it meshes with your memory of the conversation. With these big stories, sometimes it's good to have another set of eyes and ears present during the interview. It'll help to minimize errors."

Before Michael could respond, he noticed his dad taking a deep breath and looking down at the floor as he got ready to ask what would probably be a tougher question.

"Michael, I was planning to pick up Rachel for an early dinner this evening at Avanti's. It's become a special place for us since we went there on our first date. Anyhow, would you join us? After dinner, we can all head to her parents' house for the interview."

Michael nodded enthusiastically and manufactured a grin that reflected his dad's. He felt that an Oscar was warranted after this performance. And he was just getting started.

Several hours later, during the drive home at the end of the evening, Michael gazed absentmindedly out the window. He studied the pitch-black boulevard lit only by the occasional street lamp. After spending an entire evening in someone else's skin, Michael longed to enjoy the silence and process everything that had happened that day. It was understood that his father would step back and honor his son's need for quiet during those moments.

Michael reflected on his achievements since returning home as his dad drove the Civic through the quiet, empty streets, crossing from Normal into Bloomington. He realized that he had sacrificed some of his pride to adopt this awkward role and understood that he would need to maintain this act for a while longer.

But, in return, Michael had learned where the Abramowiczs lived and had scoped out their house, including the front porch that would be ground zero for the undertaking to which he was now committed. Second, and even more importantly, he had made it less likely that he would be a suspect after the bombing. When the shit hit the fan, as it most certainly would, Michael would already be on his way to Chicago, leaving behind a father who would be fervently committed to his son's innocence. Finally, on top of everything else, Michael smiled as he patted the lump inside the front pocket of his blue jeans. It was the keys to his AMC Gremlin.

CHAPTER 11

GRANT

May 1977

Despite it being a Monday afternoon, Grant had several reasons to feel celebratory. The day before, Lou Brock, his favorite baseball player on the St. Louis Cardinals, had stolen a couple more bases in his quest to break the modern-day record. While this might seem childish to some, Grant's hometown of Bloomington lay halfway between Chicago and St. Louis, forcing the locals to choose between the Cubs and the Cardinals. Grant had developed a devoted passion for the Cardinals as a small boy. Meanwhile, Rachel was a Cubs fan, which only added to the competitive nature of their relationship.

Second, and of much greater consequence, *The Pantagraph* had just published Grant's interview with the Abramowiczs the day before. The story began on the front page and continued for three pages inside the paper with text and photographs. His editor could not recall the paper ever running such a weighty story, and Grant's phone had been ringing all morning, mainly from well-wishers with a wide range of compliments. While he shrugged off comments from some of his co-workers who jokingly suggested the interview might be his ticket to a Pulitzer, Grant was pleased that the *Chicago Tribune* had agreed to run an edited version of the story the following Sunday. The timing was perfect since the national headlines from Skokie had sparked widespread interest in the Abramowiczs' story.

While all of this warranted a special dinner with Rachel, even on a Monday night, Grant understood that his son was the true source of his exuberant mood. Overnight, Michael had metamorphosized from a caterpillar into a butterfly. He was a wholly transformed kid. Instead of dark moods, he was pleasant to be around. Grant noted that rather than sequestering himself in his room, Michael spent more time downstairs. Most notably, his son's bigoted edge was suddenly gone, as though it had never existed.

Rachel was not so sure. Grant noticed how her jaw fell when she climbed into the passenger seat of his Civic and saw Michael sitting in the back with a grin that could melt glaciers. Within the first few minutes of their drive, his son earnestly apologized, but Grant could tell Rachel did not buy it from the sideways glances she kept giving him. During dinner, while they enjoyed their gondolas, a specialty sandwich piled high with cold cuts and sweet homemade bread, Rachel listened skeptically as Michael explained his change of heart.

Later that night, while Grant interviewed her parents, Rachel slipped in and out of the living room, serving drinks and other refreshments. Initially, Grant appreciated how she remained in the background, allowing her parents to sit side by side on their camelback sofa, answering questions and posing for photographs. However, when Michael chimed in, asking how they felt about Germany today, Grant noticed his girl-friend standing behind the couch with her arms crossed and lips pressed together, rolling her eyes in frustration.

Therefore, as they made their plans to have dinner at the Parkview Inn the following night, Grant intended to bring up the topic of his son. He had been exchanging the "L word" with Rachel for several months and was now considering asking her to move in with him. In his mind, a proposal was only a year or two away. However, lurking in the background was the same obstacle they had recently been avoiding. Even if Michael went away to college, he would still come home for breaks and possibly summers. Moving in with Grant meant that Rachel would also take on his son as a roommate, at least for part of the time.

Michael's significant change in perspective finally gave Grant hope that his path toward marriage was becoming clearer. He just needed to convince Rachel that this transformation was genuine. Grant decided to set realistic expectations. Rachel wouldn't have to step into the role of a stepmom; in all likelihood, she would only need to share the same roof with Michael for about a year. Still, Grant wanted Rachel to understand that his son was no longer evolving into a neo-Nazi. The more he thought about it, the more Grant realized how important tonight could be for the future of their relationship.

Hoping Rachel would spend the night later, Grant had suggested she meet him at his house, and then they would drive together to the restaurant. He called during her office hours to propose this plan, and Rachel was immediately on board. A few hours later, when the doorbell rang, Michael answered and greeted Rachel warmly. Grant was changing into more comfortable clothes at the top of the stairs to give his son some alone time with Rachel. From there, he could overhear Michael using some surprisingly mature conversational skills.

While Rachel courteously inquired about how school was going for Michael, his son skillfully redirected the conversation, asking Rachel about her classes, current research, and even her cycling workouts. Grant couldn't help but smile with fatherly pride. Not once since his son's epiphany had he sounded like the old Michael. Grant was now thoroughly convinced of his son's transformation. Hopefully, Rachel would also be impressed after spending more time with him.

Since it was a bit early when they arrived at the restaurant, and wispy clouds in the west promised a spectacular sunset, Grant and Rachel decided to park the car and take a short stroll. Miller Park was directly across the street from the Parkview Inn, so they gravitated toward its miniature lake without discussing a route, knowing they would soon pass the spot where they had first met. Grant grabbed Rachel's hand, and they scampered across South Morris Avenue with their fingers intertwined.

Once they arrived at the grassy area where Rachel had tried to change her flat tire, Grant suggested that they sit on a nearby bench to enjoy the twilight rays of the sun reflecting off the lake. He then slipped his arm around Rachel's shoulders and gently pulled her closer, a maneuver that had become as natural as breathing. She responded by softly laying her head on his shoulder.

"I love you, Rachel," Grant whispered. He could not see her face, but after hearing a soft sigh, he envisioned closed eyes and a contented smile.

"I love you too," she breathed back.

Grant reached back to gently stroke Rachel's soft, wavy hair. They took in the beautiful view in silence. It struck him that people often travel thousands of miles to exotic places like Hawaii or the Greek islands just to admire scenery that was hardly more stunning than what lay before them right now. Any thought of broaching the subject of Michael would have to wait until later. For now, Grant simply wanted to relish the moment.

Half an hour later, as darkness enveloped the outside, they sat at a table studying the menu. Then, after Rachel returned from the restroom, Grant decided this would finally be the opportune moment to bring up Michael. The Parkview Inn was the oldest restaurant in Bloomington, and it was more a family eatery than a romantic getaway. Nonetheless, Grant had been going there since he was a child, and he knew that the table next to the floor-to-ceiling wall of glass facing outside was an ideal spot for an intimate conversation.

"So," Grant began, "I'd like to discuss our future."

Rachel's eyes grew larger as she leaned forward, anticipating what was coming next. Observing her reaction, Grant felt the need to clarify.

"Rachel, I love you, and I truly believe we have a long-term future. However, to make that happen, we need to talk about the one big issue we've been avoiding.."

Rachel glanced away, and her smile faded. Following her gaze through the towering window, Grant observed the blueish-gray horizon partially hidden behind the canopy of trees. Then, he was startled by their ghost-like reflections mirrored within the sheet of glass. Grant could not see her face but observed how she was slowly shaking her head. Finally, Rachel spun around, and Grant could see her brow furrowed in concern.

"Okay, Grant, let's talk about Michael. That's the issue you're referring to, correct?"

"Yes," he pronounced, "Frankly, I no longer see Michael as an issue. But my concern is that you don't agree."

Grant paused, intertwining his fingers on the table, and stared at Rachel, waiting for her response. When none came, he decided to continue.

"Rachel, it was *your* idea for Michael to come to hear your father, and as it turned out, it was a wonderful suggestion. Yes, his question was a bit rude, and he left the auditorium in a huff, but later that evening, he had what we're both calling an epiphany, and he's been a different kid ever since."

Before Rachel could respond, he added, "Look, you two never have to be best friends. And Michael's way too old for a stepmother. He has just one more year of high school, and then he's off to college. After that, I'll be left living in the proverbial empty nest." Grant smiled mischievously as he added, "Maybe you can help fill it?"

Rachel shook her head and briefly closed her eyes. Her expression conveyed a mixture of exasperation and disbelief.

"Grant," she groaned, "I know you're not normally this naive, so I can only assume a father's love has blinded you."

"What do you mean?" Grant asked, pretending to be confused.

He understood Rachel's point but wanted her to elaborate, setting the stage for his rebuttal. Once more, a casual conversation was transforming into another debate, although this time, with more at stake.

"I *mean*," Rachel answered, "I can probably be more objective as an outsider than you can as Michael's father. Grant, you want to think he's no longer a racist so desperately that you'll believe anything he tells you. " But there's no way a bigot can suddenly stop being prejudiced any more than the sun can stop rising in the east every morning."

Grant began to reply, but before he could, Rachel placed both arms on the table, leaned forward on her elbows, and continued.

"You grew up as a white male Protestant in this lovely little cocoon called Bloomington and have probably never experienced bigotry, have you? But you've heard my parents' story, and you know what the Jews in Skokie are facing. While I was fortunate to grow up in this country, I've still faced my share of anti-Semitism. Grant, I can say with absolute certainty that no racist willingly stops being a racist. Bigots aren't snakes; they don't just shed their intolerance like a serpent molting its skin. It's too deeply ingrained. Based on my experience, eliminating the bigotry of the miscreants in Marquette Park would require a total brain transplant. As much as it pains me to say this, I think your son's become one of them."

Now, it was Grant's turn to shake his head in disbelief. He attempted to force a disarming smile but only ended up with his lips locked together in a grimace. Grant knew there was a fine line between a hearty debate and a hurtful brawl. He did not want to cross that line, but they were getting dangerously close.

"Rachel, I can't argue with anything you've said when applied to people in general. But you have to admit there are exceptions to every rule. I'm telling you, Michael is one of those exceptions."

Rachel leaned back in her chair, unwittingly putting more distance between herself and Grant. Before she could respond, the waiter, an older man likely working to supplement his Social Security, interrupted to ask for their drink order. Grant glanced toward Rachel, who gave a slight nod. He then looked up at the waiter and ordered two glasses of Cabernet Sauvignon. Once the waiter disappeared, Rachel launched a question like a guided missile.

"Why are you so convinced that Michael's the exception?"

Grant had hoped he would not need to provide evidence of his son's miraculous makeover. Still, he was prepared if necessary, and Rachel's last question provided the perfect segue to unveil specific examples demonstrating Michael's conversion. Grant felt disheartened that what had started as a dinner celebration for the publication of one of his most well-received articles had turned into an argument. However, he recognized that this conversation was essential. He and Rachel needed to find common ground about Michael.

"Okay, so you need some proof?" Grant asked as if he were preparing to cross-examine a hostile witness. "For starters, remember Michael's history teacher? She phoned the other day. Mind you, I did *not* call her; she made the effort to reach out to me with what she said was good news. That's extremely rare, you know, when a teacher actually calls home with good news."

Grant paused, realizing he had deviated from the story's main point. He took a deep breath before continuing.

"Anyhow, Mrs. Reynolds wanted me to know that during a recent class discussion about the modern Civil Rights Movement, Michael claimed it shouldn't be over because there was still much more to accomplish. She said other students disagreed, so Michael dug in his heels and passionately argued that the movement should continue until every American, black or white, had the same opportunities. Moreover, Michael insisted that someone else, like Jesse Jackson, should step forward and take over where Martin Luther King left off. According to Mrs. Reynolds, Michael was finally arguing on the right side of the issue."

"Okay," Rachel admitted, "That *sounds* like a positive step, but to me, it seems like Michael has just found another person to deceive."

"Another person to deceive?" Grant asked incredulously. "Believe me, Mrs. Reynolds is no pushover. She's an experienced educator who has seen more than her fair share of con artists. Remember she's the teacher who'd made such a fuss last fall about Michael's racism? If she's sold on Michael's transformation, then it's absolutely legit."

Grant paused, feeling satisfied with how he had defended the credibility of Mrs. Reynolds's testimony. He hoped it would make Rachel reconsider her stubborn resistance. At the very least, he wanted her to acknowledge the possibility that Michael had truly changed. Before she could respond, the waiter arrived with their bottle of red wine and then took a minute to perform the rituals of opening, pouring, and serving. More time was spent taking their food order. After the waiter finally vanished, Grant looked squarely across the table.

"Do you still think Michael is deceiving both his history teacher *and* his dad?" Grant asked in a neutral tone to avoid sounding petty or obnoxious.

"Yes, I still believe that's the most likely possibility," Rachel answered as she placed her glass of wine down, leaned back, and folded her arms. Then, she abruptly looked up, clearly eager to make a point.

"Let me ask you something, Grant," she said, appearing ready to launch her own cross-examination. "Haven't you and Mrs. Reynolds been communicating with each other throughout the school year?" When Grant nodded, she continued. "And doesn't Michael know that the two of you have been talking about him?" Again, Grant nodded hesitantly. "Then, isn't it possible that Michael deliberately took his position about the Civil Rights Movement, *knowing* she would pass it on to you?"

"That seems like quite a stretch," Grant replied defensively. "Do you really think Michael is that malicious?"

Rachel's eyes widened as she slowly began to nod. "I know you don't want to hear this, Grant, but yes, I think it's quite possible."

"Alright," Grant countered, "I've got another example for you. The other night, when I was standing at the top of the stairs about to come down, I overheard a phone conversation between Michael and, I assume, his mother in Chicago."

"Yeah?" Rachel asked skeptically, "What did you hear?"

Just as Grant was about to answer, the waiter returned with the broasted chicken. He set down their plates as unobtrusively as possible and slipped away.

"It sounded like she or someone else in her house was trying to pressure him into attending a Nazi rally. Of course, I could only hear one side of the conversation, but on Michael's end, he vigorously tried to explain why he didn't want to go. While admitting that he would not have hesitated in the past, Michael said that things had changed. I wish you could've heard him, Rachel; he was filled with passion. He stated that skin color and religion are merely superficial differences and that where it truly matters, everyone's the same. As I stood upstairs and listened, his discussion soon turned into an argument, and he ended up hanging up on the person at the other end."

Grant paused to slice his chicken. He took a bite and chewed, his expression suggesting he was waiting for a response. Rachel, who had been eating while Grant spoke, took a sip of her wine and then rose to the challenge.

"Did you hear the phone ring?"

"*What?*" Grant asked, caught off guard by the question.

"I *said*, did you hear the phone ring?"

Grant shook his head but continued chewing.

"So, Michael must've called the person at the other end of the conversation, correct?"

"Yeah, I guess so," Grant curtly answered.

"Then let's make a little wager," Rachel suggested. "I'll bet that when you get your next phone bill, there's no record of this long-distance call."

Grant swallowed hard and asked, "What are you trying to say?" His jaw was clenched, and he was unknowingly squinting.

"That Michael was speaking to a dial tone," Rachel answered in a smooth voice. "Grant, he knew you were upstairs listening. That phone call was for *your* benefit."

"Rachel?" Grant asked, more curious than angry, "Why do you keep insisting that Michael is working so hard to deceive me?"

"Because," Rachel answered with strained patience, "Michael wants you to believe he's changed. It can only work to his benefit. Didn't you already return his car keys and unground him? And as long as you're convinced that he's truly reformed, you'll stay off his back."

Grant raised his eyebrows, took a deep breath, and carefully set his silverware down on the plate. He told himself that Rachel was wrong and that she was being paranoid. Yet, a part of him admitted that she *could* be right. At the very least, Rachel had managed to introduce some reasonable doubt. Grant recognized that she would have made an excellent lawyer. Still, he felt compelled to defend his son.

"Rachel, what you're suggesting makes my son sound like some kind of sociopath, someone devoid of a conscience. I can't accept that. I *know* Michael. Except for a few years when he lived in Chicago, I raised this kid. He's merely a confused teenager trying to navigate a complicated world. That's all he is. This doesn't make him some kind of monster."

Rachel deliberately softened her tone. Grant sensed that she felt sorry, having turned their conversation upside down. What had begun with a father taking pride in his son had evolved into a debate over Michael's potential malevolence.

"Grant," she began, "There's a chance that you're right and I'm wrong—a *good* chance. But . . . what if I'm right? Is there any harm in sending Michael to a therapist, at least for an evaluation? If I'm correct, Michael could be headed down a dangerous path. And if you don't get it checked out and continue to deny at least the possibility of a problem, as remote as it might be, doesn't that make you at least partially responsible for whatever happens?"

Grant stared down at his plate. He had only eaten a few bites but pushed the rest away. Once again, an inner voice urged him to consider Rachel's premise. Instead of convincing his girlfriend that his son would no longer hinder their relationship, she had turned the tables and effectively argued that he send Michael to a shrink. Should he? Was there a chance that Rachel was right? Was Michael some kind of wacko sociopath who had successfully duped his dad into believing he no longer sympathized with neo-Nazis?

Suddenly, Grant remembered another piece of evidence. While it wasn't overwhelmingly convincing, it might be enough to sway the outcome. The armband. There was no way Rachel could claim that the armband was part of an elaborate hoax by Michael to deceive his father.

"Okay," Grant proclaimed with rising confidence, "Here's one last point to consider. Remember how I'd found the Nazi clothing in Michael's closet?"

Rachel nodded, took one last bite, and then pushed her plate aside. She had eaten more than Grant, but with a third of her chicken left, Rachel had also lost her appetite.

"Of course, I made him get rid of those clothes. However, I didn't touch the swastika armband I found in the back of his underwear drawer. He was unaware that I had discovered it, and I intentionally left it there. Like you, I initially had strong suspicions, so I wanted to see how he would handle it. You could call it a little test if you want."

Grant paused to make sure Rachel was following him. She gave a quiet nod, signaling for him to continue.

"Rachel, I found the armband in the trash the day after your father's presentation. Do you understand? Michael never knew I had discovered it. If what you're suggesting is true—that he is still secretly a Nazi—he would have kept it, right? Instead, he threw it away voluntarily."

Rachel squeezed her eyes shut for a moment and inhaled deeply. "Grant, in what room did you find the armband?"

"The kitchen," Grant immediately answered.

"And was it sitting right there on top of the trash?"

Rachel remained silent, but her eyes widened questioningly, and she sucked in her bottom lip. Grant shook his head slowly.

"Let me guess," Grant finally uttered, breaking the silence. "You think Michael planted the armband so I'd find it."

"I believe," Rachel replied thoughtfully, "There's a strong chance he did. And at the very least, you should consider the possibility."

Suddenly, a busboy appeared to clear the table, followed closely by the waiter, who left the check behind like a mailman eager to complete his route. Once the two were finally gone, Grant gazed intently at Rachel before continuing.

"Let's say you're right, Rachel. Let's say Michael's still a closet Nazi. I don't believe it's true, but for the sake of argument, let's say it is. I don't think a shrink can do anything to help the situation. Moreover, while he might join some marches wearing a Nazi uniform stashed at his mother's house, I don't believe Michael would engage in any actions that could endanger others."

"And you're a hundred percent sure of that?" Rachel inquired sympathetically.

"Yes, absolutely," Grant affirmed. However, feeling a sudden urge to reinforce his point, he added, "Rachel, until you become a mother, there's something you may not fully understand. You love your children no matter what. Whether they are right or wrong, good or evil, you never give up on them. Michael will always be my son, regardless of his actions, and I will always love him."

Rachel nodded silently. Grant, his eyes glazed with moisture, assumed she was giving up, at least for now. But after a brief moment, she launched a final attack.

"So, if you were Adolph Hitler's father, you'd still forgive him?"

"I'd still *love* him," Grant responded without hesitation. "But forgive? That's another matter." After a brief pause, while Grant managed a weak smile, he added, "Fortunately, unlike Hitler, Michael hasn't done anything that would require forgiveness."

"So far," Rachel whispered.

Grant turned to confront the darkness beyond the window. A full moon had ascended above the shadowy silhouette of the trees across the street. After a moment, he glanced at the check, pulled out his wallet, and tossed some cash onto the table. Then, with a shared sigh of disappointment, he and Rachel left the restaurant, their hands clasped together.

CHAPTER 12

MICHAEL

June 1977

For Michael, D-Day began with his father bellowing from downstairs that he was wanted on the phone. He slogged down the steps, still half asleep, wondering who would disturb his slumber at such an ungodly hour. Michael had tossed and turned in bed for hours before finally falling asleep. He knew the reason. Since he could remember, anxiety had always been the enemy of sleep, and just thinking about his plans for later that night was more than enough fuel to keep him staring at the ceiling.

As his dad impatiently handed Michael the phone, he shrugged and shook his head, indicating he had no idea who the caller was. Michael hoarsely mumbled thanks before turning his back to create a semblance of privacy. However, before speaking, Michael glanced over his shoulder to confirm that his father had returned to the kitchen.

"Hello," Michael muttered, attempting to stifle a yawn with little success.

"*Michael Parker*," the speaker at the other end pronounced with too much enthusiasm. "How've you been? Do you know who this is?"

Michael squeezed his eyes shut and quickly opened them again, hoping to shake off the fog enough to recognize the voice. Man, he hated these guessing games. Still, the voice sounded familiar. Suddenly, it hit him.

"Dale?" Michael inquired, "Is that you? Are you calling from Chicago?"

No, man," Dale quickly answered. "I just arrived in town, and I'm using a payphone at a gas station.

Michael was astonished. This was a complete surprise, and he didn't know what to ask first. Finally, the most important question came to him.

"Why are you here?"

"I woke up early this morning," Dale said. "I drove down in my new pickup truck. Well, it's not actually new, but it's new to me. It's really useful for the job I just started. I'm now working as a plumber's apprentice. Anyway, Frank asked me to drive down to see you."

"Yeah, but *why?*" Michael persisted. "I mean, don't be offended, but if this were a social call, you would've contacted me beforehand, right?"

"Actually, I'm in Normal," Dale snickered. "Man, this town's name always cracks me up."

"Okay, *Normal*," Michael responded, his patience running low. "So, *why* are you here?"

"It'd probably be better to talk about that in person," Dale answered. "Can you meet me? I'm on Main Street just south of the interstate, and there's a Micky Ds next door. How about you join me there for breakfast?"

Michael glanced toward the kitchen entrance. He heard a scraping noise, indicating his father was likely cooking something special for breakfast. For a moment, Michael attempted to formulate a plan. He realized he needed to come up with a convincing explanation for his dad. Finally, an idea struck him.

"Yeah, I know where you are. Give me about thirty minutes."

"You got it," Dale replied. "I'm looking forward to catching up."

As Michael hung up the phone, he felt a pit in his stomach. Dale had sounded friendly. Maybe too friendly? What was he doing here, and why would Frank send him? When Michael tentatively entered the kitchen, he observed his father standing beside the stove, probably making his "famous" French toast. A broad smile was painted across his face when he glanced back at his son.

"Breakfast is almost ready," his dad announced. "I hope you're hungry."

"Actually, Dad, I'm gonna take a raincheck. Maybe you can save it for later? That was a friend on the phone, and he asked if I'd join him for breakfast at McDonald's. I'd already told him yes before I realized you were making your French toast."

Michael noticed a frown on his dad's face, but it quickly vanished. He could have predicted this reaction since his father was always eager for him to form meaningful friendships. Hearing that a buddy had invited him out to breakfast would always trump French toast at home. Additionally, Michael felt a sense of satisfaction for handling the situation by simply telling the truth.

"Sure, I can save your French toast," his dad cheerfully agreed. "It'll be in the fridge; you can eat it later." Then, after a brief pause, he added, "Have a nice time."

Michael forced a smile and gave his father a mock salute. Then he spun on his heels, climbed the stairs two at a time, and ducked into the bathroom. Michael glanced at his mirror image while squirting toothpaste onto his brush. While he understood this was only a reflection, he observed that Chicago Michael had recently begun greeting him with an increasingly cynical smirk.

"So," the grinning reflection began, "Today's your big day, huh? You ready?"

"Yeah, I think so," Bloomington Michael answered. "Frank sent Dale to town to meet with me, though, so I'm curious to hear why."

"Curious or concerned?"

"Both," Bloomington Michael swiftly answered as he rinsed his toothbrush and stowed it on the rack next to his dad's.

Michael glanced down at the tiled floor. For months, he had been engaging in these morning conversations, and while it might seem bizarre to an outsider, he viewed it as a healthy form of self-reflection. Besides, doesn't everyone talk to themselves? However, his Chicago side had recently felt increasingly at odds with Bloomington Michael. Why? Was he beginning to doubt himself? When Michael looked back up at his reflection, he resolved to admit the truth out loud.

"I just hope Dale isn't planning to join me tonight. I think it would be best if I worked alone. That way, if I decide at the last minute," he admitted after a brief pause, "To pull the plug, the decision will be strictly mine.

"Pull the plug?" Chicago Michael asked, trying to mask his irritation. "Why would you do that?"

"I probably won't, but I'd like to keep my options open." Then, recalling that it's always best to be honest, at least with yourself, Bloomington

Michael added, "There are many reasons to despise the Jews. However, I've never tested this bomb, and it could kill one or both of the people living there. I don't know if I'm ready to cross that line."

"You should've thought about that a while ago, my friend, before you brought this idea to Frank. What will he say if you decide to pull the plug?" Chicago Michael raised his hands to signal air quotes as he said, "Pull the plug."

"Well," Bloomington Michael answered tentatively, "He's not a Mafia kingpin. Frank might want to send someone to help, but that doesn't mean he'll put a hit on me if I fail to complete this mission, especially since it was originally my idea, not his. Anyhow, I better get going. Dale's waiting for me at McDonalds."

Without waiting for a response, Michael ended the debate by turning off the bathroom light and proceeding to his bedroom to get dressed. Twenty minutes later, he turned his weary Gremlin into the Micky Ds parking lot, where he observed only a few cars. One of them, he noted, was a black Ford pickup that looked ready to qualify as an antique. When he entered, Michael observed Dale sitting near the back with two styrofoam trays on his table. The one before him was empty, but the other was piled with scrambled eggs, sausage, hashbrowns, and a muffin.

"*Hey*, Michael," Dale called, waving his hand like he was in the thick of a crowd.

Michael grinned and waved back to his friend. He might have misgivings about why Dale was here, but he was still pleased to see him, especially on his own turf. As Michael approached the table, he heard his stomach growl.

"I hope you don't mind," Dale announced as he stood to shake Michael's hand, "I took the liberty of buying you a Big Breakfast. Frank gave me a few bucks for food and gas, so your meal this morning comes compliments of the National Socialist Party of America."

As Michael shook Dale's hand, he observed the familiar swastika tattoo on his arm. He was making no effort to conceal it.

"This looks delicious," Michael pronounced, smiling at the tray before him. "Thanks, I'm *starving*."

As Michael picked up a plastic fork and began to jab at his food, Dale leaned back with his hands clasped behind his head. Michael noticed that his buddy had put on some weight, and now, his Chicago Bears tee shirt rode high enough to reveal the lower part of an inflated hairy gut. When Michael glanced upward, he saw a wide grin on Dale's face.

"*Man*," Dale exclaimed, "I'm really glad you introduced me to Frank Collin. Thanks to him, I've got a job and a place to stay, and I belong to a gang even better than the one in prison."

Michael nodded but could not speak with a mouth full of eggs and sausage. After swallowing some of the orange juice Dale had also provided, he finally responded.

"I'm glad everything's worked out so well. And you look *good*. Although it appears life outside prison has added some meat to your bones."

Dale glanced down and smiled sheepishly. "Yeah, I guess so."

The two friends chuckled before Michael shoveled more hashbrowns into his mouth. Then, figuring this was the right time, Dale leaned forward conspiratorially and whispered why he had shown up unannounced.

"So, Michael, Frank told me about your plan. Man, I'm impressed. I mean, I could tell you were a genius when we first met, but I had no idea you knew how to build a bomb. That's some pretty far-out shit."

Even though Michael knew the McDonald's was empty, and they were seated far from the employees back in the kitchen, he nervously scouted around the room. Michael hurriedly swallowed the last of his potatoes and leaned closer toward Dale.

"Yeah," he replied, "Well, it helps to have a good chemistry teacher." After pausing momentarily, Michael added, "So, Dale, it's great to see you and all, but why are you here?"

"To help *you*," Dale instantly answered. "Frank thought you could use another pair of hands, and when he asked for a volunteer to drive downstate, I jumped at the chance. I figured we could hang out, you know, catch up on everything. Also," Dale added while leaning closer still, "I thought this was a kick-ass plan, and I wanted to be part of it."

"Frank thought I needed help?" Michael inquired, sounding somewhat alarmed. "Did he say why?" Waiting for a response, he devoured the last bite of sausage and washed it down with his remaining orange juice.

"Look, Michael," Dale answered soberly, "I'm not going to lie. Frank's a little worried about a kid still in high school pulling off something like this. But you don't need to worry. I won't get in your way, I promise."

Michael nodded, cautiously accepting Dale's response. Meanwhile, his friend redirected the conversation.

"So, Michael," Dale whispered, absorbing his friend's paranoia and looking around the restaurant uneasily, "Where is it? Where's the bomb hidden?"

Michael grinned deviously and nodded toward his car in the parking lot. Dale turned around, following his gaze toward the green Gremlin, parked only thirty feet away. Michael could see the wheels spinning inside his brain.

"It's in your *car*?" he asked. "Is that safe?"

"No one will find it there," Michael answered. "It's in the hatch area, covered by a sliding cover so no one can see it through the window. And, yes, it's safe. Until I combine some of the chemicals and light the fuse, nothing's going to blow. There's also a five-gallon plastic canister half-filled with gasoline, but since it's sitting right above the car's gas tank, I'm not too worried."

Dale leaned back, finally feeling like it was safe to conduct an ordinary conversation. He shook his head to acknowledge the logic of Michael's response.

"So," he pronounced, "All we have to do is drive to the site tonight, combine a couple of ingredients, place it on the front porch, light the fuse, and skedaddle. Is that about it?"

Michael nodded. Then, realizing he had a partner, like it or not, he added, "Actually, Dale, why don't we transfer everything to your truck after it gets dark?" Michael glanced toward the only pickup in the lot. "My car might get recognized, but no one'll know your truck."

Dale nodded in agreement. "Yeah, that sounds good." Then, glancing down at his watch, he added, "So, we've probably got at least twelve hours to kill. Any ideas about how to spend it?"

Michael pressed his lips together and looked away. He had not intended to be a tour guide today, especially in a community his mom always referred to as "Dullsville." Michael had hoped to pack for his upcoming trip to Chicago and perhaps take a long, lazy afternoon nap. Oh well, what else could he do?

"We've got a pretty good zoo—it's not huge, but there are some cool animals." Then, after pausing to think of other ideas, Michael added,

"We also have a couple of movie theaters. Oh, and speaking of movies, have you seen Star Wars yet? I saw it the other day and would really like to see it again."

"All of that sounds good," Dale responded. "But I tell you what. Let me drive, and you give the directions. It might be better not to transport the bomb around town. Then, we'll return here tonight to pick it up."

Michael thought about it for a moment and then slowly nodded in agreement. Once again, was there really a choice? As the two stood to leave, Dale turned for the exit to the parking lot. Without thinking, Michael gathered the empty trays, napkins, and cups to deposit in the trash bin on the way out.

For the rest of the day, Dale chauffeured Michael around his hometown. They began by exploring the two universities before heading over to the zoo on Bloomington's west side. A cool front had rolled in the previous night, creating idyllic conditions for a stroll around the zoo. Most of their conversation revolved around music, television, and movies. As they pulled out of the zoo's parking lot, Dale commented on how impressive it was that a high school student knew so much about "everything."

During their discussion of politics, both agreed that Jimmy Carter was an idiot who would seriously screw up the country. When political issues arose, especially those related to race, Michael took on the role of an educator. He carefully explained affirmative action, the court-ordered busing program designed to desegregate the Boston schools, and particularly the Skokie Supreme Court case. Michael realized that Dale lacked education, but he was far from dumb. Dale even absorbed the constitutional nuances of why the Supreme Court, even though the justices might despise the Nazis, should still grant them the right to peacefully march wherever they wanted.

The evening conversation over pizza at Tobin's was mainly spent analyzing the movie they had just seen at the Normal Cinema. Like little boys, they rehashed every scene. Both Dale and Michael agreed that George Lucas was a genius. When Dale mentioned that he felt the same about Steven Spielberg due to his film "Jaws," Michael shifted back into instructional mode and stated that while "Jaws" might be a great movie, the director was Jewish. They proceeded to debate whether an artist's background should influence how people perceive their work.

As Dale drove back into Normal, silence enveloped their vehicle for the first time all day. During this pause, Michael realized they had not spoken about their evening plans since breakfast. He assumed it had to be on Dale's mind, as it was undoubtedly on his. Their escalating anxiety must have kept it simmering in the background. Soon, however, it could not be avoided.

Michael called his dad from a payphone during dinner to explain that he had spent the entire day with his buddy. He mentioned that he was now with a group that included women and men, knowing this would put a smile on his dad's face. Michael then said he would soon drop off his car, but since his friends would be waiting outside, he wouldn't come in. His father sounded a bit disappointed but didn't question his plans. Michael concluded the conversation by suggesting that he might be out late, so his dad shouldn't wait up for him.

After dropping off Michael's car, they still had time to kill. Since the university was nearly deserted in early June, Michael directed his friend to park in an empty lot at the edge of the campus. They sat in the pick-up truck for the next two hours with the windows down and the radio on. Dale produced a flask of whiskey from his glove compartment, which helped calm their nerves. He also chain-smoked half a pack of cigarettes, which increasingly annoyed Michael.

Just after eleven, they exited the vehicle and slowly strolled across the campus quad to stretch their legs. Founded in 1857, ISU was the oldest public university in the state. Its quadrangle was encircled by a wide assortment of buildings, ranging from the Ivy League-styled Fell Hall to the modern architecture of the six-story DeGarmo Building. Since the original university was established on a windswept prairie, hundreds of trees had been planted across the campus. Now, Dale and Michael strode beneath their shadows cast by a pie-faced moon.

They finally settled on a bench near the student union, and for the first time, Dale opened up about his upbringing in Cicero. Michael learned that his father had deserted the family when he was just a toddler and that his mother struggled to raise him alongside two older sisters. When Dale was young, his mother worked as a bartender most evenings, leaving him in the care of his sisters. Dale frequently had to fend for himself since the two older girls were unsurprisingly obsessed with their adolescent lives.

From the stories he heard, Michael learned about Dale's explosive temper. His first arrest was for a vicious assault in which he nearly killed another student after school. Throughout his formative years, drugs, alcohol, and fights dominated his life. When Dale was sixteen, he began to channel his anger into the boxing ring and won a few amateur bouts. After dropping out of school, he found a respectable delivery job during the day but supplemented his income with criminal activities at night.

The biggest shock came when Dale confessed to killing a store clerk one night during an armed robbery. After Michael challenged Dale's assertion that his time in prison was only for being a get-away driver, he insisted this was true. Dale contended that he was never caught for the shooting, which was a separate crime. When Michael questioned his friend about how it felt to take another life, Dale laughed it off, insisting that the clerk was reaching for a gun, so "it was either him or me."

As they returned to Dale's truck, Michael felt a growing sense of unease. Until now, everything in his life had pointed toward the act he was about to commit. Michael had come to passionately believe that the white race, the people who had built the United States and made it the greatest nation in the history of the world, were now being battered by waves of immigrants and minorities who were increasingly aggressive in demanding their share of the pie. He had also read several of the great thinkers that had influenced Hitler, including Kant, Nietzsche, and Darwin, as well as more recent philosophers, like Martin Heidegger and Carl Schmitt, who had eagerly collaborated to lend the Nazi regime a cloak of respectability. Michael had become a firmly committed Nazi, or so he believed.

But now, as he walked alongside a confessed murderer, Michael wondered if he had strayed too far into the deep water. What was he getting ready to do? Was he prepared to become a killer like the man walking beside him? Could he dismiss the gravity of taking another person's life as easily as Dale had just done? Michael understood that almost everyone encounters a pivotal moment where a single decision can shape their future. He realized that the path to Dale's truck led him directly to that crucial crossroad in his life.

When they reached the truck, Michael glanced up and saw what appeared to be a million ice crystals suspended in the night sky. Nearby security lights were off for some reason, and the empty canvas, unimpeded by clouds, exposed an endless sea of stars. Michael peeked over his shoulder and observed that the full moon had just begun its descent toward the western horizon. A warm, gentle breeze brushed through the short bristles of his hair, massaging his scalp. More than anything, Michael longed to be sleeping snugly in his bed, just as he imagined the Abramowiczs were doing.

The drive to their home took only a few minutes. Dale parked his truck around the corner, away from any streetlights. Without speaking a word, he and Michael climbed out of the truck and pulled back a tarp in the back that was concealing their illicit materials. They exchanged a look that said, "Let's get er done."

Like an alchemist, Michael knelt in the back of Dale's truck and combined the ingredients, transforming harmless chemicals into a lethal bomb. As he carefully climbed down with the device, Dale grabbed the half-full gasoline canister. Meanwhile, Michael snatched a spray can and a yardstick with his other hand."

Together, they silently made their way to the Abramowicz house. Moving like ninjas, Dale and Michael scampered up the steps to the front porch and quietly set down their bomb and gas can beneath the window just to the right of the front door. Michael pointed toward the wall on the opposite side, between the door and another window, indicating this would be a good canvas for their artwork. Dale gently grabbed Michael's arm and leaned in closer.

"Are you sure we need to do this?" he breathed. "It'll take time and increase our chances of being seen."

"*Absolutely,*" Michael shot back in an exasperated tone. "The message we're sending makes no sense unless the world knows who's sending it."

Dale nodded and reached down for the yardstick. Michael directed him where to place it against the front wall as he carefully spraypainted each of the six lines that made up a giant swastika. He could see the growing impatience on his accomplice's face, but Michael did not want to rush this step. Assuming someone saw the swastika before flames engulfed it, the infamous symbol would send an unforgettable message to the world.

Once it was completed, Michael stepped back to admire his artwork. The ivory-white backdrop accentuated the blood-red lines he had painted. Finally, he tip-toed back to the canister containing the bomb and placed it firmly against the wall beneath the window. Suddenly, he froze at the sight before him. As he was about to turn and request Dale's cigarette lighter to ignite the fuse, he observed how the full moon cast a beam directly through the window, illuminating the sleeping faces of Benjamin and Miriam Abramowicz.

Michael studied the image for a moment. Miriam was facing him, and she appeared to be smiling. Benjamin was cuddled up behind his wife with an arm draped over her midsection. Michael briefly recalled their love story and how they had met in Sobibor. More than thirty years later, they were now asleep in their home in mid-America, trusting they were safe and secure. In that moment, Michael forgot they were Jews and he suddenly realized this was a monumental mistake. Instead of asking for Dale's lighter, Michael leaned closer to whisper a message to his accomplice.

"Let's just go. We shouldn't do this. The swastika will be enough to send our message."

Dale's eyes widened. He looked at Michael in disbelief as though he was suddenly speaking in tongues. Then Dale began to shake his head. He gripped Michael by both shoulders before responding in a voice slightly above a whisper.

"Frank said you might do this. But that's alright," he added in a tone more suited for an anxious child. "That's why he sent me. I tell you what, Michael, you step aside, and I'll light the fuse."

Dale reached for his lighter, gently pushed Michael aside, and began to step toward the bomb. Without hesitation, Michael shoved back, forcing his partner away from the explosive device. He gazed at Dale like a bull glaring at a matador. This stare-down lasted several seconds before Dale landed a punch squarely to Michael's left eye, spinning him around. Before his opponent could loudly crash to the wooden floor, Dale grabbed him and gently laid Michael next to the bomb.

Dale momentarily stared down at his feet. The gas can flanked the bomb on one side while an unconscious Michael lay on the other. He then reached into his pocket, pulled out the lighter, and stooped down to ignite the fuse. Michael stirred in a daze at that moment, shook his head, and glanced up at Dale. He suddenly noticed a brilliant glow reflected in the pane of the glass window and realized it emanated from the lighter's flame.

Michael lifted his head just enough to see Dale light the fuse. He quietly reached up to his face, touched the tenderness around his eye, and winced from the pain. As he did, he saw Dale leap from the porch and vanish into the night. For a few seconds, Michael lay back, completely still and utterly alone, listening to the sizzle of the fuse and inhaling its smoke. Finally, he regained his senses.

Michael knew he was about to be blown into unrecognizable fragments. There was no time to stand, so he rolled off the porch, landed on a small azalea bush, and kept spinning. Once he reached the middle of the front yard, Michael managed to rise to his feet and ran like a gun had just started a 100-meter dash. As he crossed the sidewalk, an enormous blast propelled him forward. He flew across the street but fortunately landed on the soft grass of a neighbor's lawn.

For the second time in his life, Michael was unconscious. He had no idea how long he had lain on the spongy turf, but when he finally awoke, he heard sirens and saw dark figures racing nearby. Michael struggled to stand and then staggered over to the cover of a sprawling oak tree. Peeking around its trunk, he gazed at the Abramowicz home, which was now fully ablaze.

Disbelief washed over Michael. He had done this—almost everything—except light the fuse. But instead of pride, he felt nothing but shame. His eyes, wide with horror, mirrored the flames climbing the building, licking at the freshly painted swastika. The sirens, growing closer, punctuated the reality of his isolation. Dale, he figured, was already miles away, northbound on I-55. He was utterly alone.

As he turned to flee, Michael avoided the sidewalks beneath glowing street lamps and raced across darkened lawns. He picked up speed, putting more distance between himself and the site of the explosion. Adrenaline helped to counteract his intense headache and the stars swirling in his vision. Finally, upon crossing Emerson Street, Michael slowed down. When he arrived at his dad's house, he instantly froze. His father stood on the front porch, gazing toward the glowing sky in the west.

Michael slid behind the cover of a tree and watched nervously as his dad strode down the front stairs, climbed into his too-small Civic, and drove away. Only then did he sprint inside, race up the steps, and enter the bathroom. He bent over the sink momentarily, trying to catch his breath. When he finally glanced up, Chicago Michael grimaced at him in the mirror.

"*Wow*," he exclaimed. "That's quite a shiner you've got. You'll need a good story to explain how that happened."

"That's the least of my problems," Bloomington Michael retorted while leaning in for a closer examination and shaking his head slowly. "I need to calm down and think."

"Alright," replied Chicago Michael, "But while you do that, let me just say that you're *such* a baby. You're a total embarrassment. What will Frank and the rest of the party think? It's a good thing Dale was there to light the fuse. At least he's got some balls."

Bloomington Michael, gently probing the dark gray swelling around his eye, leaned back and stared at his reflection. He shook his head and scowled.

"That may be true," he finally responded. "Maybe I am a coward. But looking back, I wish I had never built that bomb. I just hope those people are okay."

"You mean those Yids?"

Michael glared into the mirror. Suddenly, he realized this ongoing conversation with his alter ego had to end. There was no room in his life for two Michaels. Without uttering a word, he flung open the cabinet door to make his reflection disappear. At some point, he would need to confront his mirrored image, but for now, Michael just wanted to return to the scene of the crime. He needed to learn more about the Abramowiczs.

The faucet's rush of water filled the sink as Michael drank like a man emerging from the desert and then splashed cold water on his face. He dashed down the hall, snatched a pair of dark sunglasses from his bedroom, and pondered how to explain the black eye. The fight at Tobin's had been spontaneous; a schoolmate had insulted a girl Michael was with, and when Michael intervened, he'd taken a blow. Otherwise, until the explosion shook him awake, he'd been asleep in his bed.

Twenty minutes later, Michael joined a crowd of onlookers gathered around the bomb site. He arrived just in time to see the firefighters extinguish the last flames, leaving only glowing embers and rising steam. Michael also saw an ambulance take Benjamin Abramowicz away and overheard some police officers fretting over his wife. Just as he was about to leave, he caught a glimpse of his father. As his dad clumsily stumbled into the street, Michael quickly vanished.

CHAPTER 13

RACHEL

June 1977

As Rachel brushed her teeth, she was startled by a sudden noise coming from the living room. She froze, her toothbrush sticking out of her mouth, completely motionless. Was this an intruder? Rachel was sure she had locked her front door, including the deadbolt. She had given her apartment key to only two people: her father and, more recently, Grant. Quickly, she spat into the sink, rinsed her mouth, and pushed the bathroom door slightly ajar. Rachel could feel her heart racing. With a sigh of relief, she recognized a familiar voice.

"Rachel? It's Grant. Are you awake yet?"

She grinned at herself in the mirror, pushed the dark curls flanking her forehead back behind her ears, and marched into the living room.

"Grant? What are you doing here? I didn't think I'd see you til tonight."

Seeing Grant, she instantly sensed that something was wrong. He stood still, his brow furrowed and his eyes wide and glistening. Before she could speak, he gently took her elbows and led her to sit on the couch, joining her there. Taking her hands in his, he looked directly into her troubled eyes.

"I have some bad news," he began in a rehearsed tone, "Someone exploded a bomb this morning on your parents' front porch."

Rachel leaned back, sinking into the plush cushions. She stared straight ahead, eyes vacant, attempting to process Grant's words.

"Your parents are alive and have been taken by ambulance to St. Joseph's. Your dad was treated for minor bruises and cuts in the emergency room, and he will be okay. They did not admit him. I just left your father in the ICU, waiting for news about your mom."

At the mention of her mother, Rachel broke from her trance and pivoted to face her boyfriend. Anticipating her question, Grant continued his update like a TV news reporter.

"Last I heard, your mother had yet to regain consciousness. They were still running tests when I left."

For a moment, they regarded each other in silence. Rachel tried to process the news, and Grant recognized that she needed time. She had many questions, but those could wait. For now, she simply wanted to join her parents.

Grant leaned closer and whispered, "Let me drive you to the hospital."

Rachel nodded as she rose, still wrapped in her robe. "I just need five minutes."

Ten minutes later, as Grant drove her south on Main Street from Normal to Bloomington, Rachel realized they hadn't spoken a word since leaving her apartment. Even though they sat side by side in the cab of his tiny Civic, it felt as if they were in separate cars. As they approached the hospital, they glanced at each other simultaneously.

"If it's alright with you," Grant began, "I'm going to sneak out to the office in an hour or so. I learned about the explosion early this morning when the *Pantagraph* called to assign me the story. It will only take me a couple of hours to make some follow-up calls and then write it up. In the process, I might also learn more about who planted the bomb."

Grant paused to glance at his girlfriend. Observing that she was wide-eyed and attentive, he continued.

"I'll rejoin you by lunchtime and then take the rest of the day off."

Initially, Rachel nodded in appreciation. Then, her mood shifted visibly as a thought crossed her mind.

"You've already been to my parents' house, haven't you?" Her tone was almost accusatory.

"Well, *yes*," Grant immediately replied. "As I mentioned, my paper called before dawn and sent me to cover the story."

"I feel as though you haven't shared everything, Grant. What else did you discover while you were there?"

Grant hesitated to respond. Rachel noticed his lips tighten and his chest rise as he inhaled. Grant steered into an empty parking space in front of the hospital, turned off the ignition, and faced her directly.

"Yes, there is something else. A police officer on the scene told me that he saw a large swastika spray-painted on the wall before the fire destroyed it."

Rachel winced at the image of flames engulfing her parents' house. She glared at Grant, on the verge of asking more questions, but realized this was neither the time nor the place. Although she was also tempted to ask about Michael's possible involvement, she decided that could also wait. Instead, she turned away, opened the passenger door, and climbed out of the car.

Grant silently guided Rachel to the ICU waiting room. Benjamin immediately stood when he saw his daughter and reached out for a lengthy embrace. When her dad finally pulled back, Rachel reached up to wipe away a tear streaming down his grizzled cheek. Meanwhile, Grant spotted three empty chairs in a corner beside a floor-to-ceiling picture window. Catching Rachel's eye, he gestured toward the spot. Rachel then gently shepherded her father in that direction.

Once seated, Rachel glanced around the room. The walls were paneled and decorated with several paintings, similar to the slides she showed when teaching about the Romantic Era. In one landscape, monstrous mountains overshadowed a tiny European village. In another, a massive wave hovered above a helpless sailboat, threatening to capsize the craft and drown its passengers. Rachel recollected the critical point she focused on during this lesson. Romanticism often placed people at the mercy of nature, which, in the nineteenth century, was a knee-jerk reaction to the hubris of the rising Industrial Revolution. She contrasted this idea with her parents' current situation, where they were entirely at the mercy of other people.

Turning to face her father, Rachel was struck by how much he had changed. It seemed he had aged ten years overnight, and a Band-Aid was plastered across his forehead. Benjamin stared out the window at the parking lot below. The crow's feet around his eyes had widened, and his hair was grayer than Rachel remembered. Without time for the usual brushing, tufts of hair stuck out like a scarecrow. When he finally looked at his daughter, Benjamin managed a smile that quickly faded. Rachel reached out to squeeze his hand. Hoping to distract him from his angst, she turned toward Grant with a question she knew was risky.

"Did you share with my father what you learned from the police this morning?"

Grant initially seemed confused. "About what?" he asked, trying to gather his thoughts.

"The swastika," Rachel said. "The one painted on their wall."

Grant nodded. "Yes, I did. He wasn't surprised." He glanced at Benjamin, realizing he probably should not have spoken on his behalf.

The exchange roused Benjamin from his trance, just as Rachel had hoped.

"What do you think, Dad? Was Frank Collins and his stormtroopers behind this?"

"Probably," Benjamin answered, almost in a whisper. He nodded toward her boyfriend and added, "As Grant said, I wasn't surprised by the swastika."

He was coherent but obviously in no mood to continue the conversation.

"The explosion," Grant interjected, "Was not an accident. My police friend at the scene said there were no natural gas lines near the location where it occurred, and the swastika confirmed there was a motive indicating an intentional act."

Then, steering the conversation in a new direction, Grant surprised Rachel and Benjamin with his next question.

"I understand what anti-Semitism is," he voiced. "It's simple to define. However, I've never grasped why some people are anti-Semitic. Do either of you have any insights?"

Rachel and her father exchanged a glance, silently asking who should field the question. Turning back toward Grant, Rachel observed his innocent expression, reminiscent of a young child who truly did not understand the situation. Just as she was about to speak, however, Benjamin asked his own question.

"Grant, how much Jewish history do you know?"

Rachel detected more strength in her father's voice. She sat back, pleased to let her dad take over.

"Some," Grant answered. "I took a course on the history of Western religions in college."

"And," Benjamin continued patiently, "Did you learn about Masada in that class?"

"No," Grant replied, glancing at Rachel. She slumped further in her chair with her arms folded and her eyebrows raised expectantly.

"Did you learn anything about the Jewish Revolt against the Roman Empire?" Benjamin asked, continuing with his lesson.

"Yes," Grant said with mounting confidence. "After it failed, most of the Hebrews were driven from their land, which, from that point on, scattered the Jewish people around the world."

"That's correct," Benjamin replied in his teacher's voice, which Rachel remembered from her childhood. "This was known as the Diaspora. However, in the revolt's final years, almost a thousand Jewish Zealots took refuge atop a mountain citadel in southern Israel called Masada. The Romans laid siege to this fortress but, for nearly three years, could not capture the Jewish rebels. The Jews in Masada were determined not to surrender because they would become Roman slaves, and then, they would no longer have the freedom to be Jews."

As Benjamin spoke, Rachel observed her father's face. He was fully engrossed in the lesson he was imparting. Even while his wife of over thirty years lay unconscious in the other room, he felt compelled to teach her goy boyfriend about the roots of anti-Semitism. For the moment, at least, Benjamin was not overwhelmed by grief and sorrow.

"So," her dad continued, "After employing slave labor to construct an enormous ramp and then towing a tower up to the fortress gates, the Romans were on the verge of capturing Masada. And when they finally did, Grant, can you guess what they found inside?"

Rachel resisted the urge to roll her eyes. She had heard this story so many times as a child that she thought it was as famous as the Boston Tea Party or the Alamo. Nevertheless, she did not want to spoil her dad's telling, so she remained quiet and waited while her boyfriend admitted he did not know the answer.

"They discovered almost a thousand dead Jews," Benjamin revealed. "The night before, they had all committed mass suicide rather than accept Roman enslavement and abandon their faith. And do you know that to this day, when soldiers are inducted into the Israeli military, they swear an oath that 'Masada shall not fall again.'"

Rachel observed how her father's voice became stronger as he concluded his story. A radiant smile replaced his furrowed brows and glazed-over eyes at that moment. Grant, who had been listening attentively like a child during story time, nodded in understanding and leaned back with his hands clasped behind his head.

"Dad," Rachel exclaimed, "That's a wonderful story, but maybe you should also explain how it's relevant to anti-Semitism."

Grant returned his hands to his lap and leaned forward, nodding in agreement.

"Because," Benjamin asserted with growing conviction, "Masada serves as a prime example of the resolve and fortitude of the Jewish people. For two thousand years, we have managed to survive, even though, apart from modern-day Israel, we have always been in the minority. Moreover, we have never expanded our numbers by attempting to convert Gentiles. While other civilizations have risen and fallen, we Jews have endured by steadfastly holding onto our beliefs, traditions, and values. We have upheld our strict covenant with God for thousands of years without promising external rewards like eternal life in heaven or some vision of paradise."

As Benjamin paused, Rachel and Grant exchanged glances, both impressed by his passion. Before either could speak, however, Benjamin continued, having caught his breath.

"You know, we Jews constantly fight among ourselves. We bicker over how to interpret the commandments, the Torah, the Talmud; you name it, we've argued about it. But when threatened by outsiders, we always come back together. And it's this intransigence, this steely resolve to never let Masada fall again, that ensures our survival. However, it also breeds resentment and even contempt among certain others. Therefore, over the centuries, Jews have suffered every form of oppression imaginable, including inquisitions, expulsions, pogroms, and most recently, genocide."

Rachel gazed at her father in astonishment. Even though she had heard fragments of this story throughout her life, Benjamin had never pieced it together so eloquently. Furthermore, considering her dad knew very little English when he first arrived in the United States, his grasp of the language today was impressive. The magical moment disappeared, however, when a doctor entered the waiting area and strode over to their corner.

He was young, probably just out of residency, with wavy black hair and dark eyes concealed beneath even darker glasses. Rachel thought he fit the conventional Jewish stereotype based on his appearance and mannerisms.

"Mr. Abramowicz?"

"*Yes?*"

Benjamin stood expectantly as though someone had flipped a switch, replacing his pride and enthusiasm with fear and apprehension.

The doctor motioned with his hands for Benjamin to take a seat. After glancing around, Benjamin grabbed a nearby chair and dragged it over for the young physician to join him and his family. Once seated, the doctor took a moment to catch his breath and assess his audience. Rachel instantly formed a favorable impression of his direct yet informal style.

"Hello. I'm Dr. Cohen, a neurologist. Dr. Metzger, the ER physician on duty, asked me to examine Mrs. Abramowicz. We've completed a full examination, and I'm afraid the news isn't good."

The doctor paused to allow the family to absorb his words. He glanced around the circle again, making eye contact with Grant, Rachel, and finally, Benjamin. Meanwhile, they anxiously waited for him to continue.

"We started with an X-ray, and as anticipated, Mrs. Abramowicz has a severe fracture in the upper portion of her skull. Using equipment recently acquired by this hospital, we were able to scan her brain. Unfortunately, the scan revealed significant swelling. We will intentionally keep her in a coma until the swelling subsides. For now, though, she'll remain unconscious and on life-support."

After a brief pause, the doctor asked if there were any questions. Rachel glanced at Grant and then at her father. Finally, she broke the ice.

"Doctor Cohen, will my mother ever wake up?"

"It's too early to say," the doctor responded quickly. "Her brain is severely concussed." He then looked directly at Rachel and, noticing the intense pain in her eyes, added, "In my experience, most patients with this level of swelling never regain consciousness."

"I see," Rachel replied, feeling a sense of resignation. On the surface, she seemed unexpectedly calm.

Doctor Cohen paused to see if there were any further questions. Grant glanced at his girlfriend, thinking she might have more, but

Rachel appeared lost in a daze. Meanwhile, Benjamin turned to gaze out the window, lost in a fog of his own. The doctor turned to face Grant, who nodded solemnly. Before leaving, Doctor Cohen cleared his throat and mentioned that Miriam could have visitors, but only one at a time. Benjamin stood without hesitation, nodded toward Grant and his daughter, and followed the doctor into the ICU.

Once they were alone, Grant spun around to scrutinize his girlfriend closely. "Are you okay?" he inquired.

Rachel did not respond. On the surface, she appeared hypnotized, gazing across the room at a television broadcasting a news program without sound. Inside, however, she was replaying a highlight reel of memories centered around her mother. Rachel recalled her mom's tear-filled eyes the day she escorted her daughter onto a school bus for the first day of kindergarten. She could still feel the warmth of her mother's hand in the ER when Rachel needed an emergency appendectomy. The best memory, however, was the most recent; she could still picture the sparkle in her mom's eyes as she marched across the stage to accept her doctoral diploma.

How could her mother be gone? This was the same woman who had survived the brutality of Sobibor even though the rest of her family did not. Her mom had saved her father's life by shooting a Russian soldier without hesitation beneath the snow-laden pines in eastern Poland. Since then, she had navigated the challenges of adopting another home, including mastering an entirely new language. To Rachel, no one was tougher than her parents. They had always provided a rock-solid foundation for every aspect of her life. Then suddenly, while sound asleep, her mother was violently flung across the room and plunged into a coma from which she would almost certainly never awake. In her mind, Rachel replayed the same question. How could her mother be gone?

"Rachel," Grant called out again, this time a bit louder, "Are you *okay?*"

"Yes," Rachel answered, emerging from the spell with a slight shake of her head. She reached up to wipe away tears from her eyes only to discover they were dry. Then she smiled in embarrassment upon realizing how unresponsive she had been to Grant's questions.

"I'm sorry," Rachel added. "My mind must've been a million miles away."

Grant pushed aside a strand of hair dangling over her face. Rachel glanced up and saw the alarm in his eyes.

"Are you certain?" he asked. "Because if you want me to stay, I can call the office and have them assign the story to someone else."

Rachel sat up straighter in her chair as if trying to wake from a deep sleep. "No, that won't be necessary. I'll be fine."

"Alright, I'm going to drive by the office, make a few calls, and then write up the story. I should be back within a couple of hours."

Rachel nodded and forced a smile, trying to appear stoic. She knew Grant needed to write the story about what happened to her parents.

Grant stood and glanced down at his watch. "I'll bring us back some lunch. From what I hear, the cafeteria food here is nearly inedible."

After taking a few steps, Grant stopped and turned back. "Are you sure?"

"*Yes*," Rachel quickly answered. "Now go do your job. I'll be fine."

A thought suddenly triggered something in her boyfriend. She noticed him lower his eyes and bite his lip. Grant slowly returned to his empty chair, sat gingerly, and leaned in closer.

"Rachel," he began, speaking softly as if in a confessional, "I feel like I'm to blame for what happened to your parents this morning. If I hadn't written that damn story in the *Pantagraph*, none of this would've happened."

At first, Rachel was shocked. She had just been told that her mother would probably never regain consciousness, and now she was expected to mollify her boyfriend's guilt. Rachel gazed at him intently, and they briefly locked eyes. Then Grant looked downward, appearing to Rachel like a little boy who had left the gate open, allowing the family's dog to scamper out and get run over by a car. As she reached for his hand, she quickly considered the best way to respond.

"Grant, my parents were thrilled about the article you wrote. With everything happening in Skokie, they wanted their story to be told and shared as widely as possible. And they both fully understood the risks involved. They've battled anti-Semitism throughout their lives, and you gave them another weapon. Grant, you did my parents a favor. Besides, after the article came out, I could see that they enjoyed the limelight.

Grant looked up and almost smiled. Rachel could see that her little soliloquy was having an effect.

"Still," Grant began to dispute, "If I'd never written the article . . ."

"If you had never written the article," Rachel interrupted impatiently, "There's a chance my parents would be okay right now. But they would also be more anonymous. Fewer people would know who they were or what they did, and fewer people would learn from their story."

Grant nodded. "I appreciate what you're saying, Rachel. I know this is a terrible time to bring it up, but it's been weighing on me all morning."

"Go write your story, Grant. The world needs to know what the neo-Nazis did to my parents." After briefly pausing, she added, "And, if you still feel the urge to confess, do it in your article. Let the public understand the connection between your earlier story about my parents and this morning's bombing. It's the best way to demonstrate that anti-Semitism is far from dead, even in this country. *Especially* in this country."

Grant squeezed Rachel's hand and smiled with appreciation. He stood to leave, saying, "I'll be back in a couple of hours with gondolas for lunch."

Once he left, Rachel leaned forward, glanced around the empty ICU waiting room, and buried her face in her hands. Then, suddenly, like a volcano, she erupted into uncontrollable sobs that wracked her entire body. Inside, her emotions fluctuated between rage and sorrow. Finally, needing to catch her breath, she sat up, wiped away the moisture beneath her eyes, and inhaled deeply. As she glanced over at the TV, something caught her attention, sending a chill down her spine.

On the screen, Rachel saw a swastika on the upper arm of a beady-eyed man with dark hair. She instantly recognized him; he had been all over the news recently. Why was Frank Collin being interviewed this morning? Rachel glanced around the room. She remembered having seen a remote lying around somewhere and, after standing, located it on a coffee table across the room, mixed in with some magazines.

After turning up the volume, Rachel settled into a nearby chair, stunned by the scene unfolding on the television. Collin, flanked on both sides by uniformed stormtroopers, was smugly responding to a question posed by an off-screen news reporter. Rachel could see a microphone thrust toward his chubby, round face, amplifying his self-importance. The reporter asked for Collin's prediction regarding the Supreme Court's decision on the right of his Nazis to march in Skokie.

"My lawyers," Frank Collin began, "My *Jewish* lawyers," he added with a gleam in his eyes, "Tell me the case should be decided any day now. What's more, they say our chances are excellent. They believe the Supreme Court will support the First Amendment, that it guarantees freedom for *everyone*, not just for what's currently popular."

"And what will you do after you win?" the voice asked.

Frank Collin turned to face the camera and grinned. "We'll march through the heart of that Jew town. *Peacefully*, of course. We want them to know they're not welcome in this country. We also want every white American Christian to know that Jews, Negroes, and immigrants are slowly destroying this great nation and that our movement is the only hope to prevent this from happening."

The off-camera voice politely thanked Frank Collin for his interview, and her cordial tone made it seem as if she had just interviewed an ordinary politician. Suddenly, the reporter's face appeared on the screen. In Rachel's opinion, she was young, blond, and not exceptionally bright. The reporter signed off, returning the program to the news anchor in the studio of Chicago's CBS affiliate.

Rachel pushed the power button on the TV remote like she was detonating a bomb. For a moment, she contemplated another round of weeping with her face buried in her lap. This time, however, her anger won out. Rachel stood and quietly strode across the waiting room, down the hallway to the front lobby, and through the automated doors that led outside. Seeing a wooded area on the opposite side of the parking lot, Rachel weaved between the cars, stepped up on the curb, and entered a secluded spot beneath a grove of pine trees. Looking around and seeing no one, Rachel closed her eyes, bent forward with hands cupping her mouth, and furiously shrieked like an animal caught in the viselike jaws of a trap.

CHAPTER 14

FRANK

June 1977

For days, a buzz had energized Rockwell Hall. Although Frank Collin had tried to maintain a business-as-usual approach to his daily grind at the Nazi Party headquarters, expectations were rising that the Supreme Court could hand down its decision at any moment. Usually, in May and June, the final two months of its term, the Supreme Court would meet at 10 a.m. each Monday to release its opinions. However, a decision could be announced anytime during its waning days.

Tensions nationwide had been rising since March when Frank Collin informed the Skokie police chief that his National Socialists intended to protest on the village's sidewalks. Jewish groups promptly threatened massive counterdemonstrations. One Skokie resident testified that several Jewish organizations from across the nation had planned counterprotests with an anticipated attendance of 12,000 to 15,000 and that the display of Nazi swastikas would likely incite violence.

The media also poured fuel onto the fire. Each evening, Walter Cronkite, "the most trusted man in America," updated the case's circuitous path from the Illinois lower courts to the nation's highest court. From the advice of a precocious teenager, Frank Collin had ignited a constitutional stick of dynamite. People were heatedly debating the First Amendment's limits in bars, family gatherings, and high school history classrooms across the country.

The explosive energy had infiltrated the Nazi headquarters in Marquette Park. Rockwell Hall appeared unremarkable, except for the swastika emblem displayed above the front door, positioned next to the American flag. If it weren't for the enormous racist banner draped on the west side of the building—visible from down the block—the two-story, red brick structure with its wood-paneled front would look like an ordinary tavern. Inside, however, the building hummed with excitement.

Most days, Frank Collin relished the attention. Journalists frequently contacted him for interviews or at least a quote, and Rockwell Hall residents were talking about nothing else. However, Frank was growing increasingly anxious about the impending verdict. He knew the Supreme Court's decision was final, and there would be problems to resolve regardless of the outcome. Frank also understood that, much like a child who feels down the day after Christmas, there would be a psychological letdown once the Court rendered its decision.

Frank feared that if the court sided with the Skokie Jews, he and his organization would swiftly fade back into obscurity. Conversely, a victory would bring its own challenges. If he led a march into Skokie, could the police manage the angry crowds? While a violent riot might generate beneficial publicity, it could also be life-threatening, with him at the center of the bullseye. Of course, Frank could always back down and cancel the march, but that might be seen as cowardly. The more Frank fixated on the situation, the more he wanted the Supremes to deliver its decision ASAP so he could move past all the anxiety.

Frank was also concerned about the recent bombing in Bloomington. The local media had been all over the story, which was still gaining traction. He learned that Benjamin Abramowicz had escaped with minor injuries, but his wife, Miriam, was still in a coma. That was somewhat expected; after all, bombs often kill people. However, what Frank apparently failed to communicate to Dale and the kid was that there could be no connection between the bombing and his Nazi party. So, who was the idiot who thought it would be a good idea to spray-paint a swastika on the target?

The story had yet to go national, but that was still a distinct possibility. Were that to happen, Frank was concerned about its impact on the Supreme Court's deliberations. The optics of a lethal bombing completely contradicted the party's First Amendment claim to be able to assemble peacefully. How could the National Socialist White People's Party insist on their right to a peaceful protest in Skokie while simultaneously bombing a house downstate?

Even more disconcerting was that yesterday morning, FBI agents had paid a visit to Rockwell Hall. They had no evidence, of course, and it was easy to produce alibis for everyone. Nevertheless, Frank had been trying to stay off the Feds' radar, and now, there was no telling where their investigation might lead. What if the kid was caught? Could he be trusted to keep his mouth shut? And then, there was the matter of Dale. Frank had requested a meeting with the ex-con as soon as he returned from work.

Sure enough, Frank heard a loud rapping on his office door promptly at 5:30. Looking up, he glanced at his watch. He should not have waited so long to conduct this tete-a-tete.

"Come in," Frank hollered.

The door creaked open, and Harold peeked inside. After Frank nodded, Harold entered with his right arm rigidly raised in a salute. Frank reciprocated half-heartedly.

"I've got Dale with me," he announced. Frank noticed a shadowy figure lurking behind his top aide.

"Yes," Frank replied. "Please bring him in."

The door swung open wider, brightening a spacious room lit only by the dim lamp on Frank's desk. Dale's dark silhouette, backlit by the bare light bulb in the hallway, followed Harold into the office. After motioning for Dale to sit in an empty wooden chair facing the desk, Harold moved to stand behind Frank with his arms crossed tightly. Both Harold and Frank wore identical button-down shirts, black ties, and the usual swastika armbands. In contrast, Dale was dressed in jeans and a soiled T-shirt, the same clothes he had worn to work.

Dale slumped to one side in his chair like an anxious high school student dragged into the principal's office. Frank noted the impressive bulge of the muscles in Dale's upper arms as he folded them across his chest. With a nervous look in his eyes, Dale chewed a toothpick that hung from his mouth. Frank decided to begin by lightening the mood.

"Dale, it's been a while since we've seen each other. How've you been?

"Alright," Dale mumbled uneasily.

"And how's the new job working out?" Frank inquired, determined to relax the man sitting across from him.

Dale slowly shook his head and grimaced. "Terrific," he replied sarcastically. "I work nonstop, the boss's an asshole, and the pay is barely above minimum wage. Otherwise, everything's great."

"Well," Frank replied, regretting how he had started the conversation, "Just don't do anything foolish, like returning to some of your bad habits. You won't be of any use to the party if you end up back in prison."

Dale offered a mock salute but stayed silent. Noticing that his nervous demeanor was evolving into outright disrespect, Frank concluded it was time to stop trying to appease his stormtrooper and address the issue at hand.

"Dale, do you agree that we have been quite generous since you first came to us?"

Dale appeared stunned by the question. He sat up a bit in his chair. "What do'ya mean?"

"Since coming to Rockwell Hall, Dale, haven't we provided you with a job, meals, and an inexpensive place to live?"

"Yeah," he agreed, "That's true."

"And," Frank continued, "We don't ask for much in return, do we?"

Dale nodded in agreement, sensing a trap was being set. He yanked the toothpick out of his mouth aggressively and stiffened his posture.

"No, you don't," Dale agreed. "And, in return, I've done everything you've asked. So, what's this all about? Why am I here?"

"The bombing in Bloomington," Harold answered. "The FBI has connected it to us. And do you know why?"

Dale shrugged and shook his head, feigning ignorance.

"Because you morons painted a huge swastika on the target's front porch," Harold continued. "By leaving behind a clue like that, who'd you think they'd suspect?"

"You never told us *not* to paint a swastika," Dale responded sarcastically. "Besides, it wasn't my idea; it was the kid's. He said it would send a message to the world. Michael insisted that if we were going to set off the bomb, people needed to understand its purpose. He's the one who brought the paint, and he's the one who did the actual painting."

"So," Frank interjected, "You're blaming Michael? Dale, I sent you down there to make sure the kid didn't do something foolish like this. And you left it up to him?"

"I don't know," Dale answered, looking down awkwardly. "At the time, what he said made sense."

Harold glanced at Frank and whispered, "Maybe we should bring Michael in for a little conference?"

At the mention of Michael's name, Dale perked up.

"Have you guys seen Michael?" Dale inquired.

"He's around," Harold answered. "I ran into his mom this morning, and she said he's home and staying with her." Then, in a suspicious tone, Harold asked, "Why?"

Dale hesitated. "It's just that I haven't seen him since the bombing. We separated right after, so I assumed he was still in Bloomington."

Frank stared intently at Dale, watching his newest recruit squirm in his seat. He sensed that Dale was holding something back. The ex-con had always made Frank feel uneasy; the man was an unpredictable loose cannon. Still, Frank recognized Dale's value. Like other members of their organization, he was loyal and could prove useful in certain situations, providing the muscle they sometimes needed. For now, however, Frank's main priority was eliminating loose ends that could connect the Bloomington bombing to Rockwell Hall.

"Alright," Frank declared, "What's done is done. Just be sure, Dale, that if anyone asks, you were here on the night of the bombing. We held a rally that evening, and everyone present will swear on a stack of Bibles that you were here."

Pivoting back toward Harold, Frank asked, "Can you arrange to bring Michael in for a little meeting?"

Dale went pale upon hearing this request, but neither Frank nor Harold noticed. As he stood to leave, Dale made an unusual request.

"If Michael says anything different from what I've told you, I'd like a chance to respond. Alright? As I said, the kid and I haven't spoken since we lit the fuse. I'm not sure his memory of that night will match everything I've told you."

Frank glanced at Dale with a puzzled expression and nodded. His main concern at the moment was what Michael would say if questioned by the police. Harold reached for the rotary phone on Frank's desk, knowing Gretchen's number by heart since he had recently ended a relationship with her. As Harold's finger circled the dial repeatedly, Frank waved dismissively at Dale, who quickly bolted from the office.

The following morning, Harold firmly escorted the nervous kid into the party leader's chamber, just as he had done with Dale the day before. And, once again, he stood authoritatively behind Frank Collin with his arms crossed. This time, however, Frank was in a better mood. After all, the kid was just a kid. Michael was charismatic, intelligent, and, in his own way, charming. Frank could not help but be drawn to him. He instinctively adopted a friendlier approach with Michael.

"So, Mr. Parker, how've you been?"

"Um, I'm good," he replied softly.

"So, why haven't you been around," Frank continued. "Have you been avoiding us?"

Michael's eyes widened, and he visibly inhaled a deep breath.

"Relax, Michael, I'm just kidding."

"I've been meaning to stop by," Michael asserted, appearing a bit relieved. "My mom's kept me pretty busy."

"Fair enough," Frank replied, glancing over his shoulder at Harold. "However, we'd like to discuss your actions in Bloomington. Did everything go smoothly?"

Michael nodded uncertainly but stayed silent. He glanced at Harold, who towered over him, but drew no comfort from his mannequin-like expression.

"However," Frank added, drawing out the word, "Painting the swastika wasn't such a good idea. Because of it, the police and the FBI have been snooping around, convinced we had something to do with the bombing."

"Oh," Michael whispered. "I hadn't thought about that. I just assumed that apart from harming a couple of Jews, the bomb's main purpose was to make a powerful statement."

"Yeah," Harold replied, "That's exactly what Dale said. However, he claimed that you were the one who wanted to paint the swastika and that you used that same argument with him when he questioned the idea."

"Dale? You met with Dale?"

Frank examined the troubled expression on the boy's face. Just like with Dale the day before, he instinctively felt there was more to the story. This time, he observed a spark of intelligence in Michael's eyes that he hadn't seen in Dale's. It was evident that the gears were turning in the kid's mind.

"Yes, we met with him yesterday. He indicated that everything went according to plan, although he blamed you for spray painting the swastika that has put us in the spotlight."

Frank eyed the kid warily. "Michael, is there something you're not telling us?"

Michael bit his lower lip and glanced away. Once again, Frank could tell the kid was ruminating over something. He was clearly torn about whether to share details from that night. Eventually, Michael turned back to face Frank.

"No, you know everything," Michael insisted. "And Dale's right; spray-painting the swastika was indeed my idea. He didn't want to do it, but I convinced him."

Frank glanced back at Harold before redirecting his attention to the kid.

"I appreciate your honesty, Michael." After briefly pausing, he added, "Since that night, have the police approached you about your involvement in the incident?"

"No," Michael quickly answered. "And if that ever happens, I've got a buddy from school who'll provide an alibi."

"And it should go without saying," Harold added, "That even under the most painful torture imaginable, you'll never mention our names, correct?"

"Yes, of course," Michael answered with a nervous chuckle. "But I don't see why I'd ever be investigated. My father's convinced I'd become good friends with Benjamin Abramowicz, so he'd be in my corner. Besides, who would suspect a high school kid of building a bomb like the one we used?"

Frank nodded and smiled approvingly. Before he could respond, the phone on his desk shattered the silence. He picked it up after just one ring, and shortly after saying hello, a smile spread across his face. Frank then remained quiet for a couple of minutes, occasionally nodding.

"That's terrific," he exclaimed, concluding the conversation. "I'll prepare some notes for the press conference right away."

When Frank hung up, his grin vanished, replaced by a blank expression. Lost in thought, he stared straight ahead. Michael glanced up at Harold, who shook his head and shrugged. Suddenly, Frank's electric smile returned.

"We *won*," he exclaimed. "That was our Jew lawyer. He said the decision was close, five to four. The lawyer wants us to meet him at his

ACLU office for an afternoon press conference. He said there'll probably be media from around the country."

Harold's rigid, military demeanor immediately softened, and his face broke into a broad grin as he eagerly slapped Frank on the back. "That's fantastic news," he declared.

"Yes, it is," Michael agreed. "We should choose a date right now for our march on Skokie. That way, you can announce it at the press conference."

Frank looked up, and, at that moment, his true nature was revealed, although Harold and Michael did not recognize it. Fear was evident in his wide eyes, and his lips parted as he exhaled a tense breath. Frank Collin had faced relentless harassment as a child. He was chubby and introverted, making him the perfect target for neighborhood bullies. Over time, Frank became skilled at avoiding his tormentors and learned to avoid situations that provoked fear. Deep down, however, he recognized that he was a coward. Leading a planned march with his uniformed stormtroopers into a hostile crowd of thousands of angry Jews was something he sought to avoid at all costs.

Harold turned to glance at the calendar hanging on the wall behind Frank's desk. He flipped up the June page and immediately spotted the perfect date for their march on Skokie.

"How about the Fourth of July?" he asked. "Everyone will be available, and besides, what a perfect way to celebrate our nation's birthday."

Harold glanced toward Frank, hoping for an enthusiastic response. However, the party leader was focused on Michael, looking like a man about to drown, desperate for a life preserver. Michael believed he understood. What he said next was meant to save his Führer but would shock the stormtrooper standing behind him.

"We *shouldn't* march," Michael announced forcefully. "Why give the Jew bastards a chance to counterprotest?"

Harold stared at the kid in disbelief while Frank's lips curled into a slight smile.

"You must be shitting me," Harold challenged angrily. "We've been dreaming of this day for months. Why'd we go to all the trouble of taking our case to the Supreme Court?"

"Because," Michael answered calmly as if speaking to a child, "The march into Skokie will be anticlimactic. What will we gain? We'll probably be outnumbered a hundred to one, and there's bound to be violence. If we resist, we'll come across as the evil stormtroopers. If we don't, we'll get our asses kicked by the Jews, who'll appear to be defending their home turf. Either way, we lose."

"They won't kick our asses," Harold countered. "We'll use weapons if necessary, and it'll be perfectly legal because it'll be self-defense."

Frank, who had quietly been following the debate, finally raised his hand and spoke with authority, like a judge managing a dispute between opposing attorneys.

"I understand what you're both saying, but I believe the kid's right. No matter how it goes down, marching into Skokie will *not* end well for us."

Recognizing the need to elaborate on Frank's point, Michael added the words that would later dominate their press conference.

"We've already won the Skokie battle," he declared. "In the end, our goal wasn't to march into the Jew town but to prove that we had the right to do so. What's more, we enjoyed millions of dollars of free publicity. Because the Jews in Skokie passed that foolish ordinance trying to keep us out, the whole nation paid attention while we fought our legal battle to prove them wrong. And, now that we've succeeded, we can take the higher ground and announce that in the name of preserving the peace, we'll avoid Skokie and march in Chicago instead. Everyone'll be shocked. It's the last thing they'd expect." Then, after briefly pausing, Michael added, "That's always the best strategy: keep your opponent off guard."

Frank nodded vigorously, a gleam of excitement in his eyes. Harold, standing silently behind him, looked on.

"That makes *perfect* sense," Frank agreed. "Let's go downstairs, share the good news about the Supreme Court, and then explain why we're choosing to take the higher ground and march in Marquette Park instead of Skokie on Independence Day."

To acknowledge both of his advisors, Frank nodded toward Michael when he said "higher ground" and looked back at Harold when he mentioned "Independence Day."

"However," he continued, "We should first take a few minutes to write a statement for the press conference."

Frank then fed a clean sheet of paper into his dusty typewriter and, with Michael's help, drafted an announcement expressing the party's enthusiasm for the Supreme Court's decision. This was followed by an explanation of Michael's plans to march in Chicago rather than Skokie. As expected, the statement raised some eyebrows amongst the reporters, but a few hours later, it appeared well-received on the nightly news.

By late afternoon, as Harold drove Frank back to Rockwell Hall, he initiated a conversation by posing a simple question.

"So, are you satisfied with how everything turned out today?"

"Yes," Frank affirmed while gazing straight ahead at the rush-hour traffic. "I believe Skokie was a victory on several levels. First, as the kid said, we enjoyed months of free publicity that ran from coast to coast. Second, the Court took *our* side, which means we can now march wherever we want. And finally, by choosing not to march in Skokie, we came across as morally superior to the Jews."

"That's all true," Harold agreed. "But I was also referring to the situation in Bloomington."

The satisfied smile on Frank's face gradually faded. He paused to choose his next words carefully.

"I'm still a little worried," Frank admitted. "Besides you and me, there're still two other people who know about our complicity, and if either of them decided to talk, we'd be up shit's creek without a paddle."

Harold glanced at his passenger and nodded. "I agree. You think we can trust both of them to keep their mouths shut?"

"There're no guarantees," Frank responded, "But based on our recent conversations, I *believe* we're safe. Dale's more brawn than brains, but he's got his uses. However, we'd better keep an eye on him."

"How about the kid?"

"Michael? He's brilliant. He's like a teenage Einstein."

Harold chuckled but kept his gaze fixed on a light that had been red forever. After a brief pause, Frank continued.

"The kid's still young and has some growing up to do. However, I'd take his brains over Dale's muscles anytime. We've got plenty of muscle around Rockwell Hall, but brains are at a premium."

Harold shot a skeptical glance toward his fuehrer. "I don't know," he mumbled. "It's his brains that make me nervous."

CHAPTER 15

BENJAMIN

August 1977

Every morning at six thirty, a nurse entered Miriam's room to start the day. She pulled up the blinds to let in the early morning sunlight and then checked her vitals. Thanks to donations from the Bloomington-Normal community, the hospital moved Miriam to a single room with an extra bed, allowing her husband to sleep beside her. During the night, Benjamin often climbed into bed with Miriam so the nurse would wake him to ensure he was back in his bed before Rachel arrived at seven.

Despite the prayers and well-wishes from Skokie and Bloomington-Normal, Miriam had yet to regain consciousness. The day before, when Rachel and Benjamin met with her physician, the doctor used the phrase "brain dead" for the first time. According to Dr. Cohen, there were few signs of brain activity. Miriam remained alive due to the equipment attached to her, including a ventilator that supplied oxygen. Most importantly, when Benjamin asked if there was even the slightest chance his wife would ever awaken from her coma, the doctor did not hesitate to say no.

Benjamin had gone about his daily routine like a zombie for the past two months. He filed a claim with the insurance company, agreeing to sell them the remains of his house for its original "fair market value." With his daughter's help, he purchased the basics of a new wardrobe and then moved the clothes into Rachel's spare bedroom. Benjamin showered at his daughter's apartment but spent every night in his wife's hospital room. As for his shoe store, he tapped into his savings to hire a trustworthy manager to handle its day-to-day operations. Benjamin stopped by the store for an hour or two most days but, otherwise, seldom left his wife's bedside.

The following day, when Rachel arrived, Benjamin was emotionally exhausted. He had hardly slept the night before. Around midnight, he had opened the blinds to let horizontal streaks of moonlight filter into the room, illuminating his wife's expressionless face. Benjamin gently stroked Miriam's hair for hours as she lay impassively with her eyes closed. At least at night, he could pretend that Miriam was just sleeping. He, on the other hand, had hardly slept at all.

Benjamin kept replaying the doctor's words. If Miriam was brain dead, if she was only technically alive because of machines, and if she truly would never awaken from her coma, was there any point in artificially maintaining her breathing and blood flow? Logically, the answer was an unequivocal no. Miriam was dead, and it was time for her husband to accept this fact, agree to dismantle the medical equipment, and begin planning her funeral.

Still, the ventilator's rhythm indicated that oxygen was entering Miriam's lungs as if she were breathing on her own. Additionally, the monitor next to her bed showed that her heart was steadily beating, pumping life-sustaining blood throughout her body. As Benjamin held his wife's hand, he could feel its warmth. At times, he was even convinced she squeezed his back.

With the first appearance of daylight, Benjamin gently nudged his wife, hoping to see her eyes spring open and the familiar smile brighten her face. When there was no response, he realized this would be her final day of life. The decision was made, although he would confirm it during a heart-to-heart with Rachel that morning over breakfast in the hospital cafeteria. As he studied his wife's features, illuminated by the sun's early rays, Benjamin cradled his face and began to weep softly, interrupted only when he occasionally glanced up at Miriam's dormant profile.

When Rachel entered the room at seven o'clock, Benjamin excused himself to the bathroom. A glance in the mirror confirmed that a combination of crying and sleep deprivation had left him with beet-red eyes. Benjamin thought his daughter would comment or at least ask about how he was doing. However, he appreciated that she thoughtfully overlooked her dad's unkempt appearance and focused more on her unconscious mother. After a few minutes, Benjamin, adhering to his plan, suggested breakfast in the hospital cafeteria.

Over bagels and cream cheese, Benjamin sensed that Rachel was about to ask the big question on their unspoken agenda. Before she could, he recalled a story to delay the inevitable.

"Sweetheart," he began, "Do you remember a little girl named Connie from your kindergarten class?"

With a puzzled expression, Rachel looked up from her effort to spread cream cheese evenly over her toasted bagel.

"Yeah, I guess so," she answered. "Why?"

"Do you remember what she asked one day at lunch when she noticed that your sandwich was made with matzah instead of bread?"

Rachel glanced up, trying to recall. She shook her head and returned to the part of her bagel that remained unblemished by cream cheese.

"No," she replied. "I barely remember Connie; it was a long time ago." After a brief pause, Rachel added, "I do recall, though, that she wasn't very nice."

Benjamin smiled knowingly. "No. She definitely wasn't. However, in all fairness, it probably wasn't her fault. Like most children that age, the evil that escapes their mouths usually echoes what they hear at home."

Rachel nodded in agreement and then took a hearty bite of her bagel slice, leaving behind a jagged crescent.

"So," Rachel struggled to ask with a full mouth, "What evil came out of little Connie's mouth?"

"She asked you something completely ridiculous," Benjamin replied. "She inquired whether your matzah was made from the blood of a little Christian girl."

Rachel was so shocked that she almost choked on a bite of her bagel. Once she recovered, she couldn't help but smile at the sheer ridiculousness of Connie's question.

"At the time," her father continued, "a young girl in the area had gone missing, leading to a lot of speculation about what had happened. Connie's parents held anti-Semitic views and likely had heard about the blood libel myth, which has been around for centuries. I suspect they connected that myth to the missing girl. The parents must have discussed this in front of their daughter, who then repeated it to you at school."

"Blood libel?" Rachel inquired. Before her father could respond, she answered her own question. "That's the absurd idea that Jews use the blood of Christians in their religious rituals, isn't it?"

"Yes," Benjamin replied, "And since this occurred during Pesach, and since Christians had often used the blood libel myth to explain how the Jews prepared matzah for Passover, it only made sense they'd bring it up at this time of year."

"That's *crazy*," Rachel grumbled. "How can anyone think that way in the twentieth century?"

Benjamin stayed silent but lifted his eyebrows in a way that communicated, "Really?".

"Right," Rachel agreed, shaking her head and chiding herself for momentarily forgetting what had recently happened to six million Jews. After a brief hesitation, she asked, "Dad, what's the point of your story about Connie?"

Benjamin sipped his coffee, placed the cup back on its saucer, and stared at his daughter.

"Well," he finally answered, "The point isn't about the missing girl. Unfortunately, she'd drowned in Lake Michigan, and her body washed up on a nearby beach a few days later. And, of course, there were no signs that any of her blood had been taken."

As Rachel was about to respond, Benjamin raised a hand, signaling he was not finished. "And the point's also not about Connie or her ignorant parents."

He paused once more as if trying to create suspense. After another leisurely sip of coffee, he resumed speaking.

"The point of the story is about your *mother*," he proclaimed.

Rachel leaned back in her chair, her eyes wide with disbelief. She patiently waited for her father to continue.

"When your mom heard what that little girl said to you in front of the whole class, she immediately demanded a meeting with Connie's parents and us in the principal's office. Your mother then proceeded to verbally assault those two bigots without ever giving them a chance to come up for air. At one point, I had to restrain her when Connie's father foolishly tried to defend the nonsense he had said in front of his daughter, and your mom stood up, preparing to lunge over the principal's desk."

Rachel smiled, moisture gathering beneath her eyes as she reached for her napkin.

"Your *mother*," Benjamin asserted, his voice growing a bit shaky, "Your mother never took shit from *anyone*. Most of the time, she appeared to be a simple woman, a seamstress. I think she relished that image because she wanted people to underestimate her. But, if you crossed her, especially with any form of anti-Semitism, Miriam wouldn't hesitate to shoot you right between the eyes, just like she did that Russian soldier in the Polish woods."

Rachel's glassy eyes brimmed with pride, and she was momentarily speechless. Finally, she managed to stammer out a question.

"So, whatever happened with Connie's parents?"

"I don't think they ever got a chance to speak during the conference," Benjamin answered, struggling to suppress a grin. "They just glared at us most of the time. I think they were too afraid to tangle with your mom." After pausing briefly, he continued, "They pulled Connie out of the school a short time later and then moved away. Those kinds of anti-Semites don't like living in a place like Skokie. Too many Jews."

Benjamin reached across the table to take his daughter's hand. His lips tightened into a grimace, his eyes glazed, and he inhaled deeply.

"Rachel, I think today, we need to let her go."

"Yes," she whispered, "I agree."

Rachel stood up, circled the table, and reached for her father without saying a word. The cafeteria was nearly full, and a sudden hush filled the room. For a moment, the only sound was the quiet sobs of a daughter as she enveloped her father in a tight embrace. Benjamin realized later that this likely happens often in the hospital cafeteria.

A series of painful meetings occupied the rest of their day. In the first meeting, Benjamin signed documents permitting Dr. Cohen to end the life-support measures keeping Miriam alive. The second meeting took place at a mortuary, where Benjamin and Rachel finalized the plans for the funeral scheduled for the following day. The last session was held with the rabbi of Moses Montefiore, Bloomington's only synagogue, in preparation for Miriam's service. As relative newcomers to the area and not being rigidly observant, Benjamin and Rachel did not even consider other traditions, such as sitting for seven days of Shiva.

That afternoon, Rachel drove her father back to the hospital to pick up his car, after which he followed her to her apartment. Their days at St. Joseph were finally over. Soon, Rachel would return to her duties at the university, and Benjamin would plunge himself back into running his shoe store. For now, though, they shared a bottle of wine in a daze while waiting for Grant to arrive. Neither of them felt much like eating, but they politely accepted his invitation to join him for a quiet dinner at the Parkview Inn.

As Benjamin glanced around Rachel's apartment, he realized that he had stayed with his daughter long enough. Since neither of them felt like talking, he suggested they walk down to the apartment complex's office. If there was a vacancy, he thought he would sign a lease and move in as soon as possible. At first, Rachel opposed the idea, insisting he could live with her indefinitely. However, she eventually agreed to the compromise of having her father as a neighbor.

The plan worked to perfection. It was agreed that Benjamin would move into his new home at the beginning of the month. As they ambled back to Rachel's apartment, father and daughter made plans to shop for new furniture over the upcoming weekend. Once back in Rachel's flat, they refilled their wine glasses and gazed at each other in a silent stupor. Emotionally drained, there was nothing left to say. Fortunately, Grant arrived a few minutes later.

The first topic of conversation at dinner did little to lift anyone's spirits. While writing an article about Miriam's passing for the newspaper, Grant called his friend Chuck, who works on the police force. Unfortunately, he learned there had been little progress in the bombing investigation. Due to the swastika painted on the wall, the FBI had questioned nearly everyone connected to the neo-Nazi Movement from New York to Chicago to Los Angles and even in remote areas like Montana. However, there was no evidence linking anyone to the crime.

While this update provoked an angry reaction from Rachel, her dad remained surprisingly calm. Instead of expressing rage, Benjamin focused more on the cruel irony surrounding his wife's death. As he spoke, Rachel and Grant observed how his accent thickened.

"From the time I was born," Benjamin began, "I've faced anti-Semitism. It was widespread in Poland and Russia. I understand many American Jews are the descendants of the millions who fled the pogroms at the turn of the century, but unfortunately, my family's ancestors did not join them."

Rachel glanced at Grant. Understanding that it might be beneficial for her father to talk, they silently agreed to be attentive listeners.

"The Jews in this country," he continued, "Take much for granted. At least, that's what I've always thought. While the Holocaust was slaughtering millions in Europe, American Jews were safely enjoying the blessings of their First Amendment rights. Do you know that before World War II, there were three million Jews in Poland? By 1950, that number had fallen to less than 50,000. Meanwhile, the only threat to Judaism in this country seemed to be whether too many Jews were putting up Christmas trees in December."

Benjamin paused, shook his head, and chuckled. Rachel and Grant smiled and nodded, indicating they wanted him to continue.

"As you know, Miriam and I were fortunate to survive Sobibor; most did *not*."

He looked directly at his listeners to emphasize his point. After taking a deep breath, he continued.

"We were fortunate to survive the final years of the war. The Poles, the Germans, the Russians—they all had it in for us simply because we were Jewish. After everything we'd endured, coming to America seemed like the final stroke of good luck. It felt like we'd died and awakened in heaven. Here, we could open a business, start a family, purchase a home, and live peacefully. Most importantly, for the first time, we were free from the horrors of anti-Semitism. Or at least, that's what we believed."

Benjamin observed his listeners to determine if they appreciated the irony. Rachel and Grant nodded in understanding, but neither knew how to respond. A waitress abruptly shattered the awkward silence by clearing the empty plates and leaving the check. Despite Rachel and Benjamin's best efforts, Grant managed to pick up and pay the tab. The uneasy quiet followed them into the car for most of their ride home. Making conversation the night before a funeral had been a challenge, and by this point, the trio had given up trying.

As Grant parked in front of the apartment complex, Rachel, sitting in the backseat, asked if he would like to come inside "for a little while." From the front seat, Benjamin understood that the implied message was there would be nothing but talking the night before her mother's funeral, but Rachel wasn't ready to end the evening just yet. He suspected that his daughter had something on her mind.

Once inside, Benjamin excused himself to his bedroom, respecting his daughter's need for privacy. However, Rachel's volume rose as they talked, and the sound easily penetrated the thin walls of the small apartment. Thus, Benjamin could not avoid overhearing much of their conversation, and what he heard was becoming increasingly disturbing.

After pouring two glasses of wine from the bottle that she and her father had opened that afternoon, Rachel got straight to the point.

"Grant, you mentioned at dinner that the FBI interviewed everyone involved with the Nazi Party?" After he nodded, she cautiously added, "Did that include Michael?"

Benjamin could not see Grant's face, but the prolonged silence that followed was telling. Rachel sounded like she was about to cross-examine a hostile witness. While Benjamin felt sympathy for Grant, he could not intervene.

"No," Grant finally answered, "Of course not. Why would they? He's just a high school kid."

"A *brilliant* high school kid," Rachel countered, "And one that, as you've told me, could have links to Frank Collin and his gangsters in Marquette Park. Also, since Michael lives here in Bloomington, he'd have both the opportunity and the motive."

"*Motive*? Rachel, as you know, Michael did a complete reversal regarding your parents. Yes, I'll admit he's displayed some troubling tendencies in the past, but once he met your father, everything changed. If you'll recall, he even helped me interview your parents for that piece in the *Pantagraph*."

"That's all true," Rachel conceded, "But Grant, what if it was just an act? Is that at least a possibility? What if Michael, perhaps in cahoots with those thugs in Chicago, was the one who planted the bomb? He knew all about my parents, including where they lived. Don't you think it's worth considering?"

Once again, there was a lull in the conversation. His daughter had made a serious allegation, and Grant was likely trying to find the best way to respond. In that moment, Benjamin's mind raced along several different paths. This was typically how he processed the world around him. It only took a few words—this time from a conversation he would have preferred not to overhear—to release a flood of ideas, as if someone had blown up a dam.

Benjamin's first concern was Rachel's future with Grant. He had developed a fondness for the reporter and, more importantly, had noticed how happy his daughter seemed when Grant was around. Furthermore, Rachel was not getting any younger, and her prospects in Bloomington were growing increasingly limited. Benjamin envisioned a wedding in the near future, followed by the birth of grandchildren. Now, he wondered, was all of this at risk?

His second thought was that he seriously doubted Michael could be involved in the bombing. Yes, Benjamin was grieving the death of his wife, not to mention the destruction of his home, but one should always be cautious about making unfounded accusations. Although Benjamin had known Michael for only a short time, intuitively, he failed to see how this teenage boy who had eagerly helped his dad interview Holocaust survivors could be working with the Nazis. Like so many in his generation, Michael was just a confused kid. He was no murderer.

Benjamin suspected that recent events had negatively impacted Rachel's perspective. While it was true that she was about to bury her mother, other circumstances had clearly clouded her judgment. Before the night of the bombing, Rachel had seemed hopelessly in love. Since then, however, she appeared to be on the verge of jeopardizing a life-altering relationship. Benjamin had just lost the second true love of his life that day, and he didn't want Rachel to drive away her first.

Benjamin observed that everything darkening Rachel's disposition stemmed from the Nazis. While everyone should despise them, Rachel's hatred had grown all-consuming. In Benjamin's view, her loathing had recently calcified. For starters, they threatened to march into Skokie, which, according to Rachel, would resurrect nightmares for thousands, including her parents. This was compounded by the Supreme Court voting to support the Nazis. Benjamin knew Rachel and Grant held opposite views on this issue and that their disagreement had mutated into more than just a political argument. Finally, there was the vile swastika painted on her parents' house the night of the explosion. Rachel rightfully blamed the Nazis for killing her mother, but now, for some reason, she was convinced Michael was involved. How far would her anger go?

Suddenly, Benjamin heard more words emanating from the living room. Grant was finally breaking their silence, but he spoke so softly that Benjamin drifted toward the closed bedroom door to hear better.

"Rachel, I *know* my son. For many years, he'd been a lost soul, mainly due to issues between his mother and me. And you're right; he's quite intelligent. So, even though he may not always earn the highest grades in class, he's constantly questioning everything. However, that doesn't mean he's capable of blowing up someone's home. Rachel, Michael's far from perfect, but he's *not* a killer."

Once again, Benjamin heard nothing but silence. The lapses in the conversation were as revealing as the words. This time, it was Rachel's turn to respond, and he wondered whether his daughter would pursue her inquiry any further. Benjamin hoped she would not. While he fully understood her anger, he did not want Rachel's unfounded accusation to jeopardize her chances for long-term happiness. However, her next words definitely crossed the Rubicon.

"Grant, as his father, I believe you're blinded by bias. Consider this: do you think Charles Manson's parents ever suspected what he would grow up to become?" After another pause, she added in a more threatening tone, "I believe there's a strong possibility that Michael was involved in the bombing. Grant, you owe it to me to check this out."

Benjamin winced at hearing the mention of that name. He followed the news closely and had carefully tracked the story of the Manson family. As a father, Benjamin fully understood why Grant fiercely defended his son. He appreciated why Grant could not accept that Michael was involved in the deadly bombing. Ultimately, Benjamin agreed with Grant and took his side against his daughter in this argument.

Benjamin anxiously waited to hear how Grant would respond to his daughter's emotionally charged ultimatum. However, this time, instead of receiving a verbal response from Rachel's boyfriend, the silence was shattered by the explosion of a slamming door.

CHAPTER 16

GRANT

September 1977

Grant lay flat on his back, his eyes focused on the random pattern of bumps on the popcorn ceiling. They resembled the moon's surface in the dim light of his bedroom lamp. Grant could hear Rachel's bathroom sounds from down the hall as she climbed out of the shower, brushed her teeth, and completed her other routines before rejoining him in bed. Since Michael was away in Chicago for one more day, they had the entire house to themselves.

Their evening began in the kitchen, where Grant served Rachel his "famous" spaghetti and meatballs. After moving into the living room, they viewed an episode of *The Love Boat*, a show neither would have watched alone, but its mushy romance appealed to them as a couple. Afterward, they climbed the stairs to the bedroom for a round of lovemaking. Following their usual routine, they would soon fall asleep. Grant sighed. It had been a relaxing evening, but deep down inside, he knew something was missing.

Grant felt as though the air was slowly leaking from their relationship. On the surface, Rachel remained a fun companion—thoughtful, affectionate, and always an excellent conversationalist. Recently, however, Grant realized that he was the one who always suggested the restaurants, movies, and other activities to fill their time together. While Rachel always agreed to his suggestions, she never seemed enthusiastic about them. Grant also noticed minor changes, such as how he always took Rachel's hand to hold, never the other way around. And, of course, Rachel became quiet and reserved whenever Michael was at home.

Grant observed that the changes in their relationship began right after their fight the night before Miriam's funeral. Although they reconciled shortly after, Michael continued to create tension between them. One positive development was Michael's attendance at the funeral. Dressed in his best coat and tie, he appeared genuinely mournful throughout the service at the synagogue. This display forced Rachel to suppress her concerns about Grant's son, at least temporarily.

Nevertheless, something had been missing since the funeral. From one day to the next, Rachel went through the motions of being a committed girlfriend, but a voice inside Grant told him that their days together were numbered. Even the passion in the bedroom had deflated. Grant realized that the honeymoon phase of their relationship was clearly over, but it had happened faster than expected. Now, when they made love, it was like they were just following a checklist, and the nights of going at it for hours were long gone.

Grant decided it was time to address the situation head-on. When Rachel returned, her dark hair still damp and her breath smelling of Colgate, Grant was sitting up waiting.

"I'd like to discuss something before we go to sleep."

Rachel froze, staring at Grant with wide eyes like a deer facing a hunter. She nodded for her boyfriend to continue, then cautiously climbed into bed beside him. Propping her pillow against the headboard, she lay back and turned to face Grant.

"Don't worry," Grant reassured her. "I promise this won't turn into a fight. It takes two to fight, and I refuse to be one of them. It just seems like you've grown more distant lately, and I want to understand why."

Rachel hesitated to respond; however, since Grant had stopped talking, she felt the need to fill the silence.

"Okay," she finally affirmed, "I'll concede that, yes, something *has* been bothering me. It's the same old thing, Grant. You know what it is."

"Let me guess: Michael? You still believe he was involved in the bombing, don't you?"

Rachel adjusted the straps of her nightgown, positioning herself to face Grant more directly. "Yes, I do," she replied, sensing there was nothing new she could add to support this response.

"Rachel, I've brought this subject up with Michael several times, but he continually insists he was out with a friend that night. Since we've been getting along pretty well lately, I hesitated to press him further about his involvement. However, the other night, he mentioned it again and said he would understand if I continued to push, given his past behavior. Nonetheless, Michael still maintains he had nothing to do with the bomb."

Rachel bit her lower lip but stayed silent. Grant could tell she had something on her mind, but like him, she did not want to launch another battle that, this time, would likely end their relationship.

"Go ahead," Grant encouraged, "If we're going to move forward, we've got to clear the air. So, if there's something on your mind, let's hear it."

"Alright," she agreed, "Each time you confronted Michael, what did you think he'd say? Let's say, *hypothetically*, that he actually planted the bomb. Did you think he'd come right out and admit it?"

"Rachel," Grant responded louder than intended, "I *know* my son. He wasn't lying to me. Michael's not a good actor. I also remember that he looked like he was about to cry at your mom's funeral. That also wasn't an act."

Rachel reached out and took her boyfriend's hand. She spoke in a calming tone, attempting to diffuse the situation. Although Grant felt offended by the recurring accusation, he appreciated her efforts to prevent their discussion from escalating into another full-blown battle.

"Grant, it's natural for a father to believe his son. However, as an outsider, perhaps I can see things a little more objectively?"

She briefly looked away, and Grant noticed her biting her lip again. When Rachel turned back to him, she had a conciliatory smile on her face.

"I'll tell you what," she suggested, as though launching a negotiation, "I'll give in to you on this issue provided you do one thing for me. Search his bedroom. Then, if you find nothing linking Michael either to those buffoons in Chicago or to the actual bombing, I'll believe his story too. I promise."

Grant sighed. This time, it was his turn to hesitate before answering. Rachel's proposal seemed reasonable, but Grant believed privacy was a fundamental right that should always be respected. He glanced at the digital clock and saw it was getting late.

"Rachel, you're asking me to violate a moral principle. I still get angry whenever I think about that day when I caught my mother going through my room. She claimed she was worried about all the drinking she'd heard about at my high school and just wanted to make sure I didn't have a six-pack of beer squirreled away somewhere."

"And did she find any beer?" Rachel inquired, grinning.

"Maybe," Grant answered, flashing a mischievous smile. "But that's not the point," he added, tightening his lips. "I was deeply offended. If she suspected that I had beer in my room, all she had to do was ask. I would have told her the truth. By invading my privacy, my mom showed she did not trust me."

"But," Rachel instantly retorted, "Not every teenager tells the truth like you. Also, there's quite a difference between underage drinking and setting off a bomb that kills someone."

Grant nodded, acknowledging that she had made a valid point. After glancing at the clock again and remembering their plans to meet Benjamin for an early breakfast, he considered the best response to end their debate, at least for now, and still allow for some sleep.

"Let me think about it, Rachel. I suppose every parent has to wrestle with a decision like this at some point, but it's not easy."

Rachel nodded, signaling her agreement to table the motion for now. She leaned forward for a kiss, told Grant she loved him, and then turned away to bury herself beneath the covers. Grant reached back to turn off the lamp and slid between the sheets, lying flat on his back. Within minutes, he could hear the soft purring of Rachel's breathing. He glanced over and saw her dark silhouette facing away from him. Behind her, Grant could also see a full moon peering through the open window, its soft light flooding the dark room.

Grant was still lying on his back an hour later, occasionally glancing over at Rachel's alluring profile. He could not believe how fortunate he had been to meet her. Rachel was not only spectacularly beautiful but also his intellectual equal and, currently, his best friend. When they were apart, Grant constantly thought about her. He could not recall ever feeling this way about a woman before. Grant knew that if they could get past this one issue, he would soon get down on one knee to propose. Of course, considering this issue involved the untimely death of her mother, it remained an enormous obstacle.

Now, Rachel had just given Grant a way to remove the obstacle in their path. All he needed to do was search Michael's room. But was the search justified? Only if there was a reasonably good chance that Rachel was right about Michael. Could it be that his son had been lying to him all along? Was Michael really such a talented actor? Grant wanted to trust his son just as his parents should have trusted him. However, he and Michael were not the same. Sure, he had also once been a confused teenager, but in a million years, he could never have found anything appealing about neo-Nazis.

Grant recalled what Rachel had said over a month ago. Would the parents of Charles Manson ever suspect what their son would grow up to be? If a teenager with mental health issues was in danger of harming himself or others, would the parents not have an obligation to violate his privacy? Should privacy still be sacred even when lives are at stake?

Grant knew the Supreme Court had ruled fifteen years earlier in a case called *Mapp v. Ohio* that evidence obtained from an illegal search should be excluded. This case was considered a pivotal victory for the right to privacy. However, the courts still allowed for several exceptions. Every Constitutional right has its limits; none are absolute.

Grant looked at the clock and noticed it was well past midnight. The troubling issue on his mind was preventing him from sleeping. He realized he might remain awake all night if he kept mulling it over. Moreover, Michael was coming home tomorrow, and since it would be at least a month before his son returned to Chicago, this was the perfect opportunity to search Michael's room. Grant glanced at Rachel, who was dead to the world. Quietly, he tossed off the covers, climbed out of bed, and slipped on his robe and slippers.

It took less than twenty minutes to complete the search, and Grant had not found anything suspicious. Ironically, there was a six-pack of beer high up in Michael's closet, but judging by the dust on the cans, his son had probably forgotten it was there. Grant smiled and breathed a sigh of relief, thinking about how wonderful it would be to tell Rachel that he had not found anything incriminating. He turned off the light in his son's bedroom and stepped into the hallway. Then, he caught a glimpse of his backyard through the window at the end of the hall. In the moonlight, he saw the dark outline of the old shed. It was a crumbling structure he had not entered in months, perhaps years.

Grant paused in the middle of the hallway. Climbing back into bed would be easy, satisfied that he had fully honored Rachel's request. Still, over the last few months, Grant had noticed Michael emerging from the shed on more than one occasion, though he had never given it much thought at the time. Now, a mix of conscience and curiosity prompted him to tighten the belt of his robe and head toward the steps. He retrieved a flashlight from one of the kitchen's bottom drawers, turned on the outside light, and stepped out the back door.

An invigorating rush of fresh air filled the space. The floodlight by the back door obscured the stars, yet the nearly full moon cast a grid of shadows from the high tree branches above. Grant heard only the shrill, continuous sound of crickets. Otherwise, he felt like the only person in Bloomington-Normal who was not sound asleep. Upon reaching the shed, Grant turned on his flashlight, opened the door, and cautiously peered inside.

A bicycle that Grant rarely used was concealed beneath a mesh of spider webs. Next to it leaned a weedwhacker Grant had not plugged in since hiring a kid down the street to do his lawn work. Beneath it lay the electric cable for the weedwhacker coiled around an orange plastic spool. A few other miscellaneous tools were gathered in the corner, including hedge clippers, a snow blower, and a rake.

Then Grant noticed an unfamiliar open area. What had he used to store there? Oh, that's right—the lawn mower and the gas can. He had sold the lawn mower because the kid down the street provided his own. But where was the gas can? As Grant mulled over what might have happened, the beam of his flashlight fell onto something lurking behind the weedwhacker. What was that object? He leaned down to investigate.

It was a white plastic container he had never seen before. Grant bent down to read the label—ammonium nitrate. *Holy* shit. Grant knew it was ordinarily used as a fertilizer, but he had not purchased it. More importantly, Chuck, his friend on the police force, had told him that ammonium nitrate was the primary ingredient in the bomb that had blown up the Abramowicz house. Grant gazed at the white receptacle in horror as if it were about to explode. This was Michael's.

The flashlight's beam started to tremble as Grant began to grasp the significance of the object in his hand. He shook the canister gently; it was mostly empty. Standing in the center of his shed, Grant momentarily froze in a daze. Finally, he stepped outside, still clutching the handle of the container that had once been filled with fertilizer. He slowly crossed the backyard like a sleepwalker. Once inside, Grant hid the incriminating evidence in the kitchen, tucking it away in the corner behind the refrigerator. He knew Rachel should not find out about this until he had confronted his son. Perhaps she should never know.

Grant sat down at the kitchen table, needing to think. Only later did he realize the absurdity of his initial thought. He questioned Michael's carelessness rather than considering the moral or legal implications of his actions. Why would his son, brilliant enough to build this deadly weapon, be foolish enough to leave behind such incriminating evidence?

Next, Grant shifted his focus to the pressing issue at hand: how to deal with his horrific discovery. Tomorrow was Sunday, and Michael had promised to return home by five in the afternoon after spending the weekend with his mom in Chicago. Grant decided to confront his son with the evidence as soon as he walked through the front door. What would happen next would depend on Michael's response. For now, at least, he did not want to plan any further.

Grant glanced up at the kitchen clock. It was almost 1 a.m. He stood sluggishly and approached the refrigerator, opening a half-gallon milk bottle. Without thinking, he guzzled the liquid directly from the jug, something he had told Michael countless times not to do. After placing the milk back in the fridge and closing the door, Grant noticed the fertilizer container in the corner. He pushed it further back so it was entirely out of sight. The last thing he needed was for Rachel to find it in the morning accidentally.

After Grant climbed back into bed, he noted that Rachel had not moved. She was still deep in sleep, oblivious to everything he had just experienced. Once again, Grant lay on his back, gazing at the ceiling. Still unable to sleep, his mind began to wander in a different direction. *Why* had Michael bombed the Abramowicz home? Why did he go to such lengths to create a complex plan and then work so hard to cover his tracks? What was he thinking?

Grant reflected on the fathers who felt immense pride every time their children succeeded in school, excelled in sports or achieved other accomplishments. What a remarkable feeling that must be. However, he also considered the fathers of those who ended up in prison, including those who deserved to be incarcerated but were never caught. Unfortunately, Grant realized he now belonged to that latter group. This feeling was the opposite of pride; this was shame.

Then, Grant thought more specifically about his son. Yes, Michael was a confused teenager, something Grant often told himself and others to justify the boy's erratic behavior. But that could never excuse what he had done. Michael had killed Miriam Abramowicz and was fortunate that it had not turned into a double homicide.

What was his son's motive? Was this all because he had fallen under the influence of anti-Semites? Despite his best efforts, Grant still struggled to understand the roots of anti-Semitism. While the Nazis painted Judaism as a demonic race that threatened humanity and deserved extermination, Grant, like most people, viewed it as just one religion among many. He recognized that Jews were the first to worship one God, comprised a tiny minority of the global population, and posed no threat to anyone's well-being. They had stood apart for centuries, trying to maintain Jewish traditions in a predominantly Christian world. Why have many people throughout history harbored hatred for others simply because they were different? And why had his son become one of those people?

Grant peeked at the digital clock; it was now past 2 a.m. This was turning into the longest night of his life. Grant felt exhausted, yet he could not keep his eyes closed. Then he glanced over at his girlfriend's sleeping figure. As it turned out, Rachel had been right all along. What would this mean for their relationship? Could it ever survive?

One option was to avoid telling Rachel what he discovered, but Grant quickly recognized that his conscience would never allow him to do so. For months, Rachel had insisted that Michael was deceiving him and that Grant should have monitored the situation more closely. Grant, however, had sided with Michael, naively falling for his act and believing his claims. Once Rachel discovers the truth, would she not hold the father responsible for the sins of the son? Grant shook his head, already knowing the answer.

Finally, Grant thought about his son. Michael was his only child, his flesh and blood. Together with Gretchen, he had brought this boy into the world, and as much as he might want to blame his wife, Grant realized he had also played a role in creating this monster. What Michael had done was absolutely unforgivable. However, could a child ever do something so terrible it would end a parent's love? And if the boy is viewed as an extension of the father, does Grant share some of Michael's guilt, even if only indirectly?

Grant rolled onto his side and thought about climbing out of bed. He could sneak downstairs and find something to read while his girlfriend continued to sleep upstairs. As Grant pondered his options, he eventually drifted into a deep, dreamless sleep. Five hours later, the alarm buzzed, slowly rousing him from bed. During breakfast and for several hours afterward, he forced himself to act as if everything was fine. However, his facade must have been unconvincing, as Rachel repeatedly asked if everything was okay.

Finally, by late afternoon, Rachel departed, saying she had a stack of papers to grade. Typically, Grant would have suggested taking her out for an early dinner, delivering his usual line, "After all, you still have to eat." However, today was different. Once Rachel left, Grant dragged the ammonium nitrate canister out and set it on the kitchen table. He then picked up a James Michener book, settled onto the couch in the living room, and positioned himself to greet his son as soon as Michael walked through the door.

Grant drifted off after just a few pages of *Centennial*. Shortly before five o'clock, he was suddenly roused by the jiggling of the doorknob. As Michael entered, he saw his dad sitting up and stretching. He initially wore a smile, genuinely happy to see his father. Then he observed the scowl on his dad's face. Michael gently closed the door behind him and sheepishly entered the room. He circled the coffee table and sat at the opposite end of the sofa.

"Hey, Dad," Michael said casually. After a brief pause, he asked, "Is something wrong?"

For a moment, Grant silently scowled, caught between the urge to explode with anger and the desire to sob with sorrow. Nevertheless, he took a deep breath and managed to stick to his plan. Robotically, Grant stood up, walked toward the kitchen, and then turned back, motioning for Michael to follow. Once inside the kitchen, he halted at the table and waited for his son to join him. Standing side by side and silently gazing at the nearly empty fertilizer canister, Grant finally spoke for the first time.

"I found this last night in the shed. It's a fertilizer, but I was also told that ammonium nitrate was the primary chemical used in the bomb that blew up the Abramowicz house." After pausing momentarily, he added, "I also noticed that the gasoline can I used to keep in the shed is missing. The police informed me that gasoline was the accelerant that turned the initial explosion into the fire that burned down their house."

Grant turned to face his son. Michael's expression was blank, but Grant knew his son was actively processing this information. He presumed Michael was silently weighing his options. After a moment of silence, Grant continued speaking.

"Michael, that bomb *killed* Miriam Abramowicz. Would you care to explain the role you played in her murder?"

Grant understood that his son had only two options—confess or deny. He was determined to remain in an uneasy silence for as long as it took Michael to make up his mind.

Without saying a word, Michael circled the table, set the canister on the floor, and sat in one of the kitchen chairs. He placed his hands on the table and intertwined his fingers. It was clear that Michael wanted his dad to pull out the other chair and join him. Once Grant did, Michael began to explain calmly and deliberately.

"Dad, I'll admit it: I built the bomb. I poured the fertilizer into a smaller container to mix it with the diesel fuel on the front porch. But I planned this a while ago when I was still going through my Nazi phase. And I'm not the one who actually lit the fuse; it was a member of the Nazi Party who came down from Chicago. He's the one who detonated the bomb."

Michael paused to let this sink in and to see if his dad had any questions. When none came, he continued.

"Do you remember when I received a phone call the morning of the bombing? You answered the phone and woke me up so I could take the call. Do you remember?"

Grant nodded slowly, waiting for his son to continue.

"It was from him, the guy they sent from Chicago. I told you it was a friend from school, but it was actually Dale, this guy who was supposed to help me with the bombing. I then drove to McDonald's to join him for breakfast. Do you remember any of this?"

Again, Grant nodded. "Go on."

"I spent the whole day with Dale, mostly just killing time. You might remember that I called you in the afternoon and told you I was going out with friends, but in reality, I was still with Dale. Later that night, we took the bomb to the Abramowicz house and placed it on their front porch. I'm the one who painted the swastika because I believed it would send a message. But, Dad, I was already having second thoughts throughout the day, I swear. That night, as we were preparing to set off the bomb, I happened to see the faces of Mr. and Mrs. Abramowicz through their bedroom window. They were sound asleep, and something inside told me this was wrong."

Michael paused, and Grant noticed that his eyes looked glassy. Although he remained cautious, suspecting that his son might be staging another Academy Award-winning performance, Grant felt his resolve beginning to weaken. He nodded for Michael to go on.

"Dad, it's hard to explain, but I stopped seeing them as the enemy when I saw them both cuddled together in their bed. I mean, yeah, they're Jewish and all, but in that moment, they just became regular people."

"So," Grant inquired, "What did you do?"

"I told Dale I couldn't go through with it and that we shouldn't light the fuse. He obviously disagreed as he popped me in the eye, knocking me out for a moment. While I was lying next to the bomb, Dale lit the fuse and took off. I never saw him again."

"So," Grant asked, speaking deliberately, "That's why I saw you with a black eye the following day?"

"Yeah. Dad, I feel terrible. I never thought anyone would *die*. This has been haunting me for months. I keep picturing Mrs. Abramowicz's face as she looked sleeping with her husband's arm wrapped around her. She was *so* peaceful, and I think she was smiling. I tried to pull the plug at the last moment, Dad; I really did. I know that's no excuse because, after all, I'm the one who set everything in motion, but I did try to stop it at the last minute. What's more, if I hadn't woken up when I did and rolled off the porch at the last second, I also would've died in the explosion."

Grant gazed at his son, attempting to discern the truth like a human lie detector. Despite Michael's recently discovered acting talents, Grant was still inclined to believe him. He was not trying to deny his involvement, and the details he provided contributed to a credible, cohesive story.

"So," Grant finally proclaimed, "If we went to the police, would you be willing to give up Dale? Maybe if you agree to testify against him, they'd go easier on you, especially because of your age."

"That's no longer possible," Michael exclaimed, "Dale's dead. I just found out over the weekend that the police shot him during an attempted robbery. He was leaving a 7-Eleven with less than $300 in his pocket when the police pulled into the parking lot. Dale fired at one of the officers and missed. The policeman shot back, and he didn't."

Grant raised his eyebrows and sighed. This was a lot to take in at once, and his mind went blank for a moment. Finally, Grant thought of a question.

"Michael, how did you learn this?"

"Mom told me. She's been pretty friendly with some of the guys down at the Nazi Party headquarters, and one of them told her."

"Oh," Grant responded, unable to conceal his disgust. Then, he thought of another question. "Michael, what's the Nazi Party's connection to the bombing? Maybe they should share some of the blame."

"No, Dad, it was my idea from the start. I informed them about it beforehand, and they were supportive, but except for sending Dale, the Nazis weren't involved. At least," he added, "Not in a way I can prove."

Father and son sat quietly facing each other, both unsure of what to say next. Finally, Michael broke the silence.

"Dad, I promise you I'm not the same person who built that bomb. I *tried* to stop Dale from lighting the fuse, and it almost cost me my life. I feel horrible about what happened to Mrs. Abramowicz. However, there is nothing I can do to bring her back."

Grant studied his son's face. Although Michael looked sincere, Grant no longer trusted his ability to accurately read his son's facial expressions. Part of him believed that Michael's sociopathy had gifted him with the acting skills that could win an Oscar. Moreover, it was not as if Michael had merely caused a careless accident. In this situation, feeling remorse was far from sufficient.

"Michael," Grant asserted, "You're responsible for a serious crime. A *homicide*. I hope you're not suggesting we bury this and keep it quiet."

Michael inhaled deeply and shrugged. Finally, he spoke softly and purposefully when he realized his dad was waiting for a response.

"Dad, there're two options. The first is, *yes*, we bury this information and go on living our lives. I'll finish high school in less than a year and then start college somewhere far from Chicago. In the meantime, I'll stay away from the Nazis and forswear anything that reeks of their anti-Semitism. I *promise*. What's more, to atone for what I've done, I'll pursue a career where I can help others, such as teaching or being a public defender. I might even consider going into journalism, like you did. Oh, and by the way, if we bury this, Rachel will never know about it, which means the two of you could eventually get married."

A salesman's grin crept across Michael's face as if his last point would be enough to close the sale. Grant's lips tightened into a cynical scowl, and he shook his head slowly.

"Okay," Grant replied, stretching the second syllable, "Tell me about your second option."

Michael leaned forward, looked down, and slumped in disappointment. Then, like a man facing a firing squad, he looked up at his father and continued.

"The second option is that you turn me in to the police. I'm pretty sure they'll treat me like an adult rather than a juvenile, and I'll end up getting the death penalty or, at least, spend decades in prison. My life will essentially be over either way, and I'm guessing it will destroy any chance of you and Rachel living happily ever after."

"And if we choose option two," Grant asked, "What happens to us? Will you blame me for ruining your life and never speak to me again?"

Grant leaned forward, resting his elbows on the table, and looked Michael in the eye. He waited to see if his son would threaten to end their relationship in order to avoid going to prison. As Grant waited for a response, it occurred to him that this might be the perfect test of his son's true character. Michael had just skillfully analyzed his father's two options. Was he now ready to accept his dad's decision without any repercussions?

"You're my father," Michael finally replied. "If you stand by me, I'll stand with you."

"Even from prison?" Grant asked skeptically.

"Yes, as long as you're willing to come visit me."

Tears welled in Grant's eyes as he grappled with the decision of whether to turn his son in to the police. For now, however, he found joy in the fact that Michael had just passed the most critical test of his life. Grant stood up, walked around the table, and opened his arms. Michael then rose to his feet and embraced his father tightly. At that moment, they wept together in silence.

CHAPTER 17

MICHAEL

September 1977

Panic overwhelmed Michael, triggering a wave of nausea that drove him to the bathroom. He retched the remnants of his lunch. Before he could rise from his kneeling position in front of the toilet, another wave of nausea hit him, leading to more bouts of heaving until his stomach was empty. After several minutes and with great effort, he stood and drifted before the mirror, examining the weathered face staring back at him. The moment evoked memories of the numerous conversations with his alter ego. Michael considered launching a conversation and seeking advice, but his dad interrupted by knocking on the door.

Michael opened the door and attributed his stomach problems to the deep-dish pizza he had consumed for lunch that day in Chicago. However, now that his life was suddenly teetering on the edge of a cliff, he knew it was really the stress. More than anything, Michael understood that his fate was in his father's hands. Was there any way to regain control? He needed time to think. He respectfully told his dad that he would like to lie down for a while in his room and perhaps even go to bed early. He excused himself, grabbed his knapsack, and carried it upstairs.

Once in his room, Michael collapsed onto his bed. As he lay back, gazing up at the popcorn ceiling he had come to despise, his first thought drifted to the empty canister of ammonium nitrate. How could he have been *so* careless? He had intended to wait until it was time to take out the trash to hide the canister underneath. Yet, he had completely forgotten to do this. Michael vaguely remembered wondering if his father would ever question why there was fertilizer in the lawn shed if he happened to find the empty canister. Of course, he never imagined that one day, a policeman would inform his dad about the presence of ammonium nitrate in the bomb.

Surprisingly, Michael was not that upset. It might have been different if he were a career criminal whose slip-up led to decades in prison. In that case, he would never forgive himself. Somehow, though, this was different. It was as if Michael felt relieved to be caught. The fact that it was his dad who had confronted him rather than a uniformed policeman standing at the front door made it easier to swallow. Now, the only question that remained was whether his father, his flesh and blood, would turn his only son into the police.

Michael realized that, while some men might look the other way, *his* father would turn him in the following morning. Shockingly, he did not harbor any anger. His father was a principled man, always had been. Even though it would likely end his dad's first serious romantic relationship in many years, he would still do what he believed was right. There was no way Grant Parker could do otherwise.

Michael realized he had two choices. One option was to turn himself in and face the possibility of spending much of his life in an Illinois state prison. The other option was to go on the run and create a new life far away. As he considered the second option, a grin spread across his face. At that moment, no one was looking for him; he was not yet a wanted fugitive—the idea of escaping and having the freedom to start over felt exhilarating.

Michael's escape plan was straightforward. In the middle of the night, he would drive back to Chicago. The following day, he would explain the situation to his mother, knowing her reaction would be the opposite of his father's. However, he understood he could not safely stay with her for long. Instead, Michael planned to sell his car to a local dealership for a fraction of its worth and use the money to buy a Greyhound ticket to California. Once there, he would search for a job and a place to live.

The idea was filled with uncertainties, but that was acceptable. At seventeen, much of Michael's future was shrouded in uncertainty, even under the best circumstances. He understood this was part of being a teenager. Despite this, he had an unwavering self-confidence and was ready to confront any challenges that came his way. College would have to be put on hold, maybe forever, but other opportunities awaited.

Michael could find ways to make some quick money, legal or not, and then perhaps invest in a business.

Michael reached for his alarm clock and set it for 2 a.m., planning to get a few hours of sleep before hitting the road. After that, he got up to go to the bathroom. Walking by the mirror above the sink, he caught a glimpse of his reflection and froze. The image staring back was not the familiar Michael from his past in Chicago. This was a different Michael, who appeared older and more mature. As he gazed at the image of his new alter ego, Michael noticed the face slowly shaking back and forth with a raised eyebrow and pursed lips.

"What?" Michael asked in a low voice. "Why are you looking at me like that?"

The image in the mirror stopped shaking his head, but his expression remained somber, more like a disappointed parent than a teenager. Finally, Michael's reflection spoke.

"You realize you've reached the proverbial fork in the road, right?"

"What are you talking about?"

"You're about to make a choice," the older Michael replied. "That choice will affect everything that happens to you from this day on. And whatever you decide, you'll have to live with that decision for the rest of your life."

"That's true," the teenage Michael replied, "But I've already made my decision. I choose freedom. I'm not going to prison—at least not if I can avoid it."

"But will you *really* be free?" older Michael asked, "You might remain free physically, but what about the burden you'll be carrying?."

Feigning ignorance, Michael asked, "What are you talking about?"

The image in the mirror smiled knowingly. Wrinkles spread across his forehead, and crow's feet radiated from the corners of his eyes. Michael watched as his reflection aged right before him.

"If you flee now," the aging Michael stated in no uncertain terms, "You'll forever be saddled with two weighty pieces of baggage. The first is that you'll always be looking over your shoulder. Your dad will go to the police, and you'll become a wanted fugitive. Then, no matter where you go, you'll be afraid whenever you pass a cop or hear a siren. Michael, you built the bomb that killed Mrs. Abramowicz. You think they'll ever stop looking for you?"

Michael pressed his lips together, inhaled deeply through his nose, and nodded. "Go on," he instructed.

"The other?" older Michael sneered, "You're looking right at it."

The image in the mirror paused, waiting to see if the confused teenager understood what he was saying. When nothing but a bewildered expression emerged, older Michael continued.

"Guess what, Michael, you've developed something called a conscience. You know, like that Jiminy Cricket character in *Pinocchio*? Do you remember the Disney film? Your dad took you to see it again and again when you were a kid. It was your favorite. In your case, though, you didn't get a cute little bug. You got *me*."

As Michael's eyes widened in understanding, the older Michael's expression remained unchanged.

"That's right," the reflection continued, "Every time you pass a mirror for the rest of your life, you'll see me. And I'll never grow tired of reminding you about Miriam Abramowicz. I'll flash images of how she looked, sleeping contentedly next to her husband, and then I'll contrast them with how she appeared when they loaded her into the ambulance. Before long, she'll be haunting your dreams."

Michael stepped away from the sink and moved toward the toilet. After all, he had come here to pee, not to engage in a conversation with an illusion claiming to be his conscience. However, it did not work. Although he could no longer see the image, he could still hear its voice.

"You see, Michael, that's the nature of a conscience. No matter where you go, I'll always be with you. I will be the first to greet you every morning when you brush your teeth, and my voice will be the last you hear at night when you lay your head on the pillow. Please understand, Michael, that I will never stop reminding you of what you did."

After flushing the toilet, Michael approached the sink and studied his reflection. He briefly questioned his sanity, wondering if having conversations with his reflection was normal. However, he recalled hearing many people mention that they often "talk to themselves," so he quickly dismissed his concerns.

Instinctively, Michael understood this was a battle for his soul. If he could vanquish the older version of himself or at least find a way to ignore him, there might still be a way to avoid prison. After all, he knew many people—especially those he had encountered in Marquette Park—who were never troubled by anything resembling a conscience. However, as soon as he caught sight of his reflection, Michael realized the battle was lost.

"Go back downstairs," his conscience commanded. "Talk to your dad. Tell him you're feeling better, then ask him how to proceed."

Michael nodded silently. He switched off the bathroom light, shuffled to his bedroom to turn off the alarm, and headed downstairs. His footsteps on the staircase were so soft that when he entered the living room, his father continued gazing absently at the television with the sound muted. Kojak's bald head filled the screen while he sucked on his trademark lollipop, but when his lips moved, there was no sound coming from his mouth.

For a moment, Michael studied his father's features. In the dim glow of the television, his dad appeared noticeably older. His hair was disheveled as if he had just woken up, and veins stood out on both hands. Michael stepped forward, but his dad still didn't look up; his mind seemed to be elsewhere. Michael thought he detected moisture beneath his father's eyes. He cleared his throat.

"*Oh*," Grant said, "I didn't see you there."

"I'm sorry if I startled you," Michael replied. Then, as he skirted the coffee table to join his father on the couch, he added, "How should we proceed?"

Grant concentrated on his son, initially struggling to understand the question. Eventually, he began to nod. Michael could see that his father was searching for the right words.

"I have a friend on the Bloomington police force," Grant finally responded. "His name is Chuck, and I've worked with him on many stories. I trust him completely. What's more, he's the officer investigating the explosion."

"Alright," Michael replied, sighing, "Should we call him now?"

Grant offered a faint smile. "I think we can wait until the morning," he replied. "You're not planning to escape overnight, are you?"

Michael grinned sheepishly and shook his head, waiting for his father to continue.

"First thing in the morning, I'll drive you to the police station. Chuck will take you into custody, of course, but he can probably skip some of the formalities, like the handcuffs. I'll also call an attorney who'll hopefully be able to meet us."

"An attorney?" he asked. "Do you have someone in mind?"

"Yes," his dad replied without hesitation. "His name is Jacob Robbins. We went to high school together, although we weren't friends back then. Our relationship changed when we both decided to attend Northwestern. Jake stayed an extra three years to earn his law degree before returning to Bloomington. Since then, he's become one of the best criminal defense lawyers in town."

Michael glanced up at the silent TV screen, which now displayed the news from Peoria. He struggled to process everything his dad had just said; it was all happening too quickly. Turning back to face his father, he felt uncertain about how to respond. Only one question came to his mind.

"How much will this cost?"

Grant smiled. "Don't worry about it. Jacob's an old friend, and his fee will be reasonable."

"Jacob?" Michael inquired. "Is he Jewish?"

"Yeah," his father answered warily, "Is that going to be a problem?"

"No," Michael instantly responded, "Not for *me*. But will it be a problem for him? Given the circumstances, I'd understand if he didn't want to take my case."

Grant inhaled deeply and slowly released the air from his lungs. Then he shifted to face his son directly.

"Michael, most defense lawyers don't focus on their client's guilt. Our courts operate on something called the adversarial system. The prosecutor and defense lawyer are adversaries, each trying to persuade the jury to their side of the case. This might sound strange, but neither one is really concerned with the truth. Each presents their strongest case, and then, it's up to the jury to determine the truth."

Michael already understood most of this civics lesson. However, like many people, he still questioned how a defense lawyer could represent a client known to be guilty. For now, though, he simply nodded for his dad to continue.

"Jacob won't focus on your guilt or innocence. Instead, he'll work hard to present your side of the case. In a situation like this, the prosecutor will likely be very aggressive, but as your advocate, Jacob will do every-thing possible to create reasonable doubt about your guilt or, in this case, minimize your punishment."

"Alright," Michael said, "I get it. This sounds like the same logic behind why Jewish lawyers were able to represent Nazis in the Skokie case."

Grant nodded and smiled in agreement. However, before he could respond, Michael raised a new point that redirected the conversation.

"So, what do you think Jacob will recommend? Should I even say anything to your friend on the police force if Jacob's not there?"

Grant's momentarily looked away, causing the remnants of his smile to fade. There was no easy way to respond. After a moment, Grant turned back to face his son. Before speaking, he did something that, in the past, might have made Michael a bit uncomfortable: he reached out and took his son's hand.

"Michael, are you willing to confess your role in this crime?" Before his son could respond, Grant added, "I know Jacob would advise you to stay silent and let him handle everything. That's what defense lawyers typically say. However, in this case, we both know what you did. I believe the best approach is for you to come clean, tell the truth, and then allow Jacob to negotiate the best possible sentence for you." After a pause, he asked, "What do you think?"

Michael hesitated before answering, unconsciously biting his lower lip. After reflecting on the conversation he had just had with his con-science, he finally began to nod.

"Yes," Michael agreed, "I will fully confess my role in the bombing."

"*Good*," Grant replied, squeezing his son's hand before letting go. After taking a deep breath and exhaling loudly, he continued,

"Michael, there are several factors that may help reduce your sen-tence. First, you're young. Second, you're voluntarily turning yourself in. Finally, and most importantly, there's Dale; if that part of your story checks out, it'll certainly help that you didn't light the fuse. However," he added after a brief pause and a deep sigh, "That said, there's still a good chance you will spend a significant portion of your life behind bars. There's just no getting around that."

Grant had finally voiced what they were both thinking. He reached over and grasped his son's hand again. This time, Michael squeezed back.

Then, they simultaneously pivoted to face the muted television, which had just gone to a commercial break between the weather and sports. For a minute, the only sound was the rhythmic ticking of the clock on the mantel above the fireplace. Finally, Grant turned back to confront his son.

"Whatever happens from here on out," he said, "I'll always be in your corner. Since there won't be a trial, you should quickly move through the legal process. Going to prison won't be easy, but you're strong, and you'll get through it. In the meantime, I'll visit you as often as they allow and do whatever I can to help make your time pass as comfortably as possible."

Michael nodded and even managed a wry smile. A short time later, father and son marched upstairs to prepare for bed. Neither fell asleep for several hours, and both were awake before sunrise. Grant prepared a massive breakfast with scrambled eggs, bacon, pancakes, and toast. He did not have to explain why. Soon after, Grant drove his son to the Bloomington police station, where he was fingerprinted, photographed, and taken into custody.

By midmorning, Michael had met Jacob Robbins, whom he liked instantly. His lawyer was taller than his dad and appeared athletic, even beneath his suit. Jacob had a full head of reddish curls and a neatly trimmed beard. He was in complete command, varying the pace and volume of his speech to suit the needs of any given moment. What impressed Michael the most, however, was his satirical wit. Jacob Robbins had a biting sense of humor that frequently made Michael laugh out loud, helping him to relax before his initial appearance in court.

Later that day, Michael appeared before a judge, seated beside his lawyer and directly in front of his dad. The main issue was the setting of bail. The prosecutor, an older man with a take-no-prisoners approach, argued that due to the severity of the charges, no bail should be set and that Michael should be kept in full custody. Jacob countered that Michael had come forward of his own volition and was not a flight risk.

Ultimately, the judge agreed to set bail, but it was deliberately too high for Grant to raise the necessary funds. When Jacob objected, arguing that it was unnecessary to keep a seventeen-year-old kid locked up indefinitely, the judge explained that due to the unique nature of this case, it was in the defendant's best interest to remain confined.

Michael was disappointed but understood after Jacob explained that, given the circumstances, even if he had been freed, he still could not attend school or go out in public. The local media, including *The Panta-graph*, would soon make his arrest front-page news. Once that happened, Michael would not be safe. At least inside the county jail, no one could harm him.

Michael was placed in a solitary cell, where he would only be allowed out to shower twice a week and for an hour of daily exercise in a yard the size of a postage stamp. He could have unlimited books, both from school and leisure, and he would receive daily visits from his father. Grant and Michael quickly adapted to their new routine, but they understood that it was only a matter of time before the situation worsened significantly.

Later that night, after the lights went out, Michael lay back on his cot, which occupied half the room. The small space contained a metal sink, a toilet, a small dresser, and a wooden shelf above his bed for photographs and books. Aside from that, the cell felt depressingly empty. Located at the end of a long hallway, Michael could barely hear the banter of other inmates.

Outside the room's only high window, guarded by vertical steel bars, a spotlight illuminated the courtyard below and cast a bright beam into the cell. The light was bright enough for Michael to see the polished concrete ceiling above him. The dull gray surface stretched the entire length of the tiny cell, unbroken by any lines, bumps, or indentations. Michael briefly smiled at the ironic thought that he actually missed the popcorn.

CHAPTER 18

RACHEL

September 1977

When Rachel hung up the phone, a sudden wave of apprehension washed over her. Grant had called during her office hours in the middle of the afternoon to say he would be late for their scheduled dinner. She could sense from the tone of his voice that something was wrong. Grant wasn't much of an actor—a quality Rachel usually admired. He could not hide his anxieties any more than he could keep a secret or stay quiet about a surprise. This childlike quality was typically endearing, but at the moment, Rachel felt frustrated by her boyfriend's reluctance to discuss the problem over the phone.

The rest of the afternoon passed as if everything were moving in slow motion. Rachel only managed to grade a few essays from her first major test of the semester, and researching an article she intended to submit to *The Historian* was impossible. As she drove home, Rachel felt dissatisfied with her unproductive afternoon. She had planned to barbeque steaks for dinner but decided that could wait. Although Grant had said he would arrive late, Rachel wanted to hear what he had to say first. Afterward, if everything went well, she would let him handle the outdoor grill while she prepared a salad. For now, she did not want to consider other possibilities.

After entering through the front door and setting her briefcase down, Rachel checked the mail, poured herself a glass of cabernet sauvignon, and turned on the television. She kicked off her shoes and placed her bare feet on the edge of the coffee table. As she nestled her head in the back cushion of the couch and closed her eyes, she attempted to relax. Despite Walter Cronkite's familiar voice on the CBS national news and the soothing effects of the wine, her mind kept drifting back to the brief conversation that had taken place a few hours earlier.

What did Grant mean when he said he would be late because "He had to deal with Michael?" Why did his tone sound like a blend of exasperation and sorrow? Something was *definitely* wrong. Rachel hoped it had nothing to do with the bombing of her parent's house, but her instincts suggested otherwise. Every time a car passed, she reached up to the window, drew back the curtain, and peered outside, searching for Grant's Honda.

Finally, Rachel heard a car door slam. As she saw Grant walking toward the apartment complex, her emotions were conflicted. Part of her longed to run into his arms, just like she used to do in the early days of their relationship. However, she also dreaded what he had to say. There was still enough daylight for Rachel to see his face as he approached the front steps, and she was taken aback by the worry lines etched between his eyebrows.

As Grant was accustomed to doing, he let himself into the apartment. Glancing around, he noticed Rachel lounging on the couch with a glass of wine in her hand and another glass waiting for him on the coffee table. Grant nodded with a faint smile and, in one fluid motion, circled the table, plopped down next to Rachel, picked up the wineglass, and gulped a sip like it was water in a desert. He reached over, mostly out of habit, touched her cheek and pulled her in for a kiss. Then, scanning the room, he sensed something was amiss.

"Did you want to go out for dinner?" he inquired.

"No," Rachel replied edgily, "I have some steaks for you to grill." After muting the TV and sipping her wine, she added, "But before we prepare dinner, we should talk."

Grant grimaced and nodded, indicating that he understood. Rachel sensed that something was wrong—something significant—and she wanted to address it before putting the steaks on the grill. After all, dinner might not happen if the situation was as serious as she suspected.

"What's going on?" Rachel asked. "I could tell something was bothering you when you called this afternoon. Can you share what it was?"

Grant gulped down more wine, nearly emptying his glass. He wiped his mouth and sank back into the plush cushions. Grant opened his mouth to speak but then hesitated. He was clearly struggling to find the right words, which only frustrated Rachel further. Finally, she broke the silence, aiming straight for the heart of the matter.

"It's Michael, isn't it?" she asked, frowning.

Once again, Rachel was met with silence. This time, she resolved to wait him out. Suddenly, Grant blurted out an answer in an unexpectedly loud voice.

"I just left the county jail," he announced. "Michael's been arrested."

Rachel looked up and let out a loud sigh. "What's he done this time?"

Before answering, Grant turned to face his girlfriend directly, inched closer, and took Rachel's hand in his. When he spoke, it was almost a whisper.

"Sweetheart, it's what you've suspected all along. Michael was the one who bombed your parents' house."

Although Rachel had long suspected Michael was involved in her worst nightmare, she was still caught off guard. For some reason, this was not what she had expected. She let her gaze drift toward the television. Realizing it was merely a distraction, she reached for the remote to turn it off. When Rachel finally turned to face her boyfriend, she surprisingly felt serene. Instead of expressing anger, she was overwhelmed by a wave of despair. Grant interpreted her silence as a cue to continue speaking.

"Remember how you offered to drop your suspicions of Michael if I'd search his room?" Without waiting for a response, he pressed on. "That night, after you fell asleep, I decided to search. I didn't find anything in his room, but before returning to bed, I decided to explore the shed in the backyard. Sure enough, I uncovered remnants of the fertilizer that Chuck had mentioned was used to make the bomb. I wanted to confront Michael before discussing it with anyone, so I didn't mention this to you the following day."

Rachel grabbed a Kleenex from the end table to dab what she thought was the moisture on her cheeks. Meanwhile, she continued to stare vacantly at her boyfriend's chest. Grant paused briefly but when she still did not respond, he decided to continue.

"When I confronted Michael later that night, he didn't hesitate to confess. He admitted that he'd built the bomb at a time when he was sympathetic to the Nazis. However, he also claimed—and I believe him—that he had a change of heart at the last minute and chose not to go through with it. Unfortunately, the Nazi Party had sent one of their thugs from Chicago to assist Michael. When my son refused to light the fuse, this guy punched him, knocking him out. His accomplice then lit the fuse and took off, leaving Michael unconscious on your parents' porch. If he had not woken up at the last minute, Michael would also have died in the explosion."

Rachel turned to face Grant, and for the first time, there was a trace of anger in her eyes. The scowl on her face made him stop his narration.

"Grant, are you suggesting this somehow absolves Michael for what he did?"

"*No*, of course not," Grant replied without hesitation. "He fully understands the seriousness of his actions. Michael did not argue when I told him he needed to turn himself in to the police. He's been arrested, and his bail is too high for me to secure his release."

"What about the Nazi thug from Chicago?" Rachel asked crossly. "Has he also been arrested?"

"According to Michael, this guy's dead. His name was Dale O'Connor, and he was killed by the police while holding up a convenience store. Michael just learned this during his trip to Chicago last weekend."

"*According* to Michael?"

Rachel tilted her face downward but maintained her gaze on Grant. Her expression conveyed that while she believed her boyfriend was sincere in sharing his story, he was also childishly naïve for accepting Michael's version of the facts so quickly.

"Not just Michael," Grant patiently explained. "Chuck also verified the story. There *really* was someone named Dale O'Connor who was recently shot by the police during an armed robbery in Chicago."

Rachel sighed deeply before continuing. "So, what happens next?" she finally asked.

"Michael's attorney," Grant answered, "Has suggested that if he pleads guilty, there are extenuating circumstances that might lighten his sentence."

Rachel shook her head and looked away in disbelief. This was the man she loved, someone she had thought would be her life partner. But now, he was discussing how to reduce the severity of his son's sentence.

Did Grant forget that Michael, driven by antisemitism, had built the bomb that destroyed her parents' home and killed her mother? Did it really matter who lit the fuse? Rachel felt torn between anger at Grant and pity for him. Either way, this did not bode well for their future. At that moment, all Rachel could do was echo Grant's words.

"Extenuating circumstances to lighten his sentence? What might those be?" Rachel's tone indicated she was treating Grant like a hostile witness. Still, he maintained his composure and responded patiently.

"For starters, there's his youth. His attorney told me that, in a case like this, the court will likely view Michael as an adult, not a juvenile. However, being only seventeen will still be a consideration. Second, and perhaps most importantly, is Michael's last-minute change of heart and his attempt to stop Dale, which nearly cost him his life. While Michael has no evidence to prove this point, he still tells a pretty convincing story. Lastly, Michael genuinely regrets his actions. While I don't expect you to forgive him, Rachel, he's ready to accept whatever punishment the judge gives him."

"Well, Grant, it's nice that you don't expect me to forgive your son for murdering my mother." Rachel's tone was jaded as well as sarcastic.

"No, of course, I don't," Grant replied, ignoring her mocking tone. "I just hope you can forgive *me*."

"Forgive *you*?" Rachel inquired in the same sardonic tone. "What? For ignoring all my warnings about your son? For not seeking therapy or counseling for that monster before it was too late? For being too blind and trusting to recognize what was happening right beneath your roof? Grant, if you had been more vigilant, there's a good chance Michael would soon be completing his senior year of high school, and my mother would still be *alive*."

As Rachel spoke, her voice grew louder, and her eyes squinted narrowly as if her gaze were a pair of guns aimed at her boyfriend. Her breathing began to quicken. Although seated on the couch, her posture became increasingly rigid, making her appear taller and bringing her to eye level with Grant.

Rachel's fury grew as she realized that even though Grant did not expect her to forgive Michael, *he*, apparently, was willing to do so. If excuses such as being young and misdirected were valid, then at least some blame should be directed at the parent, right? Her anger built up like magma rising in a volcano, poised to erupt.

Initially, she had aimed her wrath at Michael for his vile antisemitism and for building the bomb that killed her mother. However, the man who had fathered this killer was sitting right in front of her. Rachel knew that her boyfriend was not stupid. However, Grant's repeated denials and refusal to acknowledge what she had clearly seen had cost her mother's life.

Noticing the flush in Rachel's cheeks, the furrow in her brows, and the tension in her jaw, Grant decided to make a final appeal. He slid off the couch and knelt down on one knee. Taking Rachel's hand in his, he positioned himself as if he were about to propose.

"Rachel, you're absolutely right. I messed up, and I'm truly sorry. I did not supervise my son properly, and what he did was horrible. I wouldn't blame you if you never wanted to speak to him again. However, while my negligence as a parent played a role in what happened, can it be forgiven? From the bottom of my heart, Rachel, I apologize for my part in the bombing of your parents' house." After briefly pausing, he added, "Do you think you can forgive me?"

Rachel eyed her boyfriend suspiciously. "Grant, imagine a situation where the tavern that served a drunk driver saw him stagger out of the bar and did nothing to stop him from driving. After that driver causes a head-on collision that kills your parents, would you be able to forgive the bartender who served him?

Grant glanced away for a moment to process the hypothetical example. He casually glided back up to reclaim his seat on the couch but did not let go of Rachel's hand.

"Not right away," Grant finally replied, "But if the apology were truly heartfelt, I believe I would eventually."

"*Really*?" Rachel responded, raising an eyebrow skeptically. "Because the law wouldn't be so forgiving. Even though the bartender lacked criminal intent, he or his employer would be liable for negligence and be sued for all they were worth." Rachel paused before continuing. "I don't think I could be as forgiving as you, Grant. While you've never lost a parent due to someone else's gross carelessness, I have. That may put me in a better position to judge."

Grant nodded but remained silent. He understood what his girl-friend was saying but could not think of a response. Rachel then broke the silence.

"Grant, you mentioned an attorney. Is this someone you hired to represent Michael?"

Although he had started his update in a straightforward, news reporter style, Grant now lowered his eyes and bit his upper lip like a scolded child. Under different circumstances, Rachel might have even felt sorry for him.

"Yes," Grant replied sheepishly, "I hired an old college friend to rep-resent Michael."

Continuing in what sounded like a cross-examination, Rachel stated, "Michael just confessed to blowing up a house, which resulted in the murder of my mother and nearly killing my father. He did this solely because they were Jewish. Despite all this, you'll still do everything pos-sible to lessen his punishment?"

Grant shifted his gaze toward the front door, turning away from his girlfriend. He looked uneasy, like an animal trapped in a corner. How-ever, Rachel could sense that he was not ready to give up just yet. Instead, he glanced up as if he were contemplating a response. Over the past year, she had witnessed him behave this way during many of their "friendly" debates. Finally, he dropped Rachel's hand and turned to face her directly.

"Rachel, you know that the Constitution grants the right to an attor-ney to anyone charged with a crime. This right applies to every American citizen. Why should this be any different for my son?"

"It shouldn't," Rachel replied sharply, "But why do you feel the need to provide Michael with a lawyer? You said he would probably be charged as an adult, right? If so, why not let him take his chances with a public defender?"

In her mind, Rachel was beginning to formulate a response to Grant's request for forgiveness. If he wanted her to move past his failures as a father, then it was time for him to distance himself from his son. This was becoming non-negotiable.

"Because he's *my son*," Grant replied with increasing conviction. Rachel noticed tears gathering in the corners of his eyes.

"He's also a vicious, antisemitic murderer," Rachel argued, her temper rising. "Grant, your son built the bomb that violently hurled my mother, who was sound asleep at the time, across her bedroom, leaving her never to open her eyes again." Now, tears of anguish filled Rachel's eyes. "Isn't there a point where an evil becomes so heinous that forgiveness is impossible even from the offender's father?"

Grant gazed at his girlfriend with pleading eyes. He then reached for his wineglass on the table and drained the last few drops. In a voice that trembled as he visibly struggled to control his emotions, Grant methodically attempted to construct his own hypothetical situation.

"Rachel, I want you to take a moment to consider this scenario: What if Michael had nothing to do with the bombing? He goes off to college a year from now. In the meantime, you and I get married, and shortly after, we have a son of our own. For the next seventeen years, we dedicate every ounce of love we have to raising that child. I know you haven't had children yet, but can you imagine how powerful your feelings will be for that boy?"

Rachel nodded, feeling her anger starting to simmer down. She remained silent, curious to see where this was going.

"Let's give our son a name," Grant continued. "Let's call him Benjamin, after your father. I know that in your faith, you're not supposed to name a baby after someone who's still alive, but let's assume we've agreed to make an exception. After all, I know you worship your dad, and I also hold him in the highest regard. So little Benjamin becomes our mutual pride and joy."

Rachel nodded again, encouraging Grant to continue. As he wove more details into his narrative, Rachel was reminded of how effectively he could employ his journalistic storytelling skills off the cuff. She had always admired this talent.

"In his early years, young Benjamin is likable and charming. He's also remarkably precocious, as you'd expect from any of our offspring."

A faint smile briefly crossed Rachel's face. She quickly suppressed it, however, as she believed this was not the right time for humor.

"Unfortunately," Grant continued, "Benjamin falls in with the wrong crowd in high school. Like all teenagers, he just wants to fit in, but in this case, his social circle is made up of a group of ignorant racists. Before long, despite everything we've tried to teach him, Benjamin begins to adopt some of their bigoted beliefs. You know how teenagers can be, right? We've all been that age. They're just trying to make sense of the world, but some can take dangerously wrong turns along the way."

"Anyhow, some refugees from, let's say, a war-torn African nation settle in Bloomington. Benjamin and his gang decide to send them an ugly message that they're not welcome. And, of course, our brilliant son will be the one who devises the explosive that'll send the message. Moreover, to prove his courage, Benjamin volunteers to light the fuse that ultimately kills a mother in one of these immigrant families."

Rachel nods, her eyes widening. By now, she clearly understands the purpose behind Grant's scenario and is already preparing an answer to the question she knows is coming.

"Rachel, our son has just committed a brutal murder. Will you disown him? This is the child you bore and raised for seventeen years. Are you ready to turn your back on him? Let him take his chances with a public defender? Let him rot in jail? As a parent, I can tell you it's easy to love them when they excel in school or win trophies. It's when they screw up that your love gets tested. Rachel, this is when they'll need you the most. And the worse they mess up, the more they'll need you. Even after Benjamin has committed a horrible crime and will likely spend a significant part of his life in prison, can you really imagine not forgiving him?"

Rachel sank back into the plush cushions of her sofa, momentarily gazing at her dark gray reflection on the opaque television screen. She understood Grant's point but quickly dismissed it. Yes, Rachel could envision herself as a mother, ideally in the near future. However, there was one crucial element that Grant had omitted from his imaginary narrative. Should she bring this to his attention? If she did, it might feel like plunging a knife deep into his heart.

What she said next could either lead to marriage or end her best chance. She glanced at Grant out of the corner of her eye; he was patiently waiting for her response to his scenario. When Grant had asked how easy it would be for her to turn her back on their hypothetical son, he hadn't meant it as a rhetorical question—he clearly expected an answer.

Several images flashed through Rachel's mind: aging photographs from Sobibor, media images of Nazi marches in Chicago, her parents' house with what she imagined to be a swastika painted on its facade, the shredded remnants of their home after it was bombed, her comatose mother lying in an ICU bed, and finally, her mom's heart-wrenching funeral. Was there any way Rachel could spend her life with a man who stood by the Nazi murderer of her mother? Even more troubling, could she co-parent children with the person who had raised such a monster?

Rachel slowly turned to face her boyfriend. She licked her dry lips and inhaled deeply, pausing for a moment to gather her thoughts before responding. Even though Rachel was about to end their relationship, she wanted to express her feelings without animosity.

"Grant, I understand that it would not be easy to abandon our son if he were charged with a racially motivated murder. However, I can confidently tell you that I would never find myself in that position. Little Benjamin, as you refer to him, the son I raised, would never grow up to commit such a monstrous crime. Why? Because my values would be deeply instilled within him, and our connection would be so strong that I would know what he was up to even before he realized it."

Grant slowly shook his head. He shrugged but remained silent. Rachel noticed his deep-seated doubt reflected in the way he lifted his eyebrows, tightened his lips, and deeply inflated his lungs. The tension between them was rising like a cake in the oven. Rachel sensed that Grant was processing her words and possibly trying to come up with a response. Then, without uttering a word, he stood up, circled the coffee table, and walked out the front door. Grant never looked back. Neither of them realized at that moment that nearly thirty years would pass before they spoke again.

CHAPTER 19

BENJAMIN

October 1977

Dinner had been delicious, but Benjamin had barely noticed. Before grilling the steak to perfection, Rachel had marinated it in a homemade peppercorn sauce. She had become quite the cook. Rachel had learned the basics at her mother's apron, yet her willingness to blend creativity with traditional recipes had carried her far beyond Miriam's blintzes, borscht, and brisket. And although his daughter had invested considerable time preparing their Sunday night dinner, Benjamin's mind was elsewhere.

Their conversation at the kitchen table had mainly focused on such topics as Rachel's job, the shoe sales at Benjamin's store, and even the weather. There were also several long stretches of silence. Benjamin and his daughter were content to talk about anything except the topic that weighed heavily on both of their minds: tomorrow's sentencing hearing for Michael. The boy had fully confessed to his crime and had pleaded for the court's mercy. However, before the judge handed down a sentence, the prosecution requested a member of the family to provide a victim impact statement that would detail the long-term effects of the bombing.

Both Benjamin and Rachel welcomed the chance to discuss the consequences of Michael's crime: the loss of a beloved wife and mother, the destruction of a home filled with cherished mementos, and the psychological impact that was already evident in nightmares and deep periods of despair. Although neither openly expressed it, Benjamin suspected they both harbored a desire for at least some revenge. They called it a need to seek "justice," but deep down, it was really about getting some sort of retribution.

Benjamin appreciated that Rachel had chosen not to discuss the bombing during dinner. It had been the focal point of countless conversations in the past, and although he would soon have to address it officially on the witness stand, he felt there was nothing new to add tonight. Now, however, he was having second thoughts. As they stood side by side at the sink—one washing the dishes while the other dried—an invisible barrier seemed to have descended between them. At one point, Benjamin glanced over and caught Rachel looking back; they both forced a smile. He could sense that his daughter was uncomfortable with the silence. Perhaps it might help to talk about tomorrow, but Benjamin still hesitated to broach the subject.

After placing the last dish in the cabinet, they followed their usual routine and moved to the living room to watch television. Benjamin's favorite show was *60 Minutes*, so Rachel grabbed the remote, turned on the TV, and switched the channel to CBS, all without uttering a word. For the next ten minutes, they both watched in silence. However, since Benjamin now found it as difficult to concentrate on Mike Wallace's words as he had on the earlier steak, his gaze drifted toward a photograph on the end table.

The picture showed Rachel flanked by her parents. Benjamin recalled how Grant had volunteered to take the photograph last spring. It had been a warm day in April, so they moved outside to sit on the front porch. Now, Benjamin could not help but grin at the irony. Tomorrow, he was scheduled to testify under oath about the tragic consequences that had arisen from the photographer's son building a bomb. This bomb had destroyed the front porch and resulted in the death of one of the three people in the picture.

Suddenly, the television screen went blank. Benjamin awoke from his stupor and turned to face his daughter, who held the remote control like a smoking pistol just fired in a duel. Rachel was staring directly at her father, her eyes wide and her lips drawn slightly together.

"Alright, Dad," she pronounced, "I can always tell when something's on your mind. Right now, you seem like you're about to explode. What's bothering you? Let me guess: your testimony tomorrow?"

Benjamin glanced back at the photograph, momentarily at a loss for words. When he turned back to face his daughter, he spoke so softly that he could barely be heard.

"I had a nightmare last night."

"Well, that's only natural," Rachel replied, adopting a more compassionate tone. After briefly pausing, she added, "You should mention this tomorrow on the witness stand. Tell the court about how you hardly sleep, and when you finally do, nightmares like this torment you."

Benjamin looked at his daughter and slowly shook his head. "This nightmare wasn't about the bombing. It was about something that happened long ago, something I thought was buried in the past."

"Do you think there's a connection between this memory and the recent bombing you'll be testifying about tomorrow?" Rachel asked.

"No," Benjamin replied immediately. Then, wavering, he added, "Well, maybe. But I've been thinking about this dream all day."

"Do you still remember the dream?" Rachel inquired. "I always forget mine, even the scary ones."

"Yes, I remember every detail. Normally, I'm like you; my dreams fade quickly. But this one won't leave me alone."

"Alright," Rachel replied, "Tell me about your dream. Maybe it'll help you feel better."

Benjamin leaned forward and rested his elbows on his knees. He buried his face in his palms while inhaling deeply. After a moment, he sat up straight and turned to face his daughter.

"This won't be easy," he whispered.

"Just tell me, Dad. I'm sure it'll become easier once you begin."

"Alright," Benjamin agreed. "I'll start by describing the actual dream, but I warn you, it'll sound pretty meshuggener."

A slight smile crossed Rachel's face at the mention of one of her father's favorite Yiddish words. Meanwhile, Benjamin paused as he tried to figure out how to proceed. Finally, he recalled a line that had dominated his dream.

"Have you heard the saying, 'What goes around comes around'?"

"Yes," Rachel answered, "It generally means that if you mistreat someone, you'll eventually encounter a similar fate. It's kind of like karma, isn't it?"

"Yes," Benjamin confirmed, "Well, in my dream, a teenage boy I once knew named Aleksy kept repeating that expression over and over: 'What goes around comes around.' He would point at me each time, grinning and jumping around like a madman. I tried to run away, but I couldn't move. His voice grew louder each time he repeated those words until he was practically shouting. Eventually, Aleksy began to laugh hysterically while screaming that same phrase, until finally, I awoke in a puddle of sweat."

"Wow," Rachel exclaimed, shaking her head, "That does sound pretty meshuggener. Also, scary. But, Dad, who was Aleksy? What was he talking about? Did you do something to him in the past that might make him want to get even?"

"Yes," Benjamin admitted, nodding, "I did. And I've never shared this with anyone before." After briefly pausing, he added, "Please understand that this is not easy to talk about."

Rachel nodded with raised eyebrows, remaining silent and patiently waiting for her dad to continue. After a moment, he cleared his throat and went on.

"The last time I saw Aleksy, he was mute and staring blankly into space. He couldn't even maintain eye contact. You see, the boy had suffered a severe brain injury."

Rachel's eyes widened, and she raised a hand to cover her mouth. "*Really?*" After a brief pause, she continued, "So, now we've reached the part that's difficult for you to talk about, haven't we? Dad, what happened to Aleksy? And," she added hesitantly, "What role did you play in this story."

Benjamin nodded while glancing up at Rachel. Initially, he smiled at how quickly his daughter could assemble a puzzle. Then, as he thought back forty-three years, Benjamin's smile faded.

"To understand what happened to Aleksy," Benjamin began, adopting his story-telling mode, "You need to know about the political situation in Poland in the early 1930s. The land where I grew up lacked natural barriers and was sandwiched between two giant neighbors: Germany on the west and Russia to the east. As a result, it frequently disappeared from the map. After the First World War, the peace treaty signed in Paris revived Poland, and for a time, we actually lived under a republican form of government."

"I'm aware of all this," Rachel affirmed. "I teach history for a living, remember?"

Benjamin smiled at his daughter's chutzpah. "Okay, Miss Smarty-Pants, do you also know about the ONR?"

"No . . ." Rachel admitted, "You got me there."

"I'll spare you the Polish words that the three letters represent. In English, ONR stood for the National Radical Camp, a fascist movement known for its extreme patriotism and, as you might guess, antisemitism."

"I get it," Rachel replied, clearly pleased that the conversation had returned to a regular tone. "The same applies to the term 'Nazi.' Each letter stands for a German word that translates to 'National Socialist German Workers' Party.'" After a brief pause, she continued, "Dad, I know that fascist movements emerged in many countries during the Great Depression, including here in the United States."

Benjamin nodded as he recalled how he had begun discussing history with his daughter shortly after she learned to talk. Their conversations about the past flowed so easily that it often felt like they shared a single mind. These talks had always been among Benjamin's favorite activities, and he believed they had played a role in Rachel's decision to become a history professor.

"Well," he continued, "In 1934 when I was just nineteen, the ONR had become such a threat that the government officially banned the organization. However, it had already become a movement, especially among younger people in cities like Warsaw. I knew a group of Poles from the Academy who had formed an ONR brigade in a neighborhood that bordered the Jewish Quarter. They soon made it a practice to patrol the streets at night, looking for Jews to terrorize."

Rachel leaned back into the sofa's soft cushions. She nodded occasionally, as she often did during these conversations, signaling that her father should continue.

One night, an ONR gang came upon a boy named David. He was the younger brother of Saul, who'd been my best friend since childhood. Since he was only twelve years old, David should never have been outside after dark, but he'd gone to visit his Bubbe and stayed too late. This gang, consisting of maybe half a dozen members, began to beat him with clubs. After he fell, they continued to kick him with their jackboots. This was how these ONR squads typically operated: they would challenge one another to do terrible things they'd never do alone.

Rachel nodded but stayed silent, waiting for her dad to continue. Noticing this, he quickly resumed where he had left off.

"A short while later, Saul and I found David's body. His mother was worried when he didn't come home, so she sent us out into the night to search for him. He was so badly beaten that, at first, we couldn't tell who it was. A pool of blood encircled his head like a red halo."

Benjamin paused, still unsettled by the memory. Then, speaking almost in a whisper, he continued recounting his story.

"After the funeral, several friends joined Saul and me as we walked home from the cemetery. One of them, Isaac, suggested that we stop in a café to discuss how we should respond to David's murder. It's important to understand that we had all gone through school together, and even though some of us had jobs while others, like me, were pursuing college degrees, we still maintained a close bond. We belonged to a Jewish community in Poland that had endured for a thousand years, largely because, in difficult times, Jews typically came together to support one another. With the rise of the ONR, this appeared to be another one of those difficult times."

Benjamin paused to catch his breath. After clearing his throat and inhaling deeply, he continued.

"Isaac said he knew who was responsible for David's death. He told us that his older cousin, Bernard, who lived in an upstairs apartment on the street where the beating occurred, had heard the commotion and glanced out his window. Although it was dark, there was still enough light from a front porch to see what the older Polish boys were doing to David. Bernard said he recognized their leader, a young man named Bartek, whom everyone knew. After all, we had once attended the same academy."

"So, what did you guys decide to do?" Rachel asked. By then, she was fully absorbed in her father's story.

"It was clear that we needed to get even," Benjamin replied. "We were all aware of the saying from the Book of Exodus: 'Eye for eye, tooth for tooth, hand for hand, foot for foot.' Furthermore, we agreed that we needed to send a strong message to these Polish hooligans to ensure that they'd leave us alone."

Benjamin recognized that his tone had become harsher. He swallowed hard and paused long enough to calm himself. Finally, he spoke in a more conciliatory voice.

"At first, it was suggested we catch Bartek when he was alone. Someone knew the route he took each morning to his job at the butcher's shop. We never discussed how far we'd go with his beating, but it was understood Bartek would pay with his life for the one he'd taken. Then, someone pointed out that Bartek's gang had targeted Saul's little brother rather than one of us and that we should do the same."

Rachel drew in a deep breath and frowned. She realized that Aleksy was about to enter the story.

"I mentioned that, like Saul, Bartek had a younger brother named Aleksy, who was around fourteen. Someone in the group said they knew him and that he had been attending ONR rallies with his older brother. We didn't have to take a vote. Everyone agreed that the best way to avenge David's murder would be to go after Bartek's younger brother. We intended to ambush Alesky the following morning as he made his way to the Academy."

Rachel's eyes narrowed, her nose wrinkling. "So, is that what you did?" Benjamin felt a wave of shame wash over him as he saw the distress on his daughter's face.

"Yes," Benjamin whispered. "It was raining. Hard. When Alesky turned a corner, we pulled him into a back alley and circled him like a school of sharks. Then, one at a time, we swung our clubs. The first blow landed on the side of Aleksy's face, knocking him to the ground. When it was my turn, I aimed for his midsection but didn't use my full strength. I might've broken one of his ribs, but I just didn't have the guts to go for his skull. Others did, however, and soon, just like David, a red puddle had gathered around his head. Finally, when Aleksy had stopped moving, I tapped Saul's shoulder and suggested we go. This wasn't a Jewish neighborhood, and with the rain letting up, it was only a matter of time before we were spotted."

Rachel turned her gaze from her dad. Though she had been brought up to despise antisemitism, a look of disgust now crossed her face.

"I know," Benjamin mumbled. "What we did to Aleksy was appalling. It didn't bring Saul's little brother back to life. Instead, there were now two dead boys rather than one. Except in this case, Aleksy wasn't dead. Not quite, at least. When I later saw him in a public square, he trailed after his mother like a toddler. I heard he no longer spoke and could only respond to simple questions by nodding or shaking his head."

Rachel pressed her lips together. She could see the pain etched on her father's face. "Whatever happened to Aleksy?"

"I'm not sure," Benjamin replied. "As the situation for the Jews in Warsaw worsened, we started to keep mostly to our own neighborhoods. I met my first wife at the university, and after we graduated, we left the city and moved in with her parents in a small town to the east. You know the rest of the story. As for Aleksy, the Nazis likely sent him to one of the same death camps where they sent the Jews. After all, their concept of a master race didn't include people with his disability."

As Rachel's expression slowly changed from disgust to concern, she pondered a question that would redirect the conversation back to the present.

"So, Dad, in your dream, when that boy kept screaming, 'What goes around comes around,' do you think this was your subconscious telling you that Mom's death was your punishment for what you did to Aleksy?"

Benjamin turned to look directly at his daughter. His eyebrows arched as he drew in a deep breath, and his lower lip dropped, revealing several gold fillings. Benjamin gently rubbed both cheeks while he considered Rachel's question. He answered softly, in words that were barely audible.

"At first, Alesky's beating didn't bother me. As I said before, it was an eye for an eye, you know? But later, seeing that boy staggering across that square left an image I've never forgotten. He was the hollowed shell of his former self, and we had done that to him. Maybe it wouldn't have bothered me so much if we had only gone after Bartek, but as far as I know, Aleksy never had anything to do with David's murder. Why did he have to suffer because of what Bartek did?"

After pausing to turn away from Rachel and glance down at the floor, Benjamin added, "I've been thinking about that dream all day. And, yes, the thought has crossed my mind that your mother's murder is a punishment for my role in beating Alesky over forty years ago. What did you call it? Karma?"

Benjamin continued to stare downward, unable to face Rachel. He could never remember feeling so ashamed in front of his daughter.

"Over the years," he continued, "I've tried hard not to think about Aleksy. As you know, your mother and I survived the nightmare of Sobibor. Later, in this country, we started a business, brought you into the world, and built a life we were both proud of. Pretty soon, I could go days and even weeks without thinking about Aleksy. But every now and then, I'd see someone who looked like him, and that disturbing feeling would return—just like it did last night when I woke up from my dream."

"*Wow*," Rachel exclaimed. "I had no idea you ever did anything like this. I can see why it still haunts you."

Then, Rachel did something Benjamin did not expect. She reached out and pulled her father into a hug. For a moment, they rested their heads on each other's shoulders. When they finally drew back, Benjamin reached up to wipe his grizzled cheeks. Noticing this, Rachel said words intended to make her father feel better.

"You were *young*, Dad. The adult you've become now needs to forgive the young man you were back then."

"I wasn't *that* young," Benjamin automatically countered. "I was nineteen. Not long ago, there were men of the same age from this country who were fighting, killing, and dying every day in the rice paddies of Vietnam. They were old enough to understand what they're doing."

Initially, Rachel nodded in agreement but then smiled as a rebuttal came to mind.

"That's true, Dad. However, I've known toddlers with more maturity than some of the nineteen-year-olds in my history classes." Then, after her smile faded, she added, "But if one of my students makes a serious mistake now, should he still feel guilty about it in forty years?"

Gazing into his daughter's eyes, Benjamin, as if struck by lightning, suddenly realized what he would say on the stand tomorrow. His scowl melted away, replaced by a faint smile.

"What?" Rachel asked, her head tilting back in surprise. "Why are you smiling?"

"I've got to go," Benjamin answered.

"Why? It's still early."

"There's something I must do. And it has to be tonight."

As Benjamin stood up, his daughter did the same. She reached out to turn her father so she could face him directly.

"Wait, before you go, Dad, tell me how your nightmare relates to your testimony tomorrow. You're not going to do something meshuggener, are you?"

Benjamin gently broke free and moved toward the front door. His slight smile had blossomed into a full grin as he turned back to face her. "Meshuggener? Maybe. But I'll just be repeating what you told me tonight. Good night, Bubala, and thank you for the delicious dinner."

Without waiting for a response, Benjamin opened the door and stepped out into the chilly night. Behind him, Rachel's jaw dropped, leaving her speechless as her father vanished.

Five minutes later, Benjamin was sitting at his desk, loading a clean sheet of paper into his Smith-Corona typewriter. It took him nearly two hours to complete his project. Although the final document was only a couple of pages long, he restarted it several times because he wanted every word to be perfect. When Benjamin finally finished, he unfurled the document, read it aloud, and then prepared for bed, feeling fully satisfied with his work. This time, there was no nightmare to disturb his sleep.

Benjamin awoke early the next day, long before his alarm. He took a shower, shaved, and dressed in his best suit. After that, he poured himself a bowl of cereal, which he washed down with a glass of orange juice and a couple of cups of black coffee. He attempted to read *The Pantagraph* but found it difficult to concentrate on the news. Instead, he picked up the statement he had written the night before and reread it several times. Smiling to himself, he folded the pages and stashed them in the upper pocket of his sports coat. A few minutes later, Rachel knocked on his door to drive him to the courthouse.

During the ten-minute ride, Rachel tried to engage her dad in conversation a couple of times, but he was in no mood to talk. While the silence, particularly at red lights, might have felt awkward to many, it was not uncomfortable for a father and daughter with such a strong bond. They each got lost in their thoughts, knowing that the best time to discuss them would be after the sentencing hearing. Rachel parked in a nearby lot, and the two gingerly darted across Main Street and entered the modern, rectangular courthouse. Benjamin and Rachel had deliberately arrived early to avoid any media fanfare that might later occur on the court's front steps.

Once inside the courtroom, Benjamin and Rachel were greeted by Earl Saxon, the prosecutor handling the case, who led them to a bench directly behind the prosecution table. Earl explained that the procedure was simple. Once the judge called the court into session, he would invite the prosecution to call its witnesses. They had previously agreed to make Benjamin their only witness. As the primary victim, Benjamin could clearly articulate their reasons for seeking the harshest possible sentence.

Benjamin nervously surveyed the room, which was surprisingly plain. A few vertical windows on one side admitted angular beams of sunlight. At the front of the room, the seal of Illinois looked down upon the judge's empty desk, flanked by the American and Illinois state flags. Although the room could accommodate about fifty spectators, the benches in the gallery were mostly empty for now. To the side, the jury box resembled those seen in the movies, but Benjamin knew that, for today's hearing, it would remain vacant.

A few minutes later, Grant entered through the rear door and took a seat directly behind the defense table. Wearing a sports coat and tie, he appeared anxious. Benjamin glanced in his direction, and Grant sheepishly smiled and gave a slight wave. Benjamin politely nodded back. Meanwhile, his daughter stared straight ahead at the judge's empty seat, ignoring anyone on the other side of the courtroom. A county deputy escorted Michael through a side entrance near the jury box and led him to the defense table, where he was met by a man Benjamin did not recognize. Although Michael seemed uncomfortable in his coat and tie, he quickly relaxed once the deputy removed his handcuffs.

A short time later, the bailiff asked everyone to rise as the judge entered the courtroom. Once seated, the judge banged his gavel, declared the court in session, and briefly outlined the day's procedure for the spectators, who now filled every available seat. The judge, a surprisingly young man with a full head of black hair still free of any gray, explained that the defendant had previously entered a guilty plea. Having already reviewed Michael's presentence report, the judge would now listen to the testimonies of any victims the prosecution chose to call. By the end of the session, the judge stated he would be ready to pronounce Michael's sentence.

Shortly thereafter, the prosecutor called Benjamin to the stand. Once seated and sworn in, Mr. Saxon began with questions to identify the witness and establish his role as a victim. Benjamin asserted that he was asleep in his home at the time when the bomb exploded and that he was, in fact, the husband of the deceased victim. Next, the prosecutor sign-posted that he would ask questions about what would constitute a fair and reasonable punishment for the defendant. At that moment, Benjamin surprised everyone by raising his hand, turning toward the judge, and courteously asking for permission to read a prepared statement.

The judge was caught off guard but quickly agreed to the request, wishing to give the victim as much latitude as possible. Benjamin then retrieved the document securely nestled in his coat pocket. He unfolded it and cleared his throat. An awkward silence filled the chamber as he scanned the room. His brow was furrowed, his jaw tense, and his lips pressed tightly together.

Before starting to read, Benjamin glanced at Michael and his father, who was seated directly behind him. A hush fell over the packed courtroom as everyone strained to hear what the witness had to say. Benjamin looked down at the papers in his hand and noticed they were trembling from nervousness. Fortunately, because he had read and rehearsed it so many times, he was able to look up, take a deep breath, and speak from memory in a clear, distinct voice.

"Your Honor, we both know what Mr. Saxon wants me to say. If we continue with his questions, he will ask me to speak about the pain I've endured as a result of the defendant's actions. Until last night, that's exactly what I intended to do; believe me, it would be easy since the bomb made by this defendant cost me my beloved wife, my home, and the happiness we'd built after surviving the Nazi genocide. However, after a conversation with my daughter last evening, I've had a change of heart. Now, I want my impact statement to focus on something entirely different."

As Benjamin paused to catch his breath, he noticed several people in the audience murmuring to one another, surprised by the new direction his testimony was taking. Now that he had moved past the preliminaries, though, Benjamin was ready to delve into the heart of his statement.

"Your Honor," he continued, "Mark Twain once wrote, 'Life would be infinitely happier if we could only be born at the age of eighty and gradually approach eighteen.' Think about that for a moment. As I've grown older, I think about it all the time. It can take a lifetime to gain true wisdom, but when we're young, we often fail to realize how foolish we truly are."

Benjamin looked around the courtroom, noticing mostly blank faces. Although it was not in his written statement, he decided to reference a more recent source.

"I heard a song the other day on the car radio while driving with my daughter, and it's on my mind now because it's relevant to the point I want to make. I believe the singer was a young man named Bob Dylan. Perhaps you've heard of him?"

Benjamin understood Bob Dylan's iconic status in American popular culture. However, he took pleasure in watching how his feigned ignorance brought smiles and nods throughout the courtroom.

"The song, which I later learned is called *My Back Pages*, kept repeating, 'Ah, but I was so much older then, I'm younger than that now.' Do you understand what I'm trying to say? When we're young, we believe we know everything, but it's only as we grow older that we realize just how little we truly understood. You might be wondering why I'm bringing this up now."

The witness glanced at Michael. "I'll tell you why. This defendant was young and foolish when he committed his crime. Michael Parker was consumed by the same rage and passion that often comes with youth. While this doesn't excuse the terrible crime he committed, I don't believe he deserves the same punishment as someone who is twice his age."

Benjamin paused again, this time deliberately. Every face in the courtroom was fixated on him, anxiously awaiting his next words. He allowed the silence to linger for a few seconds.

"Last night, I was reminded that I, too, was once young and foolish. When I was only two years older than this young man and living in Poland, I also did something I regretted. However, unlike the defendant, I was never caught or punished. I was fortunate. Given a second chance, I had the opportunity to marry, raise a wonderful daughter, and grow older and wiser."

"My point is not that Michael Parker shouldn't be held accountable; rather, his age should be seriously considered when determining his punishment. The defendant was only seventeen when he committed his crime. He still has the rest of his life to gain the wisdom that comes with age. One day, he will likely reflect on his actions with regret, just like many of us who have committed unfortunate deeds in our youth."

Silence filled the chamber. Benjamin was not sure if everyone agreed with his sentiments, but a few heads nodded while others appeared to be considering his point. Encouraged by this reaction, he decided to move forward with the second idea that had come to him the night before.

"When I was just nineteen, I contributed to the hatred that existed between two groups sharing the same community. Even though I was part of a minority that had faced unwavering prejudice for centuries, my actions only added fuel to the fire. We've seen this many times throughout history. Consider the Jews and Palestinians trying to coexist in Israel, the conflict between Hindus and Muslims on the Asian subcontinent, or the battles currently raging in Northern Ireland. Each death leads to a desire for revenge, perpetuating the cycle. How long will this continue? Will the hatred ever come to an end?"

Benjamin paused and glanced at his daughter, who was slowly shaking her head. He then turned toward the judge, remembering that this was the only audience member who mattered.

"You've probably heard the quote from Mohandas Gandhi—'An eye for an eye makes the whole world blind.' When I was seventeen, I wouldn't have thought much about that saying, but, as I've mentioned, with age comes wisdom. Part of me still yearns for this boy to be sent to prison for the rest of his natural life, but that desire for revenge only fosters more hatred. It's time for this cycle of hate to end. I'm sure Miriam, my wife, would agree with me if she were still alive."

Benjamin had reached the moment when he was ready to make his request formally. He hesitated as he scanned the room. His daughter, who now fully understood what was coming, had glassy eyes and was biting her lower lip. Sitting behind his son like a shadow, Grant wore the same expectant expression as Michael. Finally, Benjamin returned his gaze to the judge, the one person in the courtroom who held Michael's fate in his hands.

"Therefore, Your Honor," Benjamin solemnly pronounced, "I urge you to show mercy to the defendant. I know the prosecution wanted me to talk about the pain this boy inflicted upon my family and me, but that would've just been stating the obvious. As you determine Michael's sentence, I ask you to keep my two points in mind: first, please consider his age, and second, understand that this is my way of advocating for an end to a timeless hatred."

Benjamin was surprised to see the judge nodding subtly. Then, the prosecutor abruptly broke the silence by announcing that he had no further questions. Benjamin assumed this meant he realized there was nothing else he could ask that would lead to the harsher sentence he sought. It was also no surprise that Michael's lawyer also had no questions. Benjamin was excused from the witness stand, and the court was recessed for thirty minutes. The judge retreated to his chambers to contemplate his final decision.

Benjamin approached his daughter with a sense of trepidation. She wore a pained expression, with tears still visible beneath her eyes. In moments like this, Benjamin often struggled to determine if his daughter was angry or just emotionally exhausted. As he drew closer, Rachel rushed toward him and wrapped her arms around her father's neck. She then whispered the words he longed to hear. "Daddy, you did the right thing. Mom would be so proud."

The commotion in the courtroom resembled the intermission of a play. While others moved around to use the restroom or gathered for conversations, Benjamin and his daughter sat on the front bench, waiting for the court to reconvene. Lost in his thoughts, Benjamin's attention gradually drifted to his right, where he noticed Grant huddling with his son. Then, to his surprise, Grant briefly looked up, and their eyes met. Although Benjamin was never good at reading lips, this time, he clearly recognized the words: "Thank you." He nodded, acknowledging their shared bond, and then both men returned to focusing on their children.

A half-hour later, the judge reentered the courtroom. He banged his gavel, reconvened the court, and announced that he was ready to pronounce the sentence. A stillness filled the room. Although Benjamin was not an attorney, he understood the significance of his recent testimony. He was the only one who had asked the judge for mercy; even the boy had not tried to lessen his own sentence. Michael had not attempted to negotiate a deal, known as a plea bargain in the American courts. He did not offer any other names, call character witnesses on his behalf, or even take the stand to apologize and request leniency. Instead, he had simply thrown himself at the mercy of the court.

The judge spoke briefly before announcing Michael's sentence. His reasoning largely echoed Benjamin's words, possibly foreshadowing a lighter punishment. Then came the pronouncement everyone anxiously awaited: twenty years with the possibility of parole. Michael nodded slowly, his expression remaining neutral. In contrast, Benjamin shook his head in disappointment, the corners of his mouth drooping; he had hoped for less.

With the final bang of his gavel, the judge adjourned the court. Suddenly, chaos erupted as everyone stood at once, and a loud buzz filled the room. Benjamin also rose and scanned the courtroom. The prosecutor was packing his briefcase and appeared to be muttering to himself. Grant was attempting to catch the words of the man standing next to Michael, both of them grinning. Meanwhile, a deputy was placing handcuffs on Michael's wrists, preparing to lead him away to his new life in an Illinois state penitentiary.

Suddenly, Benjamin felt a gentle tug on his shoulder and turned to face his daughter. Rachel gazed up at him with an expression he couldn't decipher. Benjamin realized it would take time for both of them to process what had happened in court that day and even longer to come to terms with everything that had transpired since the night of the bombing. As they approached the exit, Rachel took her father's arm to guide him out of the courtroom. She never glanced back at the defendant's father.

CHAPTER 20

MICHAEL

November 2005

It was an unexpectedly mild, spring-like day for a November burial. When Dad called last night, we decided it would be best to skip the service at Moses Montefiore Temple and go straight to the cemetery. After all, we hadn't been in contact with their family for many years. Since this was the Friday after Thanksgiving, I didn't need to take a day off from work. However, instead of bringing my family to Eastland Mall for our holiday shopping tradition, I found myself at a funeral. To brighten the day, Dad offered to serve leftovers from yesterday's Thanksgiving meal for lunch.

The surrounding countryside was mostly barren as I drove the forty miles south on Interstate 55 from Pontiac to Bloomington. Occasionally, I spotted a tractor in the distance churning corn stalks into the rich soil. The sun blazed brightly to the east, and even my sunglasses couldn't cut the glare. Driving my recently purchased Honda Civic into a steady headwind, feeling its warmth spread across the flat prairies, I popped in Bruce Springsteen's Greatest Hits CD and cranked up the volume. As I thought about the upcoming funeral, I found myself reflecting on some of the highlights of my life since the day in court when I last saw Benjamin Abramowicz.

My first days in the Pontiac Correctional Center were a nightmare. I'd heard stories about new fish being targeted as fresh prey and soon learned that this was no myth. Fortunately, my cellmate wasn't a threat because he was as new and terrified as I was. On the first night, the screams and catcalls kept us from getting much sleep. The next morning at breakfast, a giant with crazy blond hair and swastikas tattooed on both forearms approached me. He claimed he knew who I was and what I'd done.

This goliath, resembling the wrestler Dusty Rhodes, invited me to join his Aryan Brotherhood, saying they'd provide me with full-time protection. Not knowing how to respond, I must've looked like a deer caught in the headlights. However, I soon found myself surrounded by other members of the Brotherhood, like a quarterback guarded by a towering team of offensive linemen. They treated me like their quarterback, too. The Aryans were all aware of my involvement in the bombing, and if we'd been in a bar, they likely would have lined up to buy me a beer. I suppose this was the family Dale mentioned when we first met on the bus.

On the second night, the racket subsided a bit, and I was able to get some sleep. My cellmate, who I later learned had been gang-raped in the shower, soon became the bitch of an inmate who at least protected him from everyone else. Meanwhile, I was left alone. As the days went by, I fell into a routine: I attended classes in the morning and worked in a massive kitchen in the afternoons, preparing dinner for over a thousand men. It didn't take long for me to settle into a daily rhythm.

Nevertheless, it was impossible to be happy with this arrangement. The Aryan Brotherhood eventually accepted my aloofness, but since I genuinely wanted to atone for my sins on the outside, it felt wrong to accept their protection on the inside. When I finally opened up about this dilemma to my father, who was faithfully driving eighty miles round trip to visit me every week, he offered some helpful advice. Dad said that *asking* the Brotherhood for help would've been wrong. However, since they provided it without me saying a word, I shouldn't feel guilty about accepting their help. He advised me to avoid them as much as possible, to keep to myself, and to look for opportunities to make the best of a difficult situation.

That's exactly what I did, although it wasn't always easy. In July 1978, for instance, at the start of my second year in Pontiac, the worst riot in the prison's history erupted. Scores of inmates and guards were injured, several buildings were damaged or destroyed, and three correctional officers were killed. When the chaos started, I calmly found a table in the chow hall and climbed beneath it, just like in a school duck-and-cover drill. I realize it doesn't present the most heroic image, but it kept me safe and out of trouble.

By the end of the first year, I earned my high school diploma. Although it took another five years, I secured a college degree through a partnership program with Illinois State University. With a double major in corrections and counseling, my long-term goal was to use my past experiences to help others who ended up in places like Pontiac. I also kept my nose clean. After a few years, I transitioned from preparing dinners in the kitchen to tutoring in the prison's literacy program. Finally, after ten years, I successfully qualified for parole on my first attempt.

Once freed, I found work as a counselor at the same place where I'd spent the last ten years. And, with my father's help, I purchased a two-bedroom trailer in Lexington, a tiny hamlet of about two thousand people midway between Pontiac and Bloomington. Interstate 55 became my main drag. I drove north five days a week for work and south for almost everything else. Most people would probably think living in Lexington would be as exciting as life in a monastery, but after a decade spent amongst a thousand hardened felons, settling into Dullsville felt like inhabiting a utopia.

During that first year of freedom, however, my life often felt schizophrenic. Weekdays were filled with manic tales of perversely dysfunctional families, violent juvenile crimes, and Chicago street gangs. However, evenings and weekends were delightfully tranquil. I bought a television but seldom turned it on, except to watch the national news and *60 Minutes* on Sunday nights. Instead, I became an avid reader, particularly of nineteenth-century literature. By the end of that first year, I had read everything I could get my hands on by Herman Melville, Charles Dickens, Nathaniel Hawthorne, Victor Hugo, Leo Tolstoy, Rudyard Kipling, and Mark Twain.

I had a few friends at work, but the only person I truly looked forward to seeing regularly was my father. On the surface, it helped that we shared so much in common. Both of us were dedicated to jobs aimed at making a difference, we shared similar interests in literature and current events, and we both enjoyed watching the latest films released every Friday. However, beneath the surface, the real foundation of our relationship was embedded in our past.

I understood that by pleading guilty, I'd made a commitment to my father. Instead of running away from my sin, I'd chosen to stay and accept his moral guidance. In return, Dad promised that he would always be in my corner. For example, during one of his early visits, Dad urged me to write a detailed letter of apology to Benjamin Abramowicz and a separate letter to his daughter. Benjamin promptly responded, graciously accepting my apology. However, I never heard back from Rachel.

Although Dad was the center of my world, I made the conscious choice to cut Mom out. It wasn't hard because she never visited me in prison—not once. Additionally, I never heard from anyone else from Marquette Park.

According to the prison's Aryan grapevine, Frank Collin lost his position as leader of the Nazi Party in 1979 when he was convicted of child molestation. Coincidentally, he served his time with me in Pontiac, although I rarely saw him and always from a distance. Later, I learned that Collin started a new career as a writer after being paroled. He published outlandish theories about ancient peoples migrating to North America and establishing complex indigenous cultures. Unsurprisingly, no scholar took these absurd ideas seriously.

While Dad and I thrived in our careers during the day, we both slept in empty beds at night. In his case, I believe he simply gave up, thinking that no one would ever measure up to Rachel. One Sunday morning, while he was preparing breakfast, I asked him if he knew how she was doing. When he responded that she'd married a history professor at the University of Illinois, he tried to appear casual, but my dad looked like a deflated balloon. At that moment, I was convinced he would die a confirmed bachelor.

On the other hand, Dad cheerfully believed it wasn't too late for me. After months of his nagging, I joined the congregation at the town's Methodist Church, primarily to attend their social events. There, I met Martha, an English teacher at Lexington High School. It turned out that neither of us was particularly devout, but at this stage in our lives, a church dance seemed more appealing than going to a bar. Martha could be painfully shy, which likely explains why someone with doe eyes, wavy blond hair, and a honey-sweet disposition was still single ten years after graduating from Bradley University. Eighteen months later, we got married in her parents' backyard.

Reflecting on our relationship, I believe the turning point came one Saturday night in my car after a potluck dinner at the church. This was after we had gone out only a few times and had yet to agree to what people today call an "exclusive relationship." Until that point, I had kept my answers vague whenever she inquired about my past. However, I realized that if we were going to progress to the next stage in our relationship, it needed to be built on a foundation of complete honesty.

Initially, I was unsure about what disturbed Martha more: the crime that sent me to prison or the motive behind it. Nevertheless, Martha didn't leap from the car or berate me for my actions. For some reason, she made me feel at ease discussing that troubling time in my life. I broke down in tears several times over the next few hours.

We ended up spending the entire night in the front seat of my car. During our conversation, I shared with Martha the details of my parents' divorce, the dysfunction of our family dynamics, and especially the pervasive influence of Marquette Park and its rampant racism. I initially attempted to justify my behavior by claiming I was a highly impressionable teenager. However, at a certain point that night, I suddenly realized something I had never considered: Frank Collin had become a father figure to me, and I was eager to do anything to earn his approval.

During the evening, Martha was an attentive listener and skillfully asked me questions that felt therapeutic. I shared my experiences in prison, the letters of apology I had written to the victim's family, and the transformation I underwent at Pontiac. As the sun rose over a recently harvested soybean field, I gained deep insight into my past. In the process, I realized I loved Martha and wanted to spend the rest of my life with her.

It wasn't long before we sold my trailer and bought a two-story farmhouse on the edge of town. Our home was over a hundred years old and featured a wrap-around porch, two wood-burning fireplaces, and, believe it or not, a white picket fence. Additionally, Martha and I planted a sizable vegetable garden since our house sat on a two-acre lot. Occasionally, we sold some of our produce at the Bloomington farmers market on Saturday mornings.

Three years after our wedding, Martha gave birth to twins. We named our son Grant in honor of his grandfather and our daughter Debby as a tribute to Martha's beloved grandmother. Both in the eighth grade now, the kids regularly made the honor roll. We couldn't have been prouder. Martha frequently talked about how excited she was to teach them in her English class the following year.

I found myself smiling in the rearview mirror as I turned onto Veterans Parkway. After spending a decade in a maximum-security state prison, I must admit that my life now felt pretty good. However, this portrait has had one major blemish for the last twenty-eight years. Although I'd sought forgiveness from others, I had never fully forgiven myself. At my sentencing hearing, Benjamin Abramowicz stated that I was young and foolish when I committed my crime, as if that somehow partially excused my actions. However, I still vividly remember the night I saw him curled up next to his wife. Now, as I cuddle with Martha every night, my crime feels even more reprehensible.

Benjamin Abramowicz has been sleeping alone for nearly three decades, and that's all because of me. Now, when I look in the bathroom mirror each morning, I no longer see that arrogant Chicago jerk who always urged me to rebel against everything. Nor do I see that figure who called himself my conscience, even though he ultimately convinced me to turn myself in to the police. Instead, every morning, when I look in the mirror, all I see is a face filled with shame. Despite Martha's constant encouragement to forgive myself, I've found that to be impossible.

I have only shared my ongoing feelings of guilt with two people. One of them is Martha, who has shown me unconditional love and consistently tries to ease my pain. The other person who knows is my father. He understands how the memory of that night continues to haunt me, much like Marley's ghost.

I'm sure that's why he suggested we attend Benjamin Abramowicz's funeral. He probably thinks it will be helpful for me to honor the man I once wronged so gravely. Of course, Dad also knows that Rachel will be there. She's never verbally accepted my apology. Knowing my father, he likely believes that if Rachel forgave me, perhaps I could finally forgive myself. Who knows, he just might be right.

As I drove into my father's driveway, I noticed how little his house had changed over the years. Instead of the old Civic, a new Accord was parked outside, but otherwise, everything looked just as it did when I first moved here from Chicago. The front door was, as usual, unlocked. When I stepped inside, I found Dad asleep in his recliner, with a forgettable college football game playing on the television.

My father had aged considerably, looking much older than sixty-eight. Dad used to take good care of himself by running daily, eating a well-balanced diet, and rarely consuming alcohol. But that was all before 1977. Now, a wispy ring of gray encircled his head, a pot belly hung above his belt, and he was always searching for his reading glasses. Dad's job still mattered, so he'd probably never retire as the city editor of *The Pantagraph*. However, outside of work, he spent most of his free time with my family or sitting in that Archie Bunker recliner, either with a book or the television remote.

His eyes suddenly opened as I closed the door, and for a moment, he looked at me as if I were a stranger. Then, a broad smile spread across his face. He bent down to push the lever that lowered his feet, allowing him to stand up and come forward for his trademark bear hug. Ever since my release from prison, Dad had become quite the hugger. After that, he fumbled for the TV remote on the coffee table and turned off the television.

"Michael, you look *fantastic*," he exclaimed, stepping back to eye me from head to toe. It was as if he hadn't seen me in months.

"Dad, I was just here yesterday. The food from your Thanksgiving feast still hasn't fully digested."

"Well, you'd better make room because there's plenty more."

As he led me into the kitchen, I was greeted by another feast spread across the table. This time, sliced turkey was piled high on hotdog buns, accompanied by stuffing and cranberry sauce. Half a pumpkin pie was also parked off to the side. Thanksgiving had always been my father's favorite holiday, but it had become even more significant over the years. I understood why. It was a uniquely American holiday centered around traditional values such as sharing, gratitude, and family, largely free from religious influence.

I quickly realized that my joke about being stuffed was completely inaccurate. The food looked delicious. Sitting down and taking my first bite, I wondered why it always tasted better on the second day. For the next few minutes, we ate in silence. Finally, glancing up with my mouth full, I noticed a warm smile on my dad's face.

"Looks like you're having a good time," he remarked.

I looked up, swallowed hard, and wiped the mustard from my mouth with a napkin. Then, a smile cracked across my face.

"Aside from your amazing breakfasts, I don't recall you cooking so much when I was a kid," I remarked. "When did that change?"

"I took a cooking class while you were in Pontiac. Since then, I've gradually honed my skills in the kitchen. It's been a fun way to occupy my free time."

Dad didn't realize it, but his words had struck a nerve. Ever since my trial, he had been living like a hermit, and I felt responsible. I often wonder how many teenagers make foolish decisions without realizing how many people may be affected by the unforeseen ripple effects. It's akin to the Theory of Unintended Consequences but on a personal level.

Hoping to make amends for the past, I had raised the subject of his solitude many times, but he always brushed it aside. However, since he was now in a holiday frame of mind, I thought this might be a good time to try again.

"So, Dad," I began casually, "Have you thought lately about putting yourself out there again? You know, maybe a blind date or something."

I was staring at my plate, preparing to pounce on the other half of a turkey sandwich, when I realized my question had gone unanswered. Looking up, I noticed a faint smile on Dad's face. He was gazing out the window at a squirrel perched on a tree branch.

"Dad?" I asked hesitantly, "Why are you smiling?" Then it dawned on me. "Have you met someone?"

That broke his trance. He turned to face me, and his smile widened. "Maybe," he finally replied.

"Who?" I asked anxiously.

"Her name is Paula," he replied without hesitation. "She's a few years younger than I am and has been divorced for quite some time. We recently hired her as a copy editor. Paula's originally from Atlanta but moved here years ago when her husband was transferred to State Farm's headquarters. She stayed home for many years raising her kids but recently decided to return to work since her youngest just left for college in Michigan. I see her every day, and we've gotten to know each other pretty well." After a brief pause, he added, "She's really a nice woman."

Dad suddenly stopped speaking. Up until that point, everything he had said sounded rehearsed, but now he seemed at a loss for words. Perhaps he was waiting for me to ask questions.

"Nice, huh? So, have you asked her out yet?"

He looked away briefly as if this were a question he had been pondering for some time. "No," he finally answered. "I don't want to ruin a good thing. We share a lot of interests, and lately, we've been having lunch together every day. Paula's easy to talk to; she has become a good friend at work, and I wouldn't want to do anything to jeopardize our relationship. Besides," he added, "the paper frowns upon workplace romances."

I swallowed hard, shaking my head in frustration. However, Dad suddenly changed the subject before I could counter his arguments.

"Michael, did I wake you up last night?" Before I could respond, he continued, "Fred, who works the night desk, had just learned about Benjamin Abramowicz's death. Since he remembered the interview I did with him ages ago, he thought I'd want to know. The Jewish faith buries their dead quickly, so Fred wanted to share the details about his funeral as soon as possible. And, since I thought you might want to attend, I called you immediately. Sorry for the late hour."

"It's no problem," I replied, even though his call had woken us. "You're right; I definitely want to attend. However, I like your idea about keeping our distance. I wouldn't want my presence to upset anyone."

For a moment, Dad was silent. He drew a deep breath, nodded, and then reached across the table, placing his hand on top of mine. In a voice just above a whisper, he solemnly said, "If Benjamin is looking down at his funeral, I'm sure he'd be happy to see you among the mourners."

I nodded in agreement. "You know, Dad, not a day goes by when I don't think about that man and his wife. As he said in his testimony, I was young and foolish when I bombed their home, but that doesn't change the outcome. What I did to that couple was the epitome of *evil*: there's really no other way to describe it. Still, Benjamin Abramowicz asked the judge to show mercy. His testimony helped reduce my sentence and, more importantly, made it possible for me to sleep at night."

"The act itself was evil," Dad agreed. "But not the actor. You took responsibility for your actions and showed this by not trying to minimize your punishment. For instance, I believe that if you had named the Nazi thugs in Chicago who had encouraged you to commit this crime, the prosecutor might have considered reducing your sentence. However, you chose not to do that."

"Dad," I replied with mild frustration, "We've already been down this road. The bomb was *my* idea. Yes, Dale's the one who detonated it, but he was already dead by the time I could've given his name. And there was no evidence, except my word, linking the crime to Frank Collin. Besides," I added, "Giving names or anything like that would've only made it look like I was trying to weasel out of my responsibility. This was my crime, and I needed to accept its full consequences."

Dad turned to gaze out the window once again. The squirrels were still active, but he wasn't paying them much attention. We hadn't discussed the bombing in a long time, and I could tell Dad was mulling over what I'd just said. Finally, he spun around to confront me.

"The fact you're saying this almost thirty years later shows that Mr. Abramowicz made the right choice pleading for your mercy. And he unquestionably made a difference. You'd probably still be in prison had he not given that testimony." Then, after a short pause, Dad added, "You know, Benjamin Abramowicz is one of the finest men I ever knew."

"Agreed," I replied enthusiastically. "That's why I'm here now. Somehow, that man was able to find it in his heart to forgive me. The least I can do is pay my respects at his funeral." Then, almost as an afterthought, I added, "However, I'm not so sure about his daughter. She has never forgiven me."

"That makes two of us," Dad affirmed with a loud sigh. Then, glancing down at his watch, he announced, "The service at the synagogue should be about over. Why don't we head to the cemetery?"

Ten minutes later, I drove my father south on Morris Road, passing through Miller Park. Driving by the small lake, I noticed Dad intently gazing at a particular area near the water's edge. As we continued, he turned his head to keep studying the area. I considered asking him if there was something special about that spot but ultimately decided against it. A short time later, we crossed Veterans Parkway, entered the Jewish Cemetery, and parked the car. As I climbed out, I observed that Dad and I used the same motion to button our overcoats.

Although we arrived a bit early, I noticed a small crowd had gathered near a large pile of dirt. Shortly after, I saw a black hearse gliding down the narrow road, weaving through the trees that lined the cemetery grounds. As we began to walk in that direction, more cars followed the hearse, and the crowd grew dramatically as we approached the burial site. I gently guided Dad toward a grove of trees a few yards behind the crowd. This would give us a good vantage point to observe the funeral—close enough to hear the words and pay our respects but far enough away not to offend Rachel or her family.

The mid-afternoon sunshine glared bright enough to force dark glasses onto most faces. Mine were in my coat pocket, but I deliberately kept them there. I noticed that Dad did the same. We exchanged glances, but neither of us said a word. A soft murmur floated from the crowd, which had grown to at least a hundred people, but otherwise, the only sound came from the chirping of sparrows and a gentle breeze whistling through the bare branches.

Finally, the silence was interrupted by a woman's amplified voice. It was Rachel speaking into a microphone set up by the mortuary. Three decades had passed since we last spoke, but I still recognized the distinct intonation of her words. Rachel must've been standing on a platform because I could see her face above the audience. From a distance, it didn't seem like she had aged. There was probably some gray in her hair and perhaps a few wrinkles on her face, but from where I stood, they were not noticeable. I glanced at Dad, who was intently watching her. Rachel looked in our direction but did not acknowledge us.

I was initially surprised that Rachel was in charge. Given my limited experience attending funerals, I'd assumed a rabbi would conduct it, much like the ones I've seen on television or in the movies. However, I realized it made sense for her to lead the service, as no one knew the deceased better than his only child. Additionally, I figured the rabbi had already conducted the first part of the service back at the synagogue.

Rachel began by reviewing a timeline of her father's life. I knew how Benjamin and Miriam escaped from Sobibor and eventually settled in this country. However, after hearing their survival story once again, I was overwhelmed by a wave of guilt. Rachel had intended to remind the audience of her parents' incredible courage, but her words struck my conscience like a barrage of arrows. All I could think about was that while the Nazis had failed to murder her parents sixty years ago, I had completed the task with her mother and came close with her father. The taste of bile rose in my throat.

When Rachel summarized her parents' postwar years, I started to feel more at ease. I hadn't known they moved from Skokie to Bloomington to be closer to their daughter. Now that I'm a parent, I can better appreciate their sacrifices. I breathed a sigh of relief when Rachel chose to skip over the bombing and instead focused on reviewing Benjamin's final three decades. Despite our proximity, I had no idea what had happened to him after my sentencing hearing. Apparently, after selling his store, Benjamin spent his time engaged in community work, writing a memoir, and baby-sitting his grandchildren.

I glanced at Dad at the mention of grandchildren, but he didn't flinch. Maybe he already knew? If so, why hadn't he ever mentioned this? As I shifted my attention back to Rachel, she began to reminisce about her father's most notable achievements. The big surprise came near the end of her list. Locking eyes with me this time, Rachel recounted her father's testimony at my sentencing hearing. A mix of guilt and fear made it hard to breathe.

I know people cry at funerals. In my case, though, I assumed that a decade in prison had fortified me for this experience. As it turned out, I was wrong. Rachel explained how her father forgave me even before I asked for his forgiveness. She described how he "borrowed" from the Christian doctrine of "turning the other cheek" to plead for my mercy. Then she repeated her father's exact words: "It's time for this hate to end."

I felt moisture gathering beneath my eyes. A cyclone of emotions, ranging from guilt to gratitude, made it impossible to maintain my composure any longer. It was as if a bomb were ticking inside me, ready to explode. I spun around and briskly walked into the grove of trees to create some distance from the crowd. Once I found a quiet spot, I raised both hands to my face and finally allowed the dam to burst. I began to sob uncontrollably.

A short while later, I felt a hand on my shoulder. Then, my father gently spun me around and pulled me in for a smothering embrace. I had never appreciated his hug as much as I did at that moment. I buried my face in his chest and continued to weep. This went on for several minutes. Finally, when I began to calm down, Dad tenderly pulled back and gazed at me with sympathy. In the background, we could hear a man reciting something in Hebrew that I had only heard once before, at Miriam's funeral. It was the Mourner's Kaddish.

After regaining my composure, Dad and I slowly made our way back toward the crowd. The ceremony had ended, and people were beginning to head toward their cars. I glanced at Dad, silently inquiring whether we should leave as well. Before he could answer, we both looked up to see a family standing before us. Rachel was accompanied by a heavy-set man around her age and two others who were significantly younger.

"Hello, Grant," she said softly. "Hi, Michael. It's been a long time. Thank you both for coming today."

I was speechless. This was the moment I had dreaded most. Dad mumbled something consoling, but I couldn't think of anything to say.

"My father," she continued, "Would've appreciated your presence today. However, I hate to say that he wouldn't have recognized you if you'd seen him towards the end. Dad spent his final years in a nursing home, and toward the end, he didn't even know who I was."

I wondered how Rachel had managed to conduct the ceremony in such a polished and professional manner. Her lack of visible grief began to make more sense when I learned that her father's gradual decline into dementia had already provided her with ample time to grieve.

"*Oh,*" Rachel exclaimed, realizing three other people stood awkwardly beside her. "Where are my manners? Grant and Michael, this is my husband, Seth, and our children, Benjamin and Leon."

I nearly laughed when Rachel introduced Benjamin and Leon as her "children." Both appeared to be in their early twenties and towered over her.

"Seth's a history professor at the University of Illinois. After we got married, we bought a home in Farmer City, where we raised our kids."

I glanced at my father and noticed a slight smile sneak across his face. "Farmer City?" Seth, who must've read our minds, then joined the conversation.

"Many people laugh when they hear this, but it's a charming little town about halfway between Champaign and Normal. Rachel and I each drive about thirty minutes up I-74 in opposite directions, and it's quite relaxing since there's usually no traffic."

My father politely shook Seth's hand, as well as her two boys, and I followed suit. We each introduced ourselves, something Rachel had neglected to do, but Seth already seemed familiar with who we were.

"So," my dad asked, looking at Rachel's boys, "What do you guys do?"

"I'm studying history at the University of Chicago," Leon replied. "And my brother is pre-med at the University of Pennsylvania."

"We had already planned to come home for Thanksgiving," Benjamin added, "Unfortunately, we also knew there was a decent chance we'd be attending our grandfather's funeral."

"Well," I interjected, taking my turn, "We're sorry about your loss. Your grandfather was a great man who'd lived an extraordinary life."

Suddenly, an awkward silence fell over the circle. Sensing this, Rachel took charge once again.

"Hey," she declared, facing her family, "Would you guys mind waiting for me in the car for a few minutes?"

After Seth, Leon, and Benjamin had left, Rachel turned back to us. The awkwardness returned as we waited for someone to speak. Finally, it was my father who broke the silence.

"You look great, Rachel, and you have a beautiful family."

My father's tone couldn't have been more sincere. Rachel smiled uneasily and nodded, absorbing his words.

"Grant, you're also looking good," she replied unconvincingly. "And I meant what I said earlier; I'm truly grateful you came to Dad's funeral."

Rachel then turned to me, her demeanor growing more sober. She studied my face with a puzzled expression, and I realized that traces of moisture were likely still surrounding my eyes, which must've turned red.

"So, Michael," she finally asked, "How have you been?"

I hesitated. This question is asked every day; it's a common courtesy. However, in this context, the question likely concealed a hostility that had been festering for decades. Realizing this might be my only chance to express what needed to be said, I decided to take the plunge.

"I'm doing well, Rachel. Since my release from prison, I've begun working as a counselor at Pontiac, got married, and started a family of my own."

Then, shifting to what I *really* wanted to say, I briefly glanced down at my shuffling feet before looking up and continuing. There was a speech

I had been mentally rehearsing for many years, ready to deliver at this precise moment. But now that the moment had arrived, I found myself completely mute. Then I caught a glimpse of my dad, biting his lower lip and nodding like an anxious father watching his child in the school play. That's all it took for the words to start flowing from my lips.

"Rachel, I want to express how truly sorry I am for bombing your parents' house. Not a day goes by when I'm not wracked by guilt for what I did. I was seventeen when I committed that crime, and now, I'm 45. Please understand that this is *not* an excuse. However, I want you to know I am a completely different man today."

Rachel contemplated me like a governor weighing a request for clemency. She narrowed her eyes, cast a quick glance at my father, and inhaled deeply. Then, Rachel locked her gaze onto mine and slowly began to nod. Finally, without uttering a word, she reached out for a hug. As we embraced, Rachel leaned in closer to my ear and whispered the words I'd dreamed of hearing for decades: "I believe you, Michael, and I accept your apology."

When she pulled away, I glanced at Dad. His eyes were glazed, but a broad grin stretched across his face.

"It was wonderful to see both of you," Rachel pronounced as she prepared to leave. Then, just as she started to turn away, she added, "Let's meet up again sometime, you know, under better circumstances."

After she left, I tapped my dad's arm and pointed toward the car. We strolled back to the parking lot at a leisurely pace, aware that we would have much to discuss later. As I glanced over at my father, I noticed his posture was more upright, as if a weight had been lifted from his shoulders. I then realized that my own stance was mirroring his.

As we both reached for the door handles, my father broke the silence with words that pleasantly surprised me.

"You know, when we get home, I think I'll give Paula a call."

"*Really?*" I asked, unable to hide my grin.

"Yeah," he replied. "I'm a bit nervous, though. After all, it's been a long time since I've asked a woman out on a date."

After we climbed into my car and fastened our seatbelts, Dad reached over the center console and gently squeezed my shoulder. We exchanged knowing smiles. Then, we continued our conversation about the latest dating rituals all the way home.

AUTHOR'S NOTE

This is a work of fiction. However, the portrayal of Bloomington-Normal in the 1970s is based on my experiences attending Illinois State University from 1975 to 1979. Therefore, all mentioned locations, including roads, highways, university sites, parks, restaurants, and other buildings, are real and described as accurately as possible. The depictions of additional locations in Illinois, such as Marquette Park and Skokie, are also grounded in past memories.

Benjamin and Miriam's love story, which unfolds against the backdrop of the horrors of Sobibor and their escape from the death camp, is loosely inspired by the real-life experiences of Itzhak and Eda Lichtman. The main difference is that, unlike the Abramowiczs, Itzhak and Eda Lichtman settled in Israel after the war. The ONR, or National Radical Camp, was a genuine fascist movement that was outlawed by the Polish Republic in 1934. Additionally, Frank Collin is a real individual, and his plan to lead a Nazi march into Skokie resulted in the notable Supreme Court case.

ABOUT THE AUTHOR

JOE REGENBOGEN taught high school history for 40 years. He began teaching in the Ninth Ward of New Orleans in 1979, where two years later, he was named runner-up for city-wide teacher-of-the-year. After moving to St. Louis in 1984, he continued teaching in the Parkway School District in the western suburbs of St. Louis. During the final years of his career, Joe taught in a unique program for the exceptionally gifted, where his students ended their eighth-grade year by taking the AP exam in American History.

As Joe approached his retirement, he took up writing as a second career. To date, he has published six books. His first two, *Questioning History* and *Relearning History*, were intended to deepen students' understanding of the past. Joe's third book, *The Boys of Brookdale*, told the accounts of World War Two veterans who lived their final years in the same senior living facility where Joe's father resided. *Making a Difference* recounted the story of Irl Solomon and his 38-year teaching career in East St. Louis, Illinois, one of the nation's most challenging school districts. Joe's two introspective novels are Longs Peak and *Dying of the Light*.

Now enjoying his retirement, Joe resides with Dana, his wife of 45 years, in their long-time home. Together, they raised their two children, Julie, a federal public defender, and Jack, a non-profit attorney. In addition to writing, Joe currently helps Dana provide full-time daycare for their two granddaughters, Ava and Delaney.